THE LUTHIER

by
Gil Jackman

"A great violin is alive; its very shape embodies its maker's intentions, and its wood stores the history, or the soul, of its successive owners. I never play without feeling that I have released or, alas, violated spirits."

Yehudi Menuhin, *Unfinished Journey* 1976

"Tis God gives skill, but not without men's hands: He could not make Antonio Stradivari's violins without Antonio."

George Eliot

"I have a violin that was born in 1713. It was alive long before me, and I hope it lives long after me. I don't consider it as my violin. Rather, I am perhaps its violinist; I am passing through its life."

Ivry Gitlis, *The Art of Violin* 2000

SYNOPSIS

For three centuries Antonio Stradivari has been the acknowledged leader in the art of the luthier, or violinmaker. The work he did during his "Golden Period", 1698 to 1775, is without equal throughout the world and the history of violin making. Even the earlier, magnificent creations by Andrea Amarti cannot compare with this Golden Period of Stradivari.

From where then had Stradivari acquired his superb skills?

What if he had been visited one dark night around 1698 by a sinister figure out of religious myth and legend? A figure who would give him precedence over all luthiers who lived; and who had ever been and would ever be? Perhaps he came with immortality for the instrument maker that would last for all future generations to come. Suppose he brought him genius and many riches to spring from that genius; could a man like Stradivari refuse such an offer?

There is a legend that once, during this Golden Period, Stradivari made his greatest violin. It was as black as the journey to the pits of Hell and had a rare quality of sound; both euphonious and lyrical, yet not the most pleasant of musical sounds, for at times it was submediant, and at others it was dominant in a cruel, strident and discordant way.

Each of Stradivari's famous instruments that exist today, including his cellos, have an individual name; the Lipinski, the Viotti, the Messiah, the Davidoff the Khevenhuller, the Paganini - to name but a few.

It is said that the black one, the one of legend, is called the Diabolus, which name is both its description and its purpose.

Centuries passed in the slow time of humankind and in the present day a man called Harry Brogan comes into the frame. He was once a Royal Marine, part of an elite Reconnaissance Troop. He was a man with climbing and sniper skills among his other abilities; none of which qualified him for civilian employment – or did it? Following problems in his marital and private life he left the Corps and was down on his luck when he came in contact with a shadowy figure called simply Jonathon.

Using some of those skills gained in the Marines, Brogan became a successful thief. The agenda was simple, with only certain individuals being targeted; people who are dishonest, or who have allegiances to foreign powers.

Brogan, having made enough money to be comfortable, decides to retire, but fate conspires against him. He is forced into one last job, which is to find and steal a priceless violin from the Vatican at the behest of an advisor to the Pope himself.

With the aid of an expert on the Devil and all his works, Brogan steals the violin and hands it over to the priest, believing it is all finished - but it is only the beginning.

The violin is a cursed instrument. Before it can be destroyed both it and the priest disappear, and once more Brogan is enticed into stealing it from its new owner, for whom the Diabolus is essential in his own bid for diabolical power.

Only this time the task is not so easy.

PROLOGUE

(About 300 years ago)

"Their land is also full of idols; they worship the work of their own hands, that which their own fingers have made."

Isaiah 2:8

The luthier began with an internal mould.

The moulds themselves were little more than flat pieces of wood with the shape of the outline of a violin without its internal blocks. He designed them with few tools other than a ruler and compass, but even so they incorporated some fascinating mathematical relationships. The most striking of these was the recurrence of the "golden mean" (the number used by the ancient Greeks to give perfect classical proportions) as the ratio between several key widths and heights.

First onto the mould, lightly glued for future removal, were the violin's end and corner blocks. Next, the luthier used a heated iron to bend the ribs around the mould, fixing them to the blocks with glue and clamping them in place so that the four thin strips of maple formed the uninterrupted outline of the body. This became his template for tracing out the violin's shape onto the planks of spruce and maple that were to form, respectively, the instrument's belly and back. For both, the plank actually consisted of two wedges of wood cut "on the quarter." Imagine two vertical cake-slices cut from the trunk of the tree glued together at their thicker ends.

The man invariably used this technique to make his violins' bellies, so ensuring that their treble and bass sides were in balance. With the backs he varied his approach according to the wood available. For many of his earlier pieces he had made his backs from maple cut "on the slab," taking slices in planes at a tangent to the tree's growth rings. This lost the classic "figure" of quarter-cut maple (apparent horizontal stripes caused by ripples in the wood's grain) and gave a different sound to the finished violin, perhaps richer, but less highly focused. Now he mostly used quarter-cut wood: two pieces usually, often only one, if he had a large enough piece of maple.

The shapes that he had cut from the spruce and maple were now ready for working on to create the front and back plates of the violin. First the external archings: he used guides, cutting channels to match them with a long rounded gouge. Connecting these channels gave the rough exterior. A succession of finer tools finishing with a hard steel scraper led to the perfectly smooth curves of the final surfaces. The interior followed, as the craftsman, for such he was, gradually brought each plate down to its ideal thickness, thinning out from the centre toward the edge and taking great care to make front and back as thin as possible without comprising the strength of the violin.

To carve the two sound holes in the violin's belly he started with the circular finials at each end of the holes, placing them with a compass and drilling them out using a cylinder with cutting wings. A template specific to the violin's mould then gave the outline of the F that connected the finials. The simplicity of the sound holes was deceptive, for their grace and perfect proportions, together with the flawless carving was unique. The belly now needed a bass-bar attached to its interior surface. It ran about three-quarters of the length of the instrument, at its thickest in the middle and tapering down toward the ends.

At this stage of constructing the instrument, the luthier tested the "tap-tone" of back and belly to find its resonant frequency. He was aiming for something around the F below middle C for each. As well he tested the feel and flexibility of each plate in his hands. Subsequent thickness adjustment achieved what experience told him was ideal. This kind of crucial detail made the man's innate genius show through in the finished instrument. He did not make his violins according to a formula but by taking account of the specific properties of the wood he was using.

Now he started to assemble the sound box. "Lintings" (strips of willow glued along the top and bottom of the ribs) provided, with the blocks, a surface to which the plates could be glued. First was the block, using a strong adhesive, freshly made from animal hide. Now was the time to tap out the internal mould, its job finished. Two further internal attachments remained before the closure of the body: the violin's neck, by means of glue and three hand-forged nails through the top block; and the label, with its date and seal, clearly visible through the left-hand sound hole of the violin. Then, finally, he glued on the belly, using a weaker adhesive to allow for future repairs.

Many man-hours had gone into producing that neck, carved together with the peg box and scroll from a single piece of maple. Once more there was mathematics behind the scrolls. The Italian architect Giacomo Vignola had laid down principles for spirals in the sixteenth century, building on Archimede's work almost two millennia before. Our luthier's scrolls showed that he knew the work of both these men, as the central volute came out in an Archimedean spiral, with relatively tight windings, before changing to a more expansive Vignola's spiral on its outer curve. It was a glorious single sweep of two parallel grooves, narrow at the scroll's top, and expanding effortlessly in both directions away from it. The apparent inevitability of the scroll's lines, the way they drew the eye along them from every direction, and the sheer confidence and artistry underlying the carving, were all crucial to what set this luthier apart from the mere artisan. His genius was unmistakable.

The instrument was far from finished. He had cut out the back and belly so that they overlapped the ribs. This now gave him the opportunity to contour round slight irregularities in the shape of the ribs, where for example these were slightly thicker than normal, or had not followed perfectly the line of the mould. The result was an instrument whose outline initially appeared flawless; only the most careful examination revealed the imperfections inevitable in any handmade object.

Now that the final shape of the violin was complete, the luthier applied his last piece of artistry: the purling. After first tracing and then cutting the grooves around the edges of the instrument, front and back, he inserted the inlay in strips that he had previously glued together. It was at the corners that his skill was most apparent. A "bee-sting" is the sharp point of the purling seen in some instruments as it comes into the four corners of the belly and back; the belly being the arched upper surface of the sound box, made from softwood and containing the sound holes, and the back being the arched lower surface of the sound box, made from hardwood.

The characteristic bee-stings of the luthier/artist's mitres, points remarkably thin while remaining beautifully and precisely formed would be recognized in centuries to come, and the result was both delicate and confident.

The violin was now ready for varnishing.

No element of violin construction engenders more debate than this last apparently simple component. No one doubts that it is a crucial part of the look of a good violin, enhancing the natural beauty of the materials in a way that increases with age. All also agree that the wrong varnish can kill a violin's sound, deadening the vibrational qualities of its wood. But is there more to it than that? Legendary qualities have been ascribed to the Cremonese varnish that the great luthier Andrea Amarti was apparently the first to use.

For this was indeed Cremona, the year was 1699, and the craftsman working now was to become the most famous violinmaker that the world has ever known.

He was tall and thin, and habitually wore a cap of white wool in winter and one of cotton in summer. He wore over his clothes an apron of white leather when he worked; and as he was always working, his costume scarcely ever varied.

A man of strong beliefs in himself, the master craftsman was never hesitant. But now for once he showed a shy hesitancy as he gazed at two pots; one contains the standard varnish of the area, which every local luthier used with perhaps slight differences in the mix. Its golden-yellow color and faint softness to the touch owed everything to Cremonese tradition.

The other pot was of a much darker, almost black, varnish. Its constituency was more mucous; more of a gluttonous mixture than the local one. And it smelled not unlike sulphur from the pits of Hell itself.

This reminded him of whence it came.

He'd been working late in his workshop, as was his wont for he was a frugal man and saw no need to pay apprentices for work which he might well complete in his own time. The luthier himself bore witness to the appalling weather that night, and the sound of the rain beating down despite the thickness of his clay tiles was almost driving him downstairs to his warm hearth and warm wine. His visitor had been unexpected and unwelcome, unless he came with some rich commission from a worthy patron; and indeed, perhaps the strange visitor came with more than a rich commission for the luthier; but time alone would attest to that.

The tall cadaverous luthier took the stranger seriously from the very beginning, for although he was of ordinary appearance, his strangeness came from the fact that he had just entered from the veritable deluge in the street outside; yet he himself was dry as a bone. He wore no hat, yet his hair was not wet in the slightest, and although he wore no topcoat his fine tunic showed not one raindrop.

The instrument maker listened carefully to what the man had to say, and sat for long minutes considering the question the stranger had posed at the end of his short speech. It had been a simple question, requiring only a "yes" or "no" in answer. The luthier knew full well that he must reach the important decision and answer the question before the man had left. He had done so in haste, yet allowing himself time for delay and the choice of changing his mind.

Now was his final decision, and he stood gazing from one pot to the other. It was an agonizing decision, and much depended on it; his own and his family's future, his skill which would become legendary after this night, and the loss of something which would bind him to his visitor for all eternity.

Finally he picked up a clean brush and dipped it in one of the pots. He applied it liberally, yet carefully, over the length of his masterpiece. It was but the first of 40 to 50 coats of varnish he would use on the instrument before he was satisfied. The various ingredients used in the Stradivarius varnish; the resins, pigments, solvents and the other secret elixirs, are known today, but the mystery is the order in which he mixed them. As does the way in which he prepared the protective coat and this has always been a key issue, for the varnish plays a role in determining 20 to 30 percent of the sound quality. Yet, on this night of the mysterious stranger's visitation only one mystery was to stand out for the proceeding three centuries.

What was to be the color of the final application?

Stradivari's standard mix known only to himself; or the unknown one brought by the mysterious stranger comprising the color of the blackest night and the smell of the sulpherous pits of Hell itself.

CHAPTER ONE

"Do not store up for yourselves treasure on earth, where it grows rusty and moth-eaten, and thieves break in to steal it. Store up treasure in heaven, where there is no moth and no rust to spoil it, no thieves to break in and steal. For where your treasure is, there will your heart be also.

Jesus the Nazorean

(Some Ten Years Ago)

I sat on the edge of the roof and gazed out at the glittering expanse of the city, spread out below like an alien planet in Star Wars. The well-lit canyons reminded me of Luke Skywalker being chased through those other, unreal, canyons. Yet these were real, with the glistening motor vehicles containing the beautiful people rushing along to unknown but assuredly glamorous destinations; and the darker, sinister and narrower canyons behind them; which contained nothing glamorous, and where the people were certainly not in any way beautiful; especially not to themselves.

If there was any expression on my face it might have been contemptuous amusement for the denizens of this great city. That it was great I couldn't deny; that it was also rotten and filled with as many of the dregs of humanity as beautiful people, I couldn't deny either. Not that I cared; in fact at that time I didn't care about anything very much. This was not my city – it was not even my country. It was big and brash, noisy and filthy in parts, fascinating and violent in others.

It was New York, which I suppose said it all.

I glanced at my watch; the over-large luminous dial was even visible in the dark shadows in which I rested; and waited. Time to go to work, I thought, and felt neither anticipation nor apprehension. I watched, and as though on cue the lights went out beneath my feet. The side of the building was plunged into darkness as the last employee left and I sprang lightly to my feet. I was dressed in dark clothing; black pants and non-shiny windcheater; black Nike's and a ski mask rolled up on top of my head completed the ensemble. Rolling the mask down now I shrugged on the black rucksack. Even the equipment in the rucksack was black.

I liked to think I was a man who planned well.

I had done my homework on the night guard and could practically hear him as he slammed the main door, slid the bolts and turned the keys, sighing with relief. A few of these assholes took their jobs too seriously, he was probably thinking. Sure, they had more money in their current accounts than he'd seen in his whole lifetime, and it had been a long lifetime. He knew they drove the best cars; Mercedes, BMWs, fancy sports cars. But did they have to work till nine or ten o'clock EVERY frigging night?

I'd learned that Billy Deacons had fought for his country in Vietnam, an unpopular war. Now that WAS a war, not the crap they called wars these days. He'd worked in a hospital after that, most of his life in fact. Nothing heroic, he was an orderly, but he reckoned he'd made a difference in his own small way. He'd always cared for folks, had Billy, and I was not going to let anything happen to him because of tonight's job. He had a charm about him, and an eagerness to help that had made people indifferent to the color of his skin. They'd been grateful, and he'd enjoyed the connection he made with complete strangers. He'd managed to raise a small family on his small Army pension and his hospital pay. He was sixty-eight years old now, and he'd taken this job on the recommendation of his brother-in-law, Tad.

How did I know all this?

I mentioned that I liked to plan well, and I'd made acquaintance with Billy a month ago. I sidled up to him at his favorit bar, began a conversation, and after dropping the fact that I was an ex-marine myself, we became buddies. I dropped into the bar several times over the next few weeks, and it was no great trick to get his life story.

'Billy,' Tad had said to him, 'Since my sister died two years ago you has moped around here, winding yourself up som'ting chronic. Man, I hate to see you like this. Nancy was a saint, man. I know that, and you loved her dearly, but she gone now, and you got some good years left. We got a vacancy for a night watchman at the building. It's good pay and they've got one of those great wide-screen TV's in the staff room.'

He'd taken the job and told me he hadn't regretted it one bit. Something he'd never suffered from was stress, yet he could see a lot of these young people were going down that road if they weren't too careful.

I timed him as he did a final check on the fire exits on the ground floor, and then checked all the fire doors to the top of the building. It was his routine every night and he didn't deviate on this. It was what he was paid for, and he would not feel right if he didn't do his job properly, I knew. Billy Deacons was of the old school. At the top floor he walked out onto the roof and glanced around. The roof was completely bare of any impediments, except for the low-lying skylight. He stepped back into the small shack that housed the stairs and secured the door, before descending to the twenty-seventh floor and taking the elevator down to five, and the staff room.

Allowing Billy the night guard fifteen minutes to complete his routine and ensconce himself in front of the latest wide-screen and switch on the highlights of the day's football, I finally moved from my prone position on the far side of the skylight. Extracting a small clamp from my rucksack I positioned it on the glass and pulled the two levers down tight. Holding the clamp with my left hand, I drew a large circle on the glass with a diamond cutter. Putting the cutter away in my pocket I bent my knees and used both hands to grip the clamp by its handles. Straightening, I used my legs as leverage and the glass and clamp came away easily. I pulled the clamp levers up, releasing the glass, and stowed the clamp away in the rucksack. I laid the glass down in the shadows on the far side of the skylight where I'd hidden from the guard. Reaching through I opened the skylight.

Looping the long thin rope around the guardrail on the edge of the roof, I led the two ends across to the skylight. I dropped them inside and clipped both lengths onto the descendeur dangling from my harness. One step over and I was on the way down. I landed lightly in the corridor of the twenty-seventh floor. Sparing a glance up I pulled one end of the rope, which ran freely down to me. The hole in the glass was high enough to be in shadow from the lights in the corridor and was not noticeable from below. I quickly coiled the rope with an expertise learned long ago. That also went into the rucksack.

A door on my left was marked EXIT in large convenient lettering and I ducked in quickly. Down two flights and I poked my head out slowly. Another corridor, identical to the one I'd just left. I moved slowly along, not looking at the doors but counting in my head until I came to the one I wanted. Bending down I pulled a few items from a zipped pants pocket and paid attention to the lock.

A lock-picker uses two tools; a tension wrench, which is inserted into the lock and twisted to keep the pressure on the locking pins inside, and the pick itself, which pushes each pin out of the way so the lock can be turned to the open position. It can be time-consuming to push aside the pins one at a time, though, so I had been trained to master a very difficult technique called "scrubbing", in which you move the pick back and forth quickly, brushing the pins out of the way. The scrubbing system only works when the lock-picker senses exactly the right combination of torque on the cylinder and the pressure on the pins. Using tools that were only a few inches long, it had taken me less than thirty seconds to scrub open the sophisticated lock on the office door and push it open. In less time than that I was inside. Not for the first time I was grateful that I had been taught by the best, and at that time it had been legal – now it wasn't.

I shone my flashlight around. It was small and I'd taped across the top so only a needle of light beamed out. Following the directions that were in my head I made my way across the large typing room and into one of the two smaller offices at the far end. I chose the door on the right, and again it was ten seconds work with the picks to defeat the relatively simple lock.

Now came the hard part.

The massive safe in the corner was of a type that I was familiar with, and once more I followed a blueprint that was in my head. This time I used a medical stethoscope and a small box with a wire sticking out of one end and a dialled face with numbers on. Two buttons controlled the numbers. As I twirled the knobs on the dial I listened intently and as I interpreted the different clicks I recorded the numbers as they came up on the dial. That completed, the door would still not open, for there was a large old-fashioned keyhole just below the combination lock. Taking out a larger set of picks, I set to, and in the time it took me to insert the thin lengths of metal in the lock and wiggle them I was able to swing the large door open. Once more I was grateful for good training, but this time it was a man called Jimmy, and he had not been legal that time.

I shone the thin beam inside the safe and barely contained myself from whistling aloud. The top shelf was piled high with US banknotes, all with the steady gaze of Ben Franklin watching with interest for whoever might be fortunate enough to own him for a time. Personally I'd always thought he had a somewhat supercilious look for a man with no hair on top yet a luxuriant growth at the sides reaching down to his shoulders. Not that the napkin around his neck helped the image either.

I dropped down lower and shone the light into the bottom shelf. The papers which I'd come for were there, as I'd been told they would be and I'd never been let down by my source. They were in a file half an inch thick and I pulled them out, glanced at the front and was satisfied. I did not open the file because I had no interest in what it contained. It was none of my business. I had received only two simple instructions along with the plans of the building and photos of the safe. Take the file marked MADISON and help yourself to as much of the money as you can carry. It was all illegally gained and no one was going to complain.

I opened the rucksack, unzipped the extra space around the bottom edge and removed the rope. I pushed the clamp down firmly and began loading the bundles of money down as tightly as they would go. I was never a greedy person and was satisfied when I could pull the drawstring tight around the top. I pulled the flap over, strapped it, then shoved some more money into the side pockets and clipped them into place. Pulling the straps over both arms so the rucksack was resting comfortably on my back, I slung the rope over my shoulder so it lay across the pack. I didn't regret not bringing a bigger rucksack, a Bergen size even, as there was not much money left in the safe when I closed and locked it again.

I let myself quietly out of the office, again closing and locking it behind me. I smiled as I saw the sign on the door, Harold Johnson, Attorney-at-Law, and once again I had no regrets of the night's work.

I moved silently along the well-lit corridor and into the door marked EXIT and hence into the stairwell which ran from top to bottom of the building. On each landing there was a door with a bar across. I pushed it open silently and the smooth surface of the outside just as silently shut. I made a rapid descent of the metal fire stairs, my Nike's making little sound down as I took the wide steps two at a time. At the bottom I pushed out the last long ladder and was pleased at how little noise it made, although I wasn't surprised. I had oiled the hinges of the ladder myself, two days before. Posing as a window cleaner I had set up a long ladder, which I'd climbed armed with a bucket of water and the window-cleaning paraphernalia of a cloth and squeegee. No one had bothered me while I paused at the bottom of the fire escape with a spray can of lubricant.

I climbed down the ladder and pushed it back up. It ascended smoothly to its place of rest and I walked slowly off into the night. Around the corner I shoved coins into a public phone, waited until the ringing tone became a male voice who said only one word.

'Yes?'

To which I, being also a man of few words, replied with only two before I hung up.

'Mission accomplished.'

Early the next morning I handed over the mysterious package to a faceless go-between at the rendezvous point in Times Square and took a yellow cab to Penn Station from where I jumped on the Acela express to Boston. I moved along the train, exiting at the far end near the way out to the main hall of the station. By now I was wearing a cloth cap and spectacles and had turned my raincoat inside out so the once light green had now become a drab tan. I walked around the corner and jumped on a Greyhound that was due to leave a few minutes later. The ticket I'd already purchased two days previously. The bus took me north from New York to Boston's Logan airport from where I flew directly to Bermuda. There were direct flights from New York to Bermuda, but I was never one to take unnecessary chances. Not back then - not now.

I was sure the old security guard would now be ensconced in his comfortable chair in front of the wonderful new LCD screen for a while. In a couple of hours he would stretch his legs and patrol the corridors, testing the door handles but having no reason to enter any of the offices. Everything would pan out and he would return to the staff room, maybe pour himself a coffee from his flask and perhaps eat a sandwich from his lunchbox.

For a week I'd lain on the roof of an adjacent building with a set of night glasses and observed Billy as he watched the game on the wide-screen. I'd done my background checks on him and knew his every move. I knew where he was coming from and what his simple goals were in life, and had concluded that he was a good man. In fact, I knew I was going to miss his company after this night, for I could not afford to be seen around any more. No harm would come to him from my little escapade in his building for the last thing that Harold Johnson, Attorney-at-Law, would want to do was raise a ruckus on the night's events; the very last thing. Every couple of hours Billy would wander around the building. He did not have to swipe in his position and he had no obvious routine plan. I could see him appear on each floor and take the elevator up and down. With nothing visibly out of place the guard would then return to his base.

In about a year's time Billy Deacon's bank account would show a moderate increase in its funds, and the same the following year and maybe again after that. Poor Billy would be puzzled for a while. It was just in case some arsewipe DID decide to take it out on the old black guy. And I couldn't have that, now could I?

Anyway, I therefore had no reason for supposing anyone would be alerted by now or had even obtained the services of the police to be out there looking for me. Still, as I said, I was not one to take chances in my latest profession, and one I would soon be retiring from.

The plane from Boston's Logan Airport to Bermuda International Airport took two hours and landed at noon. Despite my optimistic prognostication on the state of things I still heaved a sigh of relief as I got through Customs unscathed and took a taxi to St George's. St George's was never one of the usual runs ashore when I'd been on the island before, but I knew of it.

The settlement of Bermuda, once a group of 173 small coral islands near the Gulf Stream in the North West Atlantic, is now 138 islands. It is only 259 feet at the highest point, and its colonisation began in what is now called the town of St George's nearly 400 years ago. It is an outstanding example of an early English settlement in the New World, with quaint old homes and walled gardens, walled lanes and alleys, and attractive enough to explore on foot. It was named for Juan de Bermudez, a Spanish sea captain, but because of the treacherous coral reefs was more commonly called *Islas Demonios*, the Islands of Devils. The first British castaways came ashore on St George's Island during a storm in 1609, and some believe their adventure was the inspiration for Shakespeare's "The Tempest".

I asked the driver where there was a decent hotel.

'You're sure you want a hotel, my friend?' the driver answered with a laconic question.

'Not really bothered,' his fare replied in the same laconic tone. 'Why, what have you in mind.'

'Well now, how about B&B, you being an Englishman yourself.' The driver grinned. 'They do a helluva good breakfast.'

'Sounds good to me, drive on, Mike,' I nodded, reading his name on the plate above his head.

We drove along the main thoroughfare called the Duke of York Street and turned left along a one way with the quaint appellation of Old Maids Lane, turning right into Nea's Alley where stood a lovely old colonial building called "Aunt Nea's Inn at Hillcrest" – all part of the name. I paid off Mike, added a generous tip and arranging to be picked up the next day for a tour around.

I checked in and asked a few questions of the polite owner, who handed me a map of Bermuda with historical side notes. I then took my bag to my room and strolled down into the town and along to King's Square. To the north side of the square lay the Butterfield Bank and it took me less than fifteen minutes to open an account and deposit the sum of one million and eight hundred thousand dollars in it, with no questions asked. I'd left another thirty thousand safely hidden in the room for expenses back in England. My wallet was also bulging. Gee, no fame but fortune at last.

As I walked out of the bank I glanced south across the bridge to Ordnance Island, where a large cruise ship was docked. Years ago I'd served as a marine on a tiny frigate out in these waters, and although I'd enjoyed my times on board the thought of taking a cruise did not appeal to me at all.

I walked into the White Horse on the waterfront to the right of the bridge, and sat out on the terrace sipping a

Dark and Stormy, the local brew of dark rum and ginger ale. I was in a brooding frame of mind and it revolved around many things. I had enough in the bank to retire now. Or rather, banks in the plural, because Butterfield was not my only bank account. I also had one in the Cayman Islands and another in Switzerland, never liking to have all my eggs in one basket - or one bank.

I planned on only spending a few days in Bermuda, then on to some business in England and an early retirement. I'd left the Corps with no pension. My own fault, I reflected, as I'd only done eighteen years, and the criteria when I left was twenty-two years for a full pension, and less than that – nothing. Anyone joining the Royal Navy or Royal Marines before 1975 got the same treatment.

So me being me, I'd decided to work on my own pension fund.

The marines had given me skills that were mostly useless in civilian life. Unless, that was, you became a crook. So I became a crook. I had been a member of the Climbing Wing, and then when it changed to Reconnaissance I became a recce specialist, then later it had changed again to the Mountain and Arctic Warfare Cadre, where I had to attend a basic course of eight strenuous months. This was the cause of yet another falling out on the home front.

And yet these later became the skills that gained me access to some of the most inaccessible places that guarded the things I stole. I had some simple rules that I lived by and couldn't give a toss for anyone else's rules. I didn't carry, was never tooled up on a job because you never knew what might happen and I knew that the contract security people who stood watch were not bad people, possibly inept at times, but the people who employed them on the cheap got what they paid for. They had a job to do, and if that was the best job they could find – then good luck to them.

They weren't responsible for the sins of their employers.

And in every case where I gained illegal entry and took something, the employers common denominator was in the sins they had committed. This had been another one of my rules in my chosen field of employment. I only broke into the premises of unscrupulous people. To help me in this, and like writers and movie stars, I had an agent. This faceless person had organized my talents from the start and I had come across him by chance. A fortunate chance for both of us as it turned out.

The first job I attempted was a year after I left the Corps. I had listened to the constant complaints of my wife for years about being away all the time and then coming home drunk after absences of months on end. She never asked what I'd been doing for Queen and Country, nor did she care very much. That I was risking my life time and again did not make me a hero in her eyes; merely it made me a very selfish husband. Another complaint was that I never earned as much as her sister's husband, who was already assistant bank manager; or even the man across the road who was a plumber and home every night and earned a fortune unblocking other people's drains. Shoving his hands in other people's shit I would say and she'd sneer and say at least it was respectable – I rest my case.

Eventually I threw away the eighteen years service and tried to make a go of it in Civvy Street. A not very successful try, and after nearly a year of attending the Employment Exchange every day (now called a Job Centre), and being told I lacked any job skills, I simply gave up. Weak of me, I suppose, but then... I drew my dole money; left most of it on the kitchen table then went down to the local and drank cheap Scrumpy all night on the rest. My wife hardly spoke to me and my young son I saw little of.

I lived that unsatisfying way until getting into a fight and meeting Jimmy. The one was the causation of the other.

Despite my situation I was aware that my only claim to fame would be my physical abilities, and although this awareness competed with my nasty habit of drinking every night, I kept the anomaly in mind as I ran five miles every other day. I also boxed ten rounds every intermediate day between runs in a spit and sawdust gym down the Dock Road. It was where my brothers and I had trained when we were young, and old Winston who owned and still ran it had always had a soft spot for the Brogan brothers.

One night I was in the Legs of Man on Lime Street and being down to my last couple of quid I was drinking my cider slowly. This was a good thing because by my pugilistic skills that night I made the contact that was to make my fortune. Literally.

I supposed I'd noticed the skinny bloke seated further along the bar when he first came in and I was amused at the way the man kept slurping his beer and glancing furtively around him. He reminded me of Uriah Heep, honest to God; my brothers and I had been constantly harangued by our mother to read the classics and we were all well into the various characters of classical literature. I had to admit that the appreciation of Shakespeare and Dickens had carried my brothers and me well, and gained me many distinctions in school, though a fat lot that had done me over the years. Or so I thought then.

When the two men burst through the door I'd been almost expecting it.

'Youse little turd,' one of the men hissed at the terrified man slurping his beer. His voice had that lovely lilting quality of the gutter-bred Scouse. 'We've been huntin' all over for yis.'

'Yeah,' growled the second man. 'Have you got it?'

They were quite large, wide and definitely menacing. I saw more, of course, being used to measuring up a man when he entered a ring from my early boxing days, and also from required skills in the marines. I saw two men who were in their mid-thirties, younger than myself, and going to seed. I noticed that their noses and ears showed some earlier ring experience, but this also showed they'd made contact with too many opponents' gloves, and their beer bellies and their fat faces belied any usefulness in this line except their present occupation as bully boys. I dismissed them as of no consequence.

'No,' the thin man quailed. 'I couldn't, the place was tighter than a nun's...'

'So, yis failed, did yer?' the first man was close to him now, and they kept their voices low pitched, so only their victim and I could hear. This brought me to their attention of course.

'What 'ar youse lookin' at, wack?' the second man glared at me in what he assumed was an intimidating way.

To his chagrin I laughed. 'I dunno, mate,' I threw back at him. 'The label's come off.'

'Youse cheeky bastard,' the man raised his voice and people looked up from their drinks and their conversation. He strode along the bar and loomed over me, and I took another drink from the half bottle of cider I was drinking from.

'Don't,' I warned and smiled at the man at the same time, knowing I was wasting my breath.

'Don't what?' the man asked, not bothering to look in my eyes. If he had and had seen the touch of menace lurking there he might have refrained from his next move, which was to pull his right arm back.

'Don't even think about it, arsehole,' I answered evenly, swinging into action as the other threw the punch.

My bottle came across and the man punched it instead of my face. It didn't break and so I smashed it straight into the side of his head as he held on to his damaged knuckles. I kicked back off my stool and moved against the other man who was coming along the bar.

The bigger man was used to his size intimidating people, so was surprised to see his target coming to him. He had still not recovered from the shock of seeing his chum decked so easily.

'You can turn around and walk out,' I said evenly, but naturally I knew he wouldn't take heed. He didn't so I walked straight into him and hit him with a simple combination of straight left, right hook to the ribs followed by a right cross; end of contest.

The barman had taken no part during the exchange; after all, he wasn't paid as a bouncer, was he?

'Take him out of here, mate, quick,' the barman nodded at the frightened man.

I held the man's arm as I guided him towards the door. The pub was quiet and no one moved or said anything. More than one had suffered at the hands of the two sleeping beauties on the floor and this would be reflected in their silence when the police arrived on the scene.

I took the skinny man around the corner into Lord Street and we slipped in the side door of a sleazy little place only one step up from the Union Street scrumpy dens I'd known down in Plymouth.

I ordered two pints of rough cider and stuck one in front of the little man. I'd always hated bullies, and well remembered my brothers and myself defending the smaller, more vulnerable kids at our little Catholic school. The School of Hard Knocks it was known as, and St Clare's certainly lived up to its nickname. Yet it had given the Brogan Boys, which we would always be called, the grounding that was to serve us well in later life, both in the ring and in the Royal Marines.

'Ugh,' the thin man pulled a face as he swallowed a mouthful. 'What the fuck's that? It looks like piss burrit tastes worse.'

'How long have you been a connoisseur of piss?' I growled. 'Anyway, friend, beggars can't be choosers. I'm skint so make the most of it.' I sipped my own and grimaced as I realized the other man was right.

'Ay, I'm sorry, all right? I'm grateful for what yis did in the Legs back there. I'm still a bit nervous, like. Those two are real sadistic bastards, and if their boss told 'em to break me legs, I'd be runnin' down Lime Street on me bum.'

I had to laugh at the way the man expressed himself. All Liverpudlians were comedians in their own way, though most didn't even try to be.

'Me name's Jimmy, by the way,' the man's vixen-like face took on a terrible aspect, which I suddenly realized was a smile. Don't do that too often, son, I thought. You'll scare the knickers off some old lady. 'Let me buy yis a real drink, eh?'

'Pint of Guinness would be nice,' I said immediately and tried not to sound too grateful.

Jimmy was back in a few minutes with a foaming pint of Guinness and a pint of best bitter.

'So, yer a bit down on yer luck ar yis, er...?

'Harry,' I told him, taking a deep swig of my drink before someone tried to take it away from me. It was a while since I'd had a decent pint of the black stuff. I ignored the question. 'What did Tweedledum and Tweedledee have against you then, Jimmy?'

The skinny man with the foxy face looked at me carefully for a few moments. 'Yis aren't an undercover scuffer, ar yer, Harry?'

When I shook my head Jimmy accepted it. 'I do some… work fer this feller who fixes me up with jobs, like. Sometimes when I get a bit full, I gob off a bit, and their boss, Liam Dempsey, heard about it and wanted me to do a job for him. When I told him I work through this feller, he said he doesn't go through inter…inter med…'

'Intermediaries,' I helped.

'Yis, them, aye, an anyway, one of his 'ardmen smacked me in the mouth, and Dempsey threatened that he'd get them to break me arms and legs unless I did what he wanted. Offer I couldn't refuse, wasn't it?'

'So, what went wrong?'

'I couldn't do it. The office they wanted me to get into was fuckin' miles high, and I'm, er, not very good at heights,' Jimmy pushed his mouth into the glass and drank liberally. I'd never seen anyone drink like he did. It was the same as watching a warthog at a watering hole. I'd seen one in South Africa once and the likeness was remarkable.

'A burglar, who doesn't like heights,' I gave a tight smile at the absurdity of it. 'How do you usually get in?'

'Oh, right through the front doors. Locks,' Jimmy said proudly. 'I'm a fuckin' genius at picking locks.'

'And modest with it,' I muttered. 'Why not this time?'

'Two of the biggest and most e'ficient gards I've ever bloody seen. Aren't youse bothered about heights then, Harry?' the man asked.

'Everyone is, Jimmy, unless they're nuts. But I can handle it, which is the secret. I used to be a climber and still do a bit when I can get among the rocks.'

'Reelly?' Jimmy said with interest. ''Ere, let me get some more drinks in an' don't worry about it as I'm flush at the minute.'

When he returned with the drinks he gave me, his new drinking companion, a speculative look. 'So, yis can climb, and yer can use yer mitts pretty good. What ar yis workin' at, at the moment?'

'At the moment, I'm resting between jobs,' I said flatly. 'It's been like that since I left the mob. Climbing and beating the crap out of someone are not exactly regarded as skills by Personnel Managers when you're job-hunting.'

'An 'ow long were youse in the forces for?'

When I told him, Jimmy whistled softly. 'Eighteen years, Christ, what else can you do?'

'Jump out of planes and strip any gun down in ten seconds. Escape and evasion trained; build an igloo, live off the land, and shoot the left testicle off a bumble bee at a thousand yards,' I reflected. 'Lot of use in Civvy Street, Jimmy, wouldn't you say?'

'Some of it could be useful, Harry,' the thin man said thoughtfully. 'How'd youse like ter meet me agent?'

I never did get to meet the agent, not in the flesh anyway, but from then on things began to change, and for the better. Not that they could have become much worse at that time on reflection.

'Call me Jonathon,' the voice on the open phone told me. 'No formalities here, are there, Jimmy old chap?'

'No, as yer say, Jonathon, we don't stand on cer'mony 'ere,' Jimmy coughed, spitting out his habitual fag end, then promptly lit up another one.

Jimmy had met me in the same little pub the day after our initial meeting. True to his word he'd arranged a meeting with his agent. We'd gone to an office in Dale Street, only there was little by way of an office inside. Two chairs, a sofa and a state-of-the-art telephone on a small table completed the furnishings and fittings for the entire three rooms.

'It isn't always this joint,' Jimmy told him. 'He changes the meeting places around a lot, just ter keep the fuzz away.'

'What does he look like, this bloke?' I asked him.

'Dunno,' Jimmy shrugged. 'Never met him; it's always done by phone. Sometimes he leaves a packet here, you know, instructions, plans, photos. But he never comes in person. Fuckin' rude, I call it.'

'Fucking clever, I call it,' I smiled coldly. 'He can't be implicated, can he? This place is probably rented by the month by some agency on his behalf and I'll bet they've never seen him either.'

Our discussion came to an abrupt end when the phone rang. Jimmy picked it up and pressed a button on the phone console and we were on speakerphone. A voice boomed out in the confined space of the almost empty room.

'Right, Harry. May I call you Harry? I've looked into your background, Harry, and I like what I see. One thing puzzles me though. Why now, at the age of thirty-eight and completely law-abiding, have you decided to begin a life of crime? You don't look like a criminal; there's no furtiveness about you at all. All criminals look furtive, you know.'

I looked around the room instinctively. Was the man watching me? What else did he know about me? Then I relaxed as I thought it out.

'I never actually decided to get into a life of crime,' I shrugged. I knew there must be a hidden camera somewhere, very cleverly concealed, but it had to be there. How else would the man who called himself Jonathon know what I looked like? 'But I've always had an instinct for survival and I've got to feed my family. If you've really done some background checks you will know that I haven't been doing too well lately. I get no service pension so I'm living off the dole. Every job interview I go to I'm told I don't have any job skills, no experience. How do you acquire skills and experience if no one gives you a bloody chance?'

'Quite, old boy, I'm afraid you are in what our American cousins would call a "Catch 22" situation,' the disembodied voice said sympathetically. 'However, I think we can help you out by offering gainful employment.'

'Who's this "we", Kemo Sabe?' I asked caustically, but the man on the speakerphone wasn't fooled although he did give a polite chuckle.

'I also work for someone, Harry. Don't we all, indeed? Your friend Jimmy there has been somewhat naughty in renting out his services elsewhere, but given the circumstances as explained by Jimmy last evening, and that he IS one of our best operatives, I think we can try to extricate him from the mess, don't you?'

'I did my lifesaving bit already, mate,' I snapped. 'So what are you getting at, apart from loving the sound of your own vocal cords?'

To my surprise the man gave a genuine laugh. 'You live up to your expectations, Harry. We'd like you to complete the job that Jimmy here didn't even begin. Let's say it serves two purposes. It prevents nasty Mr. Dempsey from doing awful things to Jimmy, and also gives us an opportunity to see you in action, to see how you perform on the job.'

'Why should I?' I asked rudely.

'Well, for a start you get an opportunity to help Jimmy, your new found friend, and I know you're not too well acquainted as yet, so there might not be an unbreakable bond there. But you will definitely get the opportunity to stitch up our Mr. Dempsey, who is a bit of a pratt, so you will therefore receive an expenses cheque for ten thousand pounds. I'm sure you could use it, Harry.'

I was also sure that I could, and said so.

A week later I easily climbed up the side of the tower block, stopped at the eighteenth floor where I found a window conveniently open as I'd been told, and entered. Ten minutes later I was back, long rope double looped around the steel window frame and descendeured down to the next roof where I made my exit.

Five minutes later I walked past a nondescript Ford Mondeo idling at the kerb, threw my package in through the open back window and walked around the corner where I caught a bus. The next day I would learn that an hour later the police visited the home of Liam Dempsey where they found an incriminating piece of evidence in a recent gangland slaying. Dempsey went down for twenty, and could never figure out where the evidence had come from. After all, that little tow rag, Jimmy, had been drinking in the same pub as him all night and he was the only one who could have pulled it. Or was he?

I got my ten grand and went straight home to tell my wife the good news. I actually had a well-paid job at last and maybe with money in our lives it would all be different. We'd go away on holiday first; just the three of us, and life would start anew.

So much for that, I thought, as I saw the car outside my house. The cheeky sod hadn't even bothered to hide his bloody car down the street. I should have known, Albie Lamb was always coming around on some pretext or other, and I'd seen the looks he'd exchanged with Dorothy. First I peeped in on my son, closing the door softly behind me, and then into the main bedroom where the noises were coming from.

She was riding him like a Valkrie; blonde hair tumbled around her shoulders, sweat running down her bare back.

'Oh, my God,' my wife cried. 'That's it.'

'Me too,' the man beneath her moaned, 'I'm coming too, love.'

'Not tonight you ain't, chum,' I snarled quietly, enough for the others to hear, but not enough to wake our son in the next room. I pushed Dorothy off with a powerful hand and she went bouncing off the bed, hit the wall and slid to the floor, dazed.

'Hey, no need for that, mate,' Albie half rose from the bed. 'We can sort this out like civilized people, yeah? After all, we ARE family, yeah?'

I looked at my brother-in-law incredulously, and couldn't believe the cheek of the yuppie-talking assistant bank manager. I walked towards the door then decided to hit him anyway, turned back and gave him a solid right in the nose.

'Oh, Christ. You've broken my bloody nose, oh God. What will Daphne say?'

'You'll think of something, Albie,' I turned away again, disgusted. 'Just tell her you got it for fucking her sister.'

It took me ten minutes to pack a bag, during which time I heard the door slam downstairs. A few minutes later a car started up outside and it pulled away with a roar.

I was opening the front door when I heard her voice from the staircase behind me.

'You bastard,' I heard from the staircase and Dorothy stood there with a thin robe clutched around her. 'You're an animal. How could you hit poor Albie, you know he isn't a fighting man.'

'Well, this might come as a shock, darling, but when you screw another man's wife, and in his own bed, you should expect a slap.'

'Where are you going?' She snapped. 'Away, I hope, for good. You're no use around here, always drunk, no job. You're no man, God you're pathetic. Oh God.'

God never arrived, so she sat on the stairs holding her head in her hands as I opened the front door.

'Why the hell did you have to come home early for once?' she cried

'For this,' I said softly and she looked up as five thousand pounds in notes came cascading around her. 'I came to give you this, Dorothy, and there was more. Have a nice life.'

After that it was easy, working for Jonathon.

I would receive all the details in an envelope, reconnoitre the place, and then work out a plan. This would be agreed with Jonathon, who would sometimes add a few useful suggestions, and the job would be put into practice. An untraceable cheque on a Swiss bank account would pay the money and I would then place it in one of my own accounts - all off shore of course.

Jonathon had almost begged me to stay, and I'd almost been tempted. I would miss the excitement, the adrenaline rush every time I went on a job. But I was not a greedy man and had enough now to last me for the rest of my life without the need to live frugally. I was also a cautious man, and I'd decided enough was enough.

My only regret was the loss of my son, for I'd decided that night in Liverpool when I'd walked out of my house for good, that the boy's welfare came first and being torn between parents was not the way to do it. I heard that Albie had left his wife and moved in with my ex. Dorothy had not only lost a husband, but her sister as well. I would make provision for the boy's education, as I couldn't see Albie educating a brat that wasn't his.

So I sat in the White Horse and drank my rum and gazed across at the twinkling lights on the cruise ship, not envying the people at all. I was drinking myself into a more benevolent mood, and was eventually just a man at peace with my lot and myself.

For the time being, at least, but as was apropos to the ways of man, I was never at peace with myself or my lot for very long.

CHAPTER TWO

The Manual of Discipline, one of the Dead Sea Scrolls, says that God created two great spirits, one of truth and one of perversity, the latter being the angel of darkness.

Dead Sea Scrolls

(About Ten Years Later)

I was back in Bermuda, seated in the bar of Blackbeards, a restaurant set on a small hill facing another small hill containing Fort St Catherine, which in turn overlooked the beach of the same name lying in Gates Bay. I was drinking draught Guinness in a can and enjoying myself. I had visited Bermuda often in the long ago, when I was a young marine on a warship, and then again ten years before to open an account here. I was back for some business with the bank and a week's holiday, despite that my life had been one long holiday since retiring.

True, I'd indulged myself over the years; keeping up my climbing skills in places like Arizona, some snow and ice in the Himalayas, skiing in Northern Norway and Austria. I'd dived in the sparkling waters of Tahiti, where the abundance of sea life was unequalled anywhere else on earth. I'd also kept up my daily training; running, weights, boxing many rounds on the bag and skipping.

Occasionally I'd set up rendezvous' with my brothers in some exotic spot on the planet and they'd indulged me by coming. They'd also let me take care of the bill, which after all was what brothers were for, right?

There'd been women too; some adventurous who accompanied me on my jaunts, some more sedate, and some who were just dolly birds, good for a night out but little else. In all this I'd never found a soul mate, someone I just liked to be with when the adventure was done and the shagging had stopped. Now I'd resigned myself to being a loner, with occasional lapses into female company.

Bermuda had changed, of course, in keeping with everywhere else on the planet. I'd had to adjust to the high prices, although money wasn't a problem in my immediate or foreseeable future. The Bermuda dollar was equal to an American dollar; that being the currency my money was in. The average house price was $1.6 million, but what else could you expect in a place where Michael Douglas lived, and where his kids were already enrolled in a private school. With such celebrities only the very rich and the indigenous people whose houses had been in the families for generations could afford to live. Sure, a newcomer could buy a house but it had to be priced at over two and a half million, on top of which he'd pay a whopping 25% tax and the same when he came to sell.

I'd landed at the Bermuda International Airport and dialled the number of my previous taxi-driver, Mike, whom I'd always used on my infrequent visits. The man was still driving his taxi around the islands. Twenty minutes later a gleaming black Mercedes station wagon pulled up and Mike climbed out. He grabbed me by the hand and pumped it like a long-lost friend.

'Business good eh, Mike?'

'Business very good, thanks to the cruise ships, Harry,' he grinned. 'Same place?'

'Same place,' I replied.

Mike took me straight to St George's and Aunt Nea's Inn, the place I'd stayed at several times since that first trip a decade ago. After booking in and exchanging pleasantries with the new owner and his wife, I donned my jogging sweats and ran around the Loop, the road which ran from St George's down past the cut, around Builder's Bay and along past the cemetery. Past St Catherine's Beach and the golf course and Tobacco Bay, then I followed the road along the rest of the course, past the unfinished church and dropped back into St George's. Altogether it was about three miles and at the end of it I felt so good that I decided to do it again, this time pushing it at a faster pace.

I thought about it later and wondered. It was as though I was building towards something...but what?

The following day, after a half-hour in the Butterfield Bank, I had begun with Hamilton, Bermuda's capital and a small bustling harbour town. From the old days I remembered clubs like the Forty Thieves, the Jungle Room, Four Aces, Casey's Lounge and the Clayhouse Inn. By far my favourite was the Cock and Feathers, known euphemistically by the locals as the Prick and Tickle. Sadly they were all gone now. The Mariners Club was still there, and I sampled a pint of Bass bitter from the tap while Mike went off for a lunch date somewhere else. I had told him to meet me outside the Police Station on Front Street later.

I strolled down from the Mariners along Church Street and took a right down Par-la-Ville Road, cut across the Par-la-Ville Park with its luxuriant gardens and came out on Queen Street. I ate lunch on the patio of the Lemon Tree Café, a spicy sandwich of chilli and onions and cheddar, washed down with a Gallo red wine from California.

As I continued my stroll down Queen to where it joined with Front Street, then a left to my waiting taxi, I found I was really enjoying myself. No worries, no cares; certainly no planned meetings or deadlines to be somewhere.

Why then did I have that niggling feeling in the top of my spine – the one that acted as a warning that all was not as it should be? It was a seldom thing, but also not a false-alarm thing, for it had saved my skin on many occasions. I shrugged and walked on, but my alarm zones were now on full alert.

I spent the afternoon exploring Pembroke Parish and Spanish Point, and then made it back to the lodging and a very nice, if outrageously expensive, dinner at a local restaurant. During the course of the afternoon, and glancing out of the back of the taxi often, I thought I was seeing a little too much of a white Ford Mondeo, but was not sure. I'm getting paranoid, I told myself and shrugged it off.

The next morning, following the excellent full English breakfast as advertised, Mike picked me up and we took the long drive around to the West End, part of Ireland Island. I stood sadly in what was left of the Royal Naval Dockyard where my small frigate would tie up long ago. Nostalgia was not part of my persona, but I certainly felt pangs of something as I gazed around at the handsome, centuries old Clocktower Building, now called the Clocktower Mall, holding restaurants, galleries and shops. In the Cooperage Building, once the home to craftsmen in the old trade of barrel making, now housed people of different crafts, an art gallery and an arts and crafts market.

In contrast to Hamilton and St. George's, the West End was rather pastoral. With the exception of the Dockyard, many of the attractions there were natural: wildlife reserves, wooded areas and lovely harbours and bays.

I stood and listened to the elegant guide who appeared with a cluster of Japanese tourists. '...during the post-American Revolution period, Britain found itself with neither an anchorage nor a major ship-repair yard in the western

Atlantic. Around 1809, when Napoleon was surfacing as a serious threat and British ships became increasingly vulnerable to pirate attack, Britain began construction of a major stronghold in Bermuda. The work was carried out by slaves and English convicts toiling under appalling conditions and living on prison ships. Thousands of prisoners died before the project was competed.'

I was bored now, and found it somewhat amusing that one of the Japanese was serving as interpreter for most of the rest of her group, and the singsong cadence of her voice vied strangely with the patois of the local guide. As I walked away I could still hear it.

I'd last been there in the mid-seventies, but was still surprised to see grassy lawns, trees and shrubs growing where there used to be vast stretches of concrete. A huge cruise ship was docked at the terminal especially built for it and its kind. The larger cruise ships could not get through the Town Cut; that narrow gap that had been blasted out of the solid rock, to tie up in St Georges. Private yachts floated calmly in the marina nearby.

I found my taxi and the sleeping Mike on the road outside the quaintly named Frog and Toad pub. I took a table outside near my taxi and had another pint of draught beer while I waited for the driver to wake up. Mike eventually returned to the land of the living and started to apologize but I grinned and waved my hand. I was on holiday after all.

And yet...several times I had that funny feeling in the back of my neck again, and old habits never really die; they just hide away for a while. On the way back to St George's I moved my body so I could glance out of the left-hand wing mirror. Being an old British colony the cars were still right-hand drive and they drove on the left of the road. We drove out on Pender Road and crossed the Cut Bridge onto Ireland Island South.

As we passed Loyalty Estate road on our left, then Mangrove Lane I was beginning to think my hunch was way off. My premonition turned into the real thing as we passed East Shore Road, also on the left. A nondescript white car came out behind us as we continued through Somerset Village.

'Recognize the car behind us, Mike?' I asked the driver. The chances of a local recognizing another car on the small group of islands that formed Bermuda were quite good.

'No, it looks like one of those hire for the day jobs from out by the airport.'

'Okay, mate. Drive back towards St Georges and do a few deviations, nothing fast, but let's see if he's still interested.'

By the time we'd driven the length of Middle Road, onto North Shore Road and were leaving Hamilton Parish, Mike had done a few obvious detours, but the white car was still on our tail.

'I think he likes us,' Mike grinned in the mirror.

'An amateur,' I told him. 'Know any narrow places?'

'Oh, yeah, plenty, so what's your plan?'

'Let him get close, then slam on the anchors. I'll take it from there.'

'You got it,' Mike smiled.

As we were about to go over the causeway onto St David's Island, the taxi suddenly hit the brakes and slewed across the road. I was out of the taxi and took the six yards to the other car in seconds. I yanked open the rear door and threw myself inside.

'Right,' I said menacingly, and then stared at the man seated beside me, seeing him for the first time.

The man was not perturbed in the least, merely sat in his seat smoking and gazing at me without expression, his eyes the color of the ash on his cigarette.

He was wearing a white collar.

'Hello there, Father,' I greeted cheerfully, though not feeling it, and as much to cover my surprise as to show a cheerful aspect towards the man who had been following me for two days.

'What's the deal here, mon?' the driver asked, a large black man whose aggressive accent contrasted with the polite tones of the native Bermudan.

'The deal?' I reflected. 'The deal, sunshine, is that you and God's messenger here have been following me around for the past two days. You either know why or you don't; either way you did the driving, and so you're part of it.'

'Please,' the priest said, although his tones showed he was in no way pleading. Although the English was precise, I recognized the harsh accent of middle Europe, and it brought back the halcyon days of my youth. 'I do not want trouble, and this man knows nothing, only that he drove me around.'

'Yes, around after me, and tell me, are you really a priest?' I looked at him quizzically.

Even seated I could tell the man was tall; taller than me and unlike my brothers, who were always short-arses, I stood six foot in my socks. He was around fifty I suppose, but I could have been out by a few years either side. The priest was big, corpulent though it was amply dispersed over his big frame, and with greying locks surrounding a hirsutely challenged dome. He was dressed in a simple cleric's black shirt topped with a white collar, black trousers and black jacket. The man wore a permanently beatific smile, but again, I noticed his eyes, not just for the ash-grey color, but for the lack of depth they held. Otherwise he appeared to be as perfectly pleasant as you'd expect a priest to be. Only I knew better, of course, having served my time as an altar boy.

'I am, my son,' the priest nodded gravely. 'But we cannot talk here. Will you meet me somewhere later, Mr. Brogan? I promise I'll explain everything to you to your satisfaction.'

'Where do you suggest then, padre?' I didn't show surprise that the priest knew my name, and also knew there was nowhere else to take this; I certainly didn't want to waltz into a cop shop with the priest in tow.

'You're staying in St George's, Mr. Brogan. May I suggest Blackbeard's, by Fort St Catherine? Seven o'clock all right? They have Guinness in the can, there, though nothing like the real thing, of course.'

'Of course, nothing like the real thing as the puff said to his boyfriend at the hen party.' I had now been made aware that the other man was even cognizant of my drinking habits. 'Seven o'clock tonight it is, padre.'

I climbed out of the car, which had now parked into the side of the road, and walked up to my own taxi.

The white Ford moved past us and Mike followed for a while before it turned off right to St George's Parish on St David's Island.

'Friends of yours then?' Mike caught my eye in the mirror.

'Friends?' I muttered. 'One's a priest and the other sounds like a Jamaican. I think not.'

'Ah, the white car belongs to a Jammy, eh? Thought I'd seen it before. The guy married a local girl so he could get into Bermuda. He drives his motor for private hire as they won't give him a license yet.'

'Let me guess, her big, fat and ugly, eh?' I mimicked the Jamaican driver's accent and Mike laughed loudly. 'No one locally would take her on; am I right?'

'You're dead on, mon,' Mike agreed in the same accent. 'You want me to pick you up later?'

'No, that's okay, Mike, I'm only going local.'

I glanced at my watch again. Seven-fifteen, the priest was late. At seven twenty the big man with the white collar came up the back steps of the open-air bar behind me. I could see him in the mirror, slanted above the bar, and as I'd guessed in the taxi, the priest WAS tall, at least six foot six, or maybe more. He apologized for his tardiness.

'What's your poison, padre?' I asked, trying to be polite. Politeness doesn't come naturally to some people – and I'm one of them.

'No, please,' the priest held a finger up to the barman who came immediately, to my surprise. Kenny had a habit of serving you when the mood came upon him, not when it was convenient to you the customer. 'I'll have black rum, two lumps of ice, and another Guinness for this gentleman. Tonight is on me, Mr. Brogan.'

'Thanks,' I said. 'But I always buy my own round. And out here they never call it black rum; it's referred to as dark.'

The priest shrugged, and pointed to my glass with two inches of the black stuff left in the bottom. 'How does it taste, with the thingy in it?'

'Good, but it has to be really cold, unlike the real stuff. And that thingy is called a widget. Do you know anything about it?' I was trying to be friendly, but didn't know why exactly. Probably because I was intrigued as to the priest's interest in me.

'Not a thing,' the priest shook his head as the barman placed a glass in front of him. 'I confess that it is not my pleasure.'

'Your loss then,' I nodded to the barman as he gave me a fresh one. 'I think it was Boddingtons who discovered the widget, or they bought the patent from someone who is probably now lying on the beach in the Seychelles with enough money to buy Chelsea Football Club, when Abramovitch has finished with it. I heard it has hydrogen in the widget and when you open the can and it mixes with the air outside it releases and froths up; something like that, anyway. Then they sold the patent to Guinness and just kept the rights to widget their own best bitter.'

'A lovely tale,' the priest murmured without interest and sipped his rum somewhat daintily. 'May we get a table outside?'

Without waiting for a reply he picked up his glass and carried it to a table over against the railing running around the patio. This was raised a good storey high and we had a good view of the diminutive Achilles Bay below.

'I'll begin by introducing myself, Mr. Brogan,' the tall man told me. 'My name is Zoran Milos.' He pronounced it Me-losh. 'I do not come from the land of your parents' but have been there many times. It is indeed a beautiful country. But you know that, of course, having spent many trips to the North: Belfast and Londonderry, I believe.'

I said nothing; after all, the other man was telling the story. This strange priest possessed far too much knowledge about me, and he must have had excellent sources to trace me back so far. Even to gain access to my service records would not be an uncomplicated procedure.

'Of course,' I replied. 'So you've come halfway around the world to find me. For what, may I ask? I stopped attending mass a long time ago...'

'About the time your dear Irish mother died of cancer, I believe, Mr Brogan. Though I understand that you prefer to be called just Brogan. May I call you Brogan?'

'Please yourself,' I said into my glass, but there was no antagonism in my voice, and I tossed it back and started to rise to get more. I was puzzled over this priest who knew so much about me. He was up first and laid a gentle hand on my shoulder.

'My place of residence at the moment is of no consequence, but I once worked in Vatican City, where I was close to the Holy Father himself. I'm terribly concerned about the Church at the moment, Brogan,' the well-fed jowls took on an air of sincerity, though it didn't impress me too much. Still, I'm like that. 'I work for a...little known group within the Church, dedicated to the downfall of the Devil and all his works, and have done for several decades. When I was in the Vatican I was the Holy Father's friend, and confessor; yes, even the Pope has a confessor, you know. Most people, even the Vatican dwellers, don't know who it is at any time. But we were together for so long that I think most of the inner circle guessed. My real title is Signore, but I prefer to travel incognito, and there is no one more incognito than a priest.'

To which I vaguely agreed, but made no comment. He returned from the bar a few minutes later with two refills. Milos continued as though there'd been no interruption.

'His Holiness, Simon John, is a remarkable man. He does not turn his back on the scientific works of man, and is in fact quite enthusiastic about many of the modern trappings of civilization. He refuses to get into debate about DNA, genetics, cloning, and the like, but I happen to know that he dismisses none of them. He does have strong views on birth control, celibacy and the ordaining of women into the church, and those private views might surprise you, Brogan. However, that is not what I came here to talk about. For such a modern man in so many ways, his Holiness is a staunch believer in good and evil. I see you smile, but I am not talking about the euphemistic tautology of Good and Evil; I mean God in his Heavenly grandeur, and the Devil in all his evil defiance against all that is good on the Earth.'

'You're talking superstition now, right?' I frowned. 'If there's good there must be evil, if there's a God, ergo, there must be a Devil. Balance the scales, that sort of thing? But then we get ghosties, ghoulies, vampires, werewolves, and the entire movie world of nasty creatures and beasties that go thump in the night.'

'Yes,' Milos said seriously and I stared at him for a time. 'It's all out there, my doubting friend. Not quite in the forms you grew up on in the cinema and literature, but there IS evil, in all of its perceived and hidden forms. The Devil and All His Works, in fact. What do you know of the Devil, Brogan?'

The question surprised me but I replied as though I was giving weapon training or climbing lectures to recruits.

'I know that the phrase you used just now, The Devil and All His Works, was a book by Dennis Wheatly, a writer of horror stories. That in itself says it all. Okay, have it your way; the Devil is the name given to a supernatural entity who, in most Western religions, is the central embodiment of evil. This entity is commonly referred to by a variety of other names, including Satan, Asmodai, Beelzebub, Lucifer, Mephistopheles, Prince of Darkness, Archfiend, Tempter, Anti-Christ, Common Enemy, Shaitan, Eblis, King of Hell, angel of the bottomless pit, Apollyon, Abbaddon, the foul fiend, the Evil One, Wicked O., Auld Nick, old Harry, Old Scratch, Auld Hornie, Clootie, cloven hoof, Ahriman, Angra Mainyu...shall I go on? How am I doing so far?'

'Very good,' the priest dipped his head approvingly. 'You obviously held onto your beliefs a long time after you were an altar boy.' There he goes again – the bugger's got too much information on me I thought.

'More like the horror pictures, Padre. My mother worked in the local cinema and I was always in there,' I rasped.

The Monsignor looked thoughtful for a few minutes and I left him to it as I addressed myself to my own contemplation of my glass of Guinness.

'What you just said, whether in jest or the recumbent knowledge from your days in Religious Instruction helps me to explain things to you. We want you to obtain a...item for us.'

'We? Us? As in the Church, the Pope, the Illuminati, Opus Dei...or whatever other name your secret little group goes by?'

'Christianity understands the Devil in the context of the Old Testament,' the priest changed tack, making me frown slightly, although not in confusion. 'Unlike Manichaeism which teaches a coeval dualism, Christians see the Devil as a corrupted or fallen angel. He was Lucifer, an angel in authority before the Creation, who fell because of pride and because he waged a war against Jehovah-Elohim. The key fact in understanding the Devil is that he was originally a holy being that was corrupted by misusing his free will and because of his pride.'

I was in danger of becoming bored again. All this talk of Christianity and Devils was not something I'd engaged in for a long time. Myself as the reader enjoyed mystery tales of the supernatural, but I as the man confessed to few beliefs beyond what was in my glass or on my plate. Or, as in the old days, who was trying to kill me next. The big priest was a reader of men, a skill he had to have in order to save their souls, I supposed, and he could probably tell my own state of mind. He was very astute and the man of the cloth apparently decided to get to the point before he lost me.

'I...we...want you to obtain a musical instrument for us, Mr Brogan. It is a vital thing, this instrument; a violin.'

'The Devil's Instrument,' I muttered. 'The Devil is said to have the best tunes.'

'Ah, you're a well-read man I see.'

'And the evil instrument you want me to "obtain" for you, Father?'

37

'As I said, it is a violin, Brogan'

'Just a violin?'

'No, not just a violin; it is one of the most valuable in the world, if not THE most valuable.'

'Surely not more valuable than a Stradivarius?' I said in a clever-arse voice, and drained my glass. The priest stood to get more drinks in.

'Actually it IS a Stradivarius,' the priest nodded to me, though unlike me, with no sign of smugness on his face.

I watched with a frown as he walked away. Now I WAS definitely in danger of becoming confused.

He returned, we drank, and the priest started to tell me a strange tale. About a famous violinmaker who made a pact with the Devil and made his finest ever instrument as part of the deal.

'And I suppose this violin is black.'

The priest stared at me. 'How did you know that? Very few people are aware of its existence. You're proving a surprising man, Brogan. The person who recommended you was not lying about you, was he?'

'Ah, and how is Jonathon these days?' I asked casually, covering the fact that my choice of color was merely an educated guess. I'd always been taught to hint at knowing more than you actually do. Not always the best policy, as I was about to learn with present company.

'There you go again,' Zoran Milos did not change expression. 'How would you know that, my friend? And how do you know about Stradivari?'

'Remember what I did for a living until very recently, Father?' I smiled without humour. 'Well, I did a lot of studying for my...profession. I became interested in paintings, antiques, precious objets d'art, etc. My take was often whatever I found, and I always found something that made the night's work more than worthwhile. I've heard rumours, stories, funny little tales, about all sorts of...things. One being a certain black violin. You never answered my question, by the way.'

'Jonathon's well,' the priest said with a quick smile. 'He's done work for us in the past, and when we asked him who the best man was your name was already on his lips.'

'I always felt he was working for a higher power,' I said conversationally.

'He was not contracted exclusively to us, but we were his main customers, per se. You have also done valuable work for us in the past, Brogan,' the priest told me, but to my disappointment he left it there. 'So, would you like to have some adventure once more, some adrenaline flow, and be amply rewarded into the bargain?'

I studied the Monsignor for a few moments. For some indefinable reason which I could not actually put a finger on I didn't think at that time that I liked the man, but that had no bearing on my decision.

Which was an emphatic, 'No, I don't think so, padre.'

'Your final decision, Mr Brogan?' the priest raised an eyebrow.

'What is this, "Who Wants to Be a Bloody Millionaire"?' I snapped. 'I don't need money and I've had enough adventure to last a lifetime.'

'A pity, Brogan,' the man in cloth looked quite sad. 'Altogether a great pity.'

I left him to his sadness and got two more drinks in, aware that it was my round and I liked to keep the record straight.

We got in several more rounds and drank slowly for a while, and to my surprise he did not attempt to persuade me any further, and to which I had been expecting him to pursue. We exchanged some pleasantries about Ireland, where he'd attended sabbaticals, down on the southwest coast. I had no personal memories of Southern Ireland, although my parents had apparently come from there before I was born.

Eventually Milos shook himself and rose, quite steady despite the amount of rum he'd consumed. Mind you, he was a big boy.

'I'll say goodnight then, Brogan, but will leave you my card in case you change your mind.'

He laid a visiting card on the table and I watched him walk through the bar and out into the night. That was that, I thought with satisfaction. I hadn't succumbed to the lure of another job, despite that I had nurtured some dissatisfied feelings for a time now. What was adventure anyway, except a yearning for youth, and at my age I didn't need the agro or the knocks. Though that train of thought almost had me wondering about my brothers, both a lot older than me and both out there somewhere in the nasty world, still enjoying adventures and doing exciting things. Anyway, as I've already said; I had more than enough money for my modest needs.

But something was niggling as I finished my drink and wandered back to St George's over the golf course and the steep hill past the massive darkness of the defunct hotel that had closed down some eighteen years before.

For a man with a mission who had travelled thousands of miles to make me an offer, Milos had given up very easily. Too easily, in fact, and I shrugged and told myself that it must have been when I mentioned I had enough money.

Or thought I had until the morning of my third day in Bermuda.

It started when I went into the local grocery store on the corner where the Duke of York Street collided with the Duke of Kent Street. I paid with my cheque card and it wouldn't go through.

'It's on the Butterfield Bank,' I said reasonably. 'It's as good as cash money.'

'Sorry, sir,' the young black lady said sadly. 'You must go and talk to them. Correct the mistake, eh.'

'Certainly,' I agreed with a forced smile but I started getting the vibes even then. 'I'll just leave these here, shall I?' I deposited my groceries inside her counter space and left the store, feeling that ache in my neck again – the second time in a few days.

Fifteen minutes later I left the Butterfield Bank feeling somewhat shattered. There was no money in my account. Someone had hacked in and withdrawn everything, leaving me broke, skint - penniless. But only in Bermuda and I immediately phoned Cayman and Switzerland. To my relief everything was okay there. But what kind of organisation could have the power to do something like that? I'd been shafted, but as yet I didn't know how – I suppose I was that stupid. That the mysterious priest from the Vatican was behind it was my first thought. It was too much of a coincidence that I'd been offered a job that I'd turned down because I didn't need the money then suddenly – I needed the money. I was astonished when I stopped to contemplate again what power it took to ruin a man overnight.

It put the shits up me pretty much at the same time.

Luckily I carried reserves of cash. I'd spent too many years without cash that when I had finally got my hands on some I always kept a reasonable amount around me in the folding readies variety. I was still flaming mad, however, and I've been told more than one time that me mad was not a pretty sight.

The phone rang, which I had been expecting.

'Brogan?' the voice on the phone said.

I looked at my watch and when I saw the dial read 3am I had a resurgence of the state I'd been in the night before. Hopping bloody mad.

'Mister to you, arsehole,' I replied politely.

'Say what?' the accent was unmistakably American, East coast.

'Spit it out, man. What have you got to say?'

'Hey, do nice, eh?'

'No, I don't do nice,' I did the menacing thing with my voice. 'Especially when I've just become penniless overnight and am beginning to suspect that the reason you called is to tell me that you had something to do with it on behalf of the Holy Mother church.'

'Brogan, we both know you ain't penniless, just your Bermuda account, but what we done with that we can also do with your funds in the Cayman and the place they make the cuckoo clocks.'

'Fuck you,' I hissed down the phone, perturbed now for I had no doubt that they could carry out what they said. Take it all away. 'Cut the crap and tell me what you want, as though I don't know already. You want me to work for the priest, right?'

'Wrong. If youse want it up front, you got it, Brogan,' the voice said. 'We don't give a shit what the man with the collar wants, the people I represent want it and they got leverage, okay asshole? You get the piece and your kid gets to live. It's that simple, eh?'

'Stop saying, "Eh", you sound like a Maori or a Canadian, eh?'

'You trying to be funny, pal?'

'Oh, now I'm you're pal, eh?'

'You're bugging me pal, you going to listen, or what?'

'Or what. Say again that bit about my kid.'

'Ah, got your attention, dipshit.'

'That will cost you, sunshine.'

'Cost me what, asshole?'

'Cost you a poke in the mouth when I get to meet you. I'll ask you again, what about my kid?'

'We got him, you want him back, you do what we say, Capice?'

'Capice?' despite the seriousness of the situation I couldn't help laughing. 'What, you've seen all the Scorsese films?'

'Hey, laugh all you want scumbag, but we got your kid and we expect your co-operation if you want to see him back in one piece.'

I stopped being a smart-arse as I realized what he was saying. What he HAD been saying for the length of the conversation. They had my son.

'Co-operate, how?' I asked, my throat suddenly dry despite all the wet stuff that had passed down it recently.

'If the priest asks again, you'll know,' there was amusement in the voice, and I wanted to kill him. I really did. 'Pretend to go along with him this time. He'll give you all the clues how to get to it, and when you got it, it comes to us and your kid comes back to you. Capi...you got it?'

'I got it,' I snapped and slammed the phone down.

I glanced at my watch again, though God knows why as only about ten minutes had passed on the phone call. The time in Britain would be just gone 9am and I phoned my ex. Dorothy would be up by now, preparing breakfast for Albie and my son, Phillip, who was on mid-turn break from university.

'Hello,' she answered the phone pleasantly enough, but that changed when I told her who it was. 'What the hell do you want? How dare you phone me here?'

43

'I don't have time for this, 'I almost shouted down the phone. 'I want to know where Phillip is right now.'

'Why should I tell you where Phillip is? You said you'd keep out of my son's life, and I'll make sure that you do. I don't need this...'

'This is not about you Dorothy,' I hissed down the line. 'This is about OUR son, not YOUR son, and it is very urgent I know where he is now. Please.'

The "please" put her off for a moment, then she was back to her most vitriolic accusations.

'Shut the hell up,' I yelled down the phone this time. 'I'll tell you this once, so bloody listen. I've just received a threat that Phillip might be kidnapped. Where did he spend last night? Was he home?'

'Of course he was home,' she snapped. 'What little game are you trying to pull now, you insufferable bastard. He's in his room out the back.'

'How do you know?' I was trying very hard to control my voice now and keep some calmness in it. 'Have you seen him this morning?'

'No, I haven't, but he was down the local drinking with some of his mates, and I made him a snack when he got in, and we sat in the kitchen while he ate, then he went to bed. Satisfied now?'

'No,' I snapped. 'Not until you've seen him; now go down the garden and check, please.'

That was the second "please" and it must have got to her. I heard the kitchen door slam as she went out, and could follow her route as she walked down the back-garden path to where the garage had been converted for Phillip's use. It consisted of one room, though fairly large, as it had been a double garage, the solid block variety that had come with the house. There was a small shower-room with toilet in a small cubicle in the far corner, and his bed was opposite that in the other corner. Dorothy would have knocked on the door by now, and opened it then walked over to the bed and shaken Phillip, all the while cursing me for the trouble-making arsehole that I was...

Suddenly she was back on the phone, sobbing down it and rambling incoherently. 'He's...he's gone. The bed is a mess, and there's blood on the sheets. Oh, God, this is your entire fault. Why would they take my son, my little boy? Oh, God.'

'Dorothy,' I raised my voice again to get her attention. 'Control yourself, and listen to me. They want me to do a job, some men, and they've taken Phillip to make sure I do it. Do you understand?'

'I...what kind of job?' her voice sounded small, far away. She knew nothing of what I'd been doing for the past ten years, and she was not going to find out now.

'That's not important,' I said quickly. 'What IS important is that you don't tell the police, or he'll be dead for sure. I'll do what they want and I have a feeling he'll be okay. Do you understand? Do you?'

'This is all you fault,' I let her get it all off her chest for a while, blaming me for everything, for her wasted life, for the loss of her beloved son.

She even went on about the fact that she was no longer so enamoured with the dependable Albie, who was proving himself not quite so dependable. I gathered that her sister, Daphne, had come out of it all right, having married a computer geek who turned out to be not so geeky, having just made a fortune out of selling his business. Jealousy over her sister's good fortune again raised its ugly head.

'This might take a while,' I told her finally, and even injected a modicum of kindness. She was after all the mother of my kid, and that would never change. 'Try and keep calm, I know it isn't easy, but it's for Phillip's sake. And no police please.'

She started off again on a tirade and I hung up.

'I've reconsidered your offer,' I said pleasantly. 'Meet me.'

'Oh, that won't be necessary, Brogan,' the Monsignor replied in his equally pleasant voice. It didn't quite come off over the phone, and I was sure it would be even worse face-to-face.

'Oh, but it would, Milos,' I had a dangerous edge to my voice. 'Otherwise I'm out of here.'

'Where do you suggest?' No messing around this time, though he must have known I didn't mean it. He was merely showing me that he was not afraid of a confrontation.

'There's a bench by the replica of the Deliverance on Ordnance Island, meet me there at two this afternoon.' I placed the phone carefully back on its hook. I was angry now. Bloody boiling in fact, but I would try to simmer down by two, Post Meridian. If not my son's life, then my economic future depended on it, though the latter was not so important.

The huge priest, Monsignor, or whatever the hell he was, was seated on the bench to the right of the wooden sailing ship when I arrived.

The ship was the Deliverance II, a replica of one of the two ships - the other was the Patience - built by the survivors of the 1609 wreck of the Sea Venture to carry them to Jamestown, Virginia, their original destination. I could not get over the size of the diminutive vessel. To cross the Atlantic to the coast of America in such a craft took a lot of courage.

'Turned out nice again, Padre,' I plonked himself down close to the priest.

Milos moved along the bench and flicked a speck of white from his immaculately creased black trousers. He turned to

46

face me and his grey eyes bore into mine. Eventually he backed down and looked away after reading something unsettling there. His first words threw me though, I must admit.

'Something has happened I gather, Brogan. Why have you changed your mind about my proposal?'

I studied him for a minute in turn, and then told him about my sudden change of fortune, the phone call and my own call to the UK. I finished by accusing him of being behind it all to make me change my mind.

'You really think the Vatican could be behind the kidnapping of your son, Brogan?' he said dispassionately.

We've skipped the formalities, I noticed sadly.

'Ah,' I shrugged. 'But being brought up as a Roman Catholic I have no illusions as to your power OR your scruples, you see, Monsignor.'

The other man thought for a minute. 'Yes, we DO have the power to ruin you if we wanted, and although it saddens me to admit it, some of our people only see the end, and believe that any means justify that end. I can only give you my word that we did not do this. Whoever they are, and I assure you I have no idea, the bank account was merely a warning as to how powerful they are and not to cross them. Your son being taken is their main weapon.' The sides of Milos's mouth began to curl slightly, and I sincerely hoped it wasn't about to turn into a smile, because then I would have to turn my next words into reality.

'I'm impressed with the organization behind this, whether it's Vatican primed or some other powerful outfit, but all the organizations in the world aren't going to help if I decide to kill you, Milos. You see you made a mistake if you thought I'd do something for you for money. I don't give a flying fuck about money because I was born without any. It would be kind of awkward without it, I admit, but tell your masters you went about this the wrong way. You took from me that which was mine.'

'Fine words, my friend, but entirely ineffectual because we had nothing to do with it,' he said indifferently.

'When I was a kid,' I said conversationally, and as though to myself. 'I was a skinny little runt and went to a diabolical Catholic school in Liverpool. The bigger kids picked on me a lot, stole my sandwiches and drinks, and beat me up anyway just for the hell of it. Now, I had two older brothers, tough kids both of them, and they could trounce anyone in the school, probably most of the teachers as well. I always wondered why they never came and helped me; just stood there and watched.'

'This is all very entertaining I'm sure, but...'

'Just listen padre; there's a lesson in here somewhere that you'd do well to remember. One day I'd had enough. A big kid who was about two grades ahead of me started bullying and he picked the wrong day. That was the day I'd had enough and I got stuck in; I just went straight up and hit him in the nose and it squished and blood went everywhere.'

'And he ran away and everyone left you alone after that, Brogan. Am I right? Now if you've fin...'

'Not quite,' I placed a restraining hand on his arm to prevent the man in black from rising. 'He came back at me and we then had a fight that went on for some time. He beat the snot out of me actually, but didn't walk away unscathed. In fact my brothers reckoned later that he got the worst of our exchange. You were right about one thing though, padre, no one ever picked on me again.'

'Your point in all that being...?'

'You fuck with me and I'll still be there at the end. Your lot has fucked with me, Milos.' My voice was quiet, none of

48

it carrying to the many passengers walking past in either direction, either back on board the cruise ship for one of their fifteen daily meals, or over the bridge into town. I was on my feet and half-turned away, when Milos spoke.

'Harry, Harry, how can I convince you that we are not responsible for this?' I almost believed him, and his next words gave me pause. 'Give me until tomorrow morning at 9am. I will meet you here. By that time your bank account will be restored to normal, and I would suggest that you do something quickly about protecting ALL of your assets. The people who took your son made a big mistake by gaining access to your account here in Bermuda, because we will be able to trace it through to its source. I will have the details for you of who they are and where your son is being held. It is up to you, Harry. Believe me, we will want those people out of this equation as much as you do.'

It had been the priest's turn to sound ruthless now. Strange coming from such a large tub of lard, but I was mildly impressed.

'If you do all this for me, padre,' I said slowly, 'then I will carry out the job for you, and will get your violin. Not for you, although I will be grateful, but to prevent these other bastards from getting it. You have my word on that.'

'So, closing your bank account was a warning of their power, and they also thought that by taking your son it would get your attention and make you compliant. You haven't seen your son for a long time, Harry, and if you ever planned to see him again in this lifetime, they thought you would simply do what they said. We, however, will return all of your assets and the original offer of five hundred thousand pounds still stands. I am sorry about this; it was not the way I wanted it. I find this kind of duress... unsettling.'

He must have seen the sarcastic look on my face for he gave a weak smile. 'Really, I might be a large man but I'm susceptible to much insecurity and am not a physical person.'

I didn't believe a word he said but resumed my seat and breathed deeply. 'This violin you want me to...rescue, retrieve, repatriate? Whatever. Where is it?'

He surprised me with the reply.

'The Vatican.'

'The Vatican in Rome?' I asked stupidly.

'The very same,' Milos smiled though not in a superior fashion. 'Unless you know of another one, that is?'

'Not really,' I tried a clever type of smirk, which I know didn't come off. 'Only that I know nothing about the Vatican, wherever it is. I don't know the layout or anything, and in fact I've never been there. Oh, and did I mention that I don't speak Italian? Apart from that I'm probably ideal for the job.'

He ignored me. 'One thing at a time, Harry, but first we need to get your son back, and then you can attend to this task with an unfettered mind. Until tomorrow, then.'

I'd bought a bottle of whisky at an exorbitant price and drank it in my room. My last waking thought was Devils, violins, Stradivari, and where the Hell was my life going from here on out?

The next day I booked a flight for that afternoon after downing a handful of Tylenol washed down with Bloody Mary's', which did nothing for the hangover itself but made the sting go away. Then I lay down again until it was time to meet the priest, after which Mike and his taxi would turn up when it was time for the flight back to Blighty.

Not a day had gone by in the last fifteen years when I hadn't thought about my only child. As I'd promised the day I left, I had stayed away from Phillip but had always known how he was. I'd kept in touch with one of my mates, whose wife was a friend of Dorothy's. As I'd thought, Albie had left Dorothy's sister and moved into what had been my house. Cynthia had been incapable of bearing children and Albie liked the idea of an instant family, though Phillip had not taken to him very much. Apparently he'd treated them both quite decently and provided a good living, and they'd since had a child of their own. The fact that Dorothy was now dissatisfied with Albie, taking it all out on him instead of me, should have made me feel better, but it didn't.

I still wished some things had been different.

CHAPTER THREE

The Bible warns against even BOWING to a graven image. God is a jealous God and will not share His rightful glory with another.

"I am the LORD: that is my name: and my glory will I not give to another, neither my praise to graven images."

Isaiah 42:8

The big priest had been true to his word.

We'd met the next morning at the same bench on Ordnance Island. He told me that my money was reinstalled in the Butterfield Bank and he handed me a large brown envelope. He told me that everything I needed was inside the envelope and asked if I still had his card. I told him I did and he told me to contact him when I had my son back.

That was it. He nodded and ambled off into the sunset, or wherever priests go to find their sunsets. Perhaps I'd been wrong about him all along. Perhaps he was kosher, even. Perhaps he did want the violin for the purest of reasons.

I stood up, gripping the envelope firmly, and made my way back to my lodging.

And perhaps Tony Blair didn't wear women's panties, and defer to his greedy wife, and perhaps his stooge, Prescott, should really be called "Honest John", and perhaps it never rained in East Finchley.

But I doubted all of that.

Three days later saw me in the prone position; that's lying flat on my stomach, on a small hillock and observing a bunch of wankers getting pissed. At least that was what it looked like through my binoculars. The weather was warm and they had a barbecue going by the back door of the old farmhouse. It was miles from anywhere to the east of London in what little farming country that was still left after the depredations of intensive building over the last few decades. The nearest large centre of population was Gravesend, named appropriately enough for what I had in mind for my son's kidnappers. The cheeky sods were only twenty some miles from the very heart of London. The house that Dorothy and I had moved into so many years ago was just outside Crawley, to the south of London. All they would have had to do after they'd snatched the boy was get on the M23, follow the M25 to the east and circumvent the Smoke, then out on some minor roads past Gravesend and out onto the Medway.

The intelligence I'd received from Zoltan Milos had been vague in background but precise on the logistics. The farmhouse had been rented from a local estate agent who was waiting for the rich yuppies from London to take it over as a major renovation project, and was only too happy to receive the rent for a short term let; all done by phone and an anonymous money order in the mail. The guards consisted of a local gang of wannabe's, five in number.

There were a few motorbikes and an old white van pulled up to one side of the house and five blokes prancing around the barbecue with bottles of beer in their hands and lots of noise coming out of their facial orifices. Tattoos and metal embedded in their ears, eyebrows, lips and God knows where else, appeared to be part of their uniforms.

The only thing wrong with the picture of gangbang decadence was the absence of any ladies. To enjoy a real old-fashioned barbie for crap like that would have included the presence of a number of biker chicks.

No sign of Phillip anywhere, but there again I wasn't expecting any. I had no reason to doubt that he was there. As I said, the envelope from Milos had contained everything I needed to know about the people who had taken him. All, that is, except the main man, the one who was behind all of this; the one who had taken my money from the Butterfield account, and kidnapped my son. I was still not one hundred percent convinced that Milos didn't have something to do with it, but he appeared to be doing the right things to help me out. I believe in the old adage of never looking a gift horse in the mouth. The account was back to where it should have been and I had taken his advice and transferred everything to other offshore banks, with special security IT measures on hand to prevent anything that had occurred in the past week happening again. Naturally this had not come cheap.

I quietly withdrew and left the party animals to it. It would be some time before they'd eaten and drunk their fill. They were probably celebrating the nice little earner kidnapping my son had brought them. They were rubbish of course; you could tell by the way they were acting now, no thought of the job they were supposed to be doing, even if it was a doddle in their book. But like rabid dogs they were still dangerous in the pack.

I found a pub miles away and had a Ploughman's lunch with homemade bread and pickles. It was very tasty but my appetite wasn't what it was, and the pint of real ale I had to wash down the food was just as tasteless. Not the landlord's fault, just the bitter bile rising in the back of my throat. I just hoped someone was going to get in my face before the night was out.

It was still light when I got back and the party was winding down. The burnt meat had been burned and consumed, and most of the drink had disappeared, though each of the "gang" was still holding a bottle. Some were reclining on cheap loungers obviously bought in for their temporary comfort, others just lying on the grass. In between sucking on the beers they were passing joints around.

'Fuckin' good stuff this, ain't it, fellers?' one of the culture vultures observed as he coughed over a particularly greedy inhalation.

'Fuckin' A, man, best wacky-baccy money can buy, mate,' replied a tall skinny individual with shoulder-length lank hair. 'This is Mexican Gold, old son.'

I was musing about simply walking in there, whacking a few and taking my son out, when there was an interruption from the far side of the house. The throaty sound of a performance engine as it dropped down through the gears and turned from the narrow lane into the driveway of the farmhouse.

There was little awareness from the five idiots lying around on the back lawn, for want of a better word, and even less movement.

'Who the fuck's that, then? Anyone expectin' visitors?' one wag managed to giggle through his daze.

A man suddenly burst out through the back door and began shouting, to the slow startlement of the bikers.

'You goddamn Limey dipshits,' he screamed. 'You're getting fucking well paid to carry out an easy fucking job, and what do I find but you all lying around stoned or drunk, or both. Get up, dipshits. Now.'

He emphasized the last word by kicking a few on the ground and dumped others from their loungers.

I recognized the voice right away, of course, and didn't need his signature use of "dipshits" to remind me of the nasty American prick that had told me about my son with such obvious glee, and of course further proof that I was at the right place. I'll give the little Yank his due; he showed guts the way he got stuck into the five layabouts. Every one was at least half a head taller than the American, but he pushed them out of the loungers, kicked the ones on the ground upright, and knocked bottles and spliffs out of their hands. He was raging, and in another situation I would probably have been on his side, given that a considerable sum of money had been handed over for a job to be carried out.

Only one stood up to him. The skinny one with the long hair sprang to his feet and loomed over their tormenter.

'Ere, who the bloody hell d'you thinks you are, mate?' He raised a finger to emphasis his point by prodding the smaller man in the chest.

It was the last move he did for a while.

The American, obviously a New Yorker, Bronx type by his accent, smiled, and that would have warned me for a start, but our friend with the long hair didn't seem to notice anything amiss. Until the sap, an old-fashioned word for an old-fashioned, yet effective, implement, smacked him alongside the head. He went down without a sound and the little man slapped the leather wrapped piece of soft lead against his left hand for a few seconds before yelling some more.

Basically it was more of the same, a pep talk, and I realized that I was not going anywhere with this crowd once they'd sobered up and began to measure up.

It had to be tonight, before the big change of conscience took place. After more shouting and putting the buggers in their place, the little American took off with a roar of power and ego. I stayed in position, though I wasn't as young as I once was and realized this was becoming very uncomfortable; very uncomfortable indeed.

The sky darkened and for a while I was thinking it might even rain, but on that score I was lucky. It didn't. I began to move around nine pip emma, that's 9pm, by the way. I was unarmed; a fact that I was well aware of and even felt a small amount of pride involved. Silly me.

I stood upright, shook myself and shrugged off the lethargy that had crept up on me. The grey skies that presaged rain and bad weather was creeping overhead and the boys had all gone inside. It was now or never and I knew that full well.

I moved around to the left side of the house, hoping that the two windows there did not have observers stationed. There wasn't and my line of thinking went the other way. What happened to National Service? God, these guys were pathetic.

I went to the front of the house, door wide open, and entered. They were all in the lounge, sprawled out in various stages of recovery and I couldn't believe my luck. I glanced around then walked down the passage. Nothing, so I started up the stairway that came straight ahead from the front door. On the landing I heard a toilet flush and didn't know where it came from. I stood and waited, and a door on my right opened and someone came out, zipping his pants and yawning.

My punch took him in the throat, front knuckles tight back on the palm and he went straight down with only the obligatory gurgle sound that they all make. One of my brothers, Dick, had showed me that one; he was big into the martial arts, and it always seemed to work.

In the second bedroom on the left I found my son. Phillip was lying on the bed, wrists and ankles tied to the posts and a gag in his mouth. He had a small cut above his right eye but was otherwise none the worst for his capture. I raised a finger to my lips as I cut him free and hugged him in a way I had never done before. Not that I'd had many opportunities over the years. To my surprise he hugged me back, and he nodded what I accepted as his thanks as he stepped away.

'There are only four of them left,' I told him quietly. 'You want one?'

'Yes, please,' he said solemnly, and with a certain amount of venom in his voice, so that I got the impression he meant it.

We went downstairs and were passing the lounge when one of them came out, probably for a visit to the toilet. Without thinking I knocked him back into the room, and then it was all on.

Stupid they may have been, but slow they weren't, coming out of their self-imposed visits to zonk-land. I followed the one I'd clobbered inside and kicked him in the head just to make sure. Another rolled off the sofa and fronted up, only to go down right away with a right cross to the side of his head. I heard a sound to my left and spun, but my son had already dropped the man with a left to the ribs and an elbow in the face.

I must have looked a bit gob smacked because he just grinned at me, and said, 'What? You think you got all the moves? And there's a guy behind you.'

I crouched and spun on my heels, hitting the bloke in the groin with a left and right, though one would have done. I straightened and his chin seemed to get in the way of the top of my head as he went flailing back. I used to wonder what that meant at one time, "flailing back", but he demonstrated it well, arms going like windmills as he tried to regain balance where there wasn't any.

'No, you don't,' I heard Phillip say, then a heavy sound as he hit the last one across the head with a bottle he'd picked up. God, I felt proud at that moment.

We strolled out of the front door, and in the heat of the mini-battle in the front room we hadn't heard the V6 Mustang arrive in the drive. The little Yank had obviously come back to recheck his troops.

'What the fuc...' he said as he climbed out of the car.

'Hi,' I said pleasantly. 'You must be the little arsewipe from the Bronx who kidnapped my son.'

Again, I have to say that the man had guts the way he kept on coming, and even had a big cheesy grin as he pulled the sap and came at me. I grinned back as I blocked the blow, grabbed his wrist and put it into a figure-of-four arm lock. I had the satisfaction of hearing it break, which I have to admit I did on purpose. Aren't I awful? He squealed like a little piglet; the sound most people make when one or other of their wrists are broken. I've had both broken on different occasions, though I don't recall making that bloody noise.

I picked up the sap and put it into my pocket.

'This is mine now,' I told him as I squatted down in front of him. 'You want to tell me who hired you or do you want your other wrist broken as well?'

'Contract,' he managed to spit out. 'I don't know who hired me, honest. It was a guy on the phone, gave me the details and I came down here and picked up these dipshits. Worse thing I ever did...'

'You're right about that,' I agreed. 'For some strange reason I believe you. If I ever see you again I will kill you, Capice? I know you're under contract, and that's up to you, but now you've been warned. You took my son, and that's a very personal thing. Oh, and remember what I told you about a smack in the mouth for being cheeky.'

So I smacked him in the mouth, and his big eyes were watching me in what I have to say was a very vindictive manner, but as the smack connected his eyes glazed and he fell back.

'So,' I said to my son, not believing the size he was now. 'Anything left to do?'

'No, dad,' he grinned. 'I think we've done it all.'

I must admit that I did check out the phone, and I did call the local police station, though naturally I didn't leave my name and address and told them I would not be there when they arrived but no doubt they would have warrants out on most of them. Without a complainant they probably couldn't do a lot, but like I said, they probably had warrants.

I took the Mustang around the back, hooked all the bikes on with a chain from the gate, drove it along the lane to the end, turned and came back having wrecked the bikes off road. I then belted up and drove the whole lot down a drainage ditch, car and all.

'Okay?' I said to Phillip who had watched the whole procedure, but had a big grin to let me know whose side he was on.

'Whew, Dad. Mum was right; you ARE a mean bugger when someone upsets you.'

'Mind the language,' I grinned back. 'You did good back there.'

I led him over the hill behind the farmhouse and down to the back lane where I'd left my Range Rover, and we drove off to the south.

I'll give him his due; Phillip never asked where we were going, never said a word about anything, and never asked questions but merely sat gazing out of the window as though he'd never been in a car before. I hit the A26 down to the A27 then headed west to Salisbury, onto the A303 and kept on west across southern England to Devon, where we eventually pitched up at my own little piece of what was left of the English countryside.

It was a three hundred year old single-storey cottage in the heart of the Devonshire countryside, and was located in the largest and wildest open space in southern England – Dartmoor. Dartmoor is an upland of granite rising to 2038ft at High Willhays its highest point. The River Dart and its tributaries separate two vast blocks of moorland in the north and the south, and surrounding this moorland is Dartmoor's intimate enclosed landscape containing islands of common land. The moorland itself is characterized by wide expanses of bog and smooth contoured hills often crowned by rugged tors, and here is the greatest density of prehistoric remains in north-western Europe.

Despite that mist and cloud frequently shrouded the hills and the average rainfall was high, I loved it here. Streams and rivers rise in bogs and their valleys are wide in the upper reaches; where they leave the moor they cascade down waterfalls and run through rocky gorges in steep, wooded valleys. The beginnings of any landscape are its rocks and the earth processes which act upon them, but human occupation spanning over 6000 years in these uplands has left, and continues to leave, its mark. Having said that, I'd also read somewhere that it was quite probable that Old Stone Age man, that's the Palaeolithic chap, had hunted there. But at the moment it was more recent history that had my attention.

Phillip had suggested getting in touch with his mother and telling her he was okay, and I agreed immediately. I busied myself in the kitchen but couldn't help overhearing the conversation, which was short and to the point, at least on my son's side. He stuck to the rules I'd suggested and gave out neither phone numbers nor e-mail address. I could hear his mother sobbing down the phone, and her voice went up an octave when Phillip said he was "lying low with Dad for a while", and he promised to ring her.

The idiots who'd kidnapped him had taken his mobile phone, and I had an idea that they were stupid enough to have kept hold of it. I "dropped a dime" as our cousins in the US have a habit of saying, and phoned an old mate of mine in the Met. That's the Metropolitan Police, and he was based at Scotland Yard. I told him the basic plot but said we wouldn't be pushing the kidnapping angle because there was a lot more involved.

Eddie was a good lad, an ex-marine who'd had the good sense to get out a lot earlier than me and was now a detective inspector in the Serious Crimes Squad. We'd met for the occasional drink over the years and I'd been able to put some work his way when I was thieving. He had an idea what I was up to but we never spoke of it. He just accepted the information with good grace and followed up on it, apparently making some good busts along the way and doing no harm at all to his promotion prospects.

'Sounds like a little band of clumsy burglars we've been after, Harry. I'll check it out through the cell phone and at least a stolen cell gives us reasonable cause to bust their gaff. Stay well, Harry.'

I'd never really known my son through the years, and that was understandable, but neither logical nor satisfactory. I'd decided when I left his mother that I would keep out of his life, and realized now that it had been a bad mistake.

He looked a fine boy, and his actions that day had shown that he was made of the right stuff. I could also see that when I looked at him. His looks were a mixture of both Dorothy and me, without a doubt. He had the pale eyes of his mother, and her high cheekbones, but he had also gained my pugnacious jaw and tousled head of hair.

For the first time we talked and it was good. He said nothing bitter against his mother, and neither did I. I tried tactfully to give him reasons why his mother and father had split up. It isn't easy to do that. I told him I loved him, in my own abrasive way, and I tried very hard to spare him the sordid bit at the end of it all.

'She was having it off with Albie, wasn't she?' he said to my surprise. 'Aunt Daphne told me years ago.'

I nodded.

'Did you give him a good slap?' was all he said, and I could hear amusement in his voice.

'Yes,' I acknowledged. 'A really good slap.'

I caught his eye and we laughed, and we never spoke of the matter again.

I told him why I'd brought him down to the Moor. The people behind the idiots who had kidnapped him would be watching the house where he lived with his mother and Albie.

'We can spend a few weeks here,' I told him. 'But only if you want to.'

'I'd love it,' and he sounded sincere. 'I don't have to go back to university for another month, and there's nothing I'd like better. I've never believed any of the rubbish Mum has said about you, and my two uncles, your brothers, have called me sometimes. They told me what a hero you were in the marines.'

I have a feeling I might have blushed. 'No more than them,' I murmured. 'No more than them.'

The next few days, which turned into weeks, went by like a blur.

I phoned Milos and told him the condensed version of the events that had happened. I told him my son was safe and I would honour the agreement I'd made. I asked him what he wanted me to do and I was rather surprised at his instructions.

'Spend a month studying; there's no rush, Harry. First read up on violins, visit a few places where Stradivarius are kept and study them. Know if you are looking at a Strad or an Amarti, or perhaps just a good fake. Look into the Stradivarius legend, examine the history of violins, and the great violinists through the ages; not forgetting their cousins, the cello and the viola, oh, and he made some harps as well, and a guitar or two. Most people never realized that the genius that was Stradivari had made anything other than violins.'

There was a pause on the other end of the line.

'He was a prolific worker, with more than half of his production still intact and still being played on the world stage as we speak, some three centuries after he was laid to rest. Learn to distinguish the real thing from a fake. Visit the Ashmolean and Royal Academy of Music in London, and the Palazzo Communale and the Museo Stradivriano, both in Cremona. By the way, the name of the violin I want is the Diabolus. But, Harry, keep that name very close to your chest.'

I replaced the receiver, wondering what he meant by that last bit of information. Since when did musical instruments have their own names? I would soon learn. I suddenly realized that Phillip was sitting at the kitchen table drinking coffee.

'Can I help?' was all he said. He didn't ask what it was all about, why he'd been kidnapped, anything. It was as though he took it all in his stride. He was that kind of kid.

I reached for the glass and bottle of wine and told him the whole scenario. He had become part of the deal, albeit as an unwitting pawn, but I felt he deserved to know what it was all about.

'I've spent what seems my entire life studying, Dad,' he said softly. 'And I know that you've been paying for it. The least I can do is some research for you; it's what I do, and I'm actually quite good at it.'

How could I refuse?

The next day we drove into the market town of Exeter, now a city of course, and we paid a visit to the county library. I became an instant member and we walked away with an armload of books each. I vowed to make a large donation to the library when I became mega-rich.

That night we stoked up the fire and reheated the pizzas we'd brought back with us. It turned out that my son had a complete pizza fetish, something to do with spending most of his nights at university studying, and then feeling peckish and ordering in with his mates. Ah, well, it could have been a lot worse. We began turning pages. When anything interesting turned up we would read it aloud, and anything of particular interest Phillip would take notes in some weird shorthand apparently known only to university students.

The next day he transposed them into readable material on his laptop and began making a neat pile on the coffee table. As I read them in turn I thanked the powers above for giving me a gifted son. To have had to pore through the musty library tomes themselves would have taken forever, and bored me to distraction.

The violin was a product of the late Renaissance, the result of a process of evolution, as opposed to a moment of inspiration. At the end of the fifteenth century there were only primitive instruments, which although quite good for providing dance music or accompanying voices were not meant for carrying their own tune. In 1535 Gaudenzio Ferrari was painting the ceiling of Saronno Cathedral to show not just violins, probably what we would call violas these days, but also a cello; both with just three strings. A workshop in northern Italy, which served the courts of Mantua and Ferrara, combined the peg box of the rebec, a lute-like instrument of Moorish origin, with the sound box of the lira de braccio, itself a development of the Renaissance fiddle.

I found that I was doing my best at something I'd given up years ago - studying. I sighed and flipped a page. Some aspects of my reading I found interesting but I still could not see what the jovial priest had been getting at. I flipped over a few more pages.

Under the auspices of her son, Charles IX of France, Catherine de Medici ordered a set of thirty-eight string instruments from Italy. All were made in the northern town of Cremona, already a renowned centre for this type of work. The Ashmolean Museum in Oxford has a violin from that set of Catherine de Medici's. It is a violin made in 1564, exactly 119 years before the Ashmolean was founded.

This small violin is the oldest surviving violin in the world, an exquisite piece of workmanship. Andrea Amati, who made all of the instruments in that order for France, actually made it himself. He and his family would dominate violin making for the next one hundred years. The 1564 violin has been laid on its back to fit into the case, which unfortunately hides what remains of the gilded painting with which the famous violin was decorated.

The Civic Museum in Cremona has one from the same set, but dated 1566 and was recently valued at $10 million.

I whistled through my teeth. Ten mil; Christ, what would be the value of the one I was supposed to be nicking? I talked this over with Phillip and was pleased to note that he agreed with me that a deal was a deal, no matter what the price of the violin.

Although he could not have been the violin's inventor, Andrea Amati's delicacy and awareness of geometric principles established the blueprint for others to follow. Everything of the instrument's form and function can be seen in that 1564 violin.

I poured a glass of wine from the open bottle before me. My son shook his head with a smile when I proffered the bottle, and although he'd enjoyed a glass with his pizza I gathered he was not a drinking man. A faint sound outside made me raise my head and listen more attentively, then an owl hooted nearby and I returned to the stack of notes lying between us. Phillip was adding to them all the time, and once again he surprised me with his ability to touch type.

'Girlfriend,' he'd explained laconically when I'd complimented him on it. 'Only good thing to come out of our relationship, her teaching me to type. Been very useful.'

Thinking on my own track record with relationships I made no comment; simply nodded and went back to my reading of his notes.

Antonio Stradivari was born in 1644 and established his shop in Cremona, Italy, where he remained active until his death in 1737. His interpretation of geometry and design for the violin has served as a conceptual model for violinmakers for more than 250 years.

They still say of Antonio Stradivari in Cremona, "While other makers did what they could, Stradivari did with violins as he wanted."

I paused in my reading for a moment and refilled my glass of merlot. These days I had cried off beer and spirits as part of my increased fitness regime for the forthcoming job. I now only drank wine – beer was fattening, even my beloved Guinness to a degree, and shorts like whisky and rum sometimes affected me too much. I read on.

Stradivari also made harps, guitars, violas, and cellos – more than 1,100 instruments in all, by the current estimate. About 650 of these instruments survive today. In addition, thousands of violins have been made in tribute to Stradivari, copying his model and bearing labels that read "Stradivarius". Therefore, the presence of a Stradivarius label in a violin has no bearing on whether the instrument is a genuine work of Stradivari himself.

The usual label, whether genuine or false, uses the Latin inscription Antonius Stradivarius Cremonensis Faciebat Anno (date). This inscription indicates the maker (Antonio Stradivari) the town (Cremona), and "made in the year",

followed by a date that is either printed or handwritten. A violin's authenticity (i.e. whether it is the product of the maker whose label or signature it bears) can only be determined through comparative study of design, model wood characteristics, and varnish texture.

The varnish: was a general technique known to all the Cremonese luthiers, though it was lost after the death of Stradivari. Cremonese varnish was soft to the point of fragility: grip a Strad too firmly and the palm print is clearly visible on its surface; too much rough treatment and the bare wood is exposed. The answer lay in technological progress, for the necessary drying time had been bothering the Cremonese since the time of Galileo, whose nephew ended up with an old violin because his teacher, Father Micanzio, would not wait for "the strong heat of the sun" to bring a new one "to perfection." Other woodworkers, who moved to a tougher and quicker-drying varnish that used a spirit base, felt this disadvantage and nothing would have been more natural than for luthiers to follow their lead. Stradivari, with his innate knowledge of acoustics, would have known better than to coat his violins in such a rigid substance.

I drained my glass and laid my head back with eyes closed. My (almost) photographic memory had obeyed its subliminal commands and retained the main points of my reading. So far, there was nothing I found unusual in the notes I was reading now or the web site devoted to Stradivari that Phillip had been surfing through that afternoon.

I glanced at the list of other violinmakers.

Amati, Bergonzi, Banks, Cappa, Dalla, Duke, Costa, de Salo, Duiffopruggar, Gagliano, Glass, Guarneri (Guarnerius), Gagliano, Guadagnini, Hopf, Klotz (Kloz), Maffini, Ruggieri, Tononi, Stainer, Vuillaume, Montagnana.

And then came upon the part of Stradivari's golden years, which Phillip pointed out to me and which I might have skipped over at that point.

The 'golden period' – 1700 to 1720 – when Stradivari produced his finest instruments and carried his manufacture to the highest possible finish, and when his drive for perfection led to the violins, and later cellos, that remain the most highly prized in the world. From about 1700 the workshop produced them in ever-greater numbers. Acoustically, that final design of the sound box is their most important attribute, but there is far more to them than that. The deep red of the varnish – another innovation dating to the Long Strad years – makes the golden-yellow of the Amatis and of Stradivari's earlier instruments appear insipid by comparison. The scrollwork is emphasized with black edging that when new would have proclaimed the carver's skill but has now largely worn away on violins and given an almost masculine appearance. Everything about them speaks of confidence, of the luthier's desire to draw attention to his brilliance.

The outlines are designed with taste and purity, the wood is rich and carefully selected, the arching falls off in gentle and regular curves, the scroll is carved with great perfection, and the varnish is fine and supple. The interior workmanship is no less perfect; the degrees of thickness are carefully adjusted, and are remarkable for a precision that could only have been attained by much study and experiment. Everything has been foreseen, calculated and determined with certainty.

A genius by the sounds of it, I thought, sipping on a fresh glass but still nothing sinister; certainly nothing that the Devil could be blamed for. Unless. No, I shook my head. Let's not get carried away, I thought morbidly.

Stradivari fixed the exact shape and most makers have copied the position of the sound-holes and his model since his time. He definitely settled the shape and details of the bridge, which cannot be altered in the slightest degree without in some way injuring the tone of the instrument.

I began to read through the notes, though the salient points had already been taken into my memory. Maybe I was going through it the wrong way, I thought. I began to make a list on the large A4 lined notepad in front of me, and passed them by my son vocally as I wrote.

'Stradivari. B1644 – D1737. He was 93 years old at the time of his death, a staggering age in those unhealthy times. Although his two marriages bore eleven children many did not survive infancy and others also died young.

'As a father Stradivari was prolific, but not as a maker of violins, or luthier as they were called. From his first fourteen years as an independent luthier until 1680, by now thirty-six years old, only eighteen violins are now know to exist, along with a viola, a guitar and a cello. Overall they suffer by comparison with the authoritative instruments being produced at the same time from the workshop of Andrea's grandson, Nicolo Amati.'

Phillip had been scribbling in his own tight shorthand, prior to typing it onto his laptop, and he looked at me now, tapping his pencil on his teeth.

'So, let's just see what we have here, Dad: Facts: He was producing only mediocre work in his mid-thirties. His children were dying young. He began to obsess about his own mortality. As the 1700's came along, most of the Cremona luthiers were hard-pressed to make a living – not so Stradivari, who had turned the corner and really began to prosper.'

He gave me a do-you-want-to-join-in look and I smiled and waved him on.

'Ergo: Did he make a pact with the Devil around the beginning of his "golden period?" If so – what was Stradivari's contribution? Was it the violin that the Signore wants you to get for him? As well as his immortal soul, of course.'

I was seriously impressed by my son's way of thinking, and told him so.

'They're only facts, Dad,' he shrugged. 'If you accumulate enough facts you can't help but arrive at a reasonable conclusion, although always be prepared that it might not necessarily be the right conclusion.'

I stared at him for a moment. 'What did you say you were taking in university again?'

'I didn't,' he laughed. 'Mum thinks I'm doing Art History so I can get a nice steady job in a place like Christie's or Sotheby's.'

'But you're not, right?'

'I'm not. I'm doing Criminology, as I might want to go into the Police Force. By getting Criminology first, a law degree should be easy, as I'll already have a lot of the necessary units required for Llb.'

'You've given this some thought then,' I said.

'I...yes, largely.'

I wasn't too convinced with the "largely" word, and told him so. 'I have no problem with the law, son. One of your uncles was a cop in New Zealand; it just wasn't one of my personal choices. What would you really want to do, if your choices were limitless?'

'I...' he hesitated.

'Hey, I haven't always been there, boy, but I've never been far away if you'd ever needed me. I made a decision when I left your mother to not add conflict to your life by having me pitch up every now and again and spoil the domestic bliss your new family environment might have produced. My mistake, and although this has been a drastic way of us getting together I want you to know that I'm here for you now.'

'I know that, Dad,' he smiled. 'I can't imagine Albie tackling that lot the way you did, and allowing me to have a piece of them. The truth is, I'm a bit torn between the Police and... being an actor.'

I don't know what he was expecting, and I didn't know what he'd gone through before, but I do know it took a lot of guts on his part to even come out with it.

'What's so wrong about you being an actor?' I asked with a dim look on my face.

'Well, nothing really,' he said when he realised I was not joking. 'Some people make a lot of money at it.'

'And a lot of people make some money at it,' I said before I could stop myself. 'But, in the real world you have to do what you would prefer to do, NOT what you think everyone else would prefer you to do. I'm behind you whatever your choice; and you should know that. I would agree with your mother, however, and advise you to get that degree, whatever it is. Then at least you'll have something behind you, something to fall back upon. But if you want to be an actor, then go for it. You don't want to be a dancer as well, do you?'

I said the last with a frown and we looked at each other for a while before he started laughing and shook his head. I joined in and lifted my glass, then looked up suddenly. There it was again, the sound I'd heard before. This time I knew it was no owl.

'Did you hear that?' I asked softly and received just a nod from Phillip.

I carried on talking but this time I told my son to stay where he was and just keep reading. I stood casually and stretched, then scratched my groin and went out of the door into the passage; where I moved swiftly, snatching up a walking stick out of the rack and making the back door in seconds. It was a stable door, the top being six small panels and the bottom of solid wood.

Carefully I peered out of the draped half-curtains and could see no movement. My marine training in many things was still with me, retention by familiarity the instructors' manual would say. There were five things to look for when trying to spot the enemy; and the enemy was definitely out there. Shape, shine, shadow, silhouette, and movement - the last one always being the giveaway. This time again, for I saw the shadow move over by the laurel hedge at the back. Quietly I drew back the bolts that released the top of the stable door from the bottom. I thanked my obsession with creaky doors and bolts that had caused me to spray WD40 on everything on a regular basis. I wedged my fingers in the bottom door and drew it slowly back, remembering my own thoughts on movement.

I was wearing dark blue jeans, a dark sweater over a tee shirt and black training shoes. I couldn't have been dressed any better for the task in hand as I crawled slowly out into the night. The air was cold, although it was only the end of August and I was grateful for the oiled wool of the sweater. Pulling the door to behind me I crawled to the right and crept on crawling.

At the corner of the house I ducked right and straightened up. I knew I couldn't be seen now from the hedge so ran to the back of the house and across to the barn. I still carried the walking stick in my left hand. A low hedge went from the barn to the end of the garden, where it joined up with its big brother, the laurel hedge. Ducking low I jogged along it, conserving energy for what I might meet at the other end.

I came up against – nothing. I paused for a minute, listening. I heard something over the hedge and when it dawned I couldn't believe my ears. What had sounded like stomping WAS stomping; the sound of someone trying to keep his feet warm. I had made a concealed cut through the hedge; on either side it looked compact, with a division in the middle that was off centre to each side. I had made it so I could pass through into the woods nearby. I moved slowly through, peering out at the shadowy man, still stomping his feet to keep warm.

I could see no one else around so I stepped out of the hedge and smacked the trespasser across the head with the gnarled handle of the stick. The man went down like a sack and I was on him. I pulled his belt off and strapped his hands together tightly. Then I pulled his boots off and removed his socks. Fortunately they were long, so I was able to gag the man firmly with one and tie his ankles together with the other.

I made my way along the hedge and was moving my way around the other side of the property when the light from the parlour window suddenly blinked. Someone had passed the window and I didn't think it was Phillip whom I'd left in the kitchen. I hoped to God he was all right. I moved quicker now I had a target and was heading for the back door when the outside lights blazed on, catching me like a rabbit caught in the glare of headlights. I saw the figure come out of the back door, back-dropped against the bright lights I had installed myself.

'Gotcha, mate,' a gleeful voice chuckled. 'An' I was told you were good at this sort of thing. Not - I think. Sid, over 'ere, mate, I've got the bastard.' To prove his point he cocked the handgun he was holding. Automatic, I noted.

'Getting rusty, you know,' I said conversationally. 'But it took three of you.'

'Two, actually,' the shadow in the doorway said cockily, and very obligingly. 'Sid, where the fuck are yer?'

By his accent they weren't local lads, I knew. They weren't very professional either. Already I knew there were only two of them, and I hadn't even been ordered to lose the stick yet. I was beginning to feel sorry for Sid's mate standing in front of me.

'Sid,' the man yelled again.

'Save your breath,' I snapped. 'He's out of it, and thanks to you being fucking stupid I now know you're on you own.

If you've harmed my son I'll make sure you'll never walk again, understand?'

'What? What you talkin' about?' I thought at first that the man was taken aback at my attitude, not what he'd expected at all, considering he was the one with the gun trained on his intended victim. Then I realized he'd been referring to Phillip. He'd been inside the house while I was dealing with his mate and hadn't seen my son.

'Sid, over 'ere, damn it.'

'You bloody deaf or something,' I snapped. "I just told you he's out of it. Now what do you fucking want?'

The man went silent and came down from the kitchen steps. The gun was up at full reach of his right hand, pointing at my head. The face behind the gun was livid, and I suddenly realized the man had lost it. He kept walking until the gun was a foot from me and pointing straight between my eyes.

I had the stick held loosely in my left hand, with the right stretched across my stomach and grasping the top.

'Go on, you bastard, try and hit me with it. I fucking dare you.'

I shrugged and threw the stick away to my left. The man smirked, until he felt the pain and saw the blade I held in my right hand. It was a swordstick and in the moment of discarding the case I'd drawn the blade; the case being a distraction while the steel swept up and across with an economy of effort and sent the gun flying; along with a couple of fingers which happened to be in the way.

'Oh, fuck,' the man went down on his knees, holding the damaged hand. 'Oh, shit, it fucking hurts, man.'

'Painful, is it?' I enquired sympathetically, and then kicked the man alongside the head to relieve him of the pain. It wasn't a fancy karate kick, merely a good solid plant of my foot in the man's temple. I don't do that karate shit, but one of my brother's does.

'I take it you don't need a hand then, Dad?' My son came around the end of the house grasping a pitchfork with exceptionally long tines. He looked as though he had no problem about using it.

I shook my head and smiled, 'Thanks anyway.'

When the gunman came to, groaning and trying to reach his head, realization came of his last waking moments and so did the throbbing pain of his dismembered fingers. His hands were tied in front of him, actually just the thumbs were tied with wire, and he saw there was a tourniquet around his right wrist and his finger stumps were bandaged tightly. He heard a groan to his left and saw his partner in crime, Sid, lying alongside him against the side of the cottage and also bound tightly. Both men had had their shoes and socks removed.

The outside lights were still on and their legs were also tied tightly. The author of their joint misery was sitting at a wooden barbecue table some distance away, drinking from a bottle of red wine. My son was sitting across from me, but was delicately sipping from a glass. Nothing was said for a while, until the would-be gunman rasped through parched lips.

'Don't suppose I could have a swig of that, eh, mate?'

'No,' I said coldly. 'You weren't invited here so you don't get any of the hospitality I'm fucking famous for.'

The silence went on for a long time, during which I poured from the bottle and sipped tantalizingly. Eventually it was Sid who broke, and only because of the fox.

It suddenly came trotting through my discreetly concealed hole in the hedge and straight up to me without fear. I reached down and stroked its head, while the two intruders looked on with astonishment. Even Phillip tensed up and looked as though he was about to try for an athletic scholarship. It was the biggest fox any of them had ever seen, not that they'd seen many coming from around the Smoke, but most people think of them as small creatures. Actually, my nocturnal visitors had even seen one in their own turf, Battersea, whilst driving home from a burglary in the small hours of the morning. They told me about it later, just in conversation of course.

'Big boy, isn't he?' I said conversationally. 'They usually only grow about 40 inches long, around 15 pounds at most, but he's bigger than your average Alsatian, don't you think? Probably one shafted his old lady. I wonder if he's eaten tonight. Go and sniff, feller, go on.' I waved my hand in the direction of the pair and to their horror the fox began to move their way.

'Hey, what's he doing, mate?' the gunman cried. 'Keep him away for Gawd's sake.'

The big fox went up to the pair and began sniffing around them. He even licked Sid's face, making him nearly pass out with fear. When he started on his bare feet, Sid had had enough.

'Yeah, yeah,' he yelled.

'You getting excited, Sid?' I frowned. 'Not into animals, are we?'

'Get him away from me, for Gawd's sake. I'll tell you everything.'

'I don't want to know everything, Sid,' I told him patiently. 'I just want to know what you pair of deadbeats are doing on my property. Tell me the truth and you can go – refuse and the fox will tear you to pieces and take you home in bits to his vixen and pups, though somehow I don't think his missus will think much of his taste.'

As though he could understand the fox moved back to me and sat on his haunches with what appeared to be a grin. I've learned that it's a thing that foxes do.

'There you go, was I right or what? He doesn't care for the smell, though that doesn't mean he mightn't take a mouthful later, for old time's sake, kind of. Talk for your lives, boys,' I emulated the sly grin of the fox. 'And I mean that literally.'

They did of course, and began to speak. I asked some questions and when I didn't like the answers I moved a hand and the big fox came forward licking his lips, until they promptly changed their tune and answered with more truth. At least, I thought they told the truth, which must have been hard for pricks like them, but of course fear became the catalyst here.

'So, this bloke you met in the pub, what did he look like?' I asked.

Sid shrugged. 'Ordinary kind of feller, wan'e, Johnno? White bloke, of course; don't get any darkies down our pub, do we? Keep to their own patch. He was about 40 odd, wouldn't you say, Johnno?'

Although he kept addressing questions to his mate there was usually no reply, just the occasional dip of the head. Obviously Johnno was still in a lot of pain and not a little shock.

'How much did he pay you?' I asked softly.

For a moment Sid hesitated, at which point the fox made a hectoring sound in the back of his throat as though on cue. 'F...ive hundred sobs each.'

'For killing me?' I raised an eyebrow.

'Nah, nofink like that, mister, honest,' Sid shook his head vigorously. 'Just to suss out the place, like, maybe take a few things and that; just to scare you, like.'

'No,' I said carefully. 'You were sent to look for something, weren't you?'

Sid looked at his mate, still clutching his ruined hand and rocking slightly in painful misery. He could see no support coming from that direction so gave a resigned shrug.

'Don't suppose you'd believe me, though, mister,' he muttered.

'Why not try me, Sid?' I offered.

''E told us to look for a fiddle, din 'e?'

Ah, I thought, now we're getting somewhere.

'Why would he think I had a bloody fiddle?" I hissed.

'No idea, mate,' Sid said in a low voice. 'But he kind of described it. Said it was very old, kept in a wooden case, and it was all black.'

I kept all expression from my face and studied the pinched face in front of me, pale and sallow with the deep pits of ancient acne making his cheeks look like one of the early moon shots of the craters in the Mare something.

'Supposing you had managed to find this violin,' I said softly. 'How were you going to hand it over to your contact?'

'Gave us a phone number, didn't 'e? It's a public phone box, of course, and 'e said to call him there at eight in the evenin' on a Monday or Tuesday, if we had it. Then he'd give us more instructions.'

'What if you'd found the violin?' I asked quietly. 'And I'd interrupted you?'

'Told us to kill yer, din' 'e?' Sid said with a casualness that didn't quite show in his face.

'Really,' I raised both eyebrows.

'Naturally we wouldn't 'ave done it, would we?' he said quickly.

'Naturally,' I repeated.

Then to their surprise, and no doubt my own at the time, I let them go, along with a warning that should I ever see them again I would kill them in a very slow and painful way. I advised them to disappear forever, as far as their friends and recent employer were concerned. Their car was parked along the lane leading to my property, not very well concealed and not exactly a recent mo del either; proof positive that they were not pros; sadly, they were not even successful amateurs.

Phillip still hadn't said a word as we watched them drive off and we returned to the cottage, still accompanied by my foxy friend.

'Fancy a bit of deer I've got in the fridge, mate?' I asked and the big fox appeared to nod as he trotted eagerly ahead.

One thing bothered me as I pushed through the door into the kitchen. This time they'd been amateurs, like the wankers who had kidnapped my son. Someone with clout would have found out where I lived without great trouble, but why not send the pros in? Obviously trying to try me out, or shake me down, or intimidate me even? With their failure, next time it would be professionals. Or perhaps someone might be thinking that I already had the infamous violin. Which made me realise that whoever had sent them knew exactly what I was planning.

The next morning I logged on to Google and wrote an instruction of "Vatican" in the search engine. It came back with 10,142,714 sites. Either a lot of people were trying to rubbish Catholicism or a lot of people still believed in it. I don't think it was the latter.

I read through enough to be able to get around in both Rome and the Vatican City, although why I'd bothered I didn't know. Not yet, though I had that niggling feeling. I glanced at my watch and decided it was time.

I phoned Monsignor Zoltan Milos on the number on his card. I'd already tried the line and spoken to the man twice now, so knew that the phone number at least was authentic. I wasn't in the mood so made no polite greetings but got right down to the events of the previous night.

'They were rank amateurs, Milos. Whoever sent them was not so good at choosing his lackeys. If it wasn't you, who was it?'

'Of course it was not me. Why would I want to stop you after going to such trouble to enlist your help in the first place?' He said indignantly, and it made sense, I had to admit.

'Perhaps the one who sent them was not so stupid, after all, Harry.' Ah, I thought, we're back to Harry again. 'Perhaps it was meant as a warning, knowing you'd be too good for them.'

'And if I didn't leave it alone the next ones would be real pros?'

'Exactly, Harry. So, were you able to find out from where they got the commission, contract is it?'

'It was apparently a go-between in a pub in Battersea, where they have some small reputation of sorts. Is it worth my following up on this go-between? I have his name, but I think the trail will only lead somewhere else before it disappears.'

'Yes,' the big priest replied decisively. 'You're probably right, for if the person behind it is who I think he is you're not going to track him down through the hired help. What were their instructions?'

'To look for the violin, and possibly to beat me up if I interrupted them. To kill me if they succeeded in locating the thing, though I don't think either of them had the capability to kill a sausage; probably burn the crap out of one would be all.'

'Yes, so the news would get back to whoever you were working for, and they also would be warned and possibly call off, what do you call it, "the job". This of course would leave them a clear field to go for it themselves.'

'Not to mention the other lot who kidnapped my son, so is this actually three lots of people going after the same prize. Would you like to fill me in on whom this mysterious "he" is, or who the second lot could be?'

I grunted down the phone. 'Their connections must be as good as yours for them to have found my son in the first place, then to locate me. Not even my ex-wife knows about this place, only my two brothers and no one would get it out of them. Anyway, God alone knows where they are at the moment.'

'Harry,' he spoke as though dealing with a child. 'You pay rates on the place, water bills, the television licence, etc. Anyone with an iota of patience could locate you. I have a feeling that these two groups are somehow connected; possibly not communicating with each other,' Milos said in an unusually dead voice. 'Besides, it would not be safe for you if the man I have in mind even thought you knew his name.'

'You're worried about me, I'm touched,' I rasped. 'You think it's safe for me now, after he sent two thugs after me; granted they were not very professional thugs, but still capable of committing nasty things if I'd been as stupid as they maybe thought I was. I put the fear of Christ up them and I advised them to disappear, but it's always possible their last employer will get to them first. Anyway, how did this man know I was after his bloody fiddle in the first place?'

'I don't think he did. I think his spies had seen us together in Bermuda and he sent his "unprofessional thugs" on a fishing expedition. It's not unusual for me to be followed when I travel. The way you easily took them out was proof of who, or what, you are. And by the way, it is not HIS "fiddle".'

Before he rang off, the Monsignor gave me a name and a number to call, carefully spelling it out for me. 'This is a person with whom I worked in the Vatican, and is an expert on their chosen subject. They will assist you greatly, and will also be in the right position should anything happen to me.'

'Well, if you feel like that, why not give me a clue to the identity of the man behind tonight's debacle. I assume it's the ones who took my son hostage, but how the hell did they find my address so soon? I have to tell you, Milos, I'm still not too happy about you, and I promise, if anything SHOULD happen to you, it will be me who does it, mate.'

The man of the cloth laughed down the phone without humour. He bade me goodnight.

Later, I thought how wrong my own words were to be.

CHAPTER FOUR

"It is beyond question that he (the Pope) can err even in matters touching the faith. He does this when he teaches heresy by his own judgment or decretal. In truth, many Roman Pontiffs were heretics."

Pope Adrian VI, 1523.

"Every cleric must obey the Pope, even if he commands what is evil; for no one may judge the Pope."

Pope Innocent III (1198–1216)

The next morning, proudly accompanied by my son Phillip, I drove into the old market town of Exeter, parked my car down a side road near St David's station and caught two one-ways to London. We had an overnight bag each, as we'd done some shopping for Phillip in Tavistock the day before, much to his protests. We went straight to Waterloo station on the underground. We came up in the high-domed ceiling of the main station, went out past the long row of taxis and crossed the road to Sandell Street where the imposing structure of the new Union Jack Club rose to the sky. I remembered the old Victorian building on the main road with affection, but the present one was clean and comfortable, and charged the cheapest rates for accommodation in London. I signed us both in, dumped our bags in the twin room and set out for lunch. I remembered that The Old Fire Station opposite the Union Jack Club served good sea food so I treated us both to a large platter of fruits de la mare, and I had a pint of draught Guinness while Phillip had a bottle of Corona, with a piece of lime in the top, much to my disgust.

After lunch we strolled down to the bookshop on the corner of Waterloo Road and browsed for a couple of hours, finishing up with a few purchases on our recently chosen subjects; violins and the Devil. We spent the afternoon absorbing the books on violins, and whilst not exactly John Grisham I found the subject matter quite interesting. I'd been the only one of the brothers to pass a scholarship and the inroads into the mysteries of academia had once held a fascination for me. I'd been told that I had an exceptional IQ, although true to form you were never actually told what it was. All this before the more physical aptitudes of the commandos had got to me and I'd followed my older brothers into the Royal Marines.

I muttered something that rhymed like "rollicks", and carried on reading, or was it swatting? My son chuckled into his own pages and took on a supercilious look when I frowned at him. He then read a passage that interested me not an iota, but which he seemed to find interesting.

There were many precursors to the violin. Some, such as the Ravanstron, the Rabab and the Rebec have been around since 5000 BC, and there are several others whose names are not known and which also date back to a few thousand BC. In Europe the violins history can be traced back to the 9th century, with its original possibility in Asia. The primitive form of the stringed instruments is the musical bow from which an arched stick held by a taut string is tied to its two ends. The string is divided by a loop or bridge. In order to enhance its resonance, the primitive bow was held before the mouth. In the more evolved forms, resonance enhancers included

coconut, calabash (a hollowed out dried gourd used as a recipient), tortoise shells, wooden boxes or pig bladders that were thrust tightly between the strings and the bow.

'Charming,' I muttered, producing another chuckle.

By the Middle Ages, around the 11th century, violins history indicates that the vielle and the rote had come into evidence, and were discovered as a simple reproduction of the ancient zither. The violins history in the 12th century indicates the last evolution of the vielle. It was, at that time, similar to a modern guitar in cut. It was a widely used instrument during this period due to its ease of handling, its wide tonal range, and the ease of playing the scales. Also around this time the instrument went from having one or two strings to having three or four. Some even had five, which stayed in existence until the 16th century. At that time the four-string, or true, violin became more prominent.

'Too much information,' I was already getting brain-dead from it all, and waited until he finished the chapter then suggested we go down to the bar for a nightcap.

The violins history before 1500 indicates that three other instruments appeared, one of which, the viola de gamba (held on or between the knees) is still played today. Another was a bowed instrument called the lire da braccio, and the third is called the viola da braccio, which is the direct predecessor of the violin. The viola da braccio had originally three or four strings and eventually became a four-stringed instrument all the time. It adopted other modern characteristics, such as the peg box and tuning in fifths, which allows the instrumentalist to use four fingers... The shape of the sound holes also changed from crescents to the f shape of today, and became known as the f hole.

'Or "the arsehole" to me, mate,' I muttered, and waited until he read the last line of the chapter.

At what time did the violin leave the viola da braccio family? It is hard to say....

I rose, grabbed my jacket and we trotted over to the fire station, up to the eyeballs in peg boxes, fingerboards, bridges, swan necks, tailpieces and the like. A good match on tele and a pint of Guinness would make it all go away.

At least for tonight.

The next day we visited the Royal Academy of Music, keepers of one of the most extensive collections of Strads among its impressive array of instruments of all kinds. We were early enough to join a tour of the displayed instruments, and later I sweet-talked the guide into a private tour of the Stradivarius collection. The fifty-pound note ensured we had the guide's personal and undivided attention.

As it turned out the guide was a retired music teacher from the Academy who had a love interest in the place, mainly the violins and especially the Strads and Amati's in particular. In answer to an innocuous question by moi he launched into a treatise on the bow.

'Let's say that one day you should suddenly decide that you were going to make the finest violin bow it is possible to produce, you would first have to take a ship to the port of Pernambuco in Brazil. Then you would have to set out on a long and hard journey to the interior of that great country. There, after diligent search, you would find growing in the hard and rocky ground a tree called the Brazilwood tree. You would then select a small tree, cut away the outside sapwood, and finally come to a small heart, dark red in color. This is the Pernambuco wood known to commerce.'

'How about now the place is called Recife, Professor Gibbons?' My son surprised us both by asking politely, and it was then that I saw that he had a natural ability for keeping a straight face. 'Does that alter the name of the wood?'

He must have made the right noises because the retired professor gave him an intimate smile.

'Well done, sir. You're obviously a travelled man. Even most violinists I've spoken to are hardly aware of where it is, and no; the wood is still called Pernambuco. It was selected by Tourte, the great French bow maker of the eighteenth century, as the best material for making violin bows, and nothing finer has ever been discovered. It has just the right weight for balance, the right grain structure for retaining its shape, and the right resiliency for the utmost in bow technique.'

At this point we had obviously gained his confidence with that lucky snippet of geographical knowledge, and Gibbons actually took down a long Strad and let me hold it. Despite my somewhat cynical outlook on the whole thing, I honestly felt I was in the presence of greatness – not really, I told myself but I definitely had a feeling of something. Perhaps it was just respect when I thought of the work which had gone into the making of it, and as though aware of my thoughts, Professor Gibbons expounded further on the wood used on the violins themselves as I carefully handed the instrument over to Phillip.

'Early in the development of the fine violins of Italy, the Amati and Stradivari craftsmen found there was nothing like the giant Norway spruce or Swiss pine for a violin top. These great trees grew a hundred to a hundred and fifty feet, and their grain was as even and straight as parallel beams of light. This wood filled the need for a material of great elasticity but light weight.'

Warming to his theme he took his visitors' silence for awe on the profound subject of wood. 'They didn't know then, of course, but scientists have since found out, that sound travels faster through this wood than any other, attaining a velocity through the grain lengthwise of fifteen thousand feet per second, a velocity nearly equal to that found in steel. They didn't have technical proof of this, but their trained ears told them that this spruce wood gave the best results.'

He went on to talk about the logs being cut on the quarter and sawed through the centre, then the centre edges being glued together, which gave them identical grain structure from the centre to both outside edges, the grain being so uniformly even and regular. When he explained that after three centuries of violin making nothing has been found which surpasses this wood for violin tops, even the erudite Professor Gibbons realized that he might have lost me back along the way, though not necessarily my son.

I came away not much the wiser about the private life of the man, but had a definite feeling for the genius that was Antonio Stradivari in his luthier skills, to which Phillip agreed later when we discussed it.

The next day it was the turn of the Ashmolean Museum and this time I bought return tickets to Oxford. I had never visited the University City before, so was somewhat surprised by the huge amount of bicycles everywhere. Most of them were unlocked and were simply leaning against walls and in communal racks. They were for the most part nondescript bikes of the "sit up and beg" variety, upright handlebars and not worth much as a whole. Phillip took it all in his stride and explained to me that students or anyone else for that matter, simply picked up a bike from anywhere and rode it around, then left it when they finished for the next pedestrian to become a cyclist for the day. He spoiled it somewhat by saying that the practice actually began in Cambridge, and was still going today.

I'd never read an Inspector Morse book but had often watched the TV series with John Thaw, and was almost surprised not to see piles of bodies lying around on the streets of Oxford. Morse seemed to get a fresh body every week.

The Ashmolean Museum was founded in 1683, and is the oldest institution of its kind in Britain. Beginning with Elias Ashmole's original bequest, it has gone on to establish an enviable reputation for excellence in research and teaching, with an outer appearance impressive enough to match that reputation. Wide stone steps lead up to a grand and slightly austere, classical façade. The Ashmolean is smaller than London's British Museum, and New York's Metropolitan Museum of Art, but the overall effect is similar, for the visitor feels a proper sense of awe even before stepping over the threshold.

This was my feeling upon entering, and I'd done my homework on the place. Enough to be able to chat to the guard at the front door for a while, telling him I was a journalist, Phillip was my junior, and we were researching Stradivari. His suggesting that I take the shortcut rewarded me greatly.

'Don't go up the main stairs, squire, but turn left, go to the end of the gallery, take the stairs you see on your right and the Hill Music Room is immediately at the top of the first floor. You'll probably find the room is shut, with a sign on the door blaming staff shortages, and suggesting if you really have to see the contents of the room you should check with the invigilator next door. His name's Mr. Bundige and he likes one to think he's more important than his job is, but you can butter him up, like, and he's quite knowledgeable about the place and the instruments.'

The guard graciously accepted the twenty-pound note I slipped him, "for a drink on me when you knock off work, mate," and we went up the short cut. As forecast I saw the notice on the door, which was locked, and knocked on the next door, which belonged to the invigilator.

Mr. Bundige was a short person with a big person's ego, as the guard had rightly described him, and I had no problem giving him another story about representing an anonymous benefactor, who wished to donate a large, anonymous amount to the museum and introducing him to my son. So it was that we had another personal guided tour, which in some ways was a disappointment, and in others quite enriching.

The room was only about fifteen feet by thirty feet, and there was no air conditioning, merely a fan in the far corner. The cork tiles on the floor were scuffed about, with protruding nails liable to catch the unwary foot. I saw Old Masters prominently displayed around the walls, yet with no obvious connection to music. Harpsichords and virginals stood around the walls, though they were the least interesting of the collection as far as I was concerned. One case contained bows; another included a guitar made by Stradivari; plain but beautifully executed. It was testimony to the range of the famous luthier, but far from being the piece de resistance, for in the middle of the room was a case crowded with eight violins, a viola and a bass viol.

I read that Andrea Amati in 1564, part of a commission for Charles the IX of France, made one of the violins. It is the oldest surviving violin in the world, and an exquisite piece of workmanship, and I suddenly realized that this was the one I'd read about, whose companion from the same set, though two years younger, had been valued at $10 million.

Almost every exhibit in this display would be the highlight of another museum's collection, but here they were no more than satellites to the star, the only instrument to get its own cabinet, the Messiah. Our guide informed us that every famous Stradivari possesses, and is known by, its own name. The Messiah hung suspended in its case, visible from every angle, pristine, its varnish as flawless as when Stradivari applied the last few drops in 1716. It is in mint condition because this, the most famous violin in the world and the template for countless copies, has hardly ever been played.

I then remembered the name Milos had given me for the black violin, Diabolus, and in some strange, not yet defined way, it began to come together.

'It has an astonishing tale to tell,' the rotund little man told me somewhat pedantically. However, as his astonishing tale unfolded, he relaxed more and to my surprise I found myself quite interested in what the man had to say.

'In the first part of the nineteenth century there was a mysterious individual called Luigi Terisio. He travelled all over Italy, disguised as a peddler with a pack on his back full of new violins which he offered to exchange for old ones. Dealers in Paris were amazed when he arrived there with an incredible collection, which included violins by Stradivari, and also by the earlier Amati, by Guarneri, Guadagnini and others. In the year 1854 one of these dealers, J.B. Vuillaume, heard that Terisio had died in Milan, and hurried there in the hope of being able to purchase whatever collection of instruments might remain.'

While Mr. Bundige expounded forth on the subject of the peddler dealer, I was gazing with what came close to awe in my world at the priceless examples of latter-day craftsmanship. I sensed that Phillip felt the same way.

'He was shown to the miserable room where Terisio had died, surrounded by more than two hundred violins, viols, and violoncellos by all the great masters. Vuillaume was naturally speechless with astonishment. He was then taken to a small farm where Terisio had hidden away more violins, and while he was examining this collection, he pulled open a drawer and gazed with amazement at a new Stradivari, an instrument which had never been played upon, Mr. Brogan. A descendant of Stradivari had sold this violin to Count Cozio de Salabue, who had never used it, and in whose possession it had remained until Terisio found it. It is still in mint condition just as it left the workshop in Cremona in 1716, and was presented to the Ashmolean Museum by Arthur and Alfred Hill, the foremost authorities on Stradivari.'

I looked across the room at the Messiah. 'You mean...?'

'Yes, indeed,' the man nodded with a self-satisfied beam on his face. 'The very one, and priceless, absolutely priceless, you know.'

No, I didn't know, but I did know I was soon about to steal one probably even more priceless.

If that made any kind of sense at all.

My son and I left the Ashmolean in a sombre mood. We had stood in the presence of excellence this day, and we both knew it. I was in no way a violin connoisseur; in fact I was not even sure I liked the instrument that much, but I felt awed at what I had seen and learned from the redoubtable Mr. Bundige. The man's sheer love and respect for his charges had shone through his self-important personality, and he had opened up to me as a fellow, though admittedly naïve, enthusiast.

We returned to London that afternoon and the next morning left for the West Country. After first making a plentiful cash withdrawal and visiting an old friend to collect a few purchases.

I'd known Cassidy since the first day we'd both arrived in the recruit depot at Deal in Kent. We'd hit it off from the start, both came from Liverpool and both thought we were jack-the-lads. We would soon learn that we weren't as smart as we thought we were, but somehow managed to get thrown together through most of our career. Cassidy, though I was never too sure what his first name was, for true to tradition he had acquired the nomenclature of Hopalong; the way White's had become Chalkies and Wilson's were known as Tug for the rest of their lives. Cassidy had also been known as the Armourer, for the simple reason that it was what he'd become, and had a reputation within the Corps as the best one there was. Since I began my nefarious career as a tealeaf I had purchased a quantity of stuff from him. Not firearms, for Cassidy had ventured into all kinds of lines to help an honest burglar. A lot he'd taken my advice on and a lot he'd found for himself; climbing and descending, minor charges to blow off hinges quietly, hi-tech surveillance gear, minute explosive devices that could blow up a tank, the lot. Think James Bond's supplier, Q, and you think Cassidy.

I had placed an order before lunch and picked it up afterwards. I introduced him to my son and Cassidy gave him a nod. 'You know who this arsehole is, don't you, lad?' He said.

Phillip nodded, though I could tell he was unsure of where Cassidy was taking this. 'My father?'

'Maybe, and he's also one of the Brogan Boys, legends in their own diaries. Some call them heroes, some call them arseholes. Me, I think they were a bunch of ars...'

'Thanks for the testimonial, you old git,' I hissed at him. 'But I don't need it now. Have you got the stuff?'

He did the famous Cassidy sniff and slung a bag on the counter, which I quickly checked through. It was a small dive bag and true to form it confirmed my purchases. Money changed hands, wasn't checked, and disappeared in one of Cassidy's numerous pockets.

'Good luck to yis, whatever stupid thing yer up to now,' Cassidy said amiably. 'An' give my best to those arsehole brudders of yours. I still owe one of them, but can't remember which one.'

I grinned over my shoulder at my old mate. We picked up my car at the airport and drove for the three hours it took to get to the cottage.

Never one to be accused of stupidity, I drove past the entrance to the lane and took a left to arrive at my place in a sweeping curve. I parked in tight along a high hedge and locked the car. Opening the boot I delved into the bag, pulling out two objects that I checked over carefully.

'Know anything about guns, son?' I asked.

'No,' he said honestly. 'But I'm a quick learner.'

The first gun was a Steyr GB, Austrian but no longer manufactured. There is no safety catch on a Steyr GB – the first pull needs a pressure of fourteen pounds, which is judged to be enough to avoid an accidental discharge if the gun is dropped, because fourteen pounds is a very deliberate pull. So there is no separate safety mechanism.

The second object was a suppressor – a black cylinder with maybe a final factory price of two hundred quid. It clicked in place, not like in the movies where they hold it up to their eyes and screw it on slowly, thoughtfully and lovingly. You use light, fast pressure and a half-turn and it clicks on like a lens fits a camera. It improved the weapon; improved its balance. 99 times in a 100 a handgun gets fired high because the recoil flips the muzzle upward. The weight of the silencer was going to counteract that likelihood. And a silencer works by dispersing the blast of gas relatively slowly, which weakens the recoil in the first place. The sound is loud – not a polite little spit, again like on the movies. Not unlike taking a thick phone book and smashing it down hard on a desk with all your strength. Not a quiet sound, but quieter than it could be. After there would be a strong stink of burned powder and hot steel wool inside the suppressor.

Satisfied, I held the weapon in my right hand and laid it to one side. I then took out a nine-millimetre Glock with a custom silencer and handed it to my son. I showed him the safety catch and said, 'Now all you do is point it and pull that little piece of metal there, it's called the trigger. Stay here and wait for any kind of noise, then get in the car and drive like hell until you get well away from here. Got that?'

'Got it,' he nodded. 'There's just one tiny little thing.'

'Double diminutive, I think I've been wasting my dosh at that fancy public school of yours,' I said absently. 'And that is?'

'I can't drive.' I think he was laughing at me and I resolved to sort him out later.

I picked up the Steyr and was through the hedge and running back along the line of it until I saw the top of my chimney. I approached the back door slowly and carefully, and was almost on to it when I sensed the form to my left and smelled the fox before he was on me, his tongue wiping across the line of my jaw.

'Hey, feller,' I said softly. 'Any bad people around?'

As though to assure me it was clear, the big fox trotted ahead and nuzzled the door. That was enough for me and I straightened up and strode over to the back porch sheltering the door.

I got some hamburger meat out of the freezer and defrosted it in the microwave while I poured myself a beer. Throwing the thawed meat to the fox I trotted back around to the car, but couldn't see my son. I shrugged and climbed behind the wheel, driving it up the lane and into the front yard.

I turned off the engine and felt the rim of cold steel press into my neck.

'I thought you were good at this kind of thing,' I heard Phillip say as I leaned forward over the wheel. He kept the barrel in contact with my head, reaching forward over the seat, as I half-turned, knocked his arm off aim and grabbed the Glock.

'I am,' I told him casually. 'Hungry?'

Everything seemed fine. If the fox was happy about the absence of visitors, so was I. We'd picked up a few groceries in the last petrol stop and I unpacked them and placed them in the fridge. I opened a bottle of California merlot, poured a glass, Phillip took one, and I drank mine in two quaffs. The second glass I treated with more respect, sipping instead of slurping. With the fox lying happily on the floor I threw a few lamb chops under the grill and made a salad for us both.

The fox went over and nuzzled Phillip, and I was pleased to see he responded by allowing his face to be licked and ruffled the fur behind his ears and throat. 'Someday you must tell me how you happen to have made friends with a huge fox, and how he's moved in as one of the family.'

'He IS family,' I said. 'The only family I've had for a while. Sorry, didn't mean it to sound cynical. I'm really glad you're here, Phillip, I am.'

I could hear my voice going all gruff so left it at that.

'Me too, Dad,' he said softly. 'I'm glad I'm here too.'

After dinner we went back to the studies of the life and times of Stradivari.

Looking up the master's final resting place introduced me to a history book where the author, H.V. Morton, was surprised to find a public garden and park in the centre of Cremona. He found lawns, a fountain, a bandstand, well-grown chestnut trees, polled acacias, beds of hydrangeas, and seating tastefully arranged around the area. It was like being in England or France, wrote the author, for such a garden in the heart of an ancient Italian town was unusual. He asked the history of the park and was told that an unpopular Dominican monastery, the headquarters of the Inquisition in fact, was once on the site and was pulled down shortly after the Risorgimento and the site made into a municipal garden.

While wandering around this greenery he came upon the tombstone of Antonio Stradivari, once lying in the church and now in the open air. This struck me as worthy of adding it to my meagre notes. I read on, fascinated by the stories that had accumulated around the extraordinary genius. All the finest violins by Stradivari have unblemished provenance and each, as I've said before, have their own names, such as the Viotti and the Vieuxtemps, while some are still called after their most celebrated owners such as Sarasate and Paganini.

Then Phillip came to the piece I'd been looking for all along. One Stradivari was believed to have a curse on it, but no name was put upon it and whether it was still in existence or not, no one could state to that either.

It was once owned by a professional violinist, Romeo Danni, in the eighteenth century, who bought it being unaware of its reputation of suddenly becoming silent after having played beautifully for an hour or so. This occurred during one of Danni's concerts, and he accused his rival Salvadossi with having performed some trick on him, and challenged him to a duel. Danni was killed, and then began a vendetta that would cost twenty-two lives over the years. The violin then mysteriously disappeared.

Similar stories appeared when I went on the web but I could find no running thread on one violin. Certainly not the mysterious black one which was coveted by many people and now reposed...where?

This reminded me.

CHAPTER FIVE

"The First See (Rome/Papacy) is judged by no one. It is the right of the Roman Pontiff himself alone to judge...those who hold the highest civil office in a state...There is neither appeal nor recourse against a decision or decree of the Roman Pontiff."

From today's Code of Canon Law.

"Each individual must receive the faith and law from the Church with unquestioning submission and obedience of the intellect and the will. ...We have no right to ask reasons of the Church, any more than of Almighty God. ...We are to take with unquestioning docility whatever instruction the Church gives us."

The Catholic World, August 1871, vol. Xiii, pp. 58089.

The next morning I woke with a clear head, as I always did after a night on the pure stuff, whether wine, beer or Guinness, and knew instinctively what my next move would be.

At 8am I phoned Monsignor Zoltan Milos and spoke briefly.

'I believe I'm ready to go now, so where is the violin kept?' I asked.

'We believe it is in the vaults, or catacombs you might know them as. The catacombs were the first Christian burial grounds in Rome. It is often said that the catacombs were the hiding places for Christians during the persecutions, which is not true, but this is a general misconception that probably began with 18th Century romantic literature, such as Quo Vadis. Roman Law protected all underground cemeteries and declared individual burial rights inviolable.'

'Yes, thanks for all that, but this precious instrument, this violin, is where?'

He ignored me again. Once can be forgiven as absentmindedness, but twice is downright bloody rude.

'The catacombs, the word means "the hollows" by the way, are honeycombed beneath the length and breadth of Rome. No one knows the extent, and no one knows how many more there are yet to discover. The ones below the Vatican are but a small sample of the whole. When were they built? Who knows, for underground burial was common practice among ancient Mediterranean cultures, and therefore we find underground burial tunnels in Egypt, Greece and many other lands around the Mediterranean. In Rome a pagan ipogea was discovered dating back to the Etruscan period. When Peter and Paul were preaching Christianity in Rome, there already existed pagan and Jewish catacombs; all considered sacred and protected by Roman law. Many were built upon the already existing complexes, and as the Christian community grew, new catacombs were founded, while the older ones were expanded. Over 60 catacombs have been discovered beneath Rome, with approximately one million Christian tombs.'

'All very interesting,' I said rudely. 'But now I'm bored and I asked you a question. Where is the violin, Milos? What part of the catacombs is it hidden in, and what the hell is it doing down there in the first place? This time I want an answer.'

I could imagine the large lump of clergyman stirring, his face perhaps showing his obvious annoyance at being interrupted in the full flow of dissertation. I didn't give a crap if he was annoyed or not because my main agenda was in keeping my word by getting hold of their precious violin. I was beginning to get pissed off, for I had other plans in my life, especially now that I'd got my son back, this time for good I hoped.

His next words quite surprised me, and at the same time increased my pissed off-ness even more.

'I'm afraid I haven't a clue, Harry,' his voice was sad, and I realized that this man could turn it on or off, as he felt fit. 'We know the black violin is down in the catacombs, below Vatican City itself, and it was placed there under the auspices of the Pope to protect it from being used for evil purposes, but that is all we do know.'

I felt gutted. In my naivety I thought it was a simple matter of breaking into the Vatican itself and navigating a few locked doors and delving into a few deep places. Now, the fat sod had glibly told me that they don't even have a clue about the actual whereabouts of the damn thing.

I took a deep breath and tried to act sensibly, while at the same time every nerve in my body wanted to rip the fat bastard's head off and vomit down the hole. Okay, so it wasn't a very wise thing to do, but who ever accused me of being wise. Certainly no one in my recent history.

'I thought you knew everything about the bloody thing. How did it get where it is?' I asked slowly and patiently. That was better. That showed control. But it still sucked.

'Oh, that's common knowledge among the aristocracy of the church,' Milos said knowingly, and without any apparent smugness. I was waiting for the smugness, actually, having dealt with his like before. Or thought I had. How many times can you be wrong in one lifetime, I would ask myself later. 'It was taken by the church some years ago.'

I loved that one – taken by the church – but so were so many other...things, since the advent of the Holy Mother Church.

'So, we have this...allegedly...wonderful violin, taken by the church, and...What?'

'It was taken because it was evil,' the big man said in that trim little way he sometimes had of saying things, and still managing to sound quite trite. 'The Holy Father at the time, took it upon himself to "procure" the instrument and in his haste to remove it from the world he simply had it conveyed to the catacombs and hidden securely, so no one else could ever have power over it. This knowledge has been handed down from Pope to Pope for the past 300 years.'

'Yes, but they must have some clue they leave lying around, some codeword or other, so if something happened to the current Pope, his predecessor would know where to go to, and what to look for,' I muttered.

'I'm sure you're right, Harry, I'll have Andrea look around for something like that.'

'Why can't you just go there yourself,' I asked him. 'Surely with your influence at the Vatican, having worked there, you could find out something?'

'Ah, but that would be alerting the other people who want the Diabolus,' he said softly and with so much conviction that I didn't believe a word of it. 'They keep a watch on me, I know.'

'Okay,' I muttered angrily. 'Tell me the rest.'

'The city itself and the entire place, both inside and outside, is guarded by the Swiss Guards, possibly the finest troops in the world for what they do; which is to guard the Vatican, and its entire territory, both inside and outside.'

'Oh, well, as long as there's nothing difficult about it, then. Where do I start?' I asked without expression.

Go to Rome, he'd said. Meet with Andrea Scolari, he'd said. Recover the violin, he'd said, and all will be well, he'd said. Not that I was too much into that last one. All will be well. No, it bloody well won't, I swore to myself, not while some prick had snatched my son and held him to ransom, then tried to kill me. That part sucked - big time.

The next morning Phillip told me he had to be getting back to his studies and besides, his mother would be getting worried about him. With promises to keep in touch by phone and e-mail I drove him to Plymouth airport and bought him a single to Gatwick, shoving more than enough money in his pocket for the taxi-fare to his mother's place.

The morning following I spoke to a travel agent in Exeter at 9am, and at 11am I was seated on a train from St David's station en route to Waterloo, then a shuttle to Gatwick and by 3pm I had just lifted off for Rome.

At this stage it was as far as my plans took me.

Then I remembered the name of the man in the Vatican; Andrea Scolari, the expert on the Satan, Lucifer, Devil; thing. The Devil and all his works - the words of Dennis Wheatley, whom I'd read somewhere was actually a believer in such stuff. I do not have to admit that my scoffing had diminished somewhat, and couldn't decide why it was so, nor at what stage it had happened.

We touched down in Rome and I jumped into a taxi, a small Fiat, which looked well outdated against the string of fancy Mercedes, lined up at the official cabstands but which I chose on purpose. Hey, call it a hunch. The driver, who drove like a startling reincarnation of Juan Fangio, took no time in taking me to my destination, a little boarding house about a mile from Vatican City. As with most Roman cab drivers, Fangio did his best to intimidate his touriste passenger with his maniacal driving. Although he received a generous tip he could not hide his disappointment in the nerveless demeanour of his English fare.

'Don't worry, son,' I smiled as I handed over the money. 'Stevie Wonder taught my wife to drive, so I'm used to your style. Pick me up at mi casa 8 o'clock in the morning, okay. Ciao.'

The thought of another fare with the good-natured simpleton from England brought a smile to the driver's face this time and he tooted the horn as he drove off. Another annoying habit Italian drivers had, I mused without rancour.

Rome was a place I'd visited a long time before, when I had served for a year on a frigate which parked in Genoa once and I'd gone on a bus trip to Rome with fellow SNCOs from the Royal Marines and Royal Navy.

Of course I couldn't remember much from that trip so long ago, so I'd brought a Fodor's tourist guide with me and wandered around for a couple of hours. I'd chosen the lodgings because of their proximity to the area of the Vatican. I ate around seven, early for Italians, and so had the place mostly to myself. I'd chosen a little tratorria down a back street, and enjoyed a plate of freshly made linguine, washed down with rough Chianti. As I drank the first glass of wine I thought with amusement that every American gangster movie I'd ever seen always had the main man, the capo de tutti capo standing in the kitchen with a floral pinafore around his waist and asking his next victim to taste his linguine sauce.

The next morning I was shaved, showered, dressed and out of the door by eight o'clock. I was dressed in soft fawn trousers, a dark blue shirt open at the neck, covered by a brown suede jacket. My appointment was for nine o'clock but on the day after, and I'd decided to spend the day getting intimate with the Vatican and the area around it. As I left the lodging house my taxi arrived.

I didn't need it but wanted to keep on top of everything, and a good cab driver is always worth keeping a grip on. I felt that Fangio was worth keeping a grip on.

As the cab turned left into the Via della Conciliazione I saw the magnificent view ahead. The massiveness of St Peter's Basilica, capped by the famous majestic dome, rose above St Peter's Square.

Fangio pulled into the side of Pius XII Square alongside a row of yellow cabs that were parked in front of a stone office building.

'I am not sure which entrance you require, Signor, but the Bronze Door is at the end of the right-hand colonnade,' he informed me in very good English.

'Well, Fangio, you have the excellent English, eh?' I smiled at him. 'I don't know how long I'll be so don't wait, but do you have a card?'

The driver ducked down on the floor and produced an embossed, if somewhat grubby, card with his name across it. Fabio Fangetti. I couldn't help but laugh, which drew a frown of disapproval from the owner of the little battered cab.

'Scusi, my friend, Scusi,' I apologized. 'Your magnificent driving made me dub you "Fangio", after the great racing car driver, and I see your name is similar.'

At this Fabio Fangetti also laughed, taking it as a compliment. As he drove off he waved through the window and gave the usual few toots on his horn.

I glanced at my watch and realized I was too early for visiting hours at the Vatican, according to my guidebook, and thanks to Fabio's "magnificent driving".

I found a small cafe on Via del Campiso, one of the cobble stoned ancient streets of Rome and sat outside drinking a cappuccino. Not usually a coffee drinker I'd ordered "anything with milk in it" and the cute little waitress had brought me a large cup. I was hooked instantly, nothing like the real thing. Now where had I heard that before? The place was doing good business for such an early hour, and I was to learn that in keeping with Spain and some parts of France, the workers' day began with fresh coffee at a cafe, with many having a shot of something on the side. This contempt for the judgmental mores of British and American society made me smile; so what if someone wanted something strong to kick-start his day? You seldom saw drunks in any of these Continental cities, so who had it right?

I then spent a couple of hours getting to know the area, wandering down the back streets with guide book in hand, sticking mostly to the narrow streets and back alleys and getting the lie of the land in my head. Not that I was expecting having to perform a hasty exit from the Vatican, but one thing I had learned from life was that you could never take anything for granted, become too complacent, because you never knew.

As I again walked up Via della Conciliazione I was once more confronted by the magnificence of the Basilica of St. Peter's. I deferred to the guide and learned that The Piazza San Pietro was as wide as almost three football fields, and that was the American ones not piddling soccer pitches. It could hold three hundred and fifty thousand worshippers when the Pope held mass. Two vast semicircular colonnades that stretched out from the basilica like the open arms of the Pope when he gave his benediction to the throngs below framed it.

The 284 Bernini-designed Doric columns stood forty feet tall and ran four deep around the entire ten-acre open space. I felt like a pigmy, and also had a feeling of being watched from above. I looked up and saw the scores of marble saints perched on top of the colonnades, staring down into the piazza, with soulless expressions of...what? Contempt or condemnation for what man had done with his world since the two thousand years since their Master walked upon it?

In the centre of the enormous space there rose up the obelisk brought to Rome by the Roman emperor Caligula in AD 37. Capping the eighty-five foot structure was a cross and golden ball rumoured to contain the remains of Julius Caesar himself. In any other city on earth this would have been the centre of attraction, the piece de resistance, but here, surrounded by the achievements of the greatest artists through the centuries, it was simply another wonder for the masses to gawk at. At that moment I too was one of those gawkers.

As the dome of St Peter's Basilica reached upwards to Heaven itself, back on the ground at the foot of the wide entrance steps stood a huge statue of St. Paul, holding a sword and defending the Church against her enemies. On the left was another massive statue of marble, that of St. Peter, the first Pope, holding a bunch of keys in his hands.

Everywhere I looked I saw architectural achievements that only latter-day genius could have produced. The immense, imposing wall that guarded the Vatican City ranged in height from forty to over one hundred feet. One of the several guides I now carried informed me that its medieval design was capable of defending itself against a modern military attack.

I spent the rest of the day in the more public areas of the Piazza San Pietro, the Sistine Chapel and the many museums. I hadn't known until I started studying the guidebooks the size of the Pope's cultural domain. The Vatican had a twelve-museum complex, and many apparently claimed that one of them was the largest in the world, but both the Louvre and the Smithsonian disputed this. The museums of the Vatican encompassed fourteen hundred rooms, which stretched along corridors whose total length was over four miles.

One could spend a whole year there and still not see the huge collection which had been gathered together over two thousand years. There was Etruscan art, classical statues, Renaissance paintings, books, maps, furnishings, tapestries, manuscripts, Middle Eastern artefacts, archaeology, and much more. A collectors dream and a curator's nightmare, no doubt, I thought.

The dome of St Peter's Basilica rose 390 feet into the air and Michelangelo had designed it. It had taken forty-four years to complete his amazing vision, and the Fodor's described it as the golden crown of the Church.

In the Sistine Chapel, where most people were familiar with Michelangelo's famous masterpiece on the ceiling, the sidewalls of the chapel itself also contained masterpieces by the greatest artists of their age. Botticelli, Ghirlandaio, Perugino, Rosselli, had completed magnificent frescoes spanning the length of the chapel.

A conservative estimate for the art, antiquities, gold, jewels, and of course the deeds to all of the holdings and properties of the Catholic Church from around the world, was more than forty billions dollars. This was the bit that really interested me, for no other country in the world concentrated all of their assets in such a small area. Because of this there were security measures in place that defied anywhere else in the world to equal them. The doorways were all personally monitored, as well as being covered electronically. Most of the security toys were out of sight, I noticed, so as to take nothing away from the grandeur of the contents themselves. Metal detectors were concealed, as were the radioactive sensors and electronic bomb sniffers.

Swiss Guards were stationed at all of the checkpoints and entrances. I was not so concerned by these as the others who mingled with the crowds. It was a combination of everything I had been trained to look out for, from their haircuts which were far too ordinary for the average testosterone-guided Italian, to the way they carried themselves, walked and even positioned their bodies in all the right places when they paused. These would have been the Vatican Police, and I followed one or two for a while, watching the professional way they moved through the crowds seemingly at random.

There were always two of them in each museum, one arriving as another one left.

I was very impressed, but thought I might have spoiled the moment by going up to one of them and telling him so.

I was tired by five o'clock, and God forgive me, almost bored by the continuous sights of the most precious and rare artefacts in the history of the world. I departed the Vatican, none the wiser as to the whereabouts of the damn violin, but more appreciative of the Catholic Churches worthiness in saving so much antiquity for the benefit of mankind. I knew full well that the bands of Vatican knights sent out through the ages by the Popes had not been deluded enough to believe their errands were all for the good of Mother Church, but the end was the same, surely?

I decided to walk back to my lodgings, despite the ache in both legs. This was in order to see that I could navigate the way in case of need; need to get away in a hurry. About halfway I had a brilliant dinner in a small family run tratorria, but don't ask what I had.

The next morning I had a meeting with Andrea Scolari, so a couple of hours later found me tucked up in bed reading the inevitable guidebooks and surfing my laptop. Everything you wanted to know about everything; with the exception of a black violin answering to the name of Diabolus. Nowhere was there mention of such an item, certainly not on the vast website devoted to describing the incredible treasures of the small city's museums.

It was as though the damned thing never existed.

CHAPTER SIX

The fairest harmony springs from discord,

Heraclites
540 – 480 BC

The best sort of music is what it should be – sacred; the next best, the military, has fallen to the lot of the Devil.

Samuel Taylor Coleridge
1772 – 1834

I dodged the cars speeding around the Largo del Colannato, the road bordering the two semicircular arms of Bernini's colonnade that partially enclosed St Peter's Square. I considered again that I was now in the world's smallest state; sized about one eighth of New York's Central Park. A goodly amount of people milled around the Square, mostly tourists and Christian worshippers to Rome, though with a fair sprinkling of nuns dressed in various fashions of headdress and habits. Bunches of happy students were everywhere, and they too were dressed in a variety of loud tee shirts, shorts or tattered jeans, and mainly sandals.

I went through a high arch and up a flight of stone steps to the Bronze Door, which although it was open was guarded by a Swiss Guard. The guard was wearing the official dress uniform of blue, red, orange and yellow, which gave him a distinctly Renaissance appearance. It looked decidedly poncy to me but I was well aware that their training was first class, and they were as good in their own way as many of the so-called Special Forces in the world's armies. From their expert use of the ceremonial weapon, the halberd, and the sword, they were also fully trained and equipped in modern tactics and weaponry.

The young Guard shouted "Alt" while at the same time thumping his six-foot halberd on the floor and shifting it diagonally across the doorway.

'Hello,' I spoke slowly and concisely. 'My name is Brogan and I have an appointment with Andrea Scolari.'

The Guard appeared to be either thinking over the request, or he couldn't speak a word of English. I was just deciding on the latter when a voice barked from inside. The young Swiss Guard immediately brought his fearsome weapon back to the upright position and stood back, again without saying a word.

I walked inside and over to where a Wachtmeister, or sergeant, sat at a wooden desk.

I said my name again and repeated my purpose. I extended my passport and the sergeant took it with a nod and a "grazi".

He looked at the passport photo and studied my face, before jotting down my details in a large desk log and handing back my passport. He handed me a pass with a clip at the top.

'Please wear this at all time, Signor. You can take the stairs, up two flights and turn right into the corridor. The room you want is the second on the left.'

'Thank you,' I said, and looked around for the stairs.

I heard a noise behind me and saw a Guard who had appeared from nowhere.

'This man will accompany you, Signor Brogan, 'the sergeant informed me gravely. 'Your host will be responsible for escorting you out of the Vatican at the conclusion of your business. Have a good visit.'

As we walked further into the Vatican, I remembered reading about the Swiss Guard on the plane. The Swiss Guard, or Schweizergarde, had been on duty in the Vatican since Pope Julius II asked the Swiss Diet in 1505 to provide him with a constant corps of Swiss Mercenaries.

We entered a side door that at first looked like a small alcove, and mounted a long series of steps. At last we stepped through another doorway and the Guard produced a small bunch of keys and unlocked the old yet sturdy door.

We stepped out into a vast high-ceilinged corridor, lined with statues and dark paintings in elaborate frames and turned right. Another walk and we came upon a series of doors. The Swiss Guard opened the second door on the left, a seventeenth-century carved door that had been lovingly made from a tree that probably pre-dated the Renaissance. The Guard, who had not spoken one word to me the whole time, bowed and quietly left, closing the door behind him silently and disappearing like a wraith; these boys were good I had to admit.

I looked around and thought I was in Heaven. Like the corridor we'd travelled to get here, the ceiling was miles above my head, giving the room the appearance of a vastness it didn't actually possess. Still, it was a big room, and was in fact a library. I'd always loved books, along with my brothers, and it was something acquired from our mother. Unlike my father, a plain-speaking man with an education of sorts but no particular love of books, our mother had a good education and had been a teacher in her pre-marriage years.

Rich leather was everywhere, though there were many cloth bound volumes as well. Every shelf was lined with books, with neatly printed labels defining the contents of each row. Looking up I saw there was a railed mezzanine running around the room about twelve feet high, with a ladder on wheels attached to either side. As I was gazing around the room a voice floated down from the right hand ladder.

'Scusi, Signor, un momento.'

I then noticed a pair of shapely calves descending the ladder, followed by an equally shapely backside, and when the feet contacted the floor I saw a mass of black curls surmounting a somewhat pixyish face. I knew no other way to describe that face. It wasn't the usual euphemism of elfin, for there was something more than that. It had a Puckish quality; nice features without being exactly beautiful, and there was a mischievous look about it. The mouth was too big, but so was Julia Roberts's I thought, and dismissed the negative. At first I thought she was young, in her twenties, but on close inspection, and she had definitely moved in close, I saw she was late thirties for there was an older quality about her.

She was dressed simply but appropriately, in a grey pleated skirt and a pink knitted top. Confident in her own persona she had no recourse to jewellery beyond a beautiful gold cross on a thickly woven chain about her neck which also stated her pride in her faith. Her deep tan was either genetic skin color or what it purported to be; a deep tan. She was not much above 5'2".

She laughed suddenly, a delightful sound I thought at the time. Then I realized she was laughing at me. Probably because of the way I was staring like the proverbial village idiot, I berated myself.

'I was looking for Signor Scolari,' I said politely, embarrassed at her laughter, which I had apparently set off again, and wondered what I'd done wrong.

'I am Signor Scolari,' she twinkled. I had never known a female twinkle before, but again, there was no other word to describe the way she laughed without laughing as she put the emphasis on the Signor.

'I was laughing because I wondered if you'd finished the inspection, and whether I'd passed.' She held a hand before her mouth, which detracted nothing from the overall embarrassment of the moment.

And I WAS embarrassed; big time. But she let me down easily. She advanced with her hand out and I took it, perhaps holding on more than I should but she didn't acknowledge the gesture. Nor did she relinquish it. Her voice surprised me; she sounded pure American.

'Andrea Scolari, please call me Andi, with an "I". I'm kind of the unpaid librarian around here and I take some classes, but I'm actually on sabbatical from the American School. You must be Mr. Brogan.'

It was a statement more than a question and I merely nodded. Maybe thirty-five years old, I thought.

'I'm forty-two and take a size eight, that's because I have an ample butt otherwise I'd probably be a six, and I'm 62 inches high. Any other statistics would be too much information, bub,' and she gave me that twinkle again.

I have to admit that not a lot got through to me on a scale of embarrassment, but once again I found this little lady had managed it. Of course, her American accent had a lot to do with it.

'Bub?' was all I could come up with, and she laughed.

'Why not?' she said. 'Hey, where I come from that's polite when addressing a guy.'

It was my turn to laugh now. 'I'll take your word on that, li'l lady,' I said in my best Duke accent.

She laughed back and I suddenly felt more at ease with this little Yankee bird with the nice bod and the twinkle than I had with a female for a long time.

'You like a coffee?' she asked suddenly and the safest thing I felt I could do was nod.

She led me out of the library through a door that materialized behind a pillar on the left and into a small but well-equipped kitchen.

'All mod-cons,' I acknowledged.

'This place is the only reason I do the librarian thing,' Andrea told me and said in a challenging voice. 'I'm a coffee freak - big time. I take a dozen cups a day.'

'Ah,' I said sagely. 'That explains it.'

'Explains what?' she gave me a mock frown.

'You seem rather...hyper? If that's the right expression, as I don't wish to be rude. It also accounts for the twinkle effect of course, and that's a nice thing.'

She studied me as she poured two cups of coffee. 'Hmmm, not sure if was a compliment, mister.'

'What happened to "bub"?' I asked, accepting my coffee with a nod and spooning brown sugar into the cup.

'Aw, you've moved up a notch,' she said, and I was glad to see the twinkle was still there.

'You're American,' I realized once I'd spoken that it had come out more of an accusation than either a statement or a question. 'That is, you sound...'

'Like an American? That's because I AM an American, Mr. Brogan. Italian American, of course.'

'Of course,' I smiled, trying to recover.

She picked up her coffee, to which I couldn't help but notice that she'd added neither milk nor sugar, and went out through the door again. She took me to the huge window at the far end of the library, and we sat in large comfortable chairs looking out on St Peter's Square. The tourists were just coming in through the gates.

'So, Mr. Brogan,' she looked at me, almost slyly, over the rim of her cup. 'You wanted to see me, and your entrance ticket was mentioning the name of someone I know.'

'Yes, Zoltan Milos.' I sipped my coffee and realized she was astute enough to be testing me on my contact. I was never particularly fond of coffee, but I had to admit it was spectacularly good. There again, I WAS in Italy.

'Now why would Zoltan send you to me, Mr. Brogan?'

I looked at her in surprise. 'He didn't, that is to say, not exactly. But he gave me your name and said that you would assist me in what he wanted me to take. To obtain. To do.' I must have looked rather sheepish. I frowned at my own ineptitude with words. 'That didn't quite come out right, did it?'

'Not exactly, Mr. Brogan,' she raised a pair of well-trimmed eyebrows.

'Because he said it was something very secretive, Miss Scolari,' I shrugged. I was confused, because I thought she should know everything about it.

I thought for a moment then looked at her directly.

'You're not sure of any of this, are you?'

She maintained a passive expression but I could see something beneath it; apprehension perhaps, or fear?

'I know him,' she answered guardedly. 'Your interest in him is...?'

'He approached me and asked me to carry out a...job for him.'

'And you did it because he offered you a considerable amount of money,' she raised those eyebrows again and I sensed a change of attitude, from the genial to the mildly antagonistic.

'I refused,' I stared her out, 'despite the offer of money.'

'You're a fabulously wealthy man then?'

'No, I wouldn't say that, but I have enough and I'm retired.'

'Hmm, no one "has enough" as far as I have seen, Mr. Brogan,' she murmured. 'So, you didn't take the job.'

'Eventually I did,' I told her. 'You see, Milos made me an offer I couldn't refuse.'

'And you took it,' she said with a hint of contempt.

'Oh, yes. You see, his offer was not what he would give me, but what he could do for me, that being the life of my son.'

This stopped her, and I relented. For some astonishing reason that I don't think I knew myself, I found myself telling her the whole story, well most of it, and when I'd finished, to my surprise she nodded slowly.

'Yes, that sounds like Zoltan Milos. Exactly like Zoltan Milos.' She spoke with contempt in her voice.

I was surprised, for one because I didn't expect her to believe me and for another I had also not expected her to agree with me about my opinion of the big Monsignor.

My main reason for these expectations was the name Zoltan Milos had given me, which was that of Andrea Scolari.

'Your eyes have gone skinny, Mr. Brogan,' she broke into my thoughts.

'Skinny?'

She laughed. 'My father used to say that when he told me off about something and I didn't like it. He said my eyes would go skinny.'

'You, being told off?' I said incredulously. 'I don't believe it.'

'You better believe it, buster,' she gave me a mock glare, but the twinkle came back soon after. 'I think I was a pretty bratty child.'

'You, bratty?' I began but she stopped me before I repeated my incredulous bit again.

'So, why the skinny eyes just then, Brogan?' she went back to her original track. 'Something I said about Milos you didn't agree with?'

You're smart, lady, I thought. 'No, the fact that you DID say what I agree with. You see, Ms. Scolari, Zoltan Milos also gave me a name of someone to turn to if anything happened to him, and now we've begun to believe that something HAS happened to him.'

She frowned. 'So...?'

'So, yours was the name he gave me. I didn't realize then that you were a woman.'

'And that makes a difference...why?'

'Why, because I can't exactly see someone like you being a confidante of someone like him.'

'And how would you know what "someone like him" was really like? Or "someone like me", for that matter?'

'I wouldn't, not fully, but I'm guessing that you wouldn't exactly be simpatico with what the big priest told me about his ambitions or motivations.'

'You'd be right, Harry. The only thing Monsignor Milos and I had in common was the Devil, and for totally different reasons.'

'Harry, now. What happened to bub, buster and mister?'

'You almost just graduated; more coffee, Brogan?' she offered, and I knew I'd probably just blown it.

We were discussing the Devil.

She asked me what I knew of the Satanic one and I gave the same reply as I had to Milos, some months ago. I even asked the same question when I'd finished.

'How am I doing so far?'

'Good,' she dipped her head. 'Though in classic demonology, each of these alternate names refers to a specific supernatural entity. The English word devil is derived from the Greek word Di'avolos, meaning "to slander", and the term devil can refer to a greater demon in the hierarchy of Hell. In other languages devil may be derived from the same Indo-European root word for deva, which roughly translates as "angel".

She then repeated what Milos had told me about the Devil being a fallen angel.

'In Christianity,' she continued, 'the Devil is named Satan, sometimes Lucifer, and he is a fallen angel who rebelled against God, and has been condemned to Hell. In the Bible he is identified with the serpent in the Garden of Eden, the Accuser of Job, the tempter of the Gospels, and the dragon in the Book of Revelation.'

'You believe in all that?' I asked, trying to keep the cynicism from my voice.

She frowned. 'I believe in God, therefore I suppose I must believe in the Devil. It really IS that simple, Brogan. Take music, for example, which happens to be my specialization. The esoteric school of Pythagoras taught that certain sounds could trigger different states of mind. In later centuries the church knew this; in fact there are many scripts still locked in the Vatican, and they tried to make illegal all the sounds that could bring sexual, joyful, sensual, or other feelings.'

I shook my head. 'Gosh, those old spoilsports.'

'Would you know what the link is between Black Sabbath, Wagner's Gotterdammerung, West Side Story and the theme tune to the Simpson's?'

I couldn't help laughing. 'Not that I'm a Simpson's fan myself, but what the heck have they got to do with the Devil?'

'Do you know anything about music, Harry? What music do you like?'

I considered for a moment and decided to be honest and not my usual irreverent caustic wit when asked the same question. 'I like C&W equally with Opera, but in the latter nothing too intense.'

'Intense? All opera is intense. What about modern music?'

'Crap.' I didn't hesitate on this one. 'Total crapola, lady, in my humble opinion, of course.'

'Of course,' she raised an eyebrow, a delicate gesture but quite sensuous to my eager eyes. 'Not that I believe there's a humble bone in your body. You don't like the Beatles and all the Mersey stuff?'

'Of course I do, I come from there, remember, but we're not exactly talking modern here, are we? The Mersey Beat started in the late fifties and flourished through the sixties; the Merseybeats, Billy J. Kramer, Swinging Blue Jeans...'

'Queen? Another English group I believe.'

'I like Queen,' as I said it I realized there was a defensive element in my voice.

She twinkled. 'What? A big macho man like you, into Queen? I'm shocked, Brogan.'

I grinned then. 'Why, because Fred was gay? So are half of them in the music industry. The difference between Queen and most of them was that Freddy could actually sing and they could all write songs, as well as being able to play their bloody instruments. So there.'

She laughed; a lovely sound. 'Seriously, Brogan, there's a point to my questions as I need to know your tastes before we can seriously discuss the Devil's music. So you don't like any modern music?'

'There's very little I can actually detect a tune or anything musical in it,' I shrugged. 'Most of it's just a noise to me, what's the expression "white sound"? I know it's a tolerated noise but I just don't have the ear for it.' I said diplomatically.

Then I spoiled it by adding, 'it's a crazy world when a long-haired talentless little shit playing in some second-rate group can buy a mansion and its heritage in the cream of the English countryside somewhere.'

She nodded soberly, but I didn't know whether it was because she agreed with me or not. She simply carried on with our one-sided discussion; actually it turned into a lecture from now on.

'Well, all those very diversant pieces of music rely heavily on tritones, a musical interval that spans three whole tones, like the diminished fifth or augmented fourth. This interval, the gap between two notes played in succession or simultaneously, was branded Diabolus in Musica, or the Devil's Interval, by medieval musicians and suppressed by the Church in the Middle Ages. A rich mythology has grown up around it, and many believe that the Church wanted to eradicate the sounds from its music because it invoked sexual feelings, or that it was genuinely the work of the Devil. It is a mythology much beloved of long-haired guitar wizards around the world.'

'Wow,' I injected sarcasm into the conversation, but was interested in what the lovely Italian American woman had to say despite myself. 'That explains a lot. Is your specialization in the Church to do with music, then?'

'Actually I'm more on the investigation of music as used in the Devil's work, witchcraft, superstition and the like; as you must well know by now.'

'Ah,' I said innocently.

She continued as though there had been no interruption. 'The full expression is "mi contra fa, diabolus est in musica". In modern terms this is a major 3rd against a 4th, and this was discouraged. "The Sound of Music" almost gets it right, but the mediaeval scale "ut" re, mi, fa, so, la – no seventh note – explains our word "Gammut", from the Gamma, the lowest note you could sing, to the "ut", the highest, or in other words the whole lot. False Music, "musica ficta" is nothing to do with the augmented 4th – it is a mediaeval way of describing what we would call "accidentals" that were so obvious to contemporaries it was a waste of time marking them. The result is that much mediaeval English music is not performed as it was intended when put into musical notation that people understand today.'

'Whoa,' I held a hand up. 'That's too much information there, lady.'

Andi smiled in slight embarrassment. 'Sorry, I get carried away sometimes. Basically, what I'm getting at is that music has a powerful subconscious effect, and certain notes can invoke certain internal reactions within the listener they may not be aware of. I wonder how many other "Devil's Internals" there are, and what effects they have. Coffee?'

For a moment I was confused, and then realized a coffee break was coming up and leapt at the chance to change the subject. A few minutes later we were back in the library kitchen holding cups of strong black coffee and despite the attractions of the woman in front of me, I was definitely feeling I needed out.

'It was apparently the sound used to call up the beast. There is something very sexual about the tritone.' Andi spoke as though reminiscing to herself; alternately taking small sips from her cup. 'In the Middle Ages when people were ignorant and scared, when they heard something like that and felt that reaction in their body they thought, "Oh, dear, here comes the Devil".'

I felt an irrepressible giggle rising in my guts and strove mightily to keep it under wraps.

Andi gave me a suspicious look before continuing with her talk, which her listener, me, felt was turning into a dissertation. 'The tritone has consistently linked to evil, and in mediaeval theology you have to have some way of presenting the Devil. If someone in the Roman Catholic Church wanted to portray the crucifixion, it is sometimes used there. Of course, there were musical treatises and sets of rules produced that did come to forbid the use of the interval, which was seen as wrong when it came up in choruses of monks. There are strict musical rules and you aren't allowed to use this particular dissonance. It simply won't work technically and you are taught not to write that interval, but you can read into that a theological ban in the guise of a technical ban.'

'Let me get this straight,' I felt I had to show interest in some form or other. 'You're saying that this…Devil's Interval, is a cause of evil, and makes people do things they don't want to.'

She smiled in what I thought was a supercilious way,

'For generations of Europeans and Americans the Devil was a formidable reality; the supreme embodiment of evil, vengeful, intensely malicious, ruthless and subtle. Although belief in him has decayed in proportion with the decline of belief in God, it is not by any means extinct yet. For many Christians, of all denominations, Satan remains the archenemy of God and man.

'In a book called simply, The Devil, published in 1953, Giovanni Papini accepted the evil archangel's reality and power, and maintained that he had inspired Hobbes's

Leviathan, Blake's Marriage of Heaven and Hell, Byron's Manfred and Kafka's The Trial.'

'So what, he's real?' I had to say.

'You're not listening, are you, Harry?' She gave me a withering look. 'The Devil's Interval enjoyed great popularity among composers in the 19th Century, a time when you had a lot of presentations of evil built around the tritone. It can sound very spooky, depending on how you orchestrate it. It is also quite exciting; take Wagner's Gotterdammerung for example, it has one of the most exciting scenes; a "pagan" evil scene, the drums and timpani. Harry, it's absolutely terrifying, like a veritable black mass.'

My sense of the ridiculous and my humour had disappeared under the intensity of the animated creature standing before me. 'I heard somewhere that Heavy Metal bands played the Devil's music,' I said, somewhat lamely but Andi pounced upon my words.

'Yes, there's a big connection between heavy rock music and Wagner. They've cribbed quite a lot from 19th Century music. A modern advocate of the tritone is Black Sabbath, the rock outfit led by a fellow countryman of yours, Ozzie Osbourne, particularly in their signature song Black Sabbath, supposedly a milestone in the genesis of heavy metal.'

'You've got to be joking,' I muttered. 'That pillick...'

'Yes, Harry. That pillick. That pillick has sold a fortune in records.'

'And all because he uses the tritone?' I asked sceptically.

'Just about,' she nodded. 'There's a notorious heavy metal band, Slayer, who offered tribute in an album simply called, Diabolus in Musica. It's used in film music, jazz and blues because of its association with tension and sinister things.'

'And you really believe that evil can be produced from a certain cadence of music, the way certain notes are put together?' I found it incredible that this lovely and bright woman could actually go for what she was saying.

'Oh, yes, Harry,' she said in such a level tone that I could not for a minute doubt that she believed in her own words. 'Produced from, and manifested in, a form of pure evil. Through the ages the Devil appeared before many violinists, which is where the appellation of the Devil's Instrument came from. For example, let me tell you a story in one man's own words.'

She screwed up her eyes tightly as she spoke the words as though reading them from a page before her, and I realized she had it word perfect through using it in her classes.

'"I dreamed one night in 1713 that I had made a compact with the Devil for my soul. Everything went at my command; my novel servant anticipated my every wish and surpassed all my desires. Finally I thought of handing him my violin to see what he would do with it. Great was my astonishment when I heard a sonata so singular and so beautiful, played with such superiority and intelligence, that I had never heard the like, nor even conceived that something so lovely might be possible. I felt such pleasure - rapture, surprise – that my breath failed: the violence of the sensation awoke me. I immediately seized my violin, trying to reproduce the sounds I had heard, but in vain. The piece I then composed is truly the best I ever wrote, and I called it "The Devil's Trill Sonata," (*Trillo del Diavolo, or Sonata del Diavolo*), but it is so inferior to what I heard that if I could have subsisted on other means I would have broken my violin and abandoned music for ever."

'Giuseppe Tartini's story of how he came to write his most famous composition evokes an image of violinists in league with the Devil that still echoes today, and was most likely responsible for his continuing fame, although he was a gifted violinist in his own right. He was also the owner of the massive Lipinski violin, made by Stradivari in 1715, and was probably its first purchaser. Tartini was an 18th Century violin virtuoso and his Devil's Trill Sonata was, and still is, a piece so complicated that many modern players struggle to master it. There is a song by Panseren based on the story, (with violin obbligate, of course), and a ballet (also with a solo violin part) was also based on it and performed in London in 1893.'

'There's a rather famous engraving by Boilly of Tartini's dream,' I added casually.

'Why, yes, Harry,' the woman showed surprise. 'You continue to astonish me; have you seen it?'

I laughed gently. "You know I haven't Andi; it belongs to a private collector, an Andrew McGee, if I remember right. I can tell you it was done in 1824, though.'

She continued to give me a penetrating stare, making me feel uncomfortable for a minute or two.

'What?' I growled.

'Not the rough and tough English bloke we'd like people to think, are we Brogan?'

'Back to Brogan, eh?' I said for the want of saying something. I rose, and found myself towering over Andi Scolari. I looked down at her impish face, seeing the curve of the mouth and the slant of her eyes. Tonight they were violet and for a moment I was lost in the depths.

'Beethoven's Fidelio and Mussorgsky's Night on a Bare Mountain are other examples of tritone music.'

'What?' I realized I hadn't taken my eyes off hers for several minutes.

'I said...'

'Yes,' I muttered. 'Night on a Bare Mountain.'

'At its worst Heavy Metal is hard, heavy and fast. In its purest form it demands the highest skill from guitarists and is therefore a natural progression for a lot of budding musicians. Ask anyone who plays guitar who Eric Clapton is, or Angus Young, Jimmy Page or Joe Satriani is. They'll know them all...'

I simply sat and looked at her without interrupting or giving encouragement. Our eyes met and Andi finally broke off, frowned at me, and disappeared into the kitchen with the coffee cups. When she re-entered the library her composure had returned, although her cheeks contained bright spots.

'I keep forgetting that you're really not here as a student, Harry. So how about a walk outside to blow those cobwebs away?'

'Splendid idea,' I tried my English country squire voice, of which I was quite proud of but apparently not very good at. Or so nasty cynics have told me.

We walked slowly across St Peters Square; neither of us wishing to spoil the moment by mentioning what had just taken place in the Vatican Library.

'Did you know that the Vatican state has the highest per capita crime rate of any nation on earth, more than twenty times higher than the rest of Italy?'

I looked around furtively. "You're joking, right?'

'Certainly not,' she said in a schoolma'arm voice. 'This is because they have a small resident population but millions of visitors every year. Hundreds of tourists fall victim to pickpockets and purse snatchers, and the perpetrators, who are also visitors, are rarely caught, so 90% of the crimes are never solved.'

'Wow,' I affected my astonished tone again but she ignored me.

'International mail posted in the Vatican will reach its destination far more quickly than one dropped a few meters outside the walls in an Italian mailbox. As a result more mail is sent each year, per inhabitant, from the Vatican's 00120 post code than from anywhere else in the world...'

I stopped suddenly and turned and faced the little woman with the dark curly hair. 'Enough facts and figures; some day I'll come for an excursion tour around the Vatican, but at the moment I want to talk about other things.'

'Other things?' She echoed. 'What other things?'

'Things about you, for instance,' I resumed walking. 'You said you're Italian American, but does that mean you're Italian or American?'

She looked at me almost coquettishly. 'I was born and raised in America of Italian parents. I spent most of my holidays with my grandparents here in Rome; outside, actually, in a small village on the other side of one of the seven hills. My parents spoke mostly Italian at home, so I grew up thoroughly bilingual. There, that's me, bub.'

'No, that's just the beginning,' I grinned. 'What else should I know about the indomitable Ms Scolari? Where were you born?'

'Boston, North End.'

'I thought that was where the Irish hung out?'

'Not for a long time. It's known as Little Italy now. My parents had an Italian restaurant on Hanover, which is just around the corner from Paul Revere's house, in North Square. My brother and his wife run it now, and my parents help out from time to time. I went to N. Bennet Street, a cute little Catholic school, and made my first communion at St John's Church, also in North Square. I used to spend a lot of time hanging out with my girlfriends in Quincy Market, when I wasn't working in the restaurant, or studying, or going to Jordan Hall and Symphony Hall listening to the Boston Symphony Orchestra, or getting my teeth braced. Okay, Mr. Nosey?'

'I suppose you went to Harvard?'

She stopped and looked at me with mock suspicion. 'How did you know?'

'It's the only school I know in America,' I shrugged, a bland expression on my face.

'What about Yale?'

'What about Yale? Did you go there too?'

'No, but you must have heard of it?'

'I suppose so,' I smiled. 'But surely Harvard is a business school. I didn't know they taught Devil stuff, or even music?'

'Which is why I started out with a Bachelor's in Business Administration. It was only later, after visiting the Vatican with my grandfather that I met someone who taught me there was more to life than I'd been led to expect, or had even thought about. I obtained a post working in the City's administration, and then went back to college, taking degrees in Theology, Music History and Supernatural Studies. Combined, they gave me the basis for my PhD thesis.'

'You're one clever lady, Ms Scolari,' I said admiringly, and meaning it.

'Andi, please.'

'With an "I"?'

'With an "I".'

We had reached the gardens and she led me inside. They were behind Saint Peter's Basilica and the adjoining Apostolic Palace, that series of palaces, chapels, halls and galleries that house offices, State and private apartments, and the Vatican Museums, which I'd already nosed around. The Vatican Gardens rise up the Vatican hill, occupying about half the 109 acres of the triangular-shaped walled citadel. They were stunning, and I remembered what I'd read about the Italians keep the growing things in the countryside and cover the rest with concrete. No one had told that to the people who designed and built this beautiful place, apparently.

'Like the Trinity,' Andi said as we strolled around, 'the Vatican is three in one. It is the Holy See, which can be defined as the Episcopal seat of the Bishop of Rome, readily recognized in international law and diplomacy as a sovereign entity distinct from the territorial sovereignty of the Vatican City State, which as you obviously know from all those guides you carry around with you, is the smallest sovereign state in the world.'

She smiled sweetly when she'd finished.

'Sorry, do I look that much like a tourist?' I looked up, grinning ruefully.

'Better a tourist than a schmuck,' she shrugged.

'Schmuck? What's a schmuck?'

'Hey, I'm Italian, not Jewish. How would I know what a schmuck is?'

I knew exactly what a schmuck was so dropped the question, and as we'd stopped for a breather at a flattish space near the top of the hill, I asked her what the circular tower was dominating the large fortified building ahead. Radio masts projected from the top of the tower.

'That's the Palazzina of Leo XIII,' she replied. 'It was the Vatican Observatory before they moved it to Castel Gandolfo, because of all the pollution here in the city. Now it's the headquarters of Vatican Radio, which is losing money hand over fist. And you, Brogan?'

'And me...what, Andi?'

'What's your story?'

I pretended to think for a minute. 'My grave will contain my entire life story, made up of three lines. He was born, he lived, and he died. *Finito.*'

She gave me a playful, but hard, jab in the arm. 'You don't get away with it that easy, bub. You owe me.'

'Oh, dear,' I sighed. 'She's back to "bub". I'm in deep poo.'

'Deeper than that, the only way out is to buy me a fantastic *frappe*, out through that gate over there. Plus your story, of course.'

'Of course,' I concurred; reluctantly, of course.

As we passed through the small exit gate for city cardholders only, guarded by the solitary sentry, I glanced at my watch.

'I'll do better than that,' I told her. 'I'll even spring for lunch.'

'I'm on a diet,' she almost spat at me.

'Even better,' I grinned. 'It won't cost much.'

We took our seats at a table for two outside the small cafe and although it was lunchtime and the place was reasonably full, it did not have the overcrowding of the eateries on the far side of the Vatican wall, where the main entrances were. A few people, presumably wage earners in the holy enclave, came out of the door we had exited from but no tourists entered there.

A waiter attended us quickly, and from then on it went downhill. Not exactly, for the pitcher of wine in a pottery jug arrived quickly, as did the bread, but our order was not taken for another twenty minutes and did not arrive for another twenty. Not that I was complaining. The company was good and the ambience of being in Rome, seated at a sidewalk cafe and drinking thick red wine was a change of pace after the past week or so.

'So, Harry,' she spoke in that throaty mellifluous voice that I found affected me too much. 'You were about to tell me your background.'

'Well, I was born at a very early age,' I said in a strong Scouse accent. 'In fact me mother was there at the time and me father insisted that they were smacking the wrong end, then...'

'How would you like your ears swapping over, buster,' she smiled sweetly and kept her voice down, but the threat was there so I told her a few simple truths about being brought up in a back street of Liverpool with two older brothers, a hard-working father on the docks, and a mother who was an intelligent, kind soul, but could turn into an Irish harridan when she wanted to.

'You sound like you could have made something of yourself, academically that is,' she offered quietly.

'I did make something of myself,' I told her, chewing on a delicious piece of bruschetta. 'I became one of the best thieves in the world.'

'You know what I mean,' she rebuked softly.

'Yes,' I nodded. 'I know what you mean. I was just beginning to relax into my newfound state of being a playboy when this lot came up. I still can't see why Milos wants me to steal that bloody violin. He lives in the place, presumably has access to everywhere and even if he didn't fancy getting his hands dirty himself, he could always get someone in there easily enough.'

'Well, there are certain circumstances,' she began, then shook her head and went silent. Now I WAS intrigued.

'You can't leave it there, Andi,' I tried to inject some humour with a cheesy grin, but that didn't work either.

'Zoltan Milos no longer works for the Vatican, and in fact he is denied access to the Vatican City. The reasons are complicated but do not stop his purpose being right, even though he can be somewhat odious at times. But there are... forces at work here that you could not begin to imagine,

Harry. Even I have a problem with many of them, and I have been trained my whole life to believe, and understand.'

'Believe, understand; what?' I'd really thought I had a grip on it all about twenty minutes ago, but now I had to admit I was out of it. Totally lost, in fact. Man thy name is vanity...

The starter arrived at that time, Andi had ordered aubergine and I had sliced tomatoes with mozzarella cheese and heavily seasoned with basil, which made me laugh when Andi pronounced it bas-il the way the Yanks do. This was followed eventually by pasta and pesto, and the main course of veal peccapa, and which of course was absolutely delicious.

'You're not ready for it yet,' she said with conviction in her voice. 'We need to discuss this after lunch. What do you think of the pasta?' She asked, obviously to change the subject.

'Excellent,' I said, and meant it. Not a big trencherman usually, in fact I could fill up with almost anything, I had to admit that the pasta was very good indeed. Over the next few days I would find the same, wherever we went, from the most superb restaurant to the dingiest back street caff, there was no dissing the pasta.

But as for the veal peccapa, I had suddenly discovered food.

We finished eating and Andi refused the dolci and sadly gazed after the trolley of trifles, tarts and cakes of all types disappear. As I'd also shaken my head to the wonders of the desert trolley, she ordered cappuccino for both of us. I drank the cappuccino, a habit that I have always found strange after enjoying a good meal with wine, but had to admit that the creamy coffee appeared to act as a strong digestive. I had noticed that Andi did not finish half of her pasta but made no comment. A change for me.

'Seriously, Andi, I'm very grateful for you spending this time going through this stuff with me. Whether it will provide any clues leading to the violin or not, I don't know, but there might be something that comes out of it.'

'Please, Harry,' she tossed her curls. 'Zoltan is a colleague, though I would hardly call him a friend, yet I feel his reasons are good. As for the Diabolus, I have been hearing about it for a long time, and always knew a day would come when it would have to be found, and destroyed. As a devout Catholic I think I would do practically anything to achieve that purpose.'

'Anything, eh?' I grinned.

'PRACTICALLY anything, I said,' she frowned at me. Her brows met but she couldn't keep the quirky little grin from curling the sides of her mouth.

'In that case, how about meeting me for dinner this evening?' I asked politely. 'And we can see if the two gentlemen who have been watching us through lunch turn up also, thereby confirming that they are very interested in us, and this is not just a wild, paranoid guess on my part.'

'We still have an afternoon of music and deviltry to get through, so why don't we see if you can be a good student first, and who knows?'

Again came that sweet smile, but I was amused to see that this time she was also glancing around the restaurant, albeit surreptitiously. What surprised me was that she failed to ask anything about our two erstwhile stalkers.

CHAPTER SEVEN

"The woman which thou sawest is that great city, which reigneth over the kings of the earth. Here is the mind which hath wisdom; the seven heads are seven mountains on which the woman sitteth"

(REVELATION 17:18, 9)

We were back in the teacher/student mode, with the splendid and chatty lunch but a pleasant occasion in the far recesses of memory as once again I listened to more of the same dry stuff. Albeit coming from a lovely source; the delectable Andrea's lips.

'It is of course a paradox that the violin has developed a diabolical image in popular imagination while at the same time it symbolizes the sound of tender emotions and romantic love. When people fall in love in the movies you hear violins, right? There's a very talented young violinist named Rachel Barton, and she has a CD called Instrument of the Devil. I have a copy of it and I suggest you listen to it some time. You might not like it as such, but at least you will understand what I'm talking about.

'The origins of the violin's otherworldly associations can be traced back to ancient Greek religious cults, who identified musical instruments with deities and their ethical attributes. By the 1500s violins were linked with dancing, an activity denounced by religious conservatives. Tales of demonically endowed fiddle players first emerged during the 17th Century, an image that endures in today's pop culture, and the American Record Guide critic said, and I quote, "What scares me most about this demonic-themed recording is Rachel Barton's almost inhuman violin playing...'

I smiled. 'Are you saying that this girl got her ability to play so well from the Devil?'

'Not quite, but she is certainly inspired by his tunes. The CD begins with the violin-made sounds of bells tolling midnight in Saint-Saëns' arrangement of his symphonic poem Danse Macabre, Opus 40, then she goes on to perform Tartini's Sonata in G minor that I told you about, The Devil's Trill. This version is from the 1798 first edition, as opposed to Kreisler's familiar romanticized version, of course.'

'Of course,' I said dryly. 'I hate to break up your thread, but I don't see what all this is to do with finding the bloody Strad.'

She sniffed. 'You might be surprised Mr. Harry Brogan, as well as getting a dose of culture; you might even develop a liking for such good music. Seriously, Harry, I think you should listen to this. Liszt's Mephisto Waltz is a piano piece that depicts the Devil playing a frenzied dance on the violin. Rachel performs Nathan Milstein's monstrously challenging arrangement for the solo violin. Then Bazzini's Round of the Goblins, and she plays a duet with the pianist Sinozich of Berlioz's Dream of a Witches' Sabbath from Symphonie Fantastique, Op. 14.'

'Sounds like you have a love affair with all this stuff yourself, li'll lady,' I said softly.

Andi shrugged, neither denying nor agreeing with me.

'Any normal tracks on this masterpiece?'

'They're all normal, you lunk,' she snorted. 'Just because they have some superstitious title doesn't make it any less harmonious. The Dance of Terror, from El amor brujo, depicting the ill-timed appearance of a lover's angry ghost, by Manual de Falla, is incredible.'

I rose to my feet and stood looking down at her. She colored slightly but continued talking. 'Stravinsky's Devil Dance comes from...'

I leaned down and clamped my lips on hers. After several long moments I straightened.

She gazed up at me and carried on as though there had been no interruption though I was listening to nothing she said.

'Hard to shut you up, lady,' I murmured and touched her lips with mine again, softer now, gentler. When I went to pull away this time she grabbed my lapels and pulled me down to her. This time we stayed like that for some time, and she DID shut up.

'Enough,' I pleaded. 'Can we go and eat now, please?'

For some reason she kept hitting me with her bag, again and again...

It was her choice and at first I thought she was leading me on a wild goose chase, not that I imagined there were many wild geese around these days, but considering that the Roman legions held them in great esteem as guardians of their camp sites, I wouldn't have been surprised. Bit like the Arabs with their dogs, what were they called...piards, or something? They were so valuable that when they threw a fuddle, feast, they would kill a dog as a mark of honour, though personally I could have done without it. There I go again. Who was it said that a little knowledge is a dangerous thing? As I can't remember it couldn't have been anyone important anyway.

We finally arrived, as she'd insisted that we walk, at a small tratorria not far from the Vatican as the crow flies but a bit of a schlep otherwise. It went by the title of Ristorante Fratello, which Andi told me meant the restaurant of the brothers and sisters. It was apparently a family business that had been around for many years, and originally the proprietors were the father of the present owners and his brother and sister, but now it belonged to the siblings of two brothers and two sisters. It was all too much for me so I nodded politely and tried to look interested. From extremely unimposing from the outside it was completely the opposite within. Very traditional, as though I knew the difference, but I'd seen all the movies as a kid; Doris Day and Rock Hudson on holiday in Rome, Mario Lanza making bread one day then turning into the great opera star the next, Bobby Darin courting Sandra Dee, for real as well as on the screen. Anyway, red and white tablecloths, old straw-covered Chianti bottles with candles, and the kitchen spilling over into the eating area.

Wonderful, and everyone seemed to know Andi. She spent the first twenty minutes kissing everyone, including the contents of the kitchen staff, and although she'd already told me she was bilingual, it still came as a bit of a shock hearing her rattle away in perfect Italian.

Once more I left it to Andi to order, and she did us proud. Eggplant appetizer, which she said was Antipasta di Melansane, followed by Carbonara, which she told me was pancetta, or Italian cured bacon, with cream, paprika and Parmesan, with tagliatelle noodles – more pasta.

I asked the patron to recommend a good wine and he produced Chianti that to my surprise was so delicate that it melted on the tongue. He spoke some English and I told him his choice of wine was terrific, but I was unused to this type of Chianti. He laughed and said the rough stuff was only for the touristi, though whether he was joking or not I did not know.

He insisted on plying us with the local grappa, which is the second or third pressing of the grape; mostly made from the skins, and I finally got to pay the bill among many handshakes and kisses and "you must come back to us" from the proprietor and his wife. Of course the size of the very generous tip I added might have had something to do with their well wishes, but there goes my cynical side again.

'Excellent,' I said with meaning, once we were outside. 'Absolutely excellent, little Andi.'

We began walking slowly down a poorly lit cobbled lane.

'You're drunk,' she said, though in a non-accusative way. 'Perhaps we should take a taxi.'

'Ah,' I said wisely. 'I actually DO know a taxi. Do you have a cell-phone?'

'Of course,' she pouted. 'Doesn't everyone?'

'Not me,' I grinned, holding my hands up. 'Never had the need.'

I took her phone and rang the number from memory. I'm clever like that, even when trying to appear drunk. Fabio said he'd be there in five, trying to sound like his hero, Robert de Niro.

We carried on strolling.

'You mentioned earlier about the two men at lunch,' she said in a serious manner. 'Weren't you worried about them?'

'Oh, them,' I said carelessly. 'Not really, but they're close.'

'What do you mean, close?' she looked around.

'Bad move,' I muttered. 'Looking around like that. Now they'll have to play their hand.'

'Harry, you're not making a lot of sense,' she actually snapped at me. 'What do you mean...?'

'Now,' I grinned, and saw them step out of two separate alleys to left and right.

'They're even predictable,' I told her as I moved her gently to one side and moved a few steps forward.

They didn't let me down. They moved forward from either side, treading carefully, but why bother? I wasn't going anywhere.

I went straight into the first one and dropped him with a left hook. Most people don't think about a left hook these days, but they should. It works out well most of the time.

The second idiot just came right in – so I hit him with a right, down below in the ribs, then a left as he rose and I must admit to getting a bit agitated about the whole thing so I dropped him with a right over the top.

'Got anything else in mind for a nightcap?' I mentioned, and she appeared at my side, apparently ready for something else in the adventure line. Or maybe not.

'Harry, I'm sorry, I didn't know...' she began. 'That's why you pretended to be d...'

'You have to split,' I said, 'there's a taxi here, he'll take you home.'

True to his word, Fangio was just pulling up at the end of the lane and I thrust some money into his hand and waved him on.

I saw her pale face as the taxi drew away.

I grabbed hold of the one I'd decked first and who was just coming back to the land of the living. His mate was still comatose against the wall. I spent as little time as possible questioning him, and as the quiet street where we'd met was the place of interrogation, I knew it would not have to be a prolonged thing, so I went right into nasty mode, but you really don't want to know what that is about. When I produced one of the knives that Cassidy had included in his bag of goodies and I now wore strapped to my right ankle, it showed him that I was perfectly able, and willing, to use it in the right manner, and he gave in. I suppose the fact that the long thin blade, double-edged like a Commando knife, was up his left nostril at the time helped. Actually it WAS a Commando knife.

I assumed he was intimidated, or frightened, enough to talk to me now, and I asked him about the violin and the catacombs. There was enough pale moonlight peering through beneath the close over-hanging buildings to see his eyes and they were telling me he knew exactly what I was talking about.

'I promise you,' I hissed down at the man. 'If you tell me what this is all about I'll let you go. But be warned, friend, if I ever see you again I will kill you.'

He looked at me then and I could see his brows knit together as he contemplated the odds of my telling the truth, and really letting him go. Then he disappointed me by saying just one word. 'Cobblers.' To my surprise he had an English accent, sounding like London or the Home Counties.

'Don't fuck about with me,' I hissed in his face, and put enough pressure on the knife so blood began to trickle from his nostril.

I heard a noise and turned quickly, but the second assailant was still propped up against the wall. As I turned back to my less than informative attacker, a shot rang out; closely followed by a second one and I heard a soft "thwack" as the second bullet hit my man in the chest. Now I looked at the end of the lane and saw a silhouetted figure with a rifle and what appeared to be a night-sight on top, disappear out of sight to the right.

I sprang up and was about to go after him, despite lack of a weapon, when the stricken man at my feet made a noise. At first I thought it was his death rattle, I read that expression in a book once and since then have always liked the sound

145

of it. But it wasn't, well not quite, and I leaned down with my ear close to his lips.

'Y...you're bleedin' English, ain't yer?' I confirmed this and felt around his chest. The bullet had hit him in line with the heart but through the right hand side, and judging by the blood coming from his mouth had travelled through and connected somewhere in the heart, though God knows how when I thought of the angle.

'The...bastards have shot me...the double-crossing spaghetti-yaffling, b....but ah,' his face clenched up in pain and I could see he was nearly gone. 'I...don't know what it's all about, mate, but not my business, ay? I do know I heard them muttering away in Iti the other night, and only made out a few words 'cos my Iti's lousy. Regno cavallo, the king's...steed. And cobblers...'

He slumped to the side and when I felt to the side of his jaw line there was no pulse. I moved over to the other man and he had been gone since the moment the bullet had struck. Obviously the man with the rifle was a marksman and had time to set up the first shot. It went through the side of his head and out the other side. Only high-powered ammunition could go through two layers of skull bone, and this also made sense when looking at the path through the body to reach the heart that the second shot had made.

I could hear a siren wailing somewhere far off, but it began to sound louder all the time. Time I wasn't here.

I loped off into the top of the darkened alley, turned the corner and saw a car's headlights blink on and off. At first I thought it was the pick-up for my two dead friends down the lane, and kept my knife in my right hand lying flat along the forearm. As I drew closer I recognized the small Fiat.

Fabio had come back for me, the clever chap. He got a good little retainer that night.

I spent the next morning in an Internet cafe surfing various web sites, then after a light lunch in the cafe, began poring through my guides of Rome.

Now I had an address within the city of the seven hills where the lady sitteth, to quote something from the good book. I didn't quite understand it, but could recognize a clue when I saw one. The man who had repeated the word "Cobblers" wasn't being rude, certainly not as he said it twice and on the second time it was the last word he would ever say. The king's steed got me for a while, and I was wondering if there could possibly be a pub somewhere in Rome called The King's Steed, or the Italian version I looked up in a web dictionary and put together as Regno cavallo, as the man said, when a record came on in the internet cafe, coincided with what I was reading up on, and bingo. Sometimes it all comes together. Well, not quite, as it took me another couple of hours before I had it, or thought I had.

I called on Andi early, and she appeared eager enough to see me, and ready for the next stage of the game. If such a search as we were engaged upon could by any stretch of the imagination be called a game.

But naturally she had questions first about the previous night. It would have been strange if she hadn't, of course.

Who were those men, who did they work for, what did they want, and where were they now?

Of which the only question I had the answer to was the last. They were both dead, and NO – I didn't kill them.

This was enough to silence her, but I would have been naive indeed if I thought it would still her curiosity indefinitely.

'We have a direction,' I told her, as she stirred coffee and handed me a cup. 'Tell me of the history, shortened version of course, of the catacombs.'

She shrugged and walked over to the window with the wonderful view over St Peter's Square. She was still stirring her coffee as she pondered my question.

'I suppose you don't want to know how the soil on which Rome is built is made up of volcanic origin, or that there are three strata's of which tufa is...'

'Not really,' I interjected. 'The shortened version, remember?'

'Humph,' she humphed then went on as though I was now forgotten. 'The Romans cremated their dead and deposited the ashes in a family tomb, sepulcrum, memoria, or in a vault or common sepulchre, columbarium; but the Jews living in Rome retained their traditional method of burial and imitated the rock-graves of Palestine by laying out cemeteries in the stone-like stratum of tufa around Rome. In this way Jewish catacombs were laid out and developed long before Christianity appeared in Rome.'

She paused and looked at me suspiciously, but I merely wiggled my finger in a "let's turn the pages, shall we" gesture.

'Following the year 410, when the Goths laid siege to Rome and devastated the surrounding country, it naturally put paid to burial in the catacombs, and in the following centuries Goths, Vandals and Lombard's repeatedly besieged and plundered Rome, plague and pestilence depopulated the region around the city...'

Again I did the wiggly finger thing and was just beginning to think it was working rather well when Andi glared at me, again. 'You got a problem with plague and pestilence, buster?'

I shrugged. 'Two things I can take or leave, sweetheart. But I'd rather leave if I've got a choice.'

The glare turned into a smile, the smile into a grin, then a chuckle, and the next thing we were both cackling like a pair of teenagers on their first try at pot. She came over and put her arms around me, the tight hug being a totally natural and spontaneous gesture, though me being me I didn't quite see it that way. She finally broke away, straightened her skirt with both hands in a very female way, and carried straight on.

'It was formerly believed that the early Christians used these galleries as hiding places during the persecutions. This is simply not true, for they were official burial grounds, well known to the Roman authorities, for the Romans respected the dead. Again, remember that the Romans usually cremated bodies at that time, and this was unacceptable to the Christians because of their faith in resurrection.'

'All very well, Andi,' I shook my head, 'but the period we're interested in is from 1698 to 1725.'

She frowned, those beautiful eyebrows coming together and adding new dimensions to the lovely face. Here I go, waxing poetic again.

'Why?'

'Well, Stradivari's so-called Golden Period lasted for that time. That is when he was most likely to have produced the Diabolus. Even if it had disappeared from the world scene for many years, and only found its way into the hands of the Vatican much later, we are still not interested before the Gold Period of the late 17th Century. Make sense, little one?'

'I suppose,' she acknowledged. 'Okay, I'll skip forward in time, just to please you. In 1929, the Lateran Treaty was signed, and so the Vatican became an independent state, and the Christian catacombs became Vatican territory. This also includes those discovered after 1929, mind you. Maintenance and further excavation is now the responsibility of the Pontificia Commissione di Achcheologia Sacra, the Pontifical Commission of Sacred Archaeology. They are making new discoveries all the time, and currently about 60 catacombs, 50 of them Christian, are known, but there are most probably a lot more. One of the problems is that they are often on private land, and the landowner is reluctant to report his findings to the authorities should he come across one, for the compensation for lost land is still very low.'

She stopped with a puzzled expression. 'Harry, I don't know what it is you're looking for.'

'I thought it was obvious by now,' I shrugged. 'The right catacomb, and the way into it.'

'But that's impossible without some sort of clue as to where it starts, or even where it is.'

'You're right, of course,' I said wisely.

'And not even Milos knows that,' she said almost to herself.

'No. He doesn't, does he?' I mused. 'Funny that, considering he used to live here, and had an ear to the Pope himself at one time.'

It was her turn to shrug. 'I never saw much of him, outside of overlapping classes and some research he'd ask me to do.'

'Well, I believe I have the answers to our problems,' I said modestly.

'And how did you manage that?' she said with deep sarcasm, though I wasn't sure if you could describe sarcasm as "deep". She certainly knew how to take good news well, our little Andi.

'Well, while I was questioning one of our friends from last night, I promised him that if he spoke to me I'd let him go. I think he was beginning to believe me when he was killed, obviously to keep his mouth closed, but not before he said something. A word. At first I thought he was being rude, telling me to sod off, kind of thing.'

'And the word?'

'Cobblers. He was English, London accent.' I kept a straight face and she merely frowned at me.

'The practical translation being...? And how do you know it has anything to do with why you are in Rome?'

'For a start they're both dead,' I said bluntly. 'Someone with a high-powered rifle and a night-sight shot them both right in front of me. Apparently to keep them from saying anything, and obviously because they must have known something in the first place.'

'Who...?'

'It doesn't matter,' I shook my head. 'That someone was a professional hit man, probably not involved in any of this, except to tie up the loose ends, and which he did very well.'

'But you said one of them gave you a clue,' her eyes lit up as she spoke and I realized she was now as into this as much I was.

'Yes,' I grinned. 'Yes, as I said. "Cobblers".'

I waited for her reaction, and she didn't disappoint.

'Cobblers?' she queried in a puzzled voice. 'I've hear of a peach cobbler, cherry, whatever, but they're desserts.'

'Of course they are,' I said patronizingly, and received one of those glares again.

I took pity on her and tried to explain. 'It also had two other meanings in English, that's English English,' I smiled but it didn't work. I do believe she actually growled. Totally unladylike. 'Okay, a cobbler is a man who repairs shoes.'

'That's a shoe repairman.'

'Yes, and in English slang it's a shoe repairer, a man who repairs boots and shoes. Cobblers also means "rubbish", "crap", and "bollocks" and go away in short, sharp jerks. In the English vernacular, that is.'

'And that's important...Why?' Andi asked quietly, in that wonderfully restrained way women have. 'You want to tell me what else the man said, before someone put a bullet into him?'

I gave in and stopped prating around. 'This was after he had the bullet put into him. He said, and I quote, "the king's steed".'

Andi frowned once more. 'Regno cavallo means nothing to me. You're grinning like a little chipmunk that has found a quick way of opening the coconut that he found last fall. You've solved it, right?'

I smiled modestly, as is my wont. 'Simple really. Are you an Elvis fan by any chance?'

'Actually I am,' she sniffed. 'And please understand that I am being very, very patient at this time. What is the connection between Elvis, a horse, and a supposedly diabolical violin hidden somewhere in catacombs, which, if laid end to end would be more than the length of all Italy?'

'It's funny you should mention that,' I kept to the modest persona. 'The King, could relate to Elvis Presley, yes? Of course it could.'

'So we make a list of all the people who were close to Elvis,' she suggested. 'Presupposing that you're right, that is, and which at this moment I'm not too convinced about.'

'Good thinking, but that would take an awful lot of time,' I smiled. 'Think about wives.'

'He only had one wife, Priscilla.'

'Very good,' I said condescendingly, and waited.

'The Catacomb of Saint Priscilla,' she burst out. Then the flames in her eyes went out and her animation dimmed.

'What's the matter?' I asked.

'The Catacomb of Saint Priscilla is a very small, though admittedly a very interesting, series of catacombs,' Andi shrugged. 'They're beneath a villa owned by the ancient Roman family of Arcili. Saint Priscilla was a member of the Arcili. The Catacomb contains the bodies of a number of Popes, and there are regular tours by English-speaking nuns who now live there.

'The point is, Brogan, that every inch of Saint Priscilla's catacomb has been examined by archaeologists, scientists and various seekers of the knowledge of the catacombs. Even your precious violin couldn't be hidden there.'

'Ah,' I used my wise voice. 'Remember the word "steed"? What does a horse need? Shoes on its feet of course.'

'But I know the area, there's no shoe shop anywhere around.'

'That's where the word, cobbler, comes in. A blacksmith makes shoes for a horse. The "cobbler" for horses, if you will.'

'And your point again, is...?'

'Apparently one of the old entrances to the Catacomb of Saint Priscilla is an old blacksmith's. Not running as such now, of course; it's just a derelict building, but Priscilla's catacomb extends beneath it, through its own secret entrance.'

'You know this for sure, or you're just reaching again, Brogan?' she said in a voice that was unusually cruel. At first I thought she was joking, but I found it hard to tell. 'I've just told you it's one of the smallest of all the Catacombs, and it's been inspected and dug over so often since Giovanni Battista de Rossi devoted his life to the exploration of the catacombs and the study of Christian antiquity, from around 1850. This being well after your, "Golden Period", I would have thought the Diabolus would have been found by now. If it were ever down there in the first place.'

I shrugged and told her the bottom line. 'Well, we won't know unless we go and see for ourselves, now, will we?'

'Yes, except that the entrance to the Priscilla Catacomb is nowhere near any blacksmith shop, whether defunct or not. It's along the Via Salaria, one of the oldest Roman roads that were used to transport salt from the Adriatic to the Tyrrhenian Sea. Only the first of the two levels, the older one, can be visited. After travelling through the long tunnels, you arrive at the Greek Chapel, named for the Greek writing on the walls. It's divided in the middle by an archway covered with frescoed scenes from the Old and New Testaments.'

'I'm sure they're bloody beautiful,' I muttered. 'But this is not where I believe the entrance we're looking for is located.'

She shrugged, surprisingly not put out by my little sarcasm. 'There could well be some other entrance to the catacomb, one that has not been known of for many years. But how do we find it?'

'I bought a very detailed map of the surrounding areas of Rome,' I said. 'I also downloaded a detailed map of the five Christian catacombs open to the public, which of course Saint Priscilla's is one of them. I drew in the outline of Saint Cilla's and checked for empty buildings within, or on the outskirt's of, her catacomb.'

'Clever boy,' she murmured. 'And you found...?'

I had already pulled the map from my pocket and unfolded it on her desk.

'Here,' I pointed with the tip of a pen, 'to the north is a derelict building, which apparently used to be a blacksmith's. There are other derelict buildings in the area but I got my taxi-driver's input and he tells me this was the only blacksmith's in our search area.'

'Hey, I'm impressed, Brogan. So, when do we go looking?'

'What have you got on in the morning, say about 9am?'

CHAPTER SEVEN

"Through some crack or other in the temple of God (the Vatican), the smoke of Satan has entered."

Pope Paul VI, 1972

"...we could not, therefore, avoid bringing forward...a very dark side of the history of the Papacy."

J.H. Kgnaz von Dollinger,
The Pope and the Council,
London, 1869, pp. xv, xvii.

I phoned Fabio that night and he picked me up at 8:30 the next morning, and we proceeded on to Andrea Scolari's apartment near the Vatican main gates, arriving at 9am.

First we drove to the official entrance to the Catacombs of Saint Priscilla on the Via Salaria. The tours had already started; in fact the faithful and the curious had been trampling in since 8:30am.

We drove out of the city of Rome and only ten minutes later we stopped at the beginning of the lush countryside. On the right were field of vines, and at that time of the year the grapes were huge, rich and red-black like darkest arterial blood.

To our left was what at first glance appeared to be a heap of stone blocks. I climbed out of the Fiat and moved in among them. In fact they formed a substantial part of the outline of a building, supposedly the blacksmith's shop of old. Fabio also left his taxi and came to stand beside me.

'It goes further back, Signor,' he told me quietly. 'At one time, according to my grandfather, it was a big place. At the back there they stabled horses, waiting to be...'

'Shod,' I supplied. 'For their shoes to be put on.'

'Si, that is right,' he inclined his head. 'As a child I would play in this area. My grandparents lived only a short way from here. There is nothing here now, though, Signor Harry.'

Andi had come up and joined us. Her face showed nothing; no disappointment, no anger at failure, nothing. In fact her face was devoid of expression entirely. I felt it all myself; the disappointment, the anger of failure, and something else besides. If the violin did not appear, what would be the next step for those who desired it so much? Would they go after my son again?

Then Fabio brought everything back down to the achievable with his next words.

'There is a Latino inscription you might like to see, in the back by the stables.'

'Latin?' Andi also came back to life, and spoke animatedly. 'You're sure it is Latin?'

'Si, Signorina,' the taxi driver affirmed with a degree of indignation. 'I was an altar boy. I know what Latin looks like, Signorina.'

'*Que repulisti et com Spiritu tuo*, Fabio,' I grinned at him. 'I was also an altar boy, my friend. I do not doubt you when you said you saw Latin. Please show me, and rest assured your latest tip is looking better by the minute.'

He grinned back and climbed over the rubble with alacrity. I took Andi by the arm and helped her to follow him, giving her a wink in the process. The back wall was in good condition, except for the absence of a roof, of course, but who wants to knit-pick.

To my surprise, Fabio led us out through a low arch and we went another six steps beyond the building. He stood and gazed around for a few moments, then smiled and went directly forward into a clump of bushes, which he proceeded to pull to either side, and then he disappeared.

'Signor Harry, you come,' his muffled voice came from the bushes.

I hurried forward, pushing the branches aside with both hands, and there it was.

A low slab on the ground, looking like nothing other than a paving stone, granted longer than the usual, and definitely older than most, but merely a slab. Then I saw the inscription chiselled into the top and filled in with mud and dirt, which had been quickly cleared by Fangio with the aid of a small pocket-knife.

I inspected the edges of the slab closely, and although I couldn't say for certain, the tight gap appeared to have been deliberately filled in with dirt and mud, like the inscription. This read.

'Hic iacet infra in re arcanum arcanum, origo mali ab intra, opus magnum advocatus diaboli. Custos.'

Andi arrived next to me and took in a gulp of air that came out as a gasp. Not having been a public schoolboy, and despite my altar boy Latin that was only based on religious verses, I did not have much grasp of the ancient language of Rome, and so I looked askance at her.

She did not hesitate and translated it immediately, reading in a clear voice as easily as though from the Herald Tribune.

'Here lies below regarding the secret of secrets, the source of evil from within, the masterpiece of the Devil's advocate. The Guardian.'

'Which means?' I asked.

She turned to me and spoke sarcastically. It was not a question that required an answer. 'What do you think it means. Harry? It can only mean that the Diabolus is buried beneath here.'

I looked at Fabio and he grinned and shrugged. He knew nothing of our purpose there, our mission, but he was happy to go along with whatever game we were into. I liked Fabio.

He went back to the car and came back with two tire irons and together we got the bars beneath the slab and lifted it. There was a small rush of air of a somewhat fetid nature, though not as bad as I expected. We raised the slab and tossed it over on its side.

It revealed a narrow stone staircase leading down, with solid rock on either side, and again Fangio was the man. He produced a heavy cadmium torch and we descended; me in front by popular consent; meaning that Fangio and Andi stayed back until I was down a few steps and I called back that it was safe to go. It was a short way down and then I was on a solid floor. When the others joined me Andi said for us to go ahead but to be careful. She was right to warn me, but the descending flight of steps never eventuated.

We turned back after about thirty feet, and as we approached the steps I saw that there was a cut to the right of the steps and it went back around, into the solid rock itself. Another set of steps went down, and I applied the torch and descended. At the bottom, another passage led off and about twenty feet along the narrow corridor we came to another flight of steps going down. Again we descended and came to another layer of catacombs.

'There are three levels,' Andi said, although I know she'd told me all this before. 'It's a total of around 35 to 45 feet from the lowest level to the surface; this is only about 36 feet, and we've just come to the middle stratum of soft tufa stone.'

I'd reached the bottom now and shone Fabio's torch around, the other two close behind me. We were in an obvious catacomb, the floor of compressed earth and clay, the walls and ceiling of tufa. Fabio kept crossing himself, either out of respect for the dead or fear for himself, I really didn't know, although I don't believe he was taking any of it too seriously.

I slowly moved along the passage, surprisingly wide I thought, rotating the torch from side to side. I'd read that the labyrinth of galleries is incalculable and that in a straight line they would extend the length of Italy itself, echoing on what Andi had already told me. Along the passages burial niches, cubicula, opened to the right and left, also hewn out of the tufa rock, where in the silent galleries horizontal tiers of graves rose from the floor to the ceiling. The number of graves in the Roman catacombs is estimated to be at least two million.

The graves, known as loculi, are cut out of the rock sides of the gallery so that the length of the bodies can be judged from the length of the graves. The body, wrapped in cloth, for those without a sarcophagus, was laid in the spot excavated for it, and the niche was closed by a marble slab or sometimes by large tiles set in mortar. Here there were no slabs or sarcophagi.

I remarked on this and Andi told me that throughout most of the catacombs the slabs that had once sealed them had vanished long ago, often removed to the surface for use on new buildings. As the torch beam lit up the niches there was usually just a pile of bones and decayed cloth, sometimes more than one pile of bones on top of another. There was no bad smell, only the musty, surprisingly dry, smell of the subterranean vaults.

'The early Christian name for these places of burial was koimeterion, or coemeterium, a place of rest,' Andi told us. 'This area looks long abandoned, and is probably blocked at the other end, keeping it intact for whatever purpose the Popes had in mind.'

'Like burying priceless fiddles,' I muttered. 'Where the bloody hell could they put it where it wouldn't get ruined?'

'You've probably noticed that the air down here is very dry, thus preserving the bodies for years. Now of course, the centuries and exposure to the outside air with the advent of tourists have made them crumble, but anything kept down here, away from the dust and debris, could last forever.'

'Okay, little Andi, then where is the thing,' I muttered. I was doing a lot of muttering at that time.

'Ah, here is where we have to be good detectives, Brogan,' I could see her teeth gleam through the gloom of the catacombs.

I caught on, just to prove I wasn't as stupid as she might have thought.

Inscriptions were often etched into the rock above the openings, while the art of the ancient Roman cemeteries became well known. It was also known as Paleochristian art, this funerary art including frescoes, sculptures, inscriptions and graffiti. Through this art work the early Christians left much testimony of their very profound faith in Jesus Christ.

This was being told by Andi as we explored, the torch going from floor to ceiling across and down the other side. Her voice was soft now, hypnotizing even, as she spun the story of the catacombs.

Paleochristian art stems predominantly from classical Greco-Roman art, and its period ranges from the first to the sixth century. In fact, she said, the earliest examples of Christian art are to be found within the catacombs. The majorities of marble sculptures dated from the 3rd through the 5th centuries, and are found on the sarcophagi of the catacombs. The funerary art of the catacombs reveals much about the early Christians, who they were and what they believed in. The Christians who employed artists to decorate their tombs were trying to communicate messages, seeking to bring the light of the Gospel into a dark and cold funeral chamber, where their dead lay in slumber awaiting the final resurrection.

I gave an involuntary shudder. I'd rather step into the ring with an angry Mike Tyson than even begin to contemplate the whole meaning of life as worked out by those ancient followers of Christ. I was raised on it, but buggered if I could find rhyme or reason in any of it now.

My time would come, but I was blissfully unaware of it then.

Andi was walking close to me now, and peering along the line of the torch. She was able to decipher the origins of most of the etched scrawls.

'Greek here, that's Judea over there and this, is Christian. This is a very ancient section, Harry, very ancient. It's obviously not on the tour of the Saint Priscilla Catacombs, so as I said before, the way we've come is most likely the only way down here, now.'

We carried on, and my main hope was that the cadmium batteries would last out. As though sensing my angst about such a happening, Fabio suddenly clapped me on the shoulder and grinned when I turned. He held his hand out with a small pack balanced on his palm.

'New batteries, Signor Harry, so now we can stay down here for a long time, no?'

'No,' I answered abruptly, probably too abruptly for the poor bloke, so I tempered it by smiling and hoping he could see it. 'We don't want to turn this into an expedition.'

'We don't have to,' a cool voice emerged from close by. 'Shine your torch up here, Harry.'

I did, and saw writing that had been there for a long time but there was no way of telling exactly how long that time was.

Abyssus abyssum invocat was the first line.

"One false step leads to another,' Andi translated.

'Just like that?' I queried. 'A good old English proverb suddenly confronts us in a Roman catacomb?'

'Hey, it was here before you guys knew it existed,' Andi said. 'What else is there; this was obviously telling us to look out for false clues.'

'I knew that,' I pretended to sulk, while I shone the torch on the next line.

'*Rara avis* – a rarity, that's just to titillate the seeker,' Andi was now talking mostly to herself, and arguing with it. 'The next line, *vel caeco apparent* – it's obvious - just to encourage again.'

I shone the torch closer and peered. '*Ab origine* – from the first,' I mumbled, but Andi picked up on it.

'Harry, you surprise me. You DO know more Latin than the Mass itself.'

'It's where the word Aborigine comes from, meaning the indigenous people,' I replied smugly. 'Though what the hell that's got to do with anything...'

'You might be surprised, Harry,' she said mysteriously. There was a tremor in her voice and I caught it as excitement.

'From the first...what?

'The last line, you might remember it from the Catholic mass?'

'*Ap...age Satanas,*' I read, and then had to think for a minute. 'Away with thee, Satan.'

'Well done, Harry,' she laughed softly. 'That's the biggest clue so far. Satan is being warned away from this place. He's not welcome here, but why would he come, anyway? There are only dead people here; not even people, just bones and covering cloths. There are no souls for him to take back to Hades with him. So what is it? Something that Satan coverts, something that he wants badly.'

'Great,' I said in acid tones. 'Then where the fuck is it, if you'll pardon my French?'

She laughed. 'We both know that's not French, Harry. It's close, now. Very close. Whoever first brought the Diabolus down here never expected anyone to come looking for it, so they played games covering its exact location.'

I thought for a moment, never an easy thing, but finally got it.

'"From the first" and "It's obvious"; from where we first came in.'

'You've got it, Harry,' Andi gave me a hug, and although it might well have been condescending, I took it anyway. I'm really that easy.

We moved back and up to the first flight of steps we'd come down to enter into the first level of the catacomb.

I stood at the bottom of the stone steps in silent contemplation of the problem. A single shaft of light came through from the opening above, though hardly enough to see much around us. Andi stood quietly on my left and Fabio on my right. Believing in the adage about more heads etc., I'd told him in a few words what we were looking for, and true to his irrepressible spirit he entered into the game he thought we were playing.

'We're looking at a flight of stone steps,' Andi stated the obvious, and I thought I caught a note of despair in her voice. 'Just some damn steps. So where on earth is it hidden?'

I frowned to myself as her voice had taken on a new sound, apart from the disappointment at the prospect of failure at this stage there was a quality of desperation; as though she was letting someone down, but who – apart from me?

Fabio had begun walking up the steps, tapping with the hilt of his trusty little knife, and well amused in his own way. I began walking up the steps past him, shining the torch and peering closely at each one.

'Oh, Signor Harry,' Fabio called, his voice almost a musical refrain as he sounded so proud of himself.

I paused and shone the light downwards.

'Listen, my friend,' he commanded, and tapped the stone again. And again, and again, and then the solid clunk of his knife changed to a more hollow sound. I looked down the edge of the steps, to where he was standing to my left now. Andi moved up close to him.

I was down the steps in seconds, and moved around the corner to where he stood, using my clenched fists to find the false part of the stone. My knuckles were sore on the rough stone, then the sound came again, and I handed the torch to Fangio as I wiped away the dust of years from the surface. The hollow sound had come from the farthest area from the steps, in the corner where the steps butted against the high wall before they began the descent to the second level. I had no time to think about it then but the entire set-up was wrong to what I'd been reading about the layout of the catacombs. Perhaps "wrong" was not the right word, more like "different" would be accurate.

I spoke of it to Andi.

'You're right,' she replied. 'Usually the steps would come down a level, then further on would be another set of steps, and down at the next level further on again would be the lower level of graves, as we found at the second and third levels. This business of the second lot of steps beginning around the back of the first flight of steps is very strange. Very strange, in fact.'

'Whatever,' I said impatiently.

I was busy with the tapping bit and Fabio, with a grin as big as the Acropolis, pointed to an area near the underside of the steps.

I tapped all around it, then rubbed hard around the area, then finally disappeared up the stairs. I returned shortly with one of the tire irons, and proceeded to tap the wall around the area of the hollow knocks. I rubbed the straight edge of the iron in an up and down fashion, and gradually a rectangle began to appear in the wall itself.

I then became adventurous and used the sharper edge of the tire iron to knock firmly on the rock. This wasn't rock. The iron went through, revealing a deep niche, and it turned out to be a large "tile" made of the tufa rock itself. I shone the torch inside and could see nothing. At first. Using the tire iron I knocked away all the faux stone around the edges of the hole, and then extended a long left arm holding the torch.

This time I could see something that didn't fit in with the décor of the niche. It was grey in color and for all I knew it could have been another body, most likely a member of the nobility, or even a pope. Whatever, I was hardly likely to disturb his peace on earth any more. To the touch it had a smooth feeling and I felt gingerly along its length, being rewarded with a length of string or some type of binding. Placing the torch carefully to one side, so the beam could play on the package, I used both hands to slowly pull it towards me. When it was close to the lip of the opening I nodded to Fabio and he came forward and grasped one end of the package.

Together in unison, slowly and carefully, we lowered it down onto the hard-baked floor of the catacomb. It was a lot lighter than it appeared, though still heavier than I expected – if that makes any kind of sense.

I ran my hand over the top, disturbing the dust of ages, and brushed it all away. Again, it all felt slick to the touch. It was less than a meter across and about half a meter in depth and in height it was about another half meter. The oilcloth or oilskin covering was wrapped tightly around it. I still had Fabio's knife and cut through the twine-like binding running around and across the length and breadth of the package.

I unwrapped the outer layer and inside was another covering, this time a rough canvas. Cutting through this revealed a box. A box made of lead.

'Did they have lead 300 years ago?' I asked no one in particular, but it was Andi who answered.

'Who cares?' she snapped. 'How many people do you think have seen the Diabolus over that time; each one improving on its protection?'

'Not many, I should think,' I replied shortly, matching her tight mood. 'And they would presumably have all been Popes, though it's been a long time since this place had any visitors. One thing I don't understand. Why didn't one of them destroy the damn thing, if it is supposed to be so evil, and so much a threat to the Catholic Church and its followers?'

Andi was gazing at the package with an expression of awe on her face; now she switched that gaze to me. Although the torch was shining on the package I could see that her eyes were gleaming.

'They couldn't, Harry. You see, Satan has long been in the Vatican. Babylon is a code word for Rome, and it is used that way six times in the last book of the Bible, four of the six being in Chapters 17 and 18. It is also in extra-biblical works such as Syblling Oracles and the Apocalypse of

Baruch. Eusebius Pamphilius wrote in 303 that "it is said that Peter's first epistle...was composed at Rome itself, and he himself indicated this by referring to the city figuratively as Babylon".'

'Okay,' I frowned. 'But what's this got to do with...?'

'You asked a question,' she snapped. Andi seemed to be doing a lot of snapping lately. 'A controversial figure in the Catholic church, a black archbishop named Milingo, has long accused the Vatican of harbouring Satan and his followers. In 1972 Pope Paul VI surveyed the wreckage to the Church after the Second Vatican Council, and said that Satan had entered the temple of God. Again in 1976 Paul shocked a papal audience by confiding that, "The smoke of Satan has entered the very sanctuary of St. Peter's Cathedral." Many high-ranking churchmen will say that they have not heard that anyone has seen him leave.

'He went on to explain that he had knowledge of a midnight bout, Black Satanic Mass having been conducted at the altar of St. Peter's, on the exact spot where the Pope himself regularly says mass.'

By this time I had let her waffle on, and although I was listening, had kneeled by the package and had removed the second layer of wrapping, the canvas. The box was a dull grey, but a flick with the knife revealed a shine, and what I had thought was lead turned out to be a form of zinc, which would account for the light weight. There was a hasp and a solid looking lock, which definitely did not hail from 300 years ago.

'Dr. Malachi Martin,' she continued on, and not disappointing me. 'Was a scholar and Vatican insider, and wrote in an article that Archbishop Milingo's contention that there are Satanists in Rome is completely correct. He said that anyone who was acquainted with the state of affairs in the Vatican in the last 35 years was well aware that the prince of darkness has had, and still has, his surrogates in the court of St Peter in Rome.'

I looked up at her, suddenly paying attention to what she was saying. 'You're joking, right? What you're actually saying is that there's a great conspiracy of Satanism behind the walls of the Vatican. What a load of bollocks, pardon my French.'

'That's not French,' she said automatically. 'Read it up for yourself, Harry. Now, you want to see if the Diabolus is actually there?'

'Why not?' I muttered, and attacked the lock with the tire iron. The hasp was the one to shatter, the lock still looking in a solid state. I lifted the lid.

To reveal another box, this time it was made of wood. At a glance I could see it was extremely well made, and the feel of it alone would have affirmed this. As I've said, during my period of misappropriation I became quite adept in recognizing quality pieces of objets d'art, and of course much of the earlier stuff was of excellent manufacture.

I separated the boxes and looked up at my two companions. Fangio was looking on with quiet amusement and certain anticipation, although he had no idea what we were looking for. Andi, on the other hand, had no amusement showing anywhere. She was totally absorbed in what I was doing, though perhaps revealing would be the more appropriate word. She stood back from the proceedings, which surprised me slightly but I put it down to her excitement at that time.

I bent to the box again. This time there was no hasp or lock, but a simple lever device that made the lid slowly open automatically, and I saw the Diabolus, the Devil's instrument, for the first time. It was seated comfortably in a bed of red satin, firmly wedged in by the craftsman who had made the box to house the instrument. Strangely, I had the feeling it was the same man who had made the violin itself.

It was stunning, magnificent, and incredible even. Mere words could not do it justice. To my untutored eye it was better than any I'd seen before; not at the Royal Academy of Music, the Ashmolean, nor what I had read up on about the ones in Cremona, not in any of the Museums I had visited or read about.

'Do you want to do the honours?' I asked Andi, with a nod towards the box.

To my surprise she shook her head and pointed upwards.

'We should be going,' was all she said.

I nodded absently and lifted the violin from its box.

I felt a wave of...what?...Rush over me as I touched the black wood of the instrument. It was as though it was alive though I did not believe that of course. I did not believe in religion, mysticism, the Devil or Satan. I wasn't even sure there was an old bloke lolling on the clouds above sporting a to-die-for body, and wearing a magnificent set of grey facial hair. In short, I wasn't sure what I believed in.

With reluctance I replaced the Diabolus in the receptacle that had housed it for three centuries and stood with it in my arms. Andi made as though to say something, then let it go.

'Okay, Fabio, would you like to lead the way, my friend?' I nodded towards the steps.

He grinned and went up the steps like an arrow from a taut bow. I went next with the box and Andi followed me a few steps below. At the top I went to hand the box over to Andi while I helped Fabio with the slab. For some reason she declined and muttered something about checking out the car, which made sense I supposed.

I laid the box down carefully on some flat stone and we replaced the slab, carefully filling in the gaps around the sides with dirt, as it had been when we first arrived.

At the taxi I placed it gently in the boot and packed our topcoats and bits and pieces of Fabio's around it.

We had the Diabolus, all it took now was to hand it over to Milos and I could get on with my life. Whether that included Andi at this stage, I really didn't know, but I could always dream.

Why then wasn't I feeling too warm and comfortable?

CHAPTER EIGHT

"It is beyond question that he (the Pope) can err even in matters touching the faith. He does this when he teaches heresy by his own judgment or decretal. In truth, many Roman Pontiffs were heretics."

Pope Adrian VI, 1523.

I'd contacted Milos and told him that I had his precious violin. He was suitably grateful, congratulated me, and then suggested that I go to Rome airport where I would simply hand over the violin to a contact.

'I don't think so, Milos,' I told him. 'I've gone to a considerable amount of effort to locate this thing, and I will only hand it over to you, because you I know and I don't know anyone else.'

He took some time considering this before agreeing.

'I told you in the beginning that we would reward you for your time and trouble,' he said. 'That still stands, Harry, but now we have made it a million pounds. All of the checking I've done on you indicates that you are an honourable man, Harry, in spite of your means of employment. I see no reason for you to renege on our agreement. I too am a man of my word, and I know it was against your wishes to take on the job you have done so excellently. As I've already said, I am authorized by my principles that you will now have the sum of one million pounds added to your account.'

'This was never about money, Milos,' I said shortly into the receiver. 'You know that.'

'Yes, I do, Harry,' the voice was still toneless, yet somehow to me it sounded oilier than ever. 'But it has been decided that this will keep you "sweet", I think the expression is. By your studies I'm sure you're well aware of the sort of value on this object, but to those who want it, it is a priceless thing. This should encourage you not to repeat any part of our dealings in this matter.'

He then gave me a time and place to meet him and hand over the goods at the airport. I bought a cheap holdall from a street vendor and put the box in it. At the prescribed time I met him in the main lobby of the terminal for overseas flights.

Signor Zoltan Milos was as I had seen him in Bermuda; large, fat, and with an outward appearance of jolly bonhomie.

'I understand you've had some problems, Harry, and we are grateful that you were able to work it out and arrive at a successful conclusion.'

Successful for whom? I couldn't help thinking.

We exchanged a few more words and I handed over the bag.

And that was it.

Fini.

The whole affair was out of my life forever. Or was it?

That night I had arranged to take Andi out for dinner. She'd been acting strangely for the past few days, which I put down to anxiety about the whole business. After all, before I came on the scene she had been quietly teaching, with a bit of librarianship thrown in, and since then her world had been tossed upside down. She'd been in a funny mood ever since we'd found the Diabolus in fact. So I had planned something really nice.

I picked her up and we went to one of the better restaurants in the centre of Rome, the Cossi Fan Tutte, like the opera. She was in a good mood and the dinner was delightful. As an appetizer we'd ordered baked courgettes stuffed with ham and cheese, washed down with a light Lambrusco; a very nice Lambrusco I might add. None of this cheap stuff the tarts in Liverpool order when they're having a night out in Lime Street. We kept the conversation as light as the wine until the next course arrived; fettuccine with cream and butter sauce, blanketed with shaved white truffles. I thought of the bill then mentally slapped myself when I thought of the one million pounds I'd just picked up for a few days inconvenience.

'So,' she said at last, laying her knife and fork neatly on her plate, north and south as every little student of etiquette had been taught. 'When are you going back to England, Harry?'

'That depends,' I said carefully.

'On?' She'd picked up on it right away and held her head to one side in what could only be described as a coquettish pose.

'You,' I said bluntly. 'What are your plans now?'

'Well...I...'

'You should be rewarded for your help in all this,' I said in my most serious fashion. 'I couldn't have done it without your help, and even though I didn't want it, I've been amply rewarded for the small effort I've put in. Rest assured that Fabio will be amply rewarded for his part in it.'

'That's nice,' she said, bestowing that lovely smile on me. 'As for me, I have no desire for reward or payment, for I have enough money of my own, and I also have no plans, Harry. What else did you have in mind?'

Oh, my. What else did I have in mind? The main course arriving saved me.

Andi had ordered the sautéed sweetbreads with tomatoes and peas, and I had the sautéed veal chops with sage and white wine and cream. We both had an additional accompaniment of asparagus and prosciutto bundles. It tasted wonderful.

'Hmmm, lovely,' Andi murmured as she savoured the first mouthful.

'You, hmm, do know what sweetbreads are, I take it?' I asked somewhat sheepishly.

She stared at me, and then smiled. 'Of course I do, silly man.'

We ate in a compatible silence until the next course came. By now I was well full, though I managed to get down the simple salad of field greens of mache and arugola with a light olive oil and vinegar dressing.

Over dessert and Cappuccinos; I had the Bolognese rice cake and Andi had the egg custard gelato, she told me she'd thought it over and would love to help me ease my conscience for all the trouble she'd gone to by joining me in a week's holiday at a place of my choosing, and would she need to bring a bikini with her.

I nearly choked over my coffee. Whether it was the way she put it, or the lascivious thought of little, full-breasted Andi in a bikini, I wasn't too sure, but I think I mumbled something about "yes please". Paying the bill was a blur and I'm sure I left such a huge tip they must have thought I was a Mafia cousin from Merrie England, before we arrived on the narrow pavement outside.

We had left around 12:30 and waited outside for Fabio, who had instructions to pick us up at that time. Continuing the mood and the ambiance of the evening we spoke softly about inconsequential things. I had my arm around her shoulders and she showed no objection. When the small Fiat finally arrived, some fifteen minutes late, it had no Fabio behind the wheel. My hackles arose, and I tried to cover my immediate suspicions.

'Hey, there,' I tried the drunken friendly touriste thing as I leaned in through the open window. 'Where's my man tonight?'

'Scusi, Signor Harry,' the man grinned at me. 'But my cousin Fabio is not feeling so good tonight and asked me to...stand in?...for him.'

'No problem,' I grinned back, and helped Andi into the back seat. I closed the door and moved around the front, seating myself next to the driver. Before he had a chance to shove it into gear I placed a hand behind his neck and banged his head hard on the dash. His right hand was already reaching and I grabbed it and slammed that down hard on the top of the gear lever. Now that has to hurt and he dropped the shiv he was trying to pull. You might think I'm being old fashioned by the use of that nomenclature, but it was long with a sharpened blade on either side and was definitely a shiv.

I took it and held it against his carotid, so close that I could feel the artery throb violently. I'll give Andi her due, she never once cried out, screamed, yelled, fainted, or did any of the ladylike things that so many women I've come across would have done.

'You are now going to tell me what has happened to the driver of this car, my friend,' I said in almost a whisper. 'If you don't I'm going to cut you. Comprendre?'

He nodded but I don't think he got the message because he suddenly lashed out with his left hand, bringing it across the car in a very roundabout route. I jabbed the knife into his leg and he cried out with pain, at the same time as he transferred the direction of his left fist to grab onto the wound.

'You got the message yet, my friend? I want the answer to my question, and I want it now.'

As suddenly as the first time I jabbed the knife into his other thigh, and now he definitely had the message. His head began to nod wildly and I pushed him back into his side of the car.

'Then tell me,' I injected just the right amount of venom into my voice and kept moving the shiv from hand to hand as I lay back against the other door. 'Now would be really good.'

The last word came with a snap and the wretched man actually jumped.

'Is he dead?' I asked.

The head shook from side to side. 'No, Signor.'

'Take us to Fabio,' I told him, still keeping my voice soft. 'If he's dead, so will you be. Soon, and very painfully.'

He appeared to hesitate, obviously still more afraid of his paymasters than me. That could change.

'Like I said, now would be a good time, friend, before you bleed to death,' I said reasonably and hit him on the nearest knife wound with a bunched fist. He screamed then reached for the door handle, I went to block him but he shook his head, and I realized he was too much in pain to play any more games. I jumped out and ran around the car, helping him out. He hobbled around to the boot and I was right on his elbow.

Our would be kidnapper lifted the lid of the boot and there was my little mate, Fabio, trussed up and gagged like the proverbial Christmas turkey, and with blood trickling down his face from a nasty cut on the bridge of his nose. I hit the man alongside me with a back fist and didn't bother to watch him fall. I used the thin blade to cut the little taxi-driver free, gently removed the gag and lifted him bodily out of his own boot.

He coughed and retched, cursed and fumed in Italian, then spotted the man on the ground and waded in before I could stop him, kicking and punching, even when I grabbed him around the waist and held him up in the air. I carried him around to the car and threw him in alongside Andi, with a terse, 'look after him.'

I went back to the man who had hurt him and taken his livelihood away by stealing his taxicab. I pulled him over to the wall alongside the restaurant and slapped him a few times to get his attention. It seemed to work so I dragged him to his feet.

'Okay, matey, time for you to t...'

The bullet entered the side of his head from our right, along the street where there were no lights at all.

'Not bloody again,' I muttered.

Whether the shooter had already knocked them out in anticipation of our visit, I didn't know. And I didn't care, either. I let the body fall and leapt into the driver's seat of the Fiat.

'Get down,' I shouted to the two in the back as I hit the ignition, geared into first and took off in a spray of burning rubber. I made a mental note to get Fabio some new tires. New tires, shit. I'd buy him a new taxi, poor little guy.

We gunned around the corner but I heard no further shots. Who was the shooter, I wondered? Probably sent along as backup; or rather to get rid of the evidence should things go wrong. I had no doubt it was the same shooter as before; he was too good to be yet another one. I finally stopped at the kerb in a busy, well-lighted main road and turned the engine off.

I turned round and looked at Fabio. 'How you feeling, my friend? Do you need a doctor, hospital?'

He sat upright and shook his head. 'No, Signor Harry. I thank you for rescuing me. I can drive now if you like. Did that man die?'

'Yes, they killed him, Fabio,' I told him.

He looked sad. 'I am sorry for that, Signor. He did a bad thing to me, and I don't know what would have happened if you had not realized he was lying, but I would not wish him dead.'

'He was killed by one of his friends,' I looked across at Andi, who had not said a word since we'd left the restaurant. 'I think it was the same one who shot and killed our two attackers of the other night.'

'How DID you realize he was after us as soon as we got into the taxi, Harry?' she queried.

'I knew before we got in the cab,' I told her. 'When I did my drunken act and reached in through the window I felt blood on my hands when I leaned on the door.'

'Should we call the police?' she asked.

'No,' I shook my head. 'There's not much the police can do. They'll probably find out that the bloke from tonight is some local criminal, like the other two. The shooter will be well away by now. The last thing we want is to start answering questions from the local Bobbies.'

'Why, Harry?' Andi was being very calm and very brave. 'Why is someone still trying to kill us?'

'They're not; trying to kill us, that is. If they're after the Diabolus then we're no use to them dead.'

'But surely they must know that we have it by now, and that we've handed it over,' she muttered.

'Not necessarily,' I shrugged. 'In fact, not likely, for if they knew that, what would be their point in kidnapping us? They would have taken us off somewhere and questioned us in a nasty way until we gave it up, then take us out. Remember, the only other person who knew we had found it is Milos, and it's not in his interest to broadcast the fact.'

'And me, Signor Harry,' Fabio said dubiously. 'I too know that you found this viola.'

'That's true,' I agreed, 'but the bad guys don't know that or they would have already questioned you. You have a family, my friend?'

'Si,' he said proudly. 'I have a beautiful wife and two beautiful bambini.'

'Okay, and do you have any other family in Italy, outside of Rome. Somewhere you can perhaps take a long vacation, my friend?'

'I have an uncle in the hills of Tuscany, near to Luca, Signor. He and my aunt would welcome us, for they were not blessed with bambini and they love mine very much. But, Signor Harry, without my business, how would we live? It would take a long time to get a taxi license in Tuscany.'

'Not a problem, Fabio, not a problem,' I smiled at him. 'Let's drive somewhere more secluded where we can have a drink, and as you Yanks say, make a plan,' I grinned at Andi as I said the last and she returned a weak smile.

'Are you sure you're okay to drive, mate?' I asked Fabio, and when he nodded we traded places.

I left him to it and he took us past the outskirts of the city to an all night bar cum café in the beginning of the countryside.

Wisely, and without being told, Fabio parked the old Fiat around the back in a darkened yard.

He was obviously well known by the patron, who treated us like royalty after a few words from our driver; bowing us into a quiet corner table partially hidden behind a pseudo arch.

'Drinks all around?' I asked, and Andi nodded immediately.

'I need something strong to start,' she said.

'Fabio?' I decided it was time we cemented our friendship after our little adventures together so had dispensed with the nickname I'd given him.

'Si, Signor, I too need something to...what do you say? Quieting the nerves, eh?'

I smiled at them both and ordered three double brandies. The patron scurried away and I looked around. It was pretty full, and I'd noticed the row of taxis parked outside. I mentioned this to Fabio and he nodded.

'This is where all the cab drivers come at the end of their shifts. The patron is my uncle, and his son, Alfredo, is my cousin and my good friend. We are hoping to buy a taxi between us and share the shifts. A better taxi will bring more fares.'

'The police don't bother your uncle?'

'No, Signor,' he gave one of his huge cheesy grins. 'The large table over by the bar, it is filled with many policemen who know they can come here to unwind. No one will bother them.'

'All they can drink for free, eh?' Andi said with an edge of contempt in her voice.

'No, no, Signorina,' Fabio said indignantly. 'That happens in America, I know. Once I worked there for one year, in New York, and I saw many things that I did not like, but here, everyone pays for what they drink. Sometimes my uncle brings out some pizzas and other food as a service to the late drinkers, but the police are good customers to have, as are the taxi drivers. They both have a job that takes them out on the streets, and who knows more than a taxi driver as to what is going on out there, eh? The first place the policia comes for information is where the taxi people hang out, and a big plus for my uncle is that there is never any trouble when they are here.'

'Well,' I smiled as the drinks came. 'I'm glad we got that settled.'

Andi smiled softly and murmured some words in Italian, to which Fabio nodded solemnly and said "Prego" several times. I gathered it was some form of apology, but of course I was too polite to ask. We clinked glasses and toasted each other, each drinking half of their glass at the first gulp. I finished mine in one and lifted a hand to the patron behind the bar. I held up three fingers and he hurried over with three more brandies. He also placed a pitcher of wine on the table, a bowl of olives and a jug of bread sticks.

'Looks like we're set for the night,' I said and raised my fresh drink. We did the clinking thing again and I spelled out the way I saw it going now.

'I was commissioned by Zoltan Milos to obtain an object for money and I turned it down. Then another interested party wanted it and they were not as generous as Milos; instead they kidnapped my son and would return him only in exchange for the object. Milos helped me get him back by using the vast resources of the Vatican,' I looked sidelong at Andi, 'or at least I assumed at the time that was where he accessed his information from, and he'd managed to track them down. He gave me this information with no strings attached and I got my son back. I was grateful, so promised Milos that I would go ahead and get his object, which we all know now was a violin.'

I looked at the other two. Both nodded in agreement of these facts.

'I handed over the violin and Milos insisted on giving me money, more in fact than he had promised in his initial offer. It should now be a case of living happily ever after, but the other group appears to be still after it, and have already killed three of their own rather than have them talk. I also believe there was a third, even more shadowy group, interested in it. So, this violin, this Diabolus, whether it is evil or not, and whether it has power or not, is coveted by many people; people who think we know where it is, which we do, but they don't know it is now with someone who should have it. At least, as far as we know.'

Again I looked at the other two. No fear showed in Andi's eyes, and if anything there was a look of slight amusement, but perhaps I was wrong and she was merely putting on a bold front. Fabio was also trying to put a bold front on it but I could see he was not happy.

'We have only one way to go then, folks. We have to disappear. Fabio, as far as they are concerned, is only a taxi driver who has run us around a few times, but we don't want to take chances. I suggest he takes his family and goes and stays with his uncle. Fabio, give your Fiat to Alfredo. Tell him to get used to taxiing around Rome and everything he makes is his.' I held a hand up as he went to speak. 'How do you get to Tuscany? With the brand new Mercedes we are going to buy for you tomorrow, my friend. When you get back this will all be over, and then you can buy another taxi and lease it to your cousin for a percentage of the profits and give the Fiat to a deserving cause, for there will also be a large amount of money for you to do this, and also to enable you to be independent for a while.'

Fabio's eyes were gleaming and he was shaking my hand up and down. 'What can I do to repay you, Signor Harry? How can I ever...?'

'One thing only,' I said with gravity. 'Stop calling me Signor; Harry is fine.'

'And us, Harry?' Andi leaned across and spoke softly. 'Where are we going to hide?'

'I've got just the place for us, little Andi. When was the last time you were in England?'

Fabio had driven us to my hotel where I threw my things into my bag and checked out. He then drove us to Andi's apartment, where she packed a suitcase and a few valuables and we went to a small central hotel with a discreet but useful looking concierge on duty all night.

We bade goodnight to Fabio and arranged for him to pick us up at 11:30 the next morning. I was ordering two adjacent rooms at the desk when Andi placed a hand on my arm and shook her head. She kissed me, just to make sure I got the message. I did quickly; an arsehole might well describe me, but a slow arsehole, never, and ten minutes later we were walking into a comfortable room on the third floor.

When I came out of the bathroom she was already in bed and the lights were out. I quickly stepped out of my clothes, folded them onto a chair because it's the way I was brought up, and slipped into bed next to Andi.

Soft skin came against me, then over me to rest on top.

'I forgot to pack my PJ's,' she whispered, and the next minute I was so busy doing things I hadn't done for years that I forgot to ask what PJ's were.

The next morning was more of the same, which wouldn't really interest discerning readers, as this isn't that kind of tale. Later, while Andi was in the bathroom, I rang the airport and booked two seats for Plymouth on an afternoon flight.

Over an excellent light breakfast in the room I broached the subject of reward.

'I don't want to insult you,' I said softly. 'But you were of great assistance in recovering the Diabolus, and although I did specify no payment, I was paid nonetheless. It's only fair that you share in that, like Fabio.'

'Fabio needed some reward, Harry,' she replied in the same soft tone as mine. 'Like I already told you, I do not. I'll take a rain check, and should I ever see the right pair of Dolce Gabana boots, I'll give you a call.'

'Whew,' I pulled a face. 'I wasn't planning to go THAT big.'

The phone rang and it was Fabio ringing up from the front desk. We were packed, dressed and ready to go. On my instructions we drove straight to his bank where I deposited two hundred thousand pounds in his account. We then drove to the main Mercedes dealer near the Coliseum and let Fabio take his pick of the models in the showroom. At my insistence he picked the top of the range saloon car and arranged to pick it up later. I paid by Gold Card.

It was a tearful farewell at the airport. Fabio hugged and kissed Andi, and then to my everlasting embarrassment he hugged and kissed me too.

'Thank you for everything, S...Harry,' he said tearfully.

'You earned it, my friend,' I told him, and meant it. 'It's also for your silence for the rest of your life about the violin, you understand? Comprendere? Good luck, and stay well, Fabio.'

'And you, Harry,' he held up a hand, and as we turned away he called out in an exaggeratedly puzzled voice. 'What violin is that, Harry?'

I smiled back at him and we climbed aboard.

At first I thought Andi might be game for the mile-high club, but I was too shy to find out.

Not.

CHAPTER NINE

"Pope Pelaguis (556-60) talks of heretics separating themselves from the Apostolic See, that is, Rome, Jerusalem, Alexandria plus Constantinople. *In all the early writings of the hierarchy there is no mention of a special role for the Bishop of Rome, nor yet the special name of 'Pope'*

Of the eighty or so heresies in the first six centuries, not one refers to the authority of the Bishop of Rome, not one is settled by the Bishop of Rome ...No one attacks the (supreme) authority of the Roman pontiff, because no one has heard of it."

Peter de Rosa,
Vicars of Christ: The Dark Side of the Papacy,

We arrived at the cottage just as dusk was taking over from the gentle fading sun of an English day in August. To me it was one of the best of days that my small island offered and I knew the evening would be mild, colder than the day but still pleasant.

I motioned Andi to stay in the car and began to scout around the outside of the building. Suddenly I heard a scream and spun round, the Steyr already in my right hand.

'Th...re's a big dog over there, in the bushes. He's stalking you, Brogan,' Andi hissed through the window.

'No,' I straightened. 'He's not stalking; he's guarding me. Over here, boy, come and meet haemorrhoid.'

'Haemorrhoid?'

'Well, you ARE a pain in the arse, sometimes.'

'Only sometimes?' she said sweetly, then stared at the fox and gave a little yelp. 'Oh, God, what IS that thing?'

'Quiet,' I shushed sternly. 'He'll hear you. Foxes are very sensitive creatures. You really don't want to hurt his feelings, trust me.'

'What's it doing here, Brogan?' she demanded. 'That's the biggest fox I've ever seen, and I spent vacations in the country, so I've seen plenty of them. That's no ordinary fox, mister.'

'I'm sure he'll be very pleased to know you think he's special. Now, are you going to get out of the car, or what?'

'I thought you were going to check the house out?' she said somewhat petulantly.

'No need,' I shrugged, moved to the back and opened the boot, or trunk as she kept telling me they called it in America, and removed our cases. 'If he's satisfied all's well, that's good enough for me, babe.'

'Babe,' she grumbled as she climbed out of the car. 'Where's the "babe" come from?'

'Same place as buster, and since you've been acting like one, by the way, can you cook?'

'Cook, hah, I'm Italian, aren't I?

'Good, that's a coincidence, because I've a kitchen inside.'

'And you know what you can do with that, pal. If you think I'm going to turn into a housewife just because I let you...'

The fox sat in the middle of the drive watching his friend and the strange woman bickering like two pups as they moved inside the house. Eventually the thought of hamburger meat made him give what looked like a little shrug and he strolled up the steps and through the front door.

'Tell me about your pet,' she waved her fork in the direction of the big fox.

'I call him Lupus,' I told her.

'Latin for a member of the wolf family,' she murmured.

'Oh,' I exclaimed. 'And here was me thinking it was Spanish.'

'No, you did not,' she said blandly. 'How did you end up owning a fox?'

'Like I said before, I do not own him, and he isn't a pet,' I relaxed and relented. 'Not long after I bought this place a hunt came through here.'

'A hunt?'

'Yes, you know, those people dressed up in red jackets. Riding horses and trailing a pack of hounds ready to tear apart rabbits, deer, anything; but especially foxes, which are supposedly the main reason for the hunt. "The unspeakable in pursuit of the unedible", I think Oscar Wilde put it.'

'Wise man he was, but I think it is "Inedible".'

'Whatever. They were chasing a little vixen at the time and came right into my driveway, the fox, followed by the hounds, with the riders not too far behind. The little thing was exhausted, just about done in, and collapsed on my porch.

I opened the door and dragged it inside, then kicked shit out of any hound that came up the steps.'

'And the hunters?'

'Oh, they had the cheek to complain about me interfering with their hunt, but I asked them politely and they went away without further ado.'

She gave me a sceptical look. 'You? Asked politely?'

'Sure,' I said earnestly. 'Politeness always pays, Madam. That and a twin barrel over and under shotgun, one barrel of which I discharged over their heads. They decided to pack up their indignation and scarper; that means go away. I fed the vixen some bread soaked in hot milk, made her up a little bed out of some old sheets and she slept her fright away. The next day I slipped her into the back of my car and took her out along the tracks onto the moor and left her to run back to her hide. About a week later she surprised me by just turning up one evening. She laid the carcass of a dead rabbit on the porch then trotted away.'

'Good heavens,' Andi's eyes were wide. 'What did you do with the rabbit?'

'Ate it, of course,' I stared at her, which wasn't too hard. 'She'd brought it as a present, for saving her.'

'Oh, surely you don't...'

'Of course I believe it. A few days' later she came back and we finished off the remains of the rabbit together. After that she was a regular visitor, and I always found some hamburger meat in the fridge for her. Absolutely loved it. Then she was away for a month and I was beginning to think that the bloody hunters had got her, when she arrives back in the yard, bold as brass. She came right up to me and took hold of my pants leg, very gently and pulled me towards the gate. I followed her and she took me to an old badger's sett, which she'd taken over as her den.

'Outside there was a single kit, about a month old, playing by itself. It appeared she had given birth to only one kit, whereas they usually have up to five in the litter. She also didn't seem to have a male around anywhere. Foxes breed in late winter or early spring and give birth after a two-month gestation period. Kits are born blind and weighing just a few ounces. Both the vixen and dog care for the young, with the dog doing the hunting and bringing food back for the vixen and kits. The kits leave the den after a month and are learning to hunt a couple of months later. In the autumn the family unit separates for good. Somehow, this clever little lady had done it all herself.'

'The red fox, *vulpes vulpes,* is one of the cleverest mammals,' Andi said, and went into her lecturer's mode as she began to tell me all about foxes. 'Anything else you want to know?'

I shrugged and came out with a few sentences about foxes of my own. She went to interrupt again but I continued again before she could.

'Of all the members of the family Canidae, foxes are the only canids that are not pack animals. The vixen's wail is a long, drawn-out and monosyllabic wail, almost eerie and sometimes made by the male. Gekkering is a throaty, stuttering fox noise made usually in aggressive situations. Now, is there anything YOU might want to know?'

'Yes,' she said sweetly. 'Where do you keep the pasta?'

I showed her and she began to cook, and I guessed that was her way of admitting she was a know-all or being incredibly impressed by my knowledge of foxes.

Over an excellent pasta meal thrown together with tins of things, she asked me to finish off the story of Lupus.

I shrugged. 'I don't know it all myself, and can only guess to a lot of it. I suppose the vixen had a run-in with a big dog of some kind, my guess is an Alsatian or Rottweiler, which turned into rape or consensual sex. Whatever, Lupus came along and his mother looked after him until he would be old enough to look after himself. She'd bring him by sometimes for dinner, and I always kept lots of hamburger meat in the freezer, or one of the hunters I know in the local pub would give me a haunch of venison, and I'd cook some of it up. Bizarrely enough, they both preferred their meat cooked if they had the choice.'

'Told you they were clever animals,' she sniffed.

'One day Lupus came crawling up here on his own. He was literally crawling. He'd been shot in the hindquarters and had a load of buckshot in there. He was about nine months old then.'

I paused and took a swallow of wine, still feeling the pain of that time, now years ago.

'I wrapped a blanket around his back and legs and put him into the rear seat of my car, then ran through the woods to the den. They were still there and I couldn't believe my luck. Three arseholes from Plymouth with shotguns, and they'd been out for the day, drinking since they'd been on the road, and were now pretty high. They'd come on the den during one of their quieter periods, when mother and son were playing together and one had got a lucky shot off and hit the vixen. Lupus, just nine months old, had gone straight in at them. He almost ripped the leg off one, and took a big chunk out of another's arm before they shot him. Even then he'd crawled off through the brush.

'The vixen wasn't quite dead when they chopped off her tail and cut her throat in a drunken attempt to hack off her head. At first, when they saw me, they thought they were dealing with a "fellow hunter", another country bloke who liked killing foxes for the sake of it, and they boasted about their exploits.'

I paused and took another drink of wine. 'Maybe a couple of years before I'd have been more lenient, although I've always had a soft spot for animals, and never killed unless I could use the meat. Unfortunately for them I knew foxes, and they'd just shot two of my friends. Because of the booze they'd had, and the adrenaline over their big kill, their injuries were bearable, but not after I'd kicked them around for a while. I left them there and took the distributor cap from their new Mondeo, ran back to the house and drove to the nearest vet who looked astonished when he saw the size of Lupus.

'I told him I'd be back and returned to my cottage. I left my car there and went back to the clearing. The three arseholes were still out of it, so I buried the vixen, tail and all, in the den and filled it in with rocks and soil. I then piled the visitors into their car, replaced the distributor cap and drove them up onto the moor, miles from anywhere of course, and I left them to it. They'd still not woken up but were in good physical condition mainly due to their age. I removed all their clothing. Night was coming on and it had the looks like it was going to be a cold one when they woke up.'

We were both quiet for a while and finished the meal in silence.

'Well, you know how to split up a party,' she tried to joke, but it didn't quite come off, but I was grateful to her for trying.

'Looks like the vet did a good job,' was all she said as we were washing up, together at the sink in a companionable silence.

'Yes, he worked for hours getting every piece of shot out of him, and we're still good friends today. The fox stayed with me until he was whole again, then one day he just took off. He keeps coming back to visit, though.'

Later, I made a pathetic attempt to offer Andi the spare room but she just smiled and disappeared into the bathroom. When I came out some time later, she was already curled up in my bed. That night the fox did not come into my room, like he so often did.

We stayed in the cottage for a week that moved into a second then a third, and finally a fourth week. I'd forgotten how enjoyable it was having company, no, more than that.

No offence to Lupus, my big red-haired mate, but human companionship was something else, and I made the most of it.

CHAPTER TEN

"It is better to hear the rebuke of the wise, than for a man to hear the song of a fool"

Ecclesiastes 7:5

Four weeks later I was sitting at a corner table in my local pub, trying to recover from the departure from my life of Dr Andrea Scolari that very day. She'd stayed with me for four weeks, and then reluctantly told me that she had to get back to Rome. I'd begged her not to go, saying it was not safe yet, and what was another month? But duty called and off she went.

True to Milos's word an extra million pounds had been deposited in my account in Jersey. One day I'd even left Andi alone while I tried to see my son again, but his mother had been her usual vindictive self, and although not understanding the details, had blamed me and refused to tell me anything of where Phillip was.

'It was always about YOU, wasn't it, Harry? And it still is. This time you brought your troubles to MY house and I won't have it. BLOODY STAY AWAY.'

And she'd slammed the door in my face.

I hadn't reminded her that it had been MY bloody house, mostly paid for by my marine pay all those years ago.

I nursed my pint of Guinness and was brooding again. Why, I had no idea, I just felt some dissatisfaction about the whole thing. It did not have the kind of closure I liked. They had taken my son and bankrupted me; and it had been so easily done that it was scary. The equally scary priest, Milos, although jovial on the outside had not fooled me for a moment. There was something about him; something I couldn't quite put my finger on. I suppose I still believed he was behind the initial kidnapping of Phillip and the block on my bank accounts. He was authentic as far as the Vatican was concerned, as vouched for by Andi, but what kind of priest, Signore to the Pope, okay, at one time, has to hire someone to steal an antiquity from the Vatican itself?

Something did not quite gel but every brain cell told me to leave it alone. I was on the verge of agreeing with myself when the voice broke in on my thoughts and that was that as far as being sensible went.

A voice asked how the Guinness tasted. I broke off my reveries and looked to my right to find a little man with a cheeky smile at my elbow. My first thought was that he was a Leprechaun, but then I saw that once again the man was in clerical garb.

'Not again,' I think I sighed.

'My name is Patrick Sullivan,' the little man said. He had a pronounced accent; an accent that still put shivers along my spine whenever I heard it. Expressions came easily to mind, such as; "Dod's fuckin' army", "Don't go down that road, sojer", "We know where yis family live", and the like.

The little man must have read it in my eyes, because he spoke in a softer voice.

'Although I did not live in the South, like you my parents were from there. I was actually christened Padraig, but that would have been a bit too much for the poor Prods in Belfast, as I'm sure you know only too well. And like you I began as an altar boy, well before deciding on the priesthood, Mr. Brogan.'

Another priest who knows all about me, I thought. This is becoming a habit. The priest named Sullivan continued to twitter on and I smiled despite my mood. It was an old interrogation technique I recognized from my former life. Keep on burbling and eventually the other bloke gives up and starts talking just to shut YOU up.

I said as much to the little priest, who had the grace to chuckle back. I decided I liked this one better than the big chubby one. But even then I had reservations.

'In the North I saw men with your dog-collar who were heroes,' I said conversationally. 'And I saw others who were bloody murderers, who got other men killed, and carried arms and plotted to kill young army lads.'

'You'll get no argument from me, lad; and you'll have to make up yis own mind on which type am I. Now, if you'll allow me to get the nectar in I'd like a little chat,' and without waiting for a reply the little man went to the bar. He returned with two pints of Guinness and placed them on the table in front of me.

'You're not drinking yourself then, Padre?' I asked innocently.

The priest mumbled something that sounded like "fuck you" but he was smiling and I couldn't be sure so I gave the man of the cloth the benefit of the doubt.

For a time we talked of Northern Ireland and the troubles, of Belfast and Londonderry, and of the whole wicked waste of lives and property, and of extreme religious convictions on both sides. And that the only finality in the present was the presence of armed gangs on both sides. The only good thing, if such could be called good, was that the foreign gangsters, the Russian, Kosovan and Romanian mafias could not get a foothold into Northern Ireland. Instead they were now running London, and we laughed at the irony of it all.

It was I who brought us back to the immediate present and probably spoiled the moment.

'So, padre, what would you like me to steal for you – I hope it's not a fucking piano this time.'

The little priest laughed wholeheartedly at that.

'Ah, I believe you had dealings with one of my old colleagues recently. A man named Zoltan Milos. You obtained...an instrument for him.'

'Yes, I did,' I confirmed. 'And it's your business – because...?'

'It is the Devil's Instrument, Mr. Brogan,' the priest shook his head, sadly it appeared to me.

'So they say, Father, an appellation that has followed the violin for years. I know all about it, anyway. Now why don't you follow the example of your distinguished Signore friend, and call me Harry?' I nodded.

'No, you don't understand, Harry. That particular one, the one you...obtained for Milos, THAT is the Devil's Instrument, THAT one, no other. We do not blame you for your actions, because we know what you were threatened with.'

'So why are you here?'

'I came to ask you to get it back for us, Harry.'

'Fuck you, padre,' I said without rancour. I'd about had it with violins, Devils, and especially priests.

'Fuck you too,' the priest said quietly and was halfway to the bar before I knew it.

By the time he got back with two more pints of the black stuff, I had seen the funny side of the priest telling me off in my own bad language.

'Just like that, is it?' I said to the smaller man. 'Pinch the bloody thing back again. Why not go and ask your "colleague" for it, if it's that important.'

'Difficult, Harry,' the priest said sadly. 'We can't find Zoltan Milos, and the black Stradivarius has also disappeared. It's a strong possibility that he might have been killed because of it. There again, if he is alive, then he has it in his possession, for I know he would not let it out of his sight. He would prize it unto death.'

I was silent after that one. At last I spoke. I told him the whole story as I saw little point in not. He seemed to know most of it anyway. I finished by saying, 'Surely the Pope has it, or has knowledge of it.'

The little priest sighed. 'I suppose Milos told you he was working for His Holiness, that he was a Papal Envoy and lived in the Vatican?'

I nodded my head, not puzzled after what Andi had told me, and so not altogether surprised. 'And I suppose you're also a Signore, padre?'

As when I first met Milos, I was again assailed with questions as to how the man seated opposite had gained all of this information. The answer to these unspoken questions came from Sullivan himself. He reached into the inside of the jacket he was wearing. As he laid the seal on the table I stared at it without comment. I'd seen pictures of it but never the real thing.

'It's a Papal Seal,' I managed to get out.

'That it is, Harry. That it is.' The little man beamed. 'And there's an official document that goes with it, telling the world that I'm a Papal Envoy and to give me any help I may need to perform the Lord's good work, through the proper channels of His Holiness the Pope, of course. Tell me now, did Milos show you one of these?'

I shook my head and frowned. 'Then Milos was an impostor?'

'Not completely,' Sullivan said. 'He DID live in the Vatican, he WAS a Signore, and he DID work close to the Pope.'

'Three out of three's not bad, Padre, you must admit,' I shrugged.

'Ah, but it's not that simple, Harry, for all that was once upon a time. Milos was the secretary to Cardinal Warkowsky, a fellow Slav, not the Pope himself. The Holy Father is no man's fool and is well aware of the machinations at court, I assure you. It's a long story, Harry. Let me just tell you at this juncture that Milos and his mentor, Warkowsky, although supposedly Christians, are approaching salvation by a somewhat circuitous route. They intend to use the black violin for a diabolical purpose of their own.'

'Well, if you haven't got it, and you reckon this Warkowsky hasn't got it, what about Milos simply running off and disappearing with it? Or, what about some of the others who have been after it? Like the man who kidnapped my son, for example.'

The little priest shook his head and shrugged. 'That man is the Compte Etienne Corbusier, supposedly a member of the French Aristocracy; a claim upon which we have our doubts, but that is not important now. He is a man of considerable wealth and has posted a vast sum for the acquisition of the item. The reward still stands, Harry, so we therefore assume that it is not in his hands.'

'And he has a rightful claim to it?'

'No one has a rightful claim to it,' Sullivan almost lost his air of bonhomie as his brows came together. 'Legend has it that the great luthier, Stradivari, made it as part of a pact with the Devil, and like many of his instruments it changed hands a few times in its early life, but like most transactions they have remained undocumented or recorded. The Vatican acquired it nearly 300 years ago and kept it in a secret place; a place which I assume you were clever enough to discover.'

'They were keeping it against it being used for some alleged evil purpose, I was told by Milos,' I murmured, sceptically now, and not as a question. The little priest answered it though.

'Really?' he took on an even more sceptical tone than me. 'And where did you get that piece of crap from, Brogan?'

'Well, I...' I was thrown by his question and must obviously have shown it.

'Let me shock you, or at least surprise you in some small measure. The followers of Satan have long contaminated the Vatican. These are the one who have been after the Diabolus, from within. Its whereabouts have been a well-kept secret for centuries, passed down from Holy Father to Holy Father. Some have been of the Satanic persuasion, though most have been good men. Those who have sought Satan have used one of the oldest excuses that if you can't beat them, join them.'

'You mean they pretended to follow the Devil in order to banish him for ever?' I looked at him closely, not believing a word of it.

'Not quite, but that was the gist of it in the beginning,' he smiled sadly. 'They intend to seek salvation in a roundabout way. By coming to terms with the Evil One, and conforming to his ways. A dangerous game, Harry, a very dangerous game.'

He drank from his Guinness and gazed into the glass. I thought he was done then he suddenly looked up and his eyes penetrated mine.

'A book published several years ago by a retired priest, Signore Luigi Marinelli, caused quite a stir in Italy. Gone with the Wind at the Vatican literally flew off the shelves as Italians eagerly read the stories of greedy bishops, money-laundering prelates, and especially sexual abuse. Msgr. Marinelli was the latest Vatican insider to allege that satanic rituals have been performed within the walls of the Holy See. Another book, published in recent times, was the anonymously written Blood Lies in the Vatican, also hinting at Masonic plots in Rome. It is far more than a conspiracy theory, Harry. Those behind it all have a diabolical purpose in mind, and I believe I might know what that purpose is.'

I was wondering whether it was the Guinness but felt that I was on another twisting path full of deceit and fabrication. "Diabolical purpose" fell uneasily on my ears, being overly melodramatic, yet at the same time the burden of responsibility for taking the damn thing in the first place also rested uneasily on my bloody shoulders and I knew it.

I know I must have looked uncomfortable when I spoke to the priest. 'Look, Patrick. I'm not exactly an...umm, a believer, you know. Did the usual bit as a Liverpool Irish Catholic, church every Sunday, even an altar boy for a while, but these days, I'm...I don't...er, you know what I mean.'

The priest looked at me with amusement. 'For such an erudite man you have appalling lapses at times, Harry. Yes, I know what you mean and that doesn't come into it. I believe it is the way you live your life, and the way you treat your fellow man. The church is all around us, and so is Satan. You may scoff now, but then again, you might be in for a great shock before this thing is over; when it is recovered and destroyed for good.'

'Thing?' I frowned. 'You just told me a man I knew has probably been killed over this violin, then there is another three wasted by their own man in Rome, to say nothing of the ones I disposed of to get my son back. Now you refer to it as a "thing".'

The priest looked away towards the bar. When he looked back at me there was a light in his eyes, a new expression on his face, though I could not make out what it was.

'I did not mean just the violin, Harry, though it is true it IS a thing, an accursed thing. I refer to the whole...mess, I suppose. We must find it again, and quickly, for soon it will be used for a fearsome task. I can't go into that at the moment; it would be too much for you to take in, you being a nonbeliever and all.'

I frowned into my ale. 'Suppose I believed you, Patrick, and I must confess you carry some conviction in that brogue of yours, where could I possibly begin to look for it? The last I saw of it was when I handed it over to Milos. I assumed he took it into the depths of the Vatican.'

'And you'd have been right in assuming that, Harry. But I reckon he had an agenda of his own that he was keeping, and the Vatican would have been the last place he would have taken it back to. No one inside would know of its disappearance, unless Milos had told them and that would only have been his masters.'

'Okay,' I said slowly. 'So what are you asking for this time, padre?'

'We need to find out where the Diabolus is now. There is a colleague of mine who is an expert on the nature of the Devil and his minions,' the priest said somewhat pedantically. 'If anything happens to me, promise you will get in touch. Andrea Scolari is probably the only person who will be able to help you in that event.'

'Andrea?' I repeated casually.

The little priest looked up and eyed me steadily. 'That's right. Andrea at the moment is in the Vatican library doing some pro bono cataloguing for us. Why, is the name familiar to you?'

I smiled. 'It is, very much so, padre. Milos gave me her name and she was very helpful filling in the background of the Devil, his music and the rest of the stuff. She even helped me get the violin itself. After we had it we took refuge here in my cottage, in case the ungodly were still looking for us, which I had reason to believe they were. Quite a girl, our little Andi.'

I smiled at the memory of how "quite a girl" little Andi was. The little Signore snapped me out of the pleasant reverie, and at his instigation I told him the whole story.

'Strange,' Sullivan frowned. 'I didn't know they knew each other that well, still, Andrea is an expert on the nasty one, and of course his music, don't you know, and has written a few books on the subject, so I'm sure she steered you in the right direction. She obviously did by the fact that you found the Diabolus itself.'

The little man's cheeky grin took away any perceived slight; not that I'd had any sense of perceived or misperceived slight. I just wished I hadn't heard of Stradivari and his bloody violins. A sudden thought struck me.

'I gather you and Milos weren't exactly buddies, padre, so how do you know about all this, and how did you find out about my involvement?'

The little priest merely sipped his black drink and a sly smile moved his lips as he wiped away the froth with the back of a small hairy hand. He said nothing.

'Why, that bloody Jonathon again,' I was struck with a sudden epiphany. 'The tow-rag seems to have given my name to everyone who asks.'

Patrick Sullivan smiled. "Ah, now, you can't blame Jonathon too much; with Milos he genuinely thought he was helping the church, and with me, well, we're old friends. Jonathon and I go back a long way, and he's often done jobs for us with his little army of professional...procurers. You included, I might add, Harry. There's a few good stealings you've done on our behalf over the years.'

'Us?' I enquired with a raised eyebrow, and realized it was déjà vu all over again, for I remembered a similar conversation with Milos.

'Of course, even the Holy Church needs certain services rendered sometimes, Harry.'

'And why do I get the feeling that you belong to the "end justifying the means" brigade, Patrick?' I asked.

'Of course, the other way is sinful; the "means justifying the end" is why wars are fought, why there is so much bloodshed in the world, and so much unnecessary evil. Satan relishes that philosophy. Will you humour me, if nothing else? Promise to think about it for a few days, and I'll be in here in two days time and see what you think. In the meanwhile, if you have the time, why not look up secret societies and the like.'

'What?'

The little priest misunderstood my exclamation for he elaborated. 'Study the Devil and his legends, get the feel for the possible confrontation with the entity that perhaps you're not ready for yet; for how could you be ready for that which you do not believe in? When you believe, Harry, it will make your task a lot easier.'

'Hang on a minute,' I protested. 'What task are we talking about here? I hope it isn't what I think it is. I've just gone to a considerable amount of trouble, not to mention pain, to locate and take it in the first place. In fact they're all still out there looking for me. Now you want me to do it all over again?'

The priest did not smile at my outburst this time. Instead his mood was deadly serious, and despite my conviction I found it hard not to believe in him.

'They are not looking for you any more, Harry. You were just the instrument in obtaining it for Milos. You were in danger when you were looking for it, and when you had it, but no longer. Promise me you'll do some of that reading I suggested, and I'll be in touch. Okay, me boy?'

We left it like that. I agreed and went home to reluctantly renew my studies into subjects I thought I had no interest in; at least, not in the beginning.

Once again I was struck with the similarities of my conversations with both Signores; one tall and fat, the other short...and not fat. Both wanted me to steal the same Stradivarius, both professed the importance of possessing said instrument. Both had given me the name of someone to turn to, should anything happen to them, though for one that "something" had already happened; and which thought made me think for a moment about the name I'd been given by Milos. Both swore to be the good guys in the Christian faith and on a mission for no less a figure than His Holiness himself.

I confessed to liking the little Irish priest better than the tall Slavic one, who after doing a lot of thinking on the subject, I still felt had been behind the blackmailing by taking my son. Still, I was feeling bored again and this looked like a fine opportunity to un-bore myself. And visit Rome once more before I died, or before Andi found some suave rich bastard.

I shook myself and wondered where that gloomy thought had come from.

The next morning a phone call chased my gloomy thoughts away. My son, Phillip, phoned.

'Dad, I apologise for Mum's attitude, and not giving you my new number. Some bugger nicked my mobile so I had to buy a new one and phone all my mates with the new number. She can be a right pain sometimes.'

Don't I know it, I thought, but instead said, 'well, she probably thinks she's doing the right thing.'

His silence said it all.

'So, how's varsity?'

'We don't call it "varsity" any more, Dad. It's "uni" now. Anyway, what are you up to? Did you get the whatsit?'

'Yes, handed it over, and now I've been asked to find it again.'

'You're not joking?'

'No, I'm not joking, Phillip. I wish I bloody well were.' I told him about the little priest in a few short sentences.

'But that's great news, Dad. I really enjoyed the time we had looking up all that stuff, and I get a mid-term break in a few weeks time. Can I come down and help?'

I was over the moon, and then I frowned when I thought of the danger he could be in. I told him so, but his reply was well thought out.

'How do they know you're after it again, Dad? If you trust the priest then he certainly wouldn't be telling anyone. I'll be there in a week, and the mysterious deposit I found in my account when I got back bought a neat little Beetle, which I'll come down in. Thanks for that, Dad.'

'Just a research payment,' I said gruffly. 'Look forward to seeing you, son.'

We rang off and that night I celebrated by sharing a massive steak with Lupus, done rare of course to both our likings, and a bottle of good red with myself.

Over the following two days I surfed the Internet and took more books out of Exeter City Library. I spoke with Andi both on the phone and e-mail and told her what was happening. Despite my inbuilt cynicism over such things I began to show some interest, and my notes became more in-depth.

I sat with a glass of Jameson's Irish whiskey and read over them on the afternoon before I was to meet the little Irishman from the north.

The Illuminati was an actual group that existed from 1776 until 1785.

The Illuminati – Controllers of a global network of secret societies.

Only one signer of the Declaration of Independence is known NOT to be a Freemason.

Washington D.C. was laid out and dedicated by Freemasons.

One rule of the Freemasons is that members must lie even to their wives concerning privileged knowledge and associations.

In courts Masons must lie to protect a brother they know to be guilty.

The Yalta Pact – Franklin Roosevelt, Winston Churchill and Joseph Stalin were all Freemasons.

Bilderbergers – Most secret of all secret groups with about 120 members. Annual meetings have higher security that most heads of state. Memberships include major TV news anchors, publishers of major newspapers and magazines, and corporate magnets including manufacturers of war materials.

Knights Templar – Founders of Freemasonry in Britain dedicated to the free exchange of ideas. First Grand Lodge meeting held at the Goose and Gridiron Ale House in London on June 24th, 1717. Almost from the beginning there were hidden agendas. Now known as Freemasons they were instrumental in the formation of secret organizations, and also fraternal clubs such as Rotary, Kiwanis and Odd Fellows.

The Skull and Bones Society was founded in 1832 at Yale University in New Haven Connecticut. Membership includes George H.W. Bush, William Jefferson Clinton and George W. Bush. Associated organizations: Rhodes Scholars of Oxford University, England, of which Tony Blair was a member. The originating organization for these groups The Illuminati that was founded at the University of Ingolstadt in Germany.

The Order of Skull and Bones was once called the Brotherhood of Death.

A pamphlet on Bones described the walls of the tomb as "adorned with pictures of the founders of Bones at Yale and of the members of the Society in Germany when the Chapter was established here in 1832. Skull and Bones is not American at all. It is a branch of a foreign secret society, and is a clear and obvious threat to constitutional freedom in the United States. Its secrecy, power and use of influence is greater by far than the masons, or any other semi-secret mutual or fraternal organization. Secret societies of importance are either interwoven with or in some manner related to Freemasonry.

Common goal of all of these groups and organizations: New World Order with a One World Government controlled by an elite brotherhood based upon worship of Lucifer – Satanism.

The Beginnings:

Phi Beta Kappa, the National Honours Fraternity (US) was originally the recruiting field for the Illuminati (The British East India Company) family oligarchies.

This is the way it works:

PHI – the 21st letter of the Greek alphabet.

BETA – the 2nd letter of the Greek alphabet.

KAPPA – the 10th letter of the Greek alphabet.

Then, by reducing each number to its lowest denominator via the Pythagorean Skein Method we have:

PHI = 21 = 2 + 1 = 3

BETA = 02 = 0 + 2 = 2

KAPPA = 10 = 1 + 0 = 1

Therefore PHI BETA KAPPA = 321 via the Pythagorean method.

In 1826 the East India Company dropped PHI BETA KAPPA in favour of Skull and Bones. Therefore Skull and Bones became lodge number 322.

The CYCLOPAEDIA OF FRATERNITIES states that at each Ivy League College there are three fraternities aligned with organized Freemasonry.

At Yale University it is:

Wolfs Head Society (top of the apex)

/   /

Skull & Bones   Scroll & Key Society

Therefore at Yale the Wolfs Head Society is higher on the totem pole than Skull & Bones.

Skull & Bones is connected to the University of Leipzig in Germany and the ideas of Dr Wilhelm Wundt. Wundt was a student of Frederick George Hegel, and it was Hegal who invented the Hegelian Dialectic.

PROBLEM REACTION SOLUTION

The proposed sale of Peninsular & Oriental Shipping Lines to the United Arab Emirates is the epitome of

PROBLEM REACTION SOLUTION

And let us not forget – P & O Netloyd is a direct subsidiary of the British East India Company.

My conclusion before I left for the pub later that evening was that it was all a load of nonsense. A clever man can make anything sound feasible, and yet...surely I'd read something about American presidents and their college histories...somewhere?

It would certainly explain many things that had troubled me over the years. I shook my head, threw a leftover piece of steak to the fox on my porch and hurried off for my appointment with a pint of black nectar; and of course, Patrick Sullivan.

I had arranged to meet the little priest at 7:30pm. At 8:30pm my thoughts ran blackly to the tardiness of the clergy, remembering the late showing of Milos that night in Bermuda.

As 8:30 ran into 9:30 I realized the man wasn't coming. I played several games of darts with some of the locals I knew by sight in the pub, and when closing time arrived at 11pm, I finally realized that the no-show was not a good sign. Perhaps the priest was not so wrong about his diabolical "thing" after all.

As I turned in that night, I tried to get my thoughts in order. As I've said previously, I liked the little priest, and unlike the fat Milos, I sensed the inherent goodness in the man. The Guinness following the whiskey had given me the sleeping pill I never needed. My last waking thought was; what did I do now?

Two days later I couldn't believe my eyes when a taxi drew up down by the gate and two shapely legs emerged from the back seat.

She flew into my arms and I was happy again.

We were in bed a half hour later. It was two in the afternoon and God, the shame of it. I was stroking her thigh and she was purring like a cat and alternately stroking me. I think the term "teasing" comes to mind.

'So,' she said eventually. 'You've picked up another priest, Brogan.'

'Yes, it seems to be my fate.'

'And this one wants you to…?'

'I'm sure you've guessed it by now, my dear,' I murmured.

'Surely not that awful violin again?'

'See, I knew you'd guessed it.' I wondered at her turn of phrase.

'But you had an agreement with Milos,' her voice sounded suddenly sharp.

'I did,' I agreed, moving my hand to her right breast. It felt good, so soft and silky, and the aureole was huge, with the stiffening nipple growing from the middle. 'But Milos has vanished, according to Sullivan. You DO know Sullivan, don't you?'

'Of course,' she had changed her tone and now sounded compliant, willing to listen and accept. To show her compliance her right hand had moved across my thigh and was now being very intimate with what my first girlfriend used to refer to as my "sticky-up thing." Please, I never said Liverpool girls were erudite, but they were always willing, God bless them. 'He was a nice man, always polite and friendly; quick with a joke and would often come around for some bit of research. Though I don't understand why you'd take everything he said at face value. Not that he's a liar or anything; don't get me wrong, but he surely knows more than he's telling at this stage.'

'Exactly,' I agreed, and becoming quite excited though not entirely because of the trend of our conversation. 'Let me tell you a story, little girl. Once upon a time a girl asked a boy if he thought she was pretty. He said, "No." She asked him if he would be with her forever, and again he said "No". She then asked him if she would leave would he cry, and once again he replied with a "No".

'She'd heard enough. As she walked away, tears streaming down her face, the boy grabbed her arm and said, 'Hey, you're not pretty...you are beautiful. I don't want to be with you forever...I NEED to be with you forever. And I wouldn't cry if you left...I would die.'

She stopped what she was doing and looked at me.

'You see, you have to know the full story; you have to see the whole picture, before you can judge.'

'You mean...? Sullivan has the full story and is willing to tell you?' she asked.

'Yes,' I said, putting her hand back on where it had been. 'The only trouble is; he's also gone missing.'

I'd moved my hand further up her thigh and now we both appeared on the same menu. So we left the conversation there and carried on with the coupling thing that people do, and that the readers' of certain types of books don't need to know.

The fox strolled in that evening from his surveillance position on the front porch, nestled against my leg and ate a big piece of hamburger steak that I defrosted and semi-cooked at the same time. Like his mother before him he loved the stuff. He ignored Andi as he had the first time, was polite but never went forward for a pat or a cuddle. I put it down to her being a threat to our relationship, or she was a bit frightened of him still. Foxes know these things.

It was in the evening, after Andi had made another fine meal using what rubbish I had in the fridge and the pantry, and we were settling in for the night with the superb offerings of the BBC and ITV, that we heard voices outside, and Lupus, back sleeping on the porch again began that throaty, stuttering sound called Gekkering.

'I'll shoot the bastard,' I heard the blubbering voice I recognized as my next-door neighbour from the farm just over the hill. I was out of the door in an instant, and took in the situation immediately.

Morris stood halfway along my path with a side-by-side pointing at the fox, which was on the porch with his teeth showing and his whole body quivering in the Gekkering manner

'Lower that gun or eat it,' I stepped down from the porch and placed myself between Lupus and the twin barrels of the shotgun.

'That bloody thing has been at my chickens,' Morris was a big blustery man, noted in the area for being short on temper and civility.

'No, he hasn't,' I snapped back. Morris had that habit of making people do that; snap back at him. 'He's been here with me all evening, and besides, he likes red meat and isn't too partial to chickens. He certainly wouldn't go after your skinny things.'

'Something big ripped open my chicken wire and killed the whole bloody lot.'

'I agree it had to be something big to do that,' I'd lowered my voice now, and he should have read the warning there. 'Something about the size of your bloody Dobermans perhaps, so why not take them over to the vet and get their stomach contents checked out, and I'll bet he'll find some chicken meat in there.'

'I don't need to be looking any further than that bloody fox of yourn. Taint' natural to keep one of them filthy things as a pet.'

'I'm getting pretty bloody fed up telling people he isn't a pet. He's his own master and just happens to like it here, now piss off Morris, you Devonshire twit, before I do something rude with that shotgun of yours.'

'I should listen to him, Mr. Morris,' the man with him said. 'He looks like he's losing it; such a shame for a gentle-looking man, now.'

I looked at Morris's companion for the first time. It was Signore Patrick Sullivan, no less.

'Ah, padre,' I gave him a mock-glare. 'Terrible company you're keeping these days.'

'Now then, Harry. This good gentleman offered to show me where you lived when I got out of the taxi at his place. Sure and I didn't know he was planning to shoot you, now.'

'I wasn't goin' to shoot anyone, Father,' Morris declared vehemently. 'Only that savage beast over there.'

'Savage beast?' I couldn't help laughing.   'There's only one savage bloody beast around here, Morris, and that's you. Thanks for telling me you wouldn't use it on a human, though unfortunately I have no such compunctions. That's if we class you as a human, of course.'

On my last word I moved two fast steps across the yard and snatched the side-by-side from my farming neighbour, bless him. As he reached to take it back I stepped away and shook a finger in his face. 'No, Morris, don't be silly now.'

'Harry, what are you doing out there?' came Andi's dulcet Bostonian tones from the doorway of my mansion. 'Patrick? Is that really you? Oh, come inside and leave the boys to play out there.'

Which made me turn towards her, and which left Morris feeling brave enough to try and strike me. In this he partially succeeded, but I turned into the blow and it struck harmlessly on my shoulder. I hit him in his protruding gut with the stock of his own shotgun and couldn't resist a left hook while he was doubled up in front of me. Well, I ask you...

I broke open the gun and ejected both shells, which I picked up and threw away into the brush on the other side of the lane. I checked his pockets but he had no more shells. I was tempted to break his damn gun against the trunk of a tree but destroying a man's gun could lead to him getting very pissed off and doing something stupid. I had a rain barrel, part of my attempt to look out for the environment, and there was an old saucepan hanging on a hook above it. I took it down, dipped it in the barrel and poured the cold water over the sleeping Morris's head.

He responded admirably, trying to spring to his feet and only succeeding in tripping over himself and falling backwards again. This time I helped him up and handed him his side-by-side shotgun, minus the shells.

'Take it and go, Morris,' I put on my hard man voice, a mixture of Scouse and pure nastiness. 'Come round here again with a weapon and you'll be eating your dinner through a straw for a long time. And take my advice and check those fucking dogs out before they savage something else.'

He took the shotgun and wandered off, muttering something to himself that fortunately I couldn't catch.

I followed Andi and the good Father into the house, Lupus subsiding back on the porch with a disappointed noise. I ruffled his ears and made a sympathetic sound but he was still pissed off about me getting a couple of whacks in and he didn't even get a small bite.

'Would probably have given you food poisoning, pal,' I said, but I don't think he was pacified.

Inside, I took a seat at the kitchen table and smiled somewhat bleakly at the priest. "I take it we can call off the nation-wide search for you now, padre? You seem to have been found again.'

Patrick Sullivan pulled a bottle of Tullamore Dew from his coat pocket. 'I brought a little something to apologize for me little disappearing act the other night, me boy, and leaving you to drop the black stuff all alone. Lass, would you fetch a couple of glasses, there.'

She brought over three and placed them all in front of the little priest. When he raised an eyebrow she made a noise not unlike the Gekkering sound of the fox.

'Is it too good for a woman then, Patrick, or are you trying your chauvinistic side again, because you know it doesn't work.'

'And isn't that the truth of it,' he grinned, and poured equal measures into the three glasses.

We drank each other's health slowly, savouring the strong peaty-tasting liquid.

'The reason I took off was due to a piece of information I received from one of our many spies out there. Unlike Milos, I DO work for the Vatican, and answer only to the Holy Father himself. As I told you the other night, Harry, the Vatican is not exactly riddled with the followers of Satan, but there are enough of them for people like myself to take precautions.'

'Just exactly WHO are people like you, Patrick?' I asked.

'We are on the side of God, my friend, and that's all you need to know at this stage,' he ran the bottle around our glasses again. 'I found out that Milos dropped out of sight shortly after gaining hold of the Diabolus. The instrument is also gone, disappeared along with Milos.'

'Patrick,' I stared at the little priest. 'We need to know about Milos. What was his purpose for the violin?'

He took a neat slug of his whiskey, while I ran water into a small jug for Andi and myself. 'His purpose? We believe he was one of an unholy group who has been waiting since the death of Christ to overturn the events that his death brought about. Some of them are pure evil, and want to call up the Devil or one of his disciples for their own gain, and their desire to join him in his blasphemous purposes on earth. Others, through misguided reasons, think that by calling up the unholy one, they can take a short cut to salvation, and their only wish is to join Satan on that path.'

'Hmm,' I mused. 'There are times when you wished you'd never asked the question, isn't there?'

Sullivan smiled. 'Yes, and I know you don't believe any of the answers just now, but you will, my son, you will. Anyway, I believe I know where the Diabolus is resting at the moment.'

'And where might that be?' Andi asked, taking a dainty sip of her drink.

'Up a great mountain in the French Alps, and hidden inside a virtual fortress of a Chateau, and guarded by ex-members of one of the finest Special Forces in the world. Spetznast.'

'Oh, there's nothing too difficult about it then?' I said with heavy sarcasm, which was apparently wasted on the priest.

'Not to someone with your special skills and qualities,' he beamed at me, and I got the feeling the sarcasm was now on a two-way flow.

We spent the next two hours poring over fine detailed maps of the area; maps which Patrick had just happened to bring with him. The pockets of his black raincoat were like the Tardis in Dr Who; they seemed to be filled within.

By the time we were done, my task was quite simple.

I was to travel to the area of the Chateau and explore the area around, and especially the architecture of the building itself; the Chateau Revanche, the Frenchman's folly built near the edge of the smaller massif of the Alps. To outfit myself with everything I needed for the ascent, and to work out a plan to enter the Chateau, steal a priceless violin, and extricate myself with it; oh, and both of us intact, to say the least.

CHAPTER ELEVEN

"Thou shalt not make unto thee any graven image, or any likeness of any thing that is in heaven above, or that is in the earth beneath, or that is in the water under the earth: Thou shalt not bow down thyself to them, nor serve them: for I the LORD they GOD am a jealous God..."

Exodus 20:4, 5 – King James Bible.

Three days later I was in Provence in Southern France, with Andrea Scolari as my assistant, accomplice or whatever. Here the landscape was marked by a low mountain range of limestone or schistous rock, all running from east to west parallel to the coast – the Alpilles, the Luberon, the Mont Sainte-Victoire, and the massifs of La Sainte-Baume, the Maures and the Esterel. Their white or red jagged crests, their lonely heights and deep forests, helped to give this province its epic quality. Each held some special place in its history, whether as a centre of early Christian legend or as a refuge for invaders, bandits or heretics. These were massifs redolent of mystery and magic.

At least, that was the way the guidebook described it as we pored through it while we ate sandwiches and drank coffee from a flask.

The Alpilles run for some 20 miles between the Rhone near Arles and the Durance valley. They never rise above 1,200 feet, yet their barren white crags give them the aspect of real mountains in miniature – the name itself meaning "little Alps". Long popular with rock climbers, it was here that Alphonse Daudet's comic book character Tartarin de Tarascon did his training as a mountaineer. Above all, the Alphilles have long exerted a fascination on writers and artists alike. Daudet would gaze at them philosophically from his mill in the valley below and Van Gogh when he lived at Arles painted them often, intrigued by their beautiful changing hues in the varying Provencal light.

Physically manifesting my disinterest by tossing the guide to one side, I returned my gaze to the piece of rock in front of us.

Here lay my interest in the Alphilles, a narrow section of climb consisting of rock earth and grass, with no apparent reason for ascending such a treacherous route. Thanks to the photos and hand-made maps presented to me by Signore Patrick Sullivan, I now knew better. Andi and I had spent the better part of the day wandering backwards and forwards across the rocky escarpment below, under the erstwhile pretence of bird watching. Surprising, as it might have seemed, my best route was the one before me, though I had the added advantage of the plans and photos. Some five hundred yards in from the cliff-edge lay the huge stone edifice known as Château Revanche. The area was alarmed and well patrolled by men and dogs, leaving the cliff the least expected as a means of penetration.

Which still did not make it any easier.

As I continued to look at the cliff face I now held a Baedeker's of the area, and a climbers' guide of the routes. The author had stressed that the immediate cliff below the Château Revanche was now registered as private property, but it was written with the irreverence that most climbing adventurers regarded any piece of climbable cliff that someone had dared to stress they were forbidden to use.

We'd taken the ferry across to Le Havre and rented a roomy Peugeot hatchback. On the drive down we stopped in the main town of the area, where I'd found several sports shops that specialized in climbing equipment. I bought from several of these, for by the selection of gear I had chosen it was obvious I was no novice climber, and to completely re-equip myself from scratch would have appeared suspicious.

We dumped it all in the boot of the Peugeot. A large rucksack, which I still called a Bergen, big enough to hold all the equipment and ropes I needed. A hammer and a small assortment of pitons in case I got into trouble and needed to rest or abseil down to find an alternative route. Nuts or chocks as they were once called, or friends and quad-cams in the language of the new breed of climbers. I had one of the latest descendeurs, essential for a quick getaway, and had chosen a light pair of comfortable mountain-climbing boots. I already had an earth axe that I'd made from a cut-down ice axe, with a moveable lanyard attached to the 12in handle. I'd need this in some of the middle parts and at the top of what I told Andi was called a Mixed Cliff. Mostly it is sea cliffs that are composed, not of firm rock, but a mixture of loose rock, steep earth and steep grass. For some reason best known to geologists, this part of the cliff had adopted these composites at various stages. So I'd also brought with me a light, broad-bladed earth knife.

Several ropes and some basic survival gear had completed the purchases. I would also be wearing a small pot-holing light on a headband. My final item I'd brought with me from England. This was a small ring with five loose arms, each with two broad blades. It was called a grip fast and I though it might just come in handy, which was to prove another one of my many under-statements.

219

Rooting in my pack I held up a small but powerful set of binoculars to my eyes. They looked innocuous enough but were in fact a pair of Bushnell 8 x 30s with a built-in digital camera. There were two buttons indented on the top between the lenses and I pressed the Mode on the right, turning the camera on. They were the latest toys for bird-watchers, for what you saw through the lens you could photograph at that size.

After that I traced a route up the 200 foot face; surprised at how easy most of it seemed. There were several places that could be considered crux moves, which thereby made the individual climbs into harder grades, and I clicked away on the left button taking pictures at the same high resolution as they appeared through the lenses. I was particularly interested in the long curved chimney, my own personal favourite.

I did not have to remind myself that I was not there for the sheer thrill of the climb, nor did I have to prove anything to anyone. Shit, I was nearly 49 years of age, wasn't I? The sole aim was to get up the bloody cliff; leave ropes for the descent, grab the priceless violin and get the hell out.

Easy enough, surely?

Yeah, right, I muttered to myself. One thing made it slightly more complicated, and that was the fact it would have to be a night climb. I'd done many night climbs of course, but that was during my time in the marines, and a few dozen years ago.

We returned to the car and drove away from the cliff, stopping at a small village on a hill. I parked the car, with the prominent GB sticker despite it being left-hand drive, in the central square and we sat down at an outdoor table at a nearby café. We ordered espresso and cognac and stayed there for a while with stupid tourist grins on our faces.

We were staying at a gite just outside the village, which we'd chosen from an illustrated brochure in a travel agent's office in Exeter. I liked the almost hidden drive, the sheltered converted grange, or barn, accommodation, and the fact that the owners lived in a larger house nearby on the grounds but still gave our apartment the privacy we sought. It was one of six; all within the barn conversion but each with its own separate entrance and secluded patio. There was a heated indoor pool with a small gym attached.

I was well pleased, and although we had to go through the routine of meeting the owners, who were English, to obtain the key, including a welcoming cup of coffee as an excuse for them to explain the house rules in detail, we accepted it all with good grace.

The Tomlinson's had taken early retirement. 'Made redundant, actually,' Frank Tomlinson admitted ruefully. 'Had a house in Evesham for thirty years and couldn't believe what we got for it, so we came here and bought all of this. Put a lot of work in, mind you, but it seems to be paying off now.'

Andi and I nodded dutifully, commenting appropriately on how wonderful it all was, mainly speaking the truth, and managed to get in a few low-key questions of our own.

'The Château? Well, we don't actually know the owners, do we, love?' Tomlinson shrugged at his wife. 'Heard some strange stories, but around here gossip is the order of the day. Even the maire hasn't had an invitation up there, and that IS unusual. They've even got gate guards, would you believe? Supposed to be some old member of the French aristocracy, so maybe he's got something old that's worth guarding, eh?'

Oh, you'd be right there, I thought. I hope you'll never know how much.

The next night, my reconnaissance completed, I was ready to go. Our bill was paid until the end of the week and our gear packed away in the rented car.

The night was moonless and still; ideal for my purposes. I wore the potholing light but would use it only for emergencies. I'd bound padding around the head of the hammer and the pitons were bound together with thin strips of masking tape. I'd worn the climbing boots continuously since the day I'd bought them, first immersing them in water while they were on my feet, walking around until they dried out a bit and formed themselves around the contours of both feet. Now they were like a second skin.

The plan was that Andi would see me start the climb then go back to the car and start a countdown. We reckoned on two hours if all went well. Then she would come up to the start again and help me carry the gear back to the car, for hopefully I would also be carrying a wooden violin case.

Once again.

I began the climb on loose rock, bending forward for balance, though not too much. The next pitch was earth, obviously some of the cliff head that had peeled away and collapsed years before. Here I was glad I'd worn the hardy mountain boots which I used to dig in through the grassy tufts and form steps as I swung the axe in deeply and thrust the earth-knife in as far as it could go. I paused as I made it to the next pitch of solid granite rising straight up. I threw a large tape over a projection that appeared to have been there for centuries. This I attached to myself with another tape around my chest, clipped together with a karabiner, and lay back with hands folded across my chest, probably looking like a corpse at peace with the world.

I was still only half way up the face, so the rest period was a short-lived event. The next pitch was the granite rock I was belayed onto, and I made short work of this. My brain took most of the effort; continually bringing back the lessons of the past. The nine principles of climbing I conveniently remembered by the pneumonic CASHWORTH.

Conserve energy, always test holds, stand upright, hands low, watch your feet, on three points, rhythmic movement, and think first with heels down. Rules that had saved my life more than once, and rules that had made me a good climber; but more importantly, a safe climber.

I reached with my hand and it seemed to disappear into the cliff before me. I flicked on the small light on my head. The thin beam showed that I had now gained the chimney.

Switching the light off, I disappeared into the chimney. By my calculation it ran for about thirty-five meters, wide at the bottom and narrowing after the first ten, and this I could climb easily by bridging, bracing my back against one wall and my feet against the other. Before that, however, I had to get up there. The left-hand wall seemed to be the more moderate and I started straight away. It sloped outwards at the start and I had to find secure grips for my hands, rather than holds, for at more than one time I had to swing my feet over to a more convenient spot.

By the time I'd gained the narrow part of the chimney and begun the arduous but less skilful task of bridging, the moon had decided to show some light on the scene, which I wasn't too worried about, given that I was well hidden inside the rock, both from above AND below.

Thinking of the climbing principles again also brought me to the present place in my life. My hands, instead of feeling for a hold on the solid rock now grasped a bunch of dew-laden vegetation, telling me I was now on the last pitch – the grass slope at the top. Feeding a small chock into the short vertical crack to my right, I hooked a tape through it and passed the tape over my head and under my arms. I rolled over onto my back and jammed a wired nut into another horizontal crack with a small stubai attached. This I used to thread the tape around my chest into, and closed up the screw. Lying with my back to the cliff I let out an exaggerated sigh and allowed my legs to dangle as I pulled a flask from one side of the rucksack and poured a coffee. It was not such a cold night that I needed it but it gave a semblance of normality as I hung downwards from a cliff about 140feet from the ground and some 30feet from the top, to be sipping on hot coffee as I waited to take on some unknown forces guarding an evil item. I ate a bar of chocolate, aware that I had to top up with carbohydrates, for the night had only just begun.

Replacing the flask in the Bergen I turned back to the cliff. Here I would have no protection, only my own skill in using the axe and the earth-knife in perfect co-ordination, while digging my toes in at the same moment. At times, those same times when my boots slipped back slightly, I wished I'd worn long-bladed crampons, though on reflection I knew they would have been in the way for most of the climb and continuously stopping and belaying while I put them on and took them off would have been time-consuming.

At last I could see the lighter sky appear ahead of me above the pitch black of the cliff head, and moving closer to the edge I cautiously raised my head above the curved grass.

At first I saw nothing, then some movement off to my left. As the shape became smaller I realized my luck had been in, for the patrolling guard had recently passed my present location, and if the man had a dog with him it would all have been over by now.

I pulled myself over the top and moved cautiously from left to right, taking in the immediate area of the cliff head. There were no rocks or projections of any kind within easy access of the edge and I gave myself a mental pat on the back for having the foresight to bring along the small grip-fast.

I chose a place a few yards from the cliff edge and took out the earth-knife. After carving a straight-sided horseshoe into the grass, I carefully lifted the sod back from its open side facing the cliff. I then took out the grip-fast and spread out the grapples in a fan shape, pressing each one down firmly into the hard earth. I brought my full weight to bear by standing each foot above the inverted points and using my knees to give pressure. Satisfied at last I pulled the sod back on top of the grip-fast, after first threading the long climbing rope through the ring. This went under the front of the grass sod, and when the rope was pulled from below the grip-fast would be hidden until only a close daylight search would reveal it.

I took off all of my loose, and now unnecessary, equipment and stowed it all in the rucksack. This I then tied onto a double hitch on the rope and dangled over the cliff. I was now ready for a solitary assault on the Château, less than 500 yards ahead of me with its uncompromising stark outline etched against the bleak sky in front of me.

I was soon standing beneath the high wall running around the Château. The plans of the place were fresh in my mind, as so they should be for I had been studying them all afternoon in the accommodation. My choices at this stage were limited; I could walk around the outside of the wall and hope to find some way of gaining access other than the main gate, which was well manned. Of course that way was a good chance of coming across one of the mobile foot patrols. The alternative depended very much on what my hands were feeling for now across the face of the wall.

Mortar or the lack of it, and from my initial touch I reckoned I was in luck, for although it was a well-built structure, the passing years and sea-winds had eaten away at the binding materials. There was enough depth in most of them for hands and boots. In my book to hesitate was to be doomed to failure, or to give it up and look for a better plan. There was no better plan so I proceeded to climb.

At first it was not so bad. I no longer had the burden of the rucksack, only the Steyr with its suppressor connected, and now nestling in the small of my back. Then it became apparent as I climbed that renovation work had taken place recently. The earth knife still hung at my side and I used it now to scrape away the mortar, thankful while I was doing so for the poor workmanship of the builder, who had saved well on his mixture; it was about six to one in my humble opinion. I was within feet of the top when I sensed rather that saw a figure coming towards my present position.

All I could do was hold on with both hands and trust to the rigidity of the boot toes. I thought at first the man was alone, and then saw the dark figure running in from the side. It was large, either an Alsatian or Doberman, as it was too dark to tell which. At last they passed by slowly, too slowly for me, whose arms felt like they were about to leave my body. I gained the top and lay outstretched for long moments, listening intently for noise from below as well as getting the feeling back in my arms. At last, satisfied, I hung down the other side and dropped, landing lightly on mown grass.

I ran across the lawn to the back of the building. I'd been dreading the event of a well-lighted building from surrounding searchlights tucked into the shrubs. Remembering the plans of the building and the route to the vaults, I passed under an arch and felt for the huge padlock securing an iron gate to the depths below.

In a previous time the Château Revanche had passed through many stages. Originally built as a fifteenth-century keep flanked by four towers it was owned by a family of furriers, escaping destruction during the Wars of Religion, and surviving a 200-year old vendetta with a rival family whose chateau was only a stone's throw away. This château, like many of its kind in the French countryside, was now only a neglected hummock of overgrown rubble. The word château covers the prototype feudal château-fort – the English castle – as well as the "open" unfortified country house or stately home that came in with the Renaissance. Revanche had begun life as the former, then in the early nineteenth century ruined medieval castles came back into fashion with the Romantics and it was transformed into a gleaming Hans Anderson edifice.

However, according to what I had learned about the more recent history of the place, the present mysterious owner had largely turned it back into its medieval past. Apparently its huge vaults had withstood the relentless changes in both its usage and appearance, and somehow Sullivan knew, or suspected, that the Stradivari was ensconced down there, but for what purpose he had not revealed.

The owner of the Château was a Count, allegedly.

A poor attempt on my part to learn more about the Compte Revanche had fallen on stony ground. Either none of the locals knew much about him – or they knew a lot. I believed his history went back a long time but was unable to establish it as such by finding out facts. The best I could do was finding that he was a solitary figure who had been the owner of the Château and its domains for many years, as his father before him, his granpere, and back through the portals of time.

The padlock was so easy I almost felt sorry for the guards who were going to be blamed the next day. Spetznast on guard - I didn't think so. I closed the gate behind me, setting the padlock but not locking it. Now I switched on the caving headlamp, the thin beam piercing the stygian blackness of the tomblike vault. Occasionally I would hold up a detailed plan of the vaults and check the route.

At last I emerged into a big high-ceilinged vault, and stepped back at first when my light caught the stage at the far end of the hall. It was a giant statue of a seated horned entity, eyes like twin fires and holding a thick book on its red-clothed lap. In the middle of the floor a pentacle had been drawn, or was it a pentagram. I could never remember which was which. Other items of sinister appearance and diabolical implication were displayed around the huge place, though I had little idea of what they could be used for.

At first I thought that the statue had been the centrepiece of the vault, but now I saw that there was another display on the long wall to my left. This consisted of a single glass case; its wooden frame painted or varnished pitch black. About three feet up from the floor a red curtain ran around the case. The inside was done out in red silk, and on it I assumed would have been the resting place of a certain black violin.

It was gone of course, that much I could tell at a glance but there was more. Although my terpsichorean knowledge was only very recent, I'd actually held the Diabolus in my hands once before, and could somehow tell again that I was in the presence of...something. A work of genius, perhaps, and although it was no longer there I felt it. I really did. A person of no conviction, no religious beliefs even, yet as I stared at the place it had once rested, once more my thoughts returned to that first time I'd stood before it in the catacombs, and the conclusion was the same...could this be the work of any human hands?

Unless those same hands possessed a gift which was only borrowed for their short time on this earth; and there was something else present, something I was not sure of but which I could feel. I shook off that feeling and turned to more important matters. My basic upbringing and that part of my life that I had given up to thieving, told me that you never left with nothing. Not the best philosophy in the world but at least credit me with some survival instincts.

I looked around the room and for the first time I saw something in another alcove across the room, and knew that my original feeling was for real. Somehow, and from somewhere, I suddenly knew things, or felt them.

I really did.

I moved across the room and there was a glass case embedded in the rock, and inside I gazed at a white glistening object. It was a human skull, and bore the marks of antiquity upon it, though how I knew its age I had no idea. I stared at it in a fascinated way, and had to engage in some strange mind plays to draw my attention away. From violins to skulls; something strange was certainly going on, but what? For one of the few times in my life I had little clue as to what to do next.

I delved into one of my belt fixtures and the set of lock-picks I'd brought with me opened the little brass lock that guarded the skull. I placed it in the haversack and slipped it over my neck, locating it on my back above the Steyr, which I now held in my right hand. As I turned to make my departure from the unholy place, my eyes took in the mass of signs and symbols showing high on the wall above the case I'd just looted.

The signs were executed in bright colors for the most part, but I could make no sense out of any of it; a red setting sun was an eye, then a green snake twisting around its own body, followed by the first sign again. A green and yellow bird came next, then an oblong. After that it was simply a maze of pictures and symbols, which meant absolutely nothing to me, yet it had to make sense to someone. I took out the Bushnell 8 x 30s, focused on the bright display and took several shots.

I stowed everything away and made it back to the iron-gate in a fraction of the time it had taken me to get to the great vault.

I closed the gate slowly, careful not to make a noise, and relocked the padlock. Then I turned and collected a powerful fist in the face. At the last moment of turning I had sensed the blow coming and the only thing to do was ride backwards with it. Even so it staggered me, but if the man on the other end of the fist had thought a punch on the nose would stop his opponent or even make him blink, he was mistaken. I'd had my nose broken on a regular basis when I was younger, whether in the ring or in the pub and it was now just so much pulpy flesh on my face.

Recovering quickly I lashed out with rights and lefts, driving the man back with no technical skills whatsoever.

'Ah, a toughie eh?' The man's Scots brogue surprised me for a moment, before I realized there was now a mercenary force out there following decades of Gulf Wars, Afghanistan's, Iraq's and the rest that had sprung up since my own experiences in Northern Ireland and the Falklands, not to mention my brothers' times in Cyprus, Borneo, and Aden, as well as Northern Ireland. As long as the job paid well, these boys were not too picky who the paymasters were. A point on which my brothers and I differed against the rest of the arseholes who had no morals.

Again, so much for an elite Spetznast group holding forth; when all I came up against was some Glaswegian hard man from the Argyll's or some such regiment.

I kept my mouth shut, aware there was no point in giving these people even the tiniest clue to my identity.

Instead I manoeuvred around so I had what little light from the sky behind me. I suddenly squatted and swept a leg out, catching the other man on his forward ankle and dropping him to the floor. Up, forward and a foot in the jaw put the man out but I could only wonder for how long. I'd come prepared and took a couple of plastic ties from my jacket. I pulled the man's ski mask off and pushed it in his mouth, securing it with the camouflage scarf he had around his neck. I used one tie to secure the man's hands and the other around his ankles and through the gate.

I went up a tree and found a couple of branches at the right height to get me up level with the top of the wall and leapt across. Another black mark against the Chateau's security I thought gratefully as I listened for any patrols, then hung down on the outside and dropped to the ground. I was up and sprinting immediately and soon gained the edge of the cliff. Looking back I lined up two of the keeps as I had done for markers on the way in, and felt around for the hidden gripfast. It took longer than I thought but that also said good things for the location of it. I pulled up the rucksack, and after unzipping the extension, transferred the haversack into it. I secured it tightly on my back, threaded the double rope through the descendeur around my waist and went over the cliff.

It was practically a rundown until the rock, then a straight drop, over the earth pitch and down on the rocks again. I unclipped and pulled on one side of the rope, careful not to start a small avalanche of scree and rubbish from above. The rope snaked down and I coiled and tied it quickly, throwing it over the top of the rucksack and looked around.

She'd moved up alongside me without my noticing, so busy was I with the gear.

'Are you okay, Harry,' I heard her anxious voice and gave her a quick hug. She handed me a hand torch.

'Went as though it was planned, darling,' I intoned into the darkness. 'Except the bloody thing wasn't there any more, but it had been. You take the rope and some of this extra stuff, eh?'

I switched on the headlamp and by its feeble light was able to pick my way further down the terrain until I found the narrow hunting track we'd come out on, not wanting to risk the heavy beam of the torch just yet. Every few hundred yards was a yellow notice with the red letters CHASSE written on, and I occasionally shone the narrow beam of on one to confirm our position, for I'd taken the trouble to mark them the previous day.

At last I turned downhill again and struck off across country to the tourist car park where we'd left the rental car. I congratulated Andi on finding her way back up to the cliff, then slung the rope in the boot, placed the rucksack carefully to one side, and changed my boots for comfortable loafers. The small overnight bags we'd brought over on the ferry were tucked tightly to either side of the Bergen.

Five minutes after arriving at the car we were off, making for the build-up of lights we could see down the hill.

I figured that once the alert was sounded they had little chance of finding us. They could only patrol the roads leading out of the area, check the many small airports in the vicinity, the boats on the coast, and the route into Italy. They could report the attempted theft to the authorities but somehow I doubted it. 'Pardon, M'sieur inspector, but we have had a skull with satanic implications stolen from a vault in the Château where we regularly hold Black Mass.'

Hardly.

No, unless they knew the exact car I was driving, or the route we were taking, they were stuffed. By first light we'd dropped down into Marseilles and ate breakfast near the old port. Now dressed in a white open-necked shirt with fawn slacks and brown casuals, with Andi in a light summer dress, we fit the picture as tourists; or even a couple of locals taking their leisure before a day's promenading around Marseilles. By midday we were on the coastal motorway having left Nice and Monaco behind and crossed into Italy at Menton. We stopped for lunch at a small tratorria in San Remo, and I noticed some students on motorbikes and small American flags on the packs tied on the back. Close enough to hear their talk of looking forward to climbing soon; I exchanged some conversation with them. I'd transferred all of the climbing gear now, including my boots, into the haversack.

After I'd paid the check, I took the haversack and the long rope from the car boot and presented them to the delighted students.

'Just had an unfortunate phone call from home,' I told them sadly. 'And my wife and I have to grab a plane in Torino and need to travel light, so if you guys can use any of this, you're welcome.'

Of course they could, and were suitably grateful, and I left with their thanks ringing in my ears. Perhaps they'd even sell it all when they got close to climbing country but that was okay; at least I'd got rid of it.

I left the car in Savonna, paid the extra for the rental having to be taken back to Le Havre, and caught the train to Torino. That night we flew back to London.

Andi was entertaining me during the drive back to the West Country from London later that night, aware by my mood that I was still seething over the disappearance of the violin.

Unfortunately she didn't do jokes, or even sing. What she did do was explain religious things. No doubt to a class of budding theology students she'd go down a treat, but it was all getting a bit wasted on me.

'The fish was the favourite Christian symbol, being extremely symbolic,' she was saying. 'The biblical and pagan cultural background was again important in the development of the symbol, and the New Testament abounds with references to fish. Christ told his disciples he would make them fishers of men, in the Gospels of Mathew.'

I mumbled something to be polite but don't remember what I said, and groaned inwardly when I realized it had only encouraged her.

'The most important point regarding the symbol of the fish is that in Greek the word fish was written as ICHTHYS. There are many misconceptions that the Christian used the word fish as a secret code or password. That's false, of course, and demonstrates a lack of history.

'The word fish was not a secret code, but rather formed an acrostic, which was a typical classical style of poetry by which the letters of a word were ordered to form a phrase, or vice versa. In this case we can vertically read the Greek word for fish.'

To my astonishment she was actually writing down this acrostic on a small pad she took from her purse, switched on the inside light and held it up in front of me.

I esus

CH ristos

TH eou

Y ios

S oter

Iesus = Jesus

CHristos = Christ

THeou = of God

Yios = Son

Soter = Saviour

I saw enough of it to know it made sense, but so did keeping my eyes on the road, which wasn't too easy with a notepad held up in front of them.

'Taken as an acrostic,' to my relief she put the pad back in her handbag, 'the Greek word for fish acquired a very profound meaning for the Christian. The phrase read: Jesus Christ, Son of God and the Saviour. It was the primitive credo, the fundamental article of faith because it synthesized the theological essence the true follower of Christ was called to profess.'

'Wow,' I gushed. 'That is SO interesting, but just for the time being I think I've had enough of this religious stuff. How about telling me what you have in mind to do to me when we get home?'

What she said wasn't exactly what I had in mind, but at least it was a change.

On reflection, and if I'd possessed the gift of foresight, I would have had her repeat everything she'd said about the "religious stuff".'

Unfortunately I didn't.

CHAPTER TWELVE

"It requires ingenious interpolation to derive from the simple statement "On this rock I will build my church", a Petrine office, apostolic succession, papal infallibility, and all the pomp, ceremony, and power surrounding the Pope today."

"...it required (great) skill to take statements made by a poor Carpenter to an equally poor fisherman and apply them to a regal pontiff who was soon to be called Lord of the World."

Statements taken from anti-Pope sources

'I've told you that already,' I said in a monotone to match the priest's. 'We'll meet at 10:00am tomorrow morning at the top of Devil's Tor; that should satisfy your spiritual leanings about the fallen angel, Padre.'

'But Harry, I don't understand? Do you not trust me anymore, lad?'

I thought I heard disappointment in his voice and relented somewhat as I replied. 'It's not you I don't trust, Patrick. I wouldn't put it past these people to put a task force together and attack this place. I've already told you that they have an army of mercenaries working for them, and God knows how many of them pick up a pay packet from that Chateau. At least on the Moor we have a chance, and like I told you I don't have the violin but something else that this mysterious Count might covert.'.'

I heard him sigh loudly. 'Well, I cannot say you're not right, Harry. Where is this "Devil's Tor", I'm intrigued as it has a certain ironic ring to it?'

'Dartmoor,' was my terse reply and I rang off.

I was in place at the top of the tor before first light, a small backpack with a flask and a pile of sandwiches, wedged in one of the smaller caves that had been formed by the lumps of granite that had remained on the tops of the tors from many centuries before. I had free mobility and all-around visibility. I'd even packed a couple of Ginsters' Pies, for there was no reason to be uncomfortable in the bush had been the old adage when I was in the mob.

Devil's Tor is one of the highest points on Dartmoor, which isn't saying much when you think that it is probably the bleakest place in the British Isles. We were already well into October and the weather was cold and the smell of rain was in the air. The whole of Dartmoor is the stamping ground for Royal Marines and it is here that they train for the agonizing Commando Course. I knew most of it like the shape of the face I shaved most mornings, and knew how inhospitable it could be at this time of the year. It could be a sunny morning then storm clouds would gather and sleet and hail come in. Even in the height of summer tourists would go out walking with very little gear and be caught out in a sudden downpour.

I watched the sun rise above Dartmoor, as I'd seen the sun rise above other deserts, and there were similarities here, mainly that sight of Dartmoor in the early morning that chills the blood – its lack of humanity. I remembered things, as I've already said, and can often recite whole stanzas of poetry.

Now as the sun moved across the heavens, shedding a cold light on the bleakness below, I remembered one of my mother's favourite travel writers almost without fault; H.V.Morton once wrote, "Here are no cosy acres, but miles that have not known the plough; miles that have never given food or shelter to man, woman or child, miles that are as remote from humanity as the craters of the moon; that seem to say, 'I care not for man whether he lives or dies, and though you try to the end of time you shall not tame me.' The cruelty of desert and ocean is on Dartmoor..."

It seemed a good place to see if there was going to be more of the Devil's instrument story than a simple handing over of the said piece. I used the Bushnell's to peer around the bare landscape leading up to the tor. Yes, a good place to do business – or die if you had to. I thought I saw something shine to the south, where the roads came together and there were oases of green dotted around. Good cover, but far enough away from my possy not to be concerned at any imminent danger.

It was early for many people to be about, especially the tourists, and besides this was not the season, but country folk have a habit of being about at any hour.

At nine-thirty I saw the priest begin his climb. I ignored him during the long slow climb, though I reluctantly admired the man's steadily persistent stride up to the top of the Devil's Tor. Instead I used the binoculars to focus on the area around the tor. I viewed from the back, the west and the east, as well as from the front where the man with the dog collar was gaining altitude.

By the time Patrick Sullivan had gained the top of the tor, gazing around for the man he was supposed to meet, I was reasonably satisfied that we were the only two on Devil's Tor, at that particular hour.

'Coffee?' I appeared in the doorway of the rock niche, attempting to be civil yet feeling more uptight than perhaps I should have been. After all, it was the big fat priest who I'd been suspicious of taking my son, but that had fallen flat, so now what was I thinking? That the little priest had something to do with it now? I really was getting paranoid in my old age.

'Please,' Patrick inclined his head and entered my little possy.

I poured coffee into the flasks second, smaller cup and handed it across.

'Sandwich?'

The priest smiled and nodded again.

We sat and ate our sandwiches and drank our coffee, for the entire world like two old friends who had tramped up Devil's Tor to take in the view and enjoy the exercise.

'So, what happens now, Patrick?' I asked. 'Like I told you on the phone, the item was gone when I got there, though you only have my word for that.'

'Oh, I trust you well enough, lad.' He finished eating and threw the crusts outside for the birds, then turned to face me. 'You mentioned something about another object that you thought might be a consolation prize?'

I nodded and told him the whole story about my mission to the Château. His face took on a neutral aspect when I mentioned the skull.

'I think after all your hard work,' he said, 'stealing the Diabolus then going after it again, and instead taking an alternative on impulse, you deserve an explanation about all this.'

I said nothing, merely topped up his coffee cup.

'Zoltan Milos WAS a Signore and he DID work in the Vatican. We believed that he had turned to Satan some time ago, but it took many years to prove it. I am part of a small group of priests of higher authority, who work directly for the Holy Father, answering only to him. I use the word "priest" to include anyone up to the Pope who has taken holy orders, Harry. Our task, our mission, is to ferret out those priests and civilians who we believe are in league with the Devil. This does not stop at the Vatican gates, for we are in pursuance of these people all over the world.'

He paused and sipped his coffee. I took the opportunity to scan the binoculars around the compass points from the tor. I could see no one, and nothing appeared out of place.

'So, Patrick,' I did not intend to get into a discussion about Satan dwelling in my father's mansion or any of that nonsense, so went the easier path. 'What's the real story behind this violin? After the little bit of research I've done on the Strad instruments I'd be very ready to believe that the black one they call the Diabolus was definitely done by the master himself, Stradivari. I understand that a long time ago it was taken into the Vatican for protection against it being used for evil. Why then wasn't it destroyed when they had the chance?'

I thought it a fairly reasonable question and was expecting a fairly reasonable answer, but with the little priest involved, reasonable did not come into it.

He sighed long and hard, and I knew I was in for a session of conundrums before I got anything like that reasonable answer.

'At the time it was taken into Vatican custody, the Pope was an unknown quantity, Harry. It was not known whether he was still God's servant, or if he had been already turned to the other side. Through the centuries after the same could have been said about several of the Popes. To destroy the actual violin is a simple matter. You take a match and you set it alight. But that does not destroy the evil that is inside it.'

'How can you say it's evil?' I asked. 'What has it done? What has anyone SEEN it do? Or is all this legend and myth, tall tales to woo the faithful back to the enclave.'

'Harry, Harry' the little priest shook his head. 'For a start, none of the faithful know anything about the Diabolus. Granted a few fervid admirers of Stradivari might have heard tales of his greatest creation, but for them it would be only a legend, to sit well with the rest of the legends the man had heir to. Only three centuries of Popes and their advisors know the truth of its existence, and of its power.'

I resisted the urge to laugh. 'And you've seen this power, Padraig?' This was as close as I came to calling him a liar, although I knew the man was anything but that. Merely someone who took his calling too much to heart, perhaps; or as I was to learn later, perhaps he didn't take it enough to heart.

'There is a balance of power in the world, Harry. A very fine balance at this moment in time; if there is good, there must be evil. For most of humankind that balance is within them also. The psychiatrists and many criminologists and the like believe that no one is inherently good, or bad. Perhaps, but I have seen people in my life who had been completely taken over by Satan and, in my opinion, they were pure evil. If you are a good person, and wish to destroy both the Diabolus and its power, there is a ceremony that has to be performed. It is not simple, and many of my predecessors have tried and failed.'

'And this black instrument is responsible for exactly what, Patrick?'

The little priest looked at me with a look of sympathy.

'I understand where you're coming from, lad,' he said, maintaining the sympathetic thing, which priests do very well. 'This cannot be easy to take in, and what I tell you next will not help. Would you be having a little bit of the holy spirit in liquid form around here, by any chance?'

By any chance I did, and handed him a hide flask with silver flashing at top and bottom. He held it up and examined it. '"Bisley 1986", it must have been a proud moment for you.'

'Not as proud as when I was a sniper and took out a lot of arseholes who needed taking out,' I muttered.

'Whatever,' I heard him drinking as I took a turn around the tor again. It was still quiet. Perhaps it was too quiet, I thought.

Patrick handed me back the flask and I took a nip, leaving it on the rock next to him.

'I never heard the Diabolus played of course, but I understand it is superb, yet at the same time capable of turning men's souls. I mentioned the ceremony to destroy its evil, well as in most things in this life, Harry; there is the opposite side of the coin. There are many ways to call up the Devil or one of his acolytes. One is to use one or more of the many artefacts that Satan has distributed around the globe, one of which is the Diabolus, which after all is where it got its name from. I intended to take it back to the Vatican with me, and with the Holy Father's permission we would have performed the ceremony which would destroy the evil thing for ever.'

'You tell a fine tale, Patrick,' I said thoughtfully. 'But there is no proof of the evil of the thing itself.'

'There are many tales of its evil before it was found and seized by one of the knights of the Vatican. The Diabolus had a short but bloody life after it was fashioned by the great Stradivari. As you are aware by now, Stradivari was going through a bad patch in a time of his life, and called on God to give him the genius to be the greatest luthier of all time. God did not hear him, or chose not to listen, but Satan did, and appeared before Antonio one night and a pact was made. He would indeed become the greatest violinmaker of all time, and in exchange he was to make a superlative instrument; made to the Devil's specifications, and of course, his mortal soul.

'The Devil took the instrument and passed it on. It was played superbly at the banquet of Giuseppe, the Lord of Lombardi, but with terrible effect. The Lord became ill with a hideous disease after hearing the recital, and gave up his soul in exchange for release from the pain, and that's only one of many tales I've heard over the years concerning this accursed instrument.'

I must have looked sceptical; very sceptical indeed, because Patrick Sullivan became most intense. He proceeded to inundate me with tales of terrible things that happened in the presence of the Diabolus.

'Hey, I believe you, Patrick,' I smiled at him. 'Almost. Wait here.'

'Why?' The little priest raised an eyebrow but did not otherwise appear concerned. I got the impression that he trusted me. 'You don't have the skull with you?'

'No,' I gave a tight grin. 'Of course not - it's too easy to be stupid, Patrick.'

I checked at each of my observation points and when I was satisfied went out of the narrow entrance, which had probably served as a doorway for a very long time, for during the British Ice Age Dartmoor was not covered with ice, and therefore it was quite probable that Palaeolithic man hunted there during this period, around 15,000 B.C. I was back in ten minutes and handed over the object in the haversack. I'd obtained a soft muslin bag to protect the skull and the priest hesitated for a moment, and then opened the bag in one swift movement. An audible gasp came from him as he gazed at what was inside. I noticed that unlike Milos he had no hesitation about touching such an object, which he did slowly and respectfully and with care, closed the haversack. He held it in his hand for a long minute, and I couldn't help coming out with the "Alas poor Yorick" bit from Hamlet.

Patrick laughed and shrugged in a self-deprecatory manner as he slipped it back into the protective bag then into the haversack. He raised his eyebrows and I waved a hand for him to keep it.

'You don't know what you have here, but with it our business is concluded, Harry Brogan,' he declared formerly. 'You have my gratitude, and that of the Holy Father. Tis a great pity we could not have got hold of the violin, but if this is what I think it is, we might have stopped them from their foul purpose anyway. I wish you well, Harry, in whatever direction your future lays, and if ever there is anything you need that we can be of help with, you have only to call the Vatican and give my name. I know that the value of this, like the Diabolus itself, is in excess of anything that we could put a price on, and you have our gratitude. Remember, anything we can do for you in the future. '

'Thank you, Patrick. Nothing personal but I hope that will never be necessary,' I said tonelessly. 'God speed to you.'

Only as I watched the priest walk down the hillside, the whatever relic on his back, did I have time to consider what possible use all of these people could have for a Stradivarius violin with a reputation for supreme evil, and an ancient skull of which I knew nothing. That these things were priceless of course, I knew, but I also felt that was nothing to do with the reason they were wanted by apparently everyone who knew of them.

Whatever.

I hurried down the hill, an old technique of lying back on your heels and taking great leaps forward; often, and especially in the dark, it was more a leap of faith. At the bottom I disappeared into a small copse by the crossroads. A wise move as it turned out.

I was wandering back in the general direction of the pub car park where I'd left my car when I heard a loud noise. Not a shot, not a smack, a whack or a clout, just a noise like metal hitting metal. I moved out of the trees but kept behind a high random rubble wall, that's one where they just pile up the stones on top of each other and their weight and the years' bond them together. As I neared the car park I heard a car go past and raised my head over the wall, in time to see the rear end of a large brown saloon disappear around a bend in the narrow road. I thought it was one of the latest Jags but couldn't be sure.

My car was parked over near the pub doorway next to a smart sports car; purposely so anyone would think it belonged to the pub landlord or one of the staff, perhaps even a customer who had taken a taxi home rather than risk the wrath of the law, but having used the pub often myself I knew that the local law consisted of just an elderly constable on his bike.

The hired car that I presumed Patrick had come in was aslant across the car park, with a large dent in the driver's side door. I ran to it and saw the little priest slumped across the front seat. I moved around to the other side and opened the door. I felt for a pulse in his carotid and there was one there and reasonably strong. The door of the pub opened and an elderly man stood there with a shotgun.

'Phone for an ambulance, will you please?' I called, and the man stood there and raised the weapon.

'Oh, for God's sake, Dad,' came a female voice from inside the pub. 'Would he have stayed around and tried to help the man if he was the cause of it? Go and phone for an ambulance while I'll see what I can do. Go on with you.'

The man, whom I recognized as the landlord, disappeared inside. A woman came out, aged around thirty-five or so, and walked right around to where I was leaning into the car over Patrick. I straightened up and was looking into the eyes of a woman whom I first thought of as attractive, but she was far from being merely attractive. She was downright beautiful. I felt momentary feelings of guilt, having little Andrea waiting for me not far away at home, and here I was ogling the landlord's daughter.

'Hi,' she gave me a smile that made me feel guiltier still. 'My name's Heather. Sorry about my grumpy old man, but he thinks everyone is after the money he keeps under the mattress. Now, let's see what's happened to the poor man.'

She pushed past me and bent over the little priest.

'He seems to have a good pulse,' I said firmly, just in case Heather the landlord's daughter took it upon herself to start operating.

'Hmm,' she murmured, and then asked, 'what happened here, do you know?'

'Yes, I know,' I replied, perhaps a trifle miffed at this pushy, if gorgeous, female acting like Dalzeil or Pascoe at a crime scene. 'A large car, saloon type, brown and looking like one of the new Jaguars, rammed into the side of him; so what do YOU think?'

She ignored the question.

'Ah, that accounts for the large lump on the side of his head, you know. He must have hit it against the window without breaking the glass. I see he's a priest, so why would someone who could afford the latest Jag ram into a priest?'

I'd already looked in the back of the car and on the floor. Now I went around to the boot and opened it.

'What are you looking for, Mr....?'

'Brogan, Harry Brogan, and the thing I was looking for is gone, which is the reason poor Patrick is lying there waiting for an ambulance.'

'So, you know the victim and you know what's missing, Mr. Brogan,' her voice had an edge to it. 'What would be your connection to them both and what is the missing object?'

Now I really WAS annoyed. Bloody woman had been watching too many sleuths on the tele. 'Never mind, luv. I'll talk to the coppers when they get here, so why not go back in the pub and get ready to open up? Unless you're a nurse...?'

She smiled. 'Actually I'm not, but as the first copper on the scene you can talk to me if you like. I apologize, but I never introduced myself properly just now. I'm Detective Inspector Heather Frankton.'

She turned out to be on convalescent leave from the Serious Crime Squad up in the Smoke and was taking a break in her father's hostelry. She actually became quite chatty while I was trying to wipe the egg off my face. Then of course I realised that becoming quite chatty was a police way of getting you to open up in warm-hearted reciprocal fashion. Or in this case- me.

The ambulance arrived and duly carried Patrick Sullivan off to Exeter Infirmary. I was told there did not appear to be any serious injury, but that would depend on the findings of the brain surgeon who would be examining him later in the day. The driver told me that I could probably visit the priest that evening. I thanked him and supplied his name. 'His address is the Vatican, yes the one in Rome, and he's not a priest but a Monsignor.'

When the ambulance had gone, Heather invited me into the pub for a coffee while we talked. I knew the score; I'd be doing the talking, she'd be doing the listening. The "quite chatty" period was over.

She asked how I liked my coffee, and offered something stronger if I preferred it.

'What's this?' I joked. 'Offering alcohol outside pub hours and you one of the boys in blue?'

She flashed that delightful smile again. 'For one, we open up in twenty minutes, for another this is not just a pub, it's our home and we can give anyone we like a drink. GIVE being the operative word, Mr. Brogan, as no money will change hands. Now do you want a pint or not, because I've changed my mind about the coffee and will take a G and T?'

'Silly not to,' I returned her smile. 'Guinness, please.'

While she was helping herself behind the bar, her father came in from the back. After making the phone call he had taken no further part of the business in his car park. Most probably knew his daughter would have things well in hand. He came over to the table where I was sitting.

'Apologize for not rec'nising you outside, mate. Seen you in 'ere a few times I reckon; live round 'ere do 'ee?'

'Not too far,' I told him. 'Cottage just down from the Morris farm, on the other side of the moor.'

'Oh, aye,' he nodded his head up and down. 'Nasty piece of work is that Morris. Used to make a bit of trouble in 'ere but sin' I banned him us don't see him.'

'Well done,' I grinned at him. 'With him out of the way I might make more trips over the moor to see you.'

'Be lookin' forward to it, son,' he nodded, but still the face hadn't changed expression. 'Name's Horace Frankton, but ever'one calls me Frank. Gawd knows where me mither an' faither got bloody "Horace" from.'

He went through the back of the bar and his daughter came over with the drinks.

'This makes a pleasant change,' I said, taking a thankful gulp of the black stuff.

'From what?' she asked.

'From talking to your lot in an interview room, with not a drop of Guinness in sight.'

'Ah, so you're used to being asked in for a talk, Mr. Brogan?'

'Call me Harry, or just Brogan, and yes I've been called in for a chat a couple of times; absolute cases of mistaken identity, of course. Sometimes your friends have a problem telling the good guys from the bad guys.'

'I know,' she surprised me by agreeing, albeit with a touch of cynicism, tempered with an engaging smile. 'My recent convalescence was due to my having been the recipient of a bullet fired by one of the good guys. I'll call you Brogan, as I don't know you well enough to use your first name. Now, you were going to tell me about the little priest, sorry, Monsignor, and what was stolen from him. It must have been very valuable for someone to damage their new Jaguar by ramming it into his car.'

I smiled and took a drink from my glass. 'You could buy a lot of Jaguars for what the thing was worth, though I don't know much about it myself. To me it was just an old skull.'

'You mean a HUMAN skull?'

I nodded, still smiling. 'Yes, it was a human skull, but I shouldn't think you're Cold Case lot would be interested in re-opening something that's probably more than a thousand years old, though I honestly don't know quite how old it is, nor do I know who it belonged to.'

'My goodness, how did the priest come to have it?'

'I'd like to ask you a question first, if I may?' I asked her and she nodded. 'What exactly is your position here? I mean, are you back to duty now and is this turning into your case?'

'No, not at all,' she said. 'I'm not back to duty for another month.'

'You must have been hurt pretty badly.'

'Yes, I was,' she agreed, and left it at that. 'So, from that you can see that I wish I was back, and this would be a nice start back, as you seem to know all about it. I think you probably know who took it too.'

'Not quite, but I know a man who does,' I shrugged. 'If you're not quite active yet, you could still put out an APB through the local force, couldn't you? Get everyone looking for a new Jag or similar motor, with front end damage.'

'What if they reversed into the other car?'

I shook my head. 'No, I saw the car tearing off up the lane and didn't notice any rear end damage.'

'That's okay then,' she bestowed that smile on me again. 'I already did that before the ambulance left with your friend. I said it was most likely damage to the front.'

'Good girl,' I said, a bit patronizing to use on a police inspector perhaps, but she didn't seem put out about it. 'Okay, use this as you want. Pass it on to any of your colleagues, who seem to be taking their own sweet time in getting here. But think carefully before you do, as it's a strange tale. The missing object is a...strange thing. But the world is full of collectors, even of artefacts like skulls. I sometimes find...things for those collectors.'

My last words might have sounded rather tame but I certainly wasn't going to open up to a female I'd only just met, especially one of the old Bill, even though an attractive one at that.

'So that's what you do for a living, Brogan, steal things?' She regarded me with a cold fish kind of look, one she obviously reserved for denizens of her underworld encounters. If she'd picked up on my previous occupation already, then I was very pleased that I hadn't told her more.

251

I tried to look aggrieved. 'I'm not a thief and I don't steal things. I search for, locate and liberate items and return them to their rightful owners, or the people who most have the entitlement to them in the first place.'

'That's what I said, you steal things.'

We both laughed and she very kindly left it at that. Or gave it up for the time being, which was more likely.

'Tell me, Brogan,' Heather Frankton enquired softly. 'Do you, yourself, believe that this skull, one that you have actually held in your hands, is supernatural in some way? Or that it might be cursed?'

'No,' I shook my head sadly. 'But the little priest does, and I like him.'

'And because Patrick Sullivan is into something quite sinister, in his eyes, to you that's a good enough reason to risk your life?'

'Why not?' I replied. 'We all have to die sometime. I was in the marines once, and risked my neck for silly political reasons at the time. I might as well do it this time for a good cause that the Signore seriously believes in, even if I don't myself.'

I drained my pint and stood up.

'Thanks for the drink, Heather; I'll be in for another one soon. You've got all the info about the "accident" and can pass it on to the local patrol when it gets here. I'll be dropping in to see the priest tonight and will let you know how he is.'

She saw me to the door and swung it wide to begin the lunchtime trade.

'Goodbye, Brogan. I don't think they'll have any luck finding the Jag, and without that it was just another hit and run, unless we want the whole thing shown on the TV as another "haunted" program.'

'You're so right,' I smiled. 'Let's keep it our secret.'

I drove back to my cottage thinking of Heather the double-breasted policeman. She was cool, as they say. No nonsense, told it as it was. The drive back consisted of going right across the moor, and to my shame I never even thought of the tasty little dish waiting for me until I reached the end of my lane.

I drove in the gate and parked around the back, as I usually did.

Lupus was not about and there was a silence in the cottage. I entered and looked around, by which I mean that I searched the whole place. There was nothing; no Andi and none of Andi's clothes or suitcase. There was no sign of a struggle anywhere, so I had to conclude that she'd left of her own accord.

Eventually I found the note. It had been left above the inglenook in the lounge and was quite obvious unless you were looking for a person, or a body, as I was.

No mystery; nothing sinister, she simply had to get back to her students and her extramural activities in Rome. I did wonder about her sudden exit; why she hadn't told me that morning that she was going. She knew I was meeting Patrick and that it was all over after that. We'd talked about a holiday together, somewhere in the Greek Islands, which I loved and she had never been to. Whatever; it wasn't going to happen for a while – if ever.

By 7pm I was wondering where the fox was when I heard a wail outside. The Steyr was never too far from me these days and I picked it up automatically as I went outside. Christ, talk about déjà vu.

Lupus had managed to crawl as far as the front steps but the climb up them was too much for the poor sod. There was blood on his right side but I didn't waste time examining him, I lifted him up and took him round to the car. I laid him on the back seat with some consoling words and went back inside to the phone. I phoned Julian

McVickers, my vet friend, and fortunately he was still at the practice.

'Not again,' he said, when I'd explained the situation. 'Who did you two piss off this time?' Because Julian was a public schoolboy, he actually said "orf" in that way that public schoolboys do, but I never hold that against him. After all, he doesn't hold my occasional lapses into Liverpudlian against me.

'Jules, I'll bring him right over, mate. How long are you going to be there for?'

'About 3 seconds,' he said. 'I'll be passing your place in fifteen minutes; can you staunch the blood flow and keep him calm?'

'He's like me, he's always calm,' I said. 'As for the blood flow, this isn't much to speak of.'

'Hmm,' he replied. 'He's probably lost it in the countryside, where he very wisely dragged himself off to when the shooting began. I'll bring some plasma, and see you soon. Make sure there's a dram around.'

True to form, almost exactly fifteen minutes later a sporty little Japanese job hurtles up to the door and Julian hops out. He did the business in twenty minutes and held up a small piece of lead.

'I'd say it was a .22, not high-powered so our friend here was lucky. It bounced off a shoulder bone and went out again. He'll be pretty sore for a while; right as rain in a couple of weeks. But who goes hunting with a .22? It's not going to bring down a deer, and this looks like it came from a handgun, anyway.'

'A handgun, a non-high powered .22 would be a ladies gun, surely?' I muttered.

'You'd be right,' Julian agreed. 'You had any lady friends around lately, old chum?'

'Only one,' I said slowly. 'She was staying here but I had a... task to do this morning and left early. I came back less than an hour ago and she'd packed up and gone. I thought it was strange, but with Lupus being shot, perhaps they took her.'

'They? Took her? I think you'd better uncork the bottle and tell me the story,' Julian settled himself into my best chair and looked set to stay a while.

'Don't you have to be somewhere soon?' I frowned. 'Won't Katie be waiting for you with a fine gastronomic adventure waiting on the table?'

Katie McVickers food was abominable. Julian's wife was a lovely lady, bright and always cheery, a Masters from Oxford in some obscure subject which she lectured in at Exeter University, but a cook she was not.

'No, thank God,' he said fervently. 'I get a reprieve for a few days as she's gone to stay with her folks in Hampshire for a few days. Miss her terribly, of course, but miss her cooking somewhat less.'

I laughed and dug out my secret bottle of Laphroaig that I kept for such occasions. I took the top off the bottle and flipped it away as was expected at such times. I knew Julian wouldn't bill me for Lupus, for he was too fond of the big bugger. This went both ways as the fox had a fondness for the vet too. He could pick him up onto the operating table and give him a full physical check, and Lupus would practically purr like a cat. Very few people got that close.

I was still worrying about Andi, but if someone had taken her I couldn't see them packing up all her stuff, bundling it in a suitcase and carting Andi and baggage off. There was also the note, quite chatty about her forthcoming lectures and that she'd spoken to her people on the phone and they wanted her back in a hurry.

I poured two generous tots, splashed some soda water in mine and handed him a glass and the bottle. Although he was a Scot by birth and name, he was a typical Englishman in his upbringing, education and inclination. I was always taught to add a touch of water to good Malt, as it brings out the flavour. Laphroaig being of an extremely peaty flavour, it was flavoursome on its own. Julian, however, usually drowned it with soda water.

We drank for a while and I told him the whole story, much as I had with Heather Frankton earlier. This time, however, the telling also took in the bits I'd left out for Heather, mostly about Andrea Scolari, in fact.

'Oh, shit,' I said suddenly, as I was getting to the end of my sad tale of woe, and the two acts of thievery on my part. 'I was supposed to go into Exeter and see Patrick.'

'Before you go dashing off, old chap,' Julian said sagely, 'why not give them a ring and see if the poor bloke has recovered enough to have visitors. If not, and if you're up for it, we can go and have a pub meal somewhere.'

'Sounds like a plan,' I said in my best Americanised accent.

I rang the hospital, and after being switched to three different people, and finishing up with the first one I'd spoken to, I was informed that the Signore had recovered consciousness but would be taking no visitors until the following day. They told me he would be fine but they were keeping him in over night for observation, which was consistent with a head injury.

So we went to the local pub where I believe we had a good night. Over the meal I spoke of the events of the morning, mentioning Heather Frankton.

'I know her,' Julian said, chewing on a mouthful of cottage pie. 'She was up at Oxford with Katie. Quite a clever girl, apparently; she got a first in law, then opted for the police right away. I understand she's done rather well at it.'

'Detective Inspector,' I nodded. 'Took a bullet in the line of duty and she's convalescing at her father's pub over the moor.'

'Ah, the Dartmoor Pony,' Julian drawled. 'We've been there a few times, and in fact we met Heather there for a drink and a chat, oh, about a year ago. It was just an excuse for Katie to show off her husband to her old school chum, of course.'

'Of course,' I said dryly. 'What's not to show off?'

'My point exactly, old chap, care for another?' He asked, reaching for our glasses. 'I know I do.'

The next morning I left the cottage about ten o'clock and drove to Exeter Infirmary. Julian and I had returned home to the cottage where I'd retrieved the bottle of whisky and we'd sunk it, talked a lot of shit, and he stayed the night in the spare bedroom. He'd left early, bright as a lark, humming to himself in the kitchen while he made himself breakfast, and I hated the bastard. We were both drunk that night, as we'd been drunk many times before, but Julian had remarkable powers of recovery, whereas I was not so clever on the morning after, unless I'd been solely on the Guinness.

I managed to find someone just pulling out as I got to the hospital, an incredible stroke of luck as there were never enough parking spots for the amount of traffic that went through there. Inside I went to the reception desk and gave my name, and to my surprise they allowed me straight in to see Patrick Sullivan. Apparently as soon as he came to he had been asking for me.

'How are you, Patrick?' I sat down on the single chair next to his bed.

'I've been worse after drinking a skinful of the Jameson's on top of Guinness, lad.' He managed to sit up without my help and I had to admit he didn't look too bad. 'The specialist said there's no damage to the head and there was no concussion.'

'So what happened?'

He shook his head. 'It was all a bit of a muddle. There were two cars parked up by the pub, one of which was yours, I think. I knew you wouldn't be seen dead driving the other sporty wee thing.'

I wasn't sure if that was a reverse compliment or not, whether he thought it was too poncy for me, or whether he thought I couldn't afford one. Bloody cheek.

'My hire car, the little Kia, was parked on the right by the hedge and I had to drive it around in a circle to get out of the car park. It was only as I completed the turn and I was about to leave through the gate, that this huge car came roaring out from where it had been hidden by the hedge on the left.'

'Did you see what kind of car it was, Patrick?' I asked.

'No, Harry,' he said despondently. 'It all happened so fast, and I don't keep up with the latest trends in cars. It seemed to be new, though, and it was a dark brown color. I didn't see the driver or how many were in the car.'

'Tell me, Patrick,' I asked suddenly. 'The pub where we parked our cars that day, the Dartmoor Pony, do you happen to know the daughter of the landlord?'

He gave me an odd look followed by a groan of pain as he moved in the bed, so I dropped the line of enquiry.

We talked for a while but he didn't come up with anything further. As I rose to take my leave, his small hand clutched my sleeve.

'The car is not important, Harry, nor the people in it. But the Skull, you HAVE to get it back. If they use it in conjunction with the Diabolus...D'you know the date today?'

'Yes,' I said, puzzled. 'It's the 29th October.'

'Yes, Harry,' his face looked terribly pained, but I do not think it was caused by any injury to his body. 'In two days time it is Halloween, the eve of All Saint's Day. In Britain, before Christianity, the 31st October was the eve of the New Year, when the souls of the dead were thought to visit their homes. After it became a Christian festival it was still associated with the supernatural; children carve out pumpkins or turnips into the faces of demons, although the kids of today are not aware of this.'

I made to speak but he held up his palm in a quietening gesture.

'It is a time of disquiet and disturbance of the dead and that is a time when the strength of Satan is high. Everywhere people play their games and pretend to take part in Devil worship and witches' covens dance. Some regard themselves as real followers of Satan and a few even celebrate a type of Black Mass, each one difference to the others. Very few know the real ceremony, or are aware of the power that belongs to the Evil One this night. Sadly, ALL of these misguided people are capable of summoning an amount of power to Satan, simply by taking part in anything that is against Christ.

'The people who now have the Diabolus know all this, and their plans are to come to fruition in two days time. You must stop them, Harry. You must.'

I was silent for a moment. There was no doubt in my mind that the little priest, who I'd come to respect, believed all of the rubbish he was saying.

'Tell me, Patrick, why THIS year, and why THIS time of Halloween, when they've known where the violin was for centuries and could have performed this, whatever kind of ceremony they have in mind, at any time?' I spoke quietly, soothingly, and so obviously patronizingly that he regarded me with anguish.

'Are you not aware of the date on a Tuesday in June of this year?' His voice was controlled but I could sense the effort it was to contain his frustration. 'It was the 6th of June, which is the 6th month, of the year 2006. 666, Harry, is the mark of the Antichrist himself. Much was done to summon him on that day, and the final event is on the eve of All Hallows. The playing of the Diabolus, following a Black Mass on consecrated ground, will summon up the creature that will be the Antichrist. If the skull is what I think it is that will be the next greatest gift they could hope for. They learned of its absence very soon after you took it, due to your unfortunate interlude with the security man.

'Please, Harry, you must get the violin AND the skull back so we can destroy them properly, for only when they are at the height of their powers can they be irrevocably destroyed for ever.'

So impassioned was the little priest's plea, that for a few moments there he had me going. What if he was speaking the truth; not just the truth as he THOUGHT he knew it, but the real truth? Was there something in this, after all?

Then I pulled myself together. 'And I suppose the bloody things are both back in the chateau in France by now?'

'Not at all,' he shook his head; mostly grey now but with a hint on top of the jet-black hair of the Irish. 'That's the irony of it; we practically delivered it to their doorstep. Remember what happens every year at this time, Harry, near Salisbury? Yes, the pagan celebrations at Stonehenge. That is the time that it all comes together and the Dark One is at his most powerful.'

I thought of Stonehenge, which I had visited many times. I did remember the first times I went, for it is prominent on the A303, the road I would take for the first part of my journey home to Liverpool, when I was stationed at the Commando Camp at Lympstone, or Stonehouse Barracks in Plymouth. In those early days you could walk right up among the massive stone blocks, though now of course it is well fenced off. Cordoned off and withdrawn into itself, the site of Stonehenge is an entryway into the West Country, as it predisposes the megaliths of Cornwall. I knew also that in prehistory Stonehenge was never a frontier but a centre of the Bronze Age civilization of Wessex.

I remember reading once of the awesome columns and archways of Stonehenge, built by unknown hands as a device for tracking the cycle of the sun but possibly invested with other meanings too. It is actually set in splendid isolation on the flat, chalky grassland of Salisbury Plain, some eighty miles west of London.

It is a conundrum, despite all of the research and speculation that has been foisted on it for many generations, for even the builders are still unknown. I know that over the years there have been many theories about who the builders were; Egyptians, Phoenicians, Greeks, Romans, Druids, Danes, Buddhists, Hindus, Mayans, survivors of Atlantis; even visitors from another planet have had a mention.

So, I knew Stonehenge, but what that had to do with anything I didn't have a proverbial clue. Perhaps as a place of mystery it was right; I really didn't know. But Patrick appeared to know everything, and I couldn't fault him with it.

'Harry, I like you, I really do, and I trust you. More importantly I know where your convictions and your thoughts are coming from. I want you to go to the Vatican and speak with the Holy Father.'

'Go to...and speak with...Oh, come on Patrick, you must be joking.'

'You have two days, Harry, only two days. To save us all from damnation.'

Before I left I drove to the Dartmoor Pony. Heather was there and I found her tending bar in the main lounge. It had just opened and the lunchtime crowd had yet to put in an appearance.

'Brogan, how nice to see you,' she seemed genuinely pleased to see me, but you can never tell with coppers, can you?

I ordered a pint of Guinness and a large pasty, knowing it would be a while before I had the luxury of both; certainly at the same time. She joined me in an orange squash and I shuddered at the thought.

'You look like a man who's going somewhere,' she observed with a smile.

'Now how could you possibly know that?' I smiled in response. 'You couldn't know that I've got a suitcase in the car, and there's only one way you could know that I've got an electronic ticket to Rome in my pocket, freshly downloaded from the internet this very morning.'

'And what way would that be?' she asked innocently, but never fooled old Brogan for a minute.

I took a large quaff of my Guinness and shrugged. This is not a good idea to attempt at the same time because the movement of the shoulder has a habit of shucking some of the liquid out of the glass. This happened and I saw the buxom barmaid suppress a giggle. The fact that the buxom barmaid in this case was also a detective inspector in the Met prevented my witty comeback, so I went for the jugular instead.

'After our delightful drink the other day,' I sniffed. 'Something was bugging me on the way back to my humble abode, and it took a while before I realised what it was. You mentioned Patrick Sullivan's full name, though I'd only told you his first. You know Patrick, don't you?'

'Ah, you really should have been a policeman, Brogan,' her laugh was quite genuine and definitely spontaneous;

with no embarrassment or hesitancy there at all. 'Like your brother.'

I must have stared, because she kept the laugh going for longer than was polite.

'Yes, I've known Patrick for a long time. But you I don't know, Brogan. Can I trust you? I don't know. I do know your background, and I know the suspicions that have surrounded your activities, but this present "adventure" of yours, well, it puzzles me, Brogan. I DO trust Patrick, however, and if he vouches for you, which he does, that's almost good enough for me. Another pint? Or are you in a hurry to get to the airport?'

'You know I am, Heather, but let me fill you in on a few things. As I said, the skull is very old, but it wasn't what Patrick really wanted. He was after a violin.'

I told her about its manufacture, and the legend or myth behind the supposed bargain that was made before it became the superb instrument it now was. I told her about my son being kidnapped and how the huge fat priest, Zoltan Milos, had helped me locate him, and how at his instigation I had stolen the instrument from under the noses of whomever at the Vatican knew of its whereabouts. I then spoke of Signore Padraig Sullivan, and how he had in turn convinced me to get it for him.

Now it was gone again.

Through the whole telling of it she stood and looked at me with interest, but I could tell it was not fresh interest.

'You know all this, don't you?' I broke off from the tale. 'You knew all along, in fact. You and Patrick must have laughed your bloody heads off when I suggested the meeting on Devil's Tor. It's right in your back yard.'

If I expected her to wriggle, to deny anything or make excuses, I was to be disappointed. She did none of those things, merely shrugged and put the glasses in the sink.

'You're going to be late for that plane, Brogan,' she tilted her head to one side.

I reached the door before she spoke again.

'Best of luck, Harry,' was all she said, but it was enough.

CHAPTER THIRTEEN

"Jesus saith unto him, I am the way, the truth, and the life: no man cometh unto the Father, but by me." John 14:6

"I am the LORD: that is my name: and my glory will I not give to another, neither my praise to graven images."

Isaiah 42:8

Later that day, as I was standing in line at Heathrow, I asked myself what choice I had, after all that advertising from Patrick. I'd been inhumanly processed for security reasons, shoes and belt removed, prodded, poked and generally humiliated; all for the privilege of being allowed to exchange my electronic tickets for return flights to Rome.

Before I left England - which I refuse to call the United Kingdom by the way because it isn't and hasn't been for a long time, not with Scotland and Wales treating us like shit, and even the county of Cornwall wanting independence, for God's sake, and nor would I contemplate calling it Great Britain, as it's a long time since it was anything like great -I'd called Fabio to meet me. There I go again.

After another humiliating experience with the security at Rome airport, though what I was expected to have picked up on the plane that the security at the arrivals lobby were so thorough about was beyond my little grey cells, I found a pay phone and called Andi's number. On the sixth ring I was seriously beginning to worry. That all of her belongings had gone from the cottage had not been alarming in itself, but the shooting of Lupus had definitely been cause for alarm. Her note had either been forced or forged.

After trying twice more I gave up and went out through the Arrivals gate and there he was, having promised me he'd be there the night before, sitting proudly in his new Mercedes outside with his flag down, but when I told him to drive me straight to the Vatican, main entrance, he was beside himself.

'Signore, Signore, Prego,' he wailed. 'How am to I get you into the Vaticani? Is impossible, Signore Harry.'

'You don't have to, my friend,' I told him. 'I have an appointment this time.'

'Harry, my friend, who can you know that well in the Vatican after what we did there?'

'Er, how about Pope something or other?' I grinned. 'Just drive, Fabio.'

He did, and he still didn't believe it when we got to the main entrance and the guard took my name and waved us on.

'Wow,' was all I got from Fabio. Like I said, he was a wonderful driver but a bit slow in the oligarchy of the Pope's way of doing things.

I questioned the guard who was escorting me and he told me in excellent English that the Holy Father was away from the Vatican, but would say nothing more of his whereabouts. This information really hacked me off as I expected to see him right away; after all, that was why I had come to Rome. More as an afterthought I enquired about Signorina Scolari, and was met with a frown of puzzlement by the guard.

I described Andrea and the guard appeared even more baffled. 'Signore, Scusi. Such a lady as you describe, I could not fail to remember her. And the name is not familiar to me. She does not work in the Vatican, Signore Brogan.'

I did not pursue this, for I saw no point, and such was my state of mind over the whole situation that I accepted it at face value. As far as the guard was concerned, Andrea Scolari did not exist, and never had.

I was taken up a couple of stories in the inner sanctum and deposited in a long corridor. A Signore in purple robes appeared and I was led through to an inner chamber where a man of ample girth, a broad smile and the same purple regalia confronted me.

'Good day, Mr. Brogan,' he said in excellent English. 'I am Cardinal Lumbrozzi, the private secretary to his Holiness.'

We stood and eyeballed each other for a while.

'And?' I enquired.

'And what, Signore?' he asked in return.

'And what the heck am I doing here? I take it that Signore Sullivan has been in touch with you and explained the situation, which is why I understood this visit was to see the Pope himself? I understand he is no longer in residence? I have a wedge into the Diabolus, which I thought was what you were after. We now have another problem, Your Eminence,' I backed down slightly. 'Andrea Scolari is missing. She left my house with all of her stuff and there was even a note, but further circumstances lead me to believe she is not missing of her own volition.'

Despite my annoyed tone he did not take umbrage, though neither did he give me an answer. He smiled constantly and led me to an outer room and told me to wait.

'Coffee will arrive soon, Signore,' he said as he left the room.

Which it did, of course, very expediently, and I sipped and waited in a seething fit of impatience; excellent though the coffee was.

Eventually the prelate came back and enquired as to my health, which I found extraordinary under the circumstances, but told him I was quite well. Cardinal Lumbrozzi smiled with no emotion and politely asked me to accompany him. A private elevator took us down to the Courtyard of Sixtus V. Swiss guards stood to attention either side of the elevator as we emerged. A gleaming black Mercedes with yellow and white papal pennants hanging from small masts on both front wings was waiting and we climbed aboard. The car drove slowly through the narrow arch into the Saint Damasus Courtyard, out through another narrow arch on the opposite side and down a narrow cobbled road through three small courtyards, the Pappagalli, the Borgia, and the Sentinel, overlooked by fortified ochre-colored walls.

When it reached the Square of the Oven it took the same steep road up the Vatican Gardens that I'd gone up with Andi. At the highest point of Vatican City an Alitalia helicopter, again with the papal pennant, waited. Around it were a group of prelates, altar boys and staff.

Ten minutes later I looked out on the oval-shaped blue water of Lake Albano, which partially filled a huge volcano crater, whose inner slopes were home to oaks and chestnut trees. Above the left-hand rim was Mount Cavo, and perched on the right-hand rim was the town of Castel Gandolfo, stretched back in a ragged line of red-tiled roofs from the white dome of Bernini's Church of Saint Thomas of Villanova, across a small square from the Pontifical Palace that dominated the town.

Again there was a limo waiting for us and within a few minutes we were ensconced inside the famous Castle Gandolfo, the Pope's summer retreat.

I was escorted into an inner sanctum, given spectacular coffee again, and waited, this time with decorous patience. To say I was gob smacked would have been a mis-interference of the facts. Despite what Patrick had told me, I was still surprised at the appearance of the Holy Father when he arrived in the room. He appeared jaunty, bouncing into the room like a man many years his junior. I had the feeling that the worldwide newspaper reports of his ill health, and of course his imminent death, apart from being well staged, were also part of some huge con on the Pope's part. As though he could see exactly what I was thinking, he gave me a warm smile, slightly tinged with mischief.

'Harry Brogan,' he said. 'It is good to meet you, at last. My friend and counsellor, Patrick Sullivan, has spoken of you.'

So, where did I stand now, I wondered?

'Holy Father,' I said. 'I am honoured to be here, and by your holy presence, but...'

'Please,' he said in very good English, which I learned was but one of many languages that he spoke fluently. 'I understand that you had early training in the Roman Catholic Church. I also understand that you no longer accept the faith. That is your choice, Mr. Brogan, and it is respected here, believe me. But the problem we are facing at the moment transcends all bounds of belief and understanding, for there is something that confronts us of monumental proportions. We are at risk of losing everything of Christianity to the Evil One. Whatever your beliefs, Mr. Brogan, we need your skills at this time.'

What could I say, for I was talking to the Pope himself, and as a child he was next only to God himself; the thought of actually meeting with him some day would have terrified and intoxicated all of we altar boys. But that was back then, and now it sounded like he also believed all this rubbish about violins and the Evil One.

He casually invited me to sit down in a Louis XIII chair, the beautiful brocade of which made me nervously wipe a hand across the seat of my pants, in case I'd picked up something unclean somewhere en route. The Pope made as though he hadn't noticed my reflex action but I thought I saw the ghost of a half-smile raise up the sides of his mouth.

We chatted for a while, with the Holy Father doing most of the chatting and I doing most of the listening. At the end of half-an-hour, and despite my scepticism about the whole thing, I was almost moving across to the opposite side of the beliefs I'd held for all of my adult lifetime.

I didn't know what to believe anymore.

'Patrick Sullivan heads an order which is almost secular in what its aims are, and the way in which it carries out those aims. Much as the Antichrist followers do also. The one vies with the other, the one defies the other, the one is the opposite of the other, and in most things the one is identical to the other. Except that one is evil and the other works for good.'

Once again I asked about the whereabouts of Andrea, but received only a frowned silence from Il Papa. Perhaps his silence was an answer in itself.

Cardinal Lumbrozzi reappeared and the Pope relaxed back in his brocaded chair. He was strained now; I could see it in his face. But there was still no answer to my question forthcoming. At last the Pope spoke.

'We need you, Harry Brogan, we need your skills desperately, and the fact that you are a lapsed Catholic means nothing to the Father in Heaven. He so uses the abilities of man that he cares nothing for race or creed. We Catholics are very egotistical you know; we think we have the copyright on closeness to God. Let me tell you something that I believe, Harry, and this is from the heart of an old man. I honestly believe that there is a one God who is the father of us all.

Whether we are Catholic, Protestant, Muslim or whatever, I sincerely believe that one deity watches over us all, and he doesn't care that many by different names know of him. As long as they obey a universal God that is all he wants.'

I thought it over for a moment or two, and if this man of the cloth was talking with the sincerity in which it sounded, how could I debate such profundity?

I left with the sense of having met with a great man. A man of the people, as every "sincere" politician might say and hope stupid people believed him. Yet, somehow I DID believe him.

The Holy Father gave me one piece of advice.

'You do not have to believe in God, my son,' he said intensely. 'But if you are confronted with Evil beyond the countenance of humankind, surely then you must respect the juxtaposition of good and Evil. If you are willing to be the one to prevent the ceremony then you will come into contact with this Evil, and I pray that you survive. But, dear Harry Brogan, always remember what you once were, a Christian child; indeed you were a Catholic child, and as such you have stored-up goodness within you. Be ready to use it at the right time.'

I believe I mumbled something at the time, probably some deep inanities that His Holiness would have a quiet giggle to himself about later.

'Remember, Harry, you must sight the demon before you can slay it,' were his last words before I left.

I went the same way I came in; limousine, helicopter, limo again. I asked the driver to drop me at the tratorria near where I had stayed during my first time in Rome. I made a phone call and drank wonderful cappuccino while I waited. Fabio arrived soon after and had already arranged the ticket for my return flight. He joined me in an espresso then took me straight to the airport. My small bag was still in the boot of the Mercedes. I had brought it because I did not know how long I would be staying in Rome. Even so, it would be cutting it fine for getting back in time to make arrangements for October 31st, the eve of All Hallows.

The flight back was uneventful, after a tearful farewell from my little Italian taxi-driver. I must come again when this strange affair that I was engaged in was over, he said, and stay in his poor but comfortable home and meet his wife and bambinos. He asked how the Holy Father was in his hesitant words.

'He sent his regards, my friend, and said he would pray for you and your family,' I said with a straight face.

He looked ecstatic for a moment, before he frowned at me. 'Harry, you are always teasing. Why would the Pope have ever heard of Fabio Adjani?'

'Because now he knows how you helped me when I was looking for the violin,' I said, keeping a straight face. 'I will be back some day, little Fabio, and will try to get you an audience with Papa. You have my word on that.'

And I meant it.

When I reached England I picked up the car at the airport and drove down to the West Country in a quandary.

What was right? Who was right? At that stage I didn't have a bloody clue.

I did a lot of thinking as I drove, and when I finally stopped driving by rote and took time to look around me, realized that I was driving southwest along the A303; a route that would take me right past Stonehenge itself. A long time ago the Druids inhabited Stonehenge, as I remembered from my schooling. I did say I had a good memory, though the Druids had nothing to do with the construction of Stonehenge as they arrived in Britain a long time after its construction. A certain amount of Stonehenge was built of sarsen, a type of sandstone boulder, and the rest primarily of bluestone, which is a type of blue-tinted dolerite, and later of sarsen, a variety of sandstone harder than granite. Now, here is the interesting bit; the bluestones, of which there were eighty or more slabs originally, have actually been traced to a Welsh quarry about 130 miles northwest of Salisbury Plain; the sarsen slabs were brought from the Marlborough Downs, about twenty miles north of the site. The long-distance movement of these massive rocks, some as big as fifty tons, was an astonishing feat at a time when there was no technology for this, has caused many theories and conjectures.

One of the many theories I remembered, and possibly the most feasible, given the technology at the time, or lack of it, was this. A deep V-shaped groove was made across the stone, and then they dug a trench in the ground and filled it with brushwood. The act of cutting through the rock was a remarkable operation. First they lit the brushwood and then they busily stoked it, pushing fresh wood into the trench with long poles. Soon the heat had become tremendous and the rock grew so hot that no one could touch it. After a while the rock began to glow. Finally, when the air around the rock seemed to pulsate with the heat, the men ran forward with leather buckets of water and emptied them into the V, and there was an explosion of steam. More water was slopped in and the process continued for a while until suddenly there was a great crack and as the steam cleared it could be seen that a great fissure had opened through the red-hot rock where the split had been made.

Whatever; the origins of the henge has also given rise to the mystery and superstition that surrounds the place. Soon I saw the legendary shape off to the right in the triangle where the A344 meets with the A303. Now of course there is a high steel fence, with lights shining on the massive megaliths from every angle. I pulled over to the side of the road and gazed for quite a while.

There is nothing quite like the awe-inspiring monument of Stonehenge anywhere else in the world, yet at first sight I have to say it is somewhat disappointing. It is positioned on a plain so vast that comparatively the stones seem insignificant at first. It's only when you get close to the stones that you feel so puny in comparison and it's very hard to imagine how centuries ago, and with the most primitive of tools to help them, men could have placed these huge boulders there.

I'd stopped for a pub lunch in Andover and found an excellent bookshop in the High Street. There I'd purchased a new book on the history and legends of Druids were claimed as historical Stonehenge, and I opened it now and read parts of it.

Some say the Druids constructed it, and as I've said previously, most historians agree that they arrived here too late to have done so. Druids were not exactly English, as they derived from the elite Celtic priests who along with their people had swept westwards from the continent to populate Britain as far back as 2000 B.C. They were known in France as the Gauls, and their connection to Stonehenge was so puzzling because their reputation for bloody sacrifices was well known down through the ages, and this produced a paradox. For how could men who held with such repugnant religious practices have produced such superb work as the circular doorways of Stonehenge? I well remembered from my school years that the early chroniclers told of them being a sinister fraternity dedicated, to quote the Roman Publius Cornelius Tacitus, to inhuman superstitions and barbarous rites. They are mentioned by many of the ancient Roman authors, who portrayed them as overseeing bloody religious rituals, and so the Druids are often thought of as having a primarily religious function, and are often called "priests".

Diodorus called them "philosophers", while Strabo called them "bards and soothsayers, with a reputation for mediation". Julius Caesar wrote about the Druids in his Gallic

Wars, stating that they made human sacrifices to their gods by constructing huge wicker cages in human form, "whose limbs, woven out of twigs, they fill with living men and set on fire, and the men perish in a sheet of flame". Diodor Siculus, a contemporary of Caesar, wrote of Druid rituals in which the priests would kill a man by a knife-stab in the region above his midriff, and after his fall they foretell the future by the convulsions of his limbs and the pouring of his blood.

All in all the early Druids were blood-thirsty philosophers and astronomers, and many scholars and researchers through the centuries have often attributed the building of Stonehenge to them, as a temple to their own rituals. Yet I remembered a teacher once telling us of Inigo Jones, the seventeenth-century architect, who disputed this big time, saying, "I find no mention that they were studious in architecture or anything else conducing thereunto". He allowed that the Druids may have been philosophers and astronomers, but those were branches of learning "consisting more in contemplation than practice".

After centuries of neglect in the wake of first Roman and then Christian suppression, the Druids were rediscovered during the Renaissance when the revival of interest in ancient Greek and Latin writers brought attention to the works of Pliny, Tacitus and Julius Caesar and their descriptions of the Celtic world. First in France in the sixteenth century and then in England, the ancient Celts and Druids were claimed as historical ancestors. By the seventeenth century, a new romantic image of Druids began to emerge in French and English literature.

As I gazed at the massive stones lit up by searchlights in a ghostly way, I remembered that famous men down through the ages had revived the cult of Druidism and it had been passed on. William Stukeley, a physician, an antiquarian and an orthodox Christian, had started resurgence in the whole Stonehenge/Druid association, and founded a "social club" calling it the Society of Roman Knights. Stukeley even went so far as to call himself Chyndonax, after a fabled French Druid high priest. Architect John Wood, who rebuilt the city of Bath, declared Stonehenge "the great sanctuary of the Archprophet of Britain." And the Druidophile Henry Hurle, taking the revivalist movement to its logical conclusion, founded in 1781 the Ancient Order of Druids.

But sitting there in my car, staring at the eerie megaliths framed against the night sky, with the whole superstitions of Stonehenge laid out before me in either reality or the book on my lap, I got to wonder. Was it actually Stukeley around the 1720s who reformed the Druids, or had they always been there, and in turn had recruited him?

I turned to the more recent history of Stonehenge and the year 1915 popped up; the year that the campaign in the Balkans had failed and all chances of ending the coming conflict had ceased to be. In Salisbury's New Theatre an auctioneer announced in dramatic tones:

'Lot 15, ladies and gentlemen; Stonehenge'.

The Antrobus family had suddenly ceased to be, for the heir had been killed somewhere on a faraway battlefield and his father, Sir Edmund, had now died also; some said of grief. Therefore the estate with no surviving heir was now for sale, and it included a huge piece of Salisbury Plain, including the legendry Stonehenge. It had nearly been sold a decade earlier, when John Jacob Astor, an American, had tried to buy it for the British Museum, and for the amazing sum of twenty-five thousand pounds sterling. Sir Edmund Antrobus, fearing it would become under the control of a government department refused to sell.

By act of Parliament Stonehenge was also protected against demolition and export. Two years later the Church of Universal Bond had tried to transfer ownership to a company called the Druids and Antiquarians.

The bidding that day was rather disappointing, reaching six thousand pounds then stopping. On impulse a local man put his hand up, and Mr. Cecil H.E. Chubb of Bemerton Lodge, Salisbury, became the owner of Stonehenge for the sum of six thousand, six hundred pounds. In 1918 he gave it to the British nation, and I noted ironically that the then Prime Minister, Lloyd George, made him a baronet the same year.

Impressed as I had always been with the appearance of Stonehenge I wasn't so impressed with its history, and I eventually drove on, confused that this entire violin business was producing more mysteries than it was explaining.

I arrived at the cottage late, yet all of the house lights were on and a black Mercedes people carrier gleaming in the outside spotlights. I approached warily and felt a large presence rub against my right leg. Lupus didn't appear to be perturbed in any way so although I was aware that I had visitors I concluded I had friendly visitors. I was also pleased to note that he'd more or less recovered from his recent injury.

'Let's see if there's some food left in the fridge, shall we mate?' I said to the fox and he seemed to nod as he trotted ahead, nuzzling the door open.

We walked into the living room and there were three people sitting there watching the news on TV and drinking Jameson's; not mine, though the glasses were. My best ones, I noticed.

'Do I get one of those or have I run out of glasses?' I asked.

Patrick waved a hand in front of a big grin, but his two companions were on their feet in a minute; reaching for weapons as their eyes caught sight of Lupus.

'Don't even think about it, gents,' I said, taking a couple of paces forward and covering my friend the fox. 'He'll have your throats out before you clear the holsters and I'll take what's left.'

Patrick said something sharply in Italian and they both relaxed, somewhat sheepishly. They were strapping young

277

men, early thirties, clean-shaven and good looking. They looked like they could do the business and I assumed that they were Patrick's bodyguards by order of the Pope following his misadventure in the car park.

Then I saw they both wore dog collars.

'Scusi, Signore, Scusi,' one of them said. 'We did not know it was your friend.'

'That's okay,' I smiled. 'At least you did not call him my pet, which is a mistake many people make. Indeed, he IS my friend, not my pet. Excuse me a moment, he's hungry.'

I grabbed some hamburger steak from the freezer and stuck it in the microwave to defreeze. Then fetched an empty glass and went back in the lounge where I placed it noisily in front of the Signore.

'You run out of hands, lad?' he frowned in mock vexation. 'Pour your bloody own.'

Which I did and shook my head at him. 'Padraig, I've just had an audience with your mate, the Papa.' I did a reasonable Belfast accent; of course I should be able to after the time I'd spent there. 'What a nice man, a true gentleman. Do you really think you're in contention for his job one day with that terrible mouth of yours?'

'As much as the chance of you ever becoming an altar boy again,' and this time as he smiled his face took on the expression of a prowling barracuda. 'So, what decision did you come to after chatting with Il Papa?'

'Hey,' I shrugged. 'How do you say "no" to the Pope?'

'With great difficulty?' he grinned, and stuck his hand out. I took it and the bargain for my service was struck.

The room visibly relaxed, meaning his two acolytes, as I clinked glasses with everyone and had a good slurp of the decent stuff, then looked enquiringly at the little priest.

'So, who let you out of hospital, Patrick?'

'After I got rid of the headache I was in fine fettle, Harry. I only had to complain twice about the food and they kicked me out. The police came to see me in hospital, but no one glimpsed the car, despite the lass phoning it all in to the local law and them doing one of those APB things.'

'The lass?' I asked, though I had a good idea who that was.

'Aye, Heather, the landlord's daughter, as though you didn't know,' he grinned. 'I saw you looking at her.'

'You know she happens to be a cop, and a detective-inspector at that,' I told him somewhat sharply. 'Besides, Andrea and I have an understanding.'

He gave me a strange look but said nothing.

Just then I felt a nudge against my leg and realized I'd forgotten about the fox's supper. I patted his head in apology, opened the microwave and tossed the large piece of meat on the kitchen floor. It was made of large slabs of Delabole slate from Cornwall and had stood the test of time so well that one piece of meat wasn't going to discolor it.

Patrick poured more whiskey but I noticed he left the young men's glasses alone.

'These lads,' he nodded to them, 'are part of my little circle, Harry. You don't need all the details but they are both ordained priests, though more secular than religious at this time of their lives. They fight the Lord's good fight and are good at what they do. There are many more of them.'

'You're saying they kill, Patrick?' I took a glug, which is a bit larger than a slurp, rolled it around my mouth and then swallowed it slowly. 'In the name of the Lord it may be, but it's still a mortal sin, which threatens their souls, does it not?'

The little priest nodded. 'You're right, of course. But they are willing to chance it in their quest to defeat the Evil one.

When they have achieved their aim Il Papa will grant them a dispensation and they will be whole again.'

I said nothing. I had discovered at a very early age there was no use arguing with a priest, and certainly not one engaged on a mission. They had their ways.

'These lads are yours for the mission, Harry. There's more if you need them, but I thought you'd rather go in low key, as it were. Better that way, avoid a lot of heavy contact; in and out quickly.'

'Tell me, Patrick,' I looked at him steadily. 'What rank were you in the Army below the border before donning the black suit?'

'There's no avoiding yer suspicious nature, now, is there lad?' he gave an ironic little smile. 'I was once a company commander, actually.'

I was never to know more about his association with the IRA than that.

Each of the young priests gave me a rundown on their qualifications. Before taking orders they had been in the Alpini, the Italian crack Alpine troops with whom I'd done exercises on occasion, and their reputation was indeed well deserved. Antonio, he of the saturnine visage had been something of a biathlon champion, representing his country in the Winter Olympics and was a crack shot. Having performed at that sport myself in modest inter-services competitions, I was impressed. His fair-haired companion, Alain (that's French, I said. My father was French, he told me), obviously from the north of Italy, was also a marksman and had been a karate instructor in the army.

Both had gone on to obtain University degrees after they'd been ordained, and I was surprised to learn that they were both in their middle thirties, as I'd thought them younger.

'The last time we met, Harry,' the little priest said. 'You spoke of the load of strange markings on the wall of the vault where they'd been keeping the violin. Can you describe them at all, as Antonio here has some knowledge of that kind of thing?'

'I can do even better than that, Padraig old son,' and I rose and went into my bedroom. The Bushnell's were lying in my pack under the bed and I took them out.

I returned to the living room and picked up my laptop from its case behind the sofa. I set it up on the table, plugged into the mains and connected the binoculars cum digital camera into the system via one of the USB ports. A few minutes later I was able to bring up the photos I'd taken of the mysterious wall symbols in the Chateau Revanche.

The three priests gathered around as I flipped through the various pictures.

'I know this,' Antonio said quietly. 'They are hieroglyphs, the writing of the ancient Egyptians. Take the first row; the "eye" you see there is actually a mouth, and stands for "r". The twisted green snake is "o", the half red sun is "t", the bird is a vulture, representing "a", and that hook-like symbol can be a folded cloth or a door bolt, meaning "s".

'So, we have "ROTAS",' I wrote down. 'Which means...?'

The priest took the pen from me and began jotting words down across the page. Sometimes he would frown for a moment then remember the letter for the symbol and carry on. He was good, and soon had the following list of words in front of him.

ROTAS

OPERA

TENET

AREPO

SATOR

'Very good,' I couldn't help a touch of the famous Brogan sarcasm creeping into my voice. 'But it still means sod all.'

'Ah now, that's where you'd be wrong, laddie,' Patrick suddenly joined the conversation, a touch of excitement in his voice. 'By themselves the words have no significance, except that an observant reader might notice they form a palindrome, for they can be read the same way back to front. More important here is that we're looking at the old established freemasonry of the religion of Mithras the bull god, whose doctrines of self-discipline and sacrifice was popular with the army. To every Christian at that date they had a well known significance, dating back to the time before the Emperor Constantine in the last century when Christians had been persecuted for their faith.'

He too took up the pen and underneath the previous deciphering of Antonio he began to scribble an arrangement of words.

'The secret of these five words is that they can be arranged to read:

```
                    P
                    A
                    T
                    E
                    R
        P A T E R N O S T E R
                    O
                    S
                    T
                    E
                    R
```

The little priest beamed around the table and was obviously disappointed in the reaction he received, or should I say non-reaction. I for one was lost somewhere back there in the time of Constantine. The two younger priests were actually beginning to nod now; as though they were actually cottoning on to what Padraig Sullivan was saying.

'Well, don't you see it now, Brogan? When the arrangement is completed, two letters remain unused: A and O, which stood for Alpha and Omega, the Greek biblical description of God; an ancient rubric, to be sure, but a sure sign of what we are dealing with here. These people have corrupted the meaning of the religion of Mithras.'

'Or,' said Alain. 'They are of that cult in the present day.'

We sat late into the night and made an initial plan; simple enough but it seemed reasonably effective. Once again Patrick had the information we needed, which was the location in Britain of the people who owned the Château Revanche in France. It was deja vu all over again, for the target was a large forbidding place in the country, Houghton Hall.

'About all we know, boyo,' Patrick said. 'It belonged to a rather reticent family of the aristocracy for a long time, since it was built in fact. Suddenly the old boy died, apparently last of the line, and it was sold to someone just as reticent as the original owners. Spends long periods away and that's all we've been able to learn.'

'All sounds very fishy to me, Patrick,' I shook my head. 'We obviously need more information about the place and that's where my people skills come in.'

I smiled beguilingly but the little priest was having none of it. 'What you mean, lad, is that during your previous unsavoury and dishonest life you learned special ways of gaining knowledge about your target residences.'

'Something like that, yes,' I grinned. 'Come on, Lupus, we're turning in. Unless you've got other plans in the great outdoors, that is.'

By the way he made for my bedroom door he obviously hadn't, though the inclement weather outside might have had something to do with it rather than a desire for my soothing company.

'No doubt you gents know where all the spare beds are by now, not to mention a couple of sofas, so make yourselves comfortable.'

They bid me goodnight but made no attempt to turn in themselves. Having had a flight and a drive myself I was knackered so said goodnight in turn. When I pushed my door to, I never close it in case Lupus wants to get out during the night, I left the three Catholic clergymen intent on a discussion in Italian. Without being modest I somehow knew it involved me.

The next morning we ate a leisurely breakfast and left around ten o'clock. We'd decided to take both cars, with Patrick riding with me in my 4 x 4 and the boys bringing up the rear. There was a dual purpose in this, as I would be navigating and they would be running interference should it be necessary. We might also need the second car later.

We travelled through a countryside I knew well. It was England, as I knew her. Forget the recent interlopers; foreigners, mainly from Continental Europe but also from countries where many of them had not been political victims but the aggressors, pretending to be asylum seekers and claiming vast amounts of money and sending it back to their countries of origin. But let us not go there, because it makes my blood boil, all of this money being given away to arseholes when old people who were born and bred in England are getting sweet F.A.

We picked up the double-carriageway of the A30 east of Okehampton and carried on east, circumventing Exeter to the south and picking up the A30 again just past the M5 motorway heading north. At Honiton I dropped down onto the A35 and along the coast road, passing the old carpet town of Axminster, and then Bridport and at Dorchester went northeast on the A354. We stopped off on the road to Blandford Forum for lunch, after which we carried on northeast on the A354, moving now through the county of Wiltshire and nearing Salisbury around two in the afternoon.

Much of the country we'd gone through was rich stock-broker country these days: the land of property millionaires and yuppies, the quasi-countrified people who had a Merc for the alpha male, and a 4 wheel drive something for the little wife, who would pick up their 2.5 kids from the right public school with their 1.25 Labradors in the back of the wagon. She would also be correctly dressed in a rough blue jersey, no makeup, green wellies, and in winter would be wearing a green waterproof coat with a corduroy collar.

Enough, already, I thought; don't let your prejudice show.

We drove into the ancient town of Salisbury and booked into a second-rate hotel off the High Street so not to draw attention. We split up and I wandered around town on my own, the others trying to casually locate our target. Around seven we met up in the small hotel bar and ate a decent meal in the dining room, the clerical hit-men wearing their clerical collars, Patrick also wearing his trademark black with the white collar; and me wearing my usual cynical smile.

The fare was traditional but well prepared. It was a set menu, with two choices; take it or leave it. It consisted of generous helpings of steak and kidney pie, with tenderised lumps of steak and slivers of kidney packed inside homemade pastry along with rich ale gravy. It came with mashed potatoes and peas, one of my favourites, and carrots and string beans on the side for the really hungry. The younger priests ate as though they'd been fasting for weeks, while Patrick ate sparingly and I sunk an average portion. I don't eat dessert but the dog-collared pair downed two helpings of figgy duff.

I wondered where they put it all until the next morning when the three of us drove out of the city and went for a run on the plains of Salisbury. They left me standing after about three miles and I jogged slowly back to the car and sipped strong coffee from a flask. I was listening to the eternal Wogan on the car radio when they returned an hour later. They were dripping in sweat but by their demeanour I guessed they'd be ready for another ten miles after a ten minute rest and their pulse rate would be in the low sixties.

After a shower and change of clothes, no dog collars this time, we climbed in their car and meandered around the country lanes and as if by chance we passed our target at a leisurely pace but kept on going. This allowed me to take half a dozen quick snaps from the back window of the car. After lunch in a pub near the bus station, on the quaintly named Blue Boar Row, the three clergymen decided to drive up to Stonehenge and do the tourist bit. Back at the hotel I got out the yellow pages and flipped to the biggest section, that of the real estate offices. A dozen calls later and I finally got one that acceded to my request of the agents who had sold the place.

'Clifton & Webb, Real Estate Bureau,' breathed a public school voice. 'How may we be of service?'

I held back a titter, never having heard an estate agency called a "bureau" before, and being an old movie buff I knew of Clifton Webb of course. I told him I was an Inland Revenue inspector and was trying to ascertain who had last sold the Ashenbrook Manor. He sounded delighted when I used my best sinister voice and told him confidentially that I was investigating the whole deal; buyers, sellers and agents.

'Oh, indeed I do,' he squealed. 'Baverstoke, Haskins and Perry, about three months ago, and we just knew that someone would get onto them eventually. You know, they never even allowed it to go on the market. Many of us feel there was some kind of stitch-up which ruins things for all of us in the profession.'

Without recourse to my usual sarcasm I enquired politely as to how his suspicions were founded; at which point he became somewhat vague so I thanked him and rang off. I donned a suit and tie and phoned Patrick's room to tell him what I was up to. Not that I was too sure myself.

The premises of Baverstoke, Haskins and Perry were situated in a prime spot on the High Street, and surrounded by banks, insurance offices, other estate agents and dozens of charity shops. The latter are a purely British institution and all get tax-free benefits and are also rate-free. Those that don't own their premises outright, usually pay a low rent. Little old ladies work in them for no wages, and they make a fortune. In the bigger towns and cities, buses take groups of senior citizens around on guided tours of the charity shops. Anyway, my point is that only the aforementioned groups can afford to dwell in the High Street anywhere in this Sceptred Isle anymore.

I walked in as though I owned the place and counted at least a dozen agents sitting behind big desks and speaking softly and eloquently to potential clients.

There was a front desk with a receptionist ensconced. She was a large bespectacled woman in her thirties, with golden hair straight from the bottle and too much makeup. When she spoke it came as a shock, for she had an incredibly sexy voice, albeit was all public school.

'How may I help?' she purred, and I wondered if she'd worked her way through school as one of those telephone voices who wanted to know what you were wearing now and describing in avid detail what she was doing, all for twenty quid for five minutes. It really was that sultry sounding.

'Hmm,' I bestowed my best smile upon her. 'That perfume, it's very familiar, it's not...?

'" An Evening in Picardy", yes,' she breathed.

'Of course,' I said. "My late...used it. I'm sorry, it brings back such painful memories, you know.'

I put on my pathetic look, thinking that my bloody fox wouldn't even wear it, but by the look in her eye I knew I had her.

Putting on my best upper crust accent, the one I'd practiced over the years, I introduced myself as Timothy Tancredy, producer of documentaries, and told her I was making a film about Britain's historical heritage and how the present high property price trend was affecting the sales of these. I mentioned that I was terribly impressed with their recent sale of Houghton Hall and she positively preened.

'I'm in negotiations with the present owner to film there,' I told her in a conspiratorial voice. 'I'd really like to do some homework first, you understand, and wondered if you had any sales brochures, plans or the like.'

Of course she had, and would love to loan them to me. Perhaps I'd also like the details of some other splendid properties they just happened to have on their books at the moment? Of course I would. I left with an armload of sales brochures, plans and lots of other stuff of the like. I also left the no-longer-young, dyed-blonde receptionist with a warm glow and a subtle promise of more of me later. Not.

I arrived back at the hotel and phoned Patrick and his acolytes. They were now returned from their sightseeing trip and about five minutes later joined me in my room. I then spread my booty out on the table in the middle of the room and spent a few minutes on explanations. We spent an hour poring over the stuff I'd brought back, and began to form a more tangible plan.

It was now less than two days before October 31st; which was the eve of All Hallows and I suddenly remembered something I had to do back in Devon. I also vaguely remembered Andi telling me that the great festival of Samain was the Celtic name for Halloween, though why that should be significant I had no idea.

At the time.

I made a brief farewell to Patrick, who showed no surprise but nodded wisely, and I promised faithfully, by a God I no longer had a lot of faith in, to be back in plenty of time for our quest.

I decided to take the quicker route of the A303 and booted the pedal, arriving home in a few hours. That's one of the few remaining good things about Britain. It doesn't take you days and many visits to a Motel 6 or Ramada Inn to get somewhere. I saw a car in the drive and some gear on the bed in the spare room. My son joined me a short time later. When I asked where he'd been he said he'd been out exploring with Lupus. I was pleased that my son and my best mate were getting on, and wished it were the same with the fox and Andi.

'He certainly knows his way around this place, Dad,' Phillip said. 'He showed me everything.'

'Such as?' I enquired with a smile.

'Well,' he replied with a grin. 'I can't tell you, because he mightn't want you to know some of the places we went to.'

'You cheeky little arsehole,' I grinned back. 'Now, come and tell me what you think of this lot.'

I laid out all of the brochures, plans and stuff I'd acquired during my visit to Salisbury. Our last conversation had been about the dwelling that was to become our target, and although I couldn't isolate the particular place at that time, he said he'd do his "research thing". A touch of pride came over me again when five minutes into the conversation he showed me that he'd done just that. He'd brought himself up to scratch with the background of the English country house.

And this was certainly a classical example of a classic English country house. English because it was in England and country house because it was a mansion built in the country - sorry, couldn't resist. The term "country house" is synonymous with "historic house", though naturally houses of historical interest may also be found in any British towns and cities.

The country house as a style of building rose up in the relative peace and prosperity of the Tudor age, Phillip quoted. There was no longer a requirement for defence of domestic buildings so the aristos began lavishing their money on houses designed to impress their friends and families. The heyday of the country house was the 18th century and most of the surviving examples are from that period. The predominant style of the early 18th century was Palladian, based on the classical designs of Andreas Palladio, and fostered by Lord Burlington among others. My son referred to notes only moderately but bugger me if he didn't have an even better mind for recall that his old man.

Then we came to the interesting part; for me at least, with my imminent incursion into one. Generally they were situated on rising ground, with gardens stretching up to the back door from parklands below. They were classical in style, with a large central portico and strong vertical lines on the exterior. It was in the interior that the traditional country house really shone. Ornate furnishings were designed to impress, with generally a large entry hall leading on to living rooms meant specifically for show. Bedrooms and dressing rooms were upstairs, with the kitchen and servants quarters relegated to the basement; very inconvenient but quite magnificent.

'Thank you, Phillip,' I stood up. 'This is exactly the kind of place Houghton Hall is like. Quite possibly too much information in some of that but generally very rewarding for what I need to know.'

'So, when you going in to do the deadly deed, Dad?' He asked with a grin.

'Phillip, I'm shocked,' I scolded with mock seriousness. 'Just what do you think I'm going to do with this information?'

'Nick something?' he replied carelessly, and I knew I'd have to have a long conversation with my son quite soon.

'Can I come?' there was eagerness in his voice that part of me relished but the rest didn't really want to hear.

I shook my head, then realized he deserved something other than a negative, so I sat down and told him the whole story – well, most of it.

We compromised in that he would stay in the cottage, feed Lupus and keep an eye on the place until I got back. Which would be in a few days – I hoped.

The next morning, early, as I was preparing to return to Salisbury, I received a surprise visitor.

The car looked exactly like it was – an unmarked cop car.

Heather looked good. Not quite stunning, although that could have been because she was in mufti wearing a severe grey suit, sensible shoes and had her hair up. The bloke with her had no such excuse for being on duty for I felt he would have worn the same tired blue suit and rumpled shirt if he was going to a wedding, or a funeral. The latter would have been more apt because he already had the right expression. Mournful. He was about fifty with a face that could have been formed from a lump of play dough, and a pasty type of pallor.

'Hi,' I said carefully. 'Back at work already?'

'I've been returned to duty, yes, Mr. Brogan.'

Oh, dear, I thought, such formality.

'Now why would that be?' I asked nonchantly.

'Apparently pressure has been applied to my superiors from someone in the Salisbury area. A very influential person, so I was told. This person stated that he has an original Stradivarius violin, worth a lot of money and he has been informed that someone intends to steal it.' She gazed at me with a bland expression, but having been treated to a more sociable side of her, it appeared more like something green and slimy had emerged from her Caesar salad and was daring to affect an escape the long way across her plate. I tried not to squirm under that gaze.

'Really?' I pretended to muse. 'Now why would that have anything to do with me, I wonder?'

'You once mentioned a violin to me, Mr. Brogan, a very valuable violin.'

'Ah yes,' I was getting pissed off now. I prefer to say it straight out, not this arsing around the way the fuzz do it. 'I believe I told you a winsome little tale about a Stradivarius that had a curse on it. Worth about 20 million I think I said. Come on Heather, surely you didn't believe me?

'Yet worth a lot more to someone who believes in the supernatural,' she said dryly and I saw her companion swallow hard as he tried to pretend he knew exactly what was going on. 'By the way, this is Detective Inspector Millerchip from Special Branch.'

'What a fertile imagination you do have, Inspector,' I shrugged, ignoring the belated introduction. 'How on Earth does any of this have to do with anything? Or perhaps you've found the Jag, in which case that's great police work and I'm very impressed.'

'Can we go inside, Brogan?' she asked.

I led the way inside and offered coffee, which they both declined. We sat at the kitchen table and I looked at Heather enquiringly.

To my surprise she looked almost embarrassed for a moment, before appearing to force herself into her official mode.

'A leading political figure, living in the Salisbury area, has had an interview with the Commissioner of the Metropolitan Police,' she said slowly and carefully, as though she was attempting to convince herself of the facts herself before passing them on. 'He lives in a big house, is filthy rich and states that he owns a certain violin, a Stradivarius worth a large amount of money, and he believes that someone is going to try and steal it. He has asked for police protection to guard this item.'

'And you're here because...?' I asked, as though I didn't know.

'Don't be a wisearse, Brogan,' the male version of Deputy Dog, or is it Dawg, growled.

I turned and gave him my hard look. 'What?'

'I said...'

'I know what you said, Captain Sensible,' I retorted. 'I just don't know what made you think you could come into my house and call me names.'

'We know about you, Brogan,' he said with what he probably considered a touch of menace in his voice.

'You know WHAT?' I did a better job of putting the menace in my voice. 'I've never seen the inside of a police station, never been arrested and certainly never been charged with anything, so tell me what you know about me.'

'All right, boys,' Heather snapped. "That's enough testosterone for now. Bob, Mr. Brogan is not a suspect for anything. At the moment. You look as though you're going somewhere, Brogan.'

'Yes,' I smiled. 'I do, don't I?'

'Morning,' my son's voice came from the doorway leading to the outside of the cottage, though how long he'd been there no one had apparently noticed. Lupus was standing at his side, looking at the male detective inspector with distain. 'Thought you'd be gone by now, dad.'

'My son,' I said unnecessarily. I noted the look of surprise on Heather Frankton's face before it disappeared and was replaced by a radiant smile that to my annoyance had my son almost blushing.

Millerchip was still looking apprehensively at the fox, which was gazing back at him with flat emotionless eyes, a sure sign that he had not taken to the man. Good judge of character, old Lupus.

'Well, thank you for your time, Brogan,' Heather said politely, yet her voice was still tinged with…what? Suspicion, perhaps? Not that I could blame her too much.

I walked them out to their car and waited until Detective Inspector Millerchip settled himself behind the wheel and fiddled with the seat and the mirror the way blokes like him always do. I spoke softly to Heather as we made our way around the back of the car to the passenger side.

'Leave me a card, phone number or something so I can reach you at short notice if I need to.'

She stopped and looked me straight in the eyes. 'So there is something going down, Brogan.'

'That's as much as I'm saying, Heather,' I stared right back at her. 'This is too big and involves too many people for me to start blabbing right now. I'll promise you this much; if it goes as we think it will then it's bigger than any of us, but I'll let you be one of the first to know. Take whatever steps you like then, but I swear this is a whole lot more than a mere theft, even if the Strad IS worth a fortune. We're talking about the Salisbury area, but don't contact anyone locally unless you'd bet your life on him or her because we don't know how high up this goes. Let me correct that; we know it's bloody high but not the individuals involved, and there could well be high-ranking policemen placed in the right positions.'

'Take this, Brogan,' she startled me by saying and I felt something thrust into my hand. It was a small cell phone. 'Press the dialling button and it will automatically reach me. It has no other contact numbers.' Her words were accompanied by a rather sage look. 'Take care, Brogan. You don't know what you're dealing with.'

I held the door open for her and she accepted the small gesture with good grace and swung her legs inside before I closed the door. I returned to the kitchen deep in thought. Reprising the visit I thought that perhaps it had all been for the benefit of the guy from London. Why the hell would they send an inspector from Special Branch down here? Maybe Heather's participation was simply to warn me. I couldn't get over her last words, "You don't know what you're dealing with".

Was it just a general caution or did she know in fact know what we were dealing with?

'Coffee afore you shove off, maister?' Phillip gave a reasonable impression of the local dialect and I saw he'd made a fresh pot. I accepted and sunk into thought again as he poured two cups and brought them to the table.

'Bit of an arsehole that copper, wasn't he?' he observed and I nodded without remonstrating about his turn of speech. After all, when you're right, you're right.

'Talking of which,' he said.

'Talking of arseholes or cops?' I smiled.

'Both,' he grinned. 'I read in the paper last week about a woman who was belting down the road and passed over a bridge, only to find a cop with a radar gun on the other side lying in wait.

'The cop pulled her over and walked up to the car with that patronizing smirk we all know and love, and he asked.

'What's your hurry?'

'I'm late for work,' the woman replied.

'Oh, yes,' he sniffed. 'And what do you do?'

'I'm a rectum stretcher,' she said with a straight face.

'The cop frowned disbelievingly. 'So what does a rectum stretcher do?'

'Well,' she said. 'I start by inserting one finger, then work my way up to two fingers, then three, then four, then get my whole hand in. I work from side to side until I can get both hands in; then slowly but surely I stretch it until it's about 6 feet wide.'

'And just what the hell do you do with a 6 foot arsehole?' he snorted.

'You give him a radar gun and park him behind a bridge...'

I couldn't stop laughing at that. 'You made that up you little bugger.'

He shook his head and looked solemn. 'No, at the end of the article it said; Traffic Ticket $95,

'Court Costs $45,

'Look on the Cop's face...........PRICELESS

'For everything else, there's MasterCard......'

I took a mock smack at his head, but his little story had achieved its purpose for I'd snapped out of my pensive mood after the visit of the fair Heather and her horrible colleague. Talk about Beauty and the bloody Beast…

At last I was ready to go and again it took only around three hours to return along the 303 to Salisbury Plain. I took a right past Winterbourne Stoke onto the A360, passing Old Sarum on the left and into Salisbury. I located Patrick and brought him up to speed on the events in Devon and to my relief he had no incidents to report.

Then he spoilt things by casually mentioning that there was a ball at Houghton Hall beginning at 7:30pm the following evening – the feast of All Hallows.

'Obviously it's being done as a diversion from the main business of the night. There'll be cars coming and going all night, and not all of the guests will be part of the Compte's followers they will also be part of the cover. The ceremony will take place at Stonehenge, no doubt about that. I'll not bore you with details, Harry, but the location and the timing are what these people have been preparing for over two millennia. Some time after the henge was first built, its astronomers made a discovery: that the moon in its orbit round the earth does not follow a single path, but that it oscillates from side to side in a subtle cycle of its own; repeated every nineteen years.

'It is one of the greatest secrets in the sacred sayings of the priests, that the moon goddess only shows the same face, on the same day, once in nineteen years. For although the solar year does not divide neatly into twenty-nine-day lunar months, a coincidence between solar and lunar years could be arranged on a long count of nineteen years – a discovery ascribed to Meton the Greek around the time of Christ. When the Romans first landed in the isles of Britain they were disgusted with the sacrificial rites of the Celts and their Druid priests, and their great God, Dagda, the protector of the tribe, who took pleasure in changing into unlikely shapes and playing tricks on mankind. The young

Vespassian when he visited island Britain gave a decree to exterminate them...'

'That's very interesting, Patrick,' I growled at him. 'But I don't need another history lecture; I'm about up to here with them. Tell me what this ceremony consists of – the shortened version for God's sake.'

He muttered something under his breath and I thought of how it would be if I sat him and Andi down together and let them lecture each other for a few weeks, or would it be more like months?

'The present day Druids you might have read about are simply quasi-religious groups who are harmless and carry out their little pagan rites without harming anyone. Tonight's lot is totally different. For one they are not Druidic in any shape or form. Their society goes back to the dawn of humankind, their strange rites and beliefs changing over the years but always having one goal; the exaltation of Lucifer and his lordship of the Earth.'

I left it at that, not coming back with any snappy retorts or anything. The next day was the 31st of October, and we spent it mainly in trying to look casual and leisurely before the night came looming and things would start to happen.

CHAPTER FOURTEEN

"And they worshipped the dragon which gave power unto the beast: and they worshipped the beast, saying, "Who is like unto the beast?" Who is able to make war with him?"

Revelation 13:4

Simple as it was the plan meant that I would go in first, with the other two forming back-up by following me and flanking out to provide cover if needed. Once I'd gained entry to the place they'd come in and together we'd explore; looking for the now oft-stolen violin.

The time was ten o'clock at the moment of entering. We had lain in wait for a while opposite the well-manned main gate and had seen the entrance of more cars than you'd see in half-a-dozen well-stocked dealerships. We'd also noted the presence of several uniformed policemen in the vicinity of the front gate.

Our plan, as I've said before, was simple. Over the wall and through the depth of bushes and deciduous trees that surrounded the well-laid lawns and flowerbeds, which in turn surrounded the mansion-cum-fortress. It was discreetly done, the open lawns and miniature flowerbeds giving all-round vision to anyone watching from the building; and I had no doubt that there were many pairs of eyes peering out from the dark windows. I lay on my stomach and used the night scope I'd brought with me to try and detect movement in those windows. I felt the presence of the priests as they fanned out to either side of me. I had reservations about it being a comforting presence, however, as I was by now well used to working on my own. That was unfair and I realized it at the instant I allowed it to go through my mind.

I'd seen that the house was surrounded by arc-lights focused onto the house itself, but to my relief only the front were shining, presumably to give a great bas-relief to the darkened sides and back.

I moved to my right through the bushes, barely hearing my backup team of the priests as they matched my change of direction. The rear of the imposing building was darker, but that meant even more chance of night detection apparatus of some kind. In the end I took a deep breath, mouthed, "sod it", and raced across the finely manicured lawn.

Surprisingly I was still alive after my little heart-stopping piece of exercise and had to grin when I thought of the two young men feeling very frustrated as they waited to join me but were also waiting for the shot in the night which betokened my demise. It was not to be, I realized as I eased my way around the building testing the windows, surprisingly modernized for such a superb old building, until an ancient casement type in what was most likely a scullery rewarded me. Not a major problemo as it would at least get me inside the house. I was getting to be a mite nervous wandering outside in the dark. Call me paranoid, but...It must go with the territory – that of being a thief.

The thin blade from my leg sheath slid easily along the usual casement hollow between sashes and a helpful prod from moi on the lower window helped it to find the catch and move it forward. I clambered inside (yes, I said clambered because the window was about four feet from the ground level outside and I was not feeling my usual gymnastic self – all right?). I was correct the first time and was in a scullery, or dairy in the old terminology, so felt my way slowly around the room until I encountered the door. It was locked, of course, which was why they hadn't bothered changing the window, but it was the work of a couple of seconds to open it. Remember, an expert trained me. Pity he wasn't an expert in looking out for the old Bill, but that's another story.

I switched on my pencil torch and shone the thin beam of red light quickly around the room behind me, also flashing it at the window and sending it out as a message to the priests that I was inside. I turned the knob and slowly entered what appeared to be a narrow hallway running to the front of the house. I stood motionless for a few moments, getting the feel of the place and allowing my built-in radar to ascertain if it was safe or not. It usually worked well on my behalf and this time was no exception, only...I did not feel settled and thought at first it might be that I was in an alien place, with little or no knowledge of what to expect. The plans of the house were etched into my brain but I had no similar awareness of the people who might have been inside.

I finally moved, keeping tight to the right side of the passage and looking for a door leading to the lower depths of the house. The estate agent's plans had shown large cellars below the house, as would be attributable to any such dwelling of the period. But surely three months wouldn't have been enough to carry out any major changes.

A sudden epiphany struck me at this point, albeit too bloody late as usual.

The house had changed hands only three months ago – not really time to convert the cellars into something like the one in France, or get the house into some kind of security order, but this brought forward the interesting bit about the exchange of deeds, etc; from whom and to whom. Interesting, I mused, but too late for anything to come of it at that time. Yet I couldn't help wondering if the new owner was also the old owner, and there was a reason behind the whole thing.

I shook myself. Of course there was.

I found the cellar steps through a door on the left of the passage I was negotiating, and wondered how many other entrances there were leading down to the subterranean depths. From the plans I'd seen, surprisingly vague considering the age of the house and the fine Palladian ancestry attached to both the design and supposedly sumptuous interior, I knew that the space below the house almost equalled the proportions above. High-ceiled vaults apparently contained fine examples of barrel vaulting with the original brickwork in amazing condition. Being on a hill also prevented the curse of all under-house spaces the world over; incipient damp, if not actual flooding.

The thin beam of red light gave onto surprisingly wide and generously proportioned steps leading down to the depths below. Sconces were set every few feet and I judged by their design that they were probably electric, though the last thing I wanted was to bring unwanted attention by turning them on. I also thought about waiting for the priestly pair to show up but preferred to stay on my own for the time being.

The flight took me down a fair distance, or depth as it turned out to be. I flashed the pencil torch around and found only a main passage leading forward. So I followed it. It wound down for quite a distance, before levelling out and becoming an even wider passage. As I progressed the condition of the passage became more established and progressed from an initial stone floor with carved out walls to Delabole slate floors and walls of a thick tiled variety. Some doors led off from here; stout oaken doors of ancient lineage, their antiquity showing in their thickness and blackened appearance. I had no time to explore, much as

I would have loved to, but crept on remorselessly – a man on a mission no less.

At the end were heavy double doors taking up the whole width of the passage. I admit to hesitating for a minute, and then pressed on. I turned the massive handle on the right hand door and it slowly opened as I applied muscle. Surprisingly there wasn't a sound, betokening well-maintained and oiled hinges.

I had switched off the thin beam of red light as I'd pulled open the door and was met with Stygian darkness. I walked forward and something heavy enshrouded me. I controlled my sudden rush of adrenaline and with it my breathing. Reaching out I felt thick cloth, of the nature of velvet, and realized they must be curtains enclosing the doors. I felt around near the middle and found where they divided and became two. I gently prized them apart and gave myself a small aperture to look through.

It was a vast chamber, far bigger than any mere cellars might have been if constructed during the original building of the house. It was a cavern built on massive proportions and well lighted by large wall sconces giving out powerful illumination that could only be achieved by electricity. Although on a much larger scale it put me in mind of the one I'd seen in the Châteaux in France. This was also lined with bricks, of the small Elizabethan type, and they rose to the ceiling far above to become complicated barrel vaulting of a highly professional standard. It too was filled with artefacts around the base of the walls, with flags and standards flying high above attached to the higher reaches of the wall.

And although the place had in it some five hundred people it was not exactly packed, and in the chamber, cavern or hall ten times as many could have been contained quite substantially. The present congregation was gathered at the far end from where I peered through the curtains. I couldn't tell whether they were all men or all women; for each one wore a long brown robe with a cowl pulled well down over their faces, and of course they were all turned away from me.

From where I stood I could see little, only the packed throng of brown garments in front of which appeared to be a high dais or podium. As I watched a figure appeared from somewhere at the far end, behind the dais, and even before he mounted the steps to the top I could guess by the height that it was Zoltan Milos or perhaps there was another vertically non-challenged type around. At the same time I heard a sound behind me and moved back to the door. I had left it ajar and glancing back along the passage I saw a light shining on the floor.

I went out through the door again, closing it gently behind me, and then crouching in the shadows to the left. My luck was in as I saw only one shape behind the glow of the torch. Although it was a pencil flashlight like mine, it gave out a generous beam, and I was afraid that if he moved it up at all it couldn't help but light up my position. I need not have worried for it turned out to be a man by the way he was scurrying along the wide passageway, and he was obviously late and hurrying to catch up with whatever was happening in the hall.

I waited until he had grasped the door handle in both hands and was beginning to pull when I reached him. My hands went over his shoulders, met and clasped, with the thumb knuckles caressing his carotid arteries on both sides. As his hands went up to prize mine away I drew them towards me, the knuckles pressing into his carotids, closing them down and restricting the flow of blood to the brain. Without that blood, unconsciousness was not an option, and if the pressure used was continuous and sustained, death would occur next. Not knowing the man I decided prudently on the first choice and seconds later he was out of it.

I lowered him to the ground and looked around. I remembered a small doorway to the right side about thirty yards from the main doors and dragged him there. He was about my height but a lot heavier, and most of it felt like fat. The door was unlocked and led into a small storage area for cleaning gear. I stripped off the brown robe and donned it. The loser of our one-sided match was about sixtyish, wearing a well-cut suit by one of the leading tailors of the moment; not that I'd have much of a clue about that. Being mean and lean I can still wear them off the peg, and do.

He had a gold Patek watch and was obviously a toff. Despite my time limitations I took out his wallet and flipped it open. I let my breath out in a small whistle as I saw the name on his driving license. A High Court judge no less. I secured his wrists with his expensive leather belt and his ankles with his not less expensive paisley tie. Conveniently he wore socks of the long variety, so one was bundled up in his mouth and the other just tied around his head to keep it in place. I used my lock picks to secure the door as I left.

A minute later I was just entering the curtains, letting them fall behind me. I walked softly across the empty stretch of floor to reach the motionless brown throng. A couple of heads turned in my direction as I took my place at the rear but I could not see them so assumed they could not see me.

Milos, for such it was, had taken his place at a lectern on the dais. He had thrown back his cowl; such was the man's obvious confidence in what he was a part of, and what he was now embarked on.

'Friends; I welcome you from the distant lands which many of you have travelled from. I welcome you from the community of nations, which we all here enjoy membership of. Most of you here tonight have reason to be grateful to our society, as have many down through the ages. We have been accused of belonging to many secret societies in our long history; The Priory of Sion, also know as the Prieure de Sion, or the Order de Sion; the Order of the Temple, the Knights Templar; Order of the Ship and the Double Crescent; the Rosicrucian

Order, or the Rose-Croix; Order of the Holy Sepulchre; Order of the Golden Dawn; The Illuminati; Bilderbergers; The Skull and Bones Society; The Rhodes Scholars of Oxford University, Opus Dei, and of course the Freemasons.'

His heavy gaze swept slowly around the room, and although he could not see any individual (I at least prayed that he could not) they could see him, and that was what it was all about.

'We are none of these things – yet we are ALL of them. We have infiltrated into those and many others. It is the Eve of Allhallows. The Great Father is becoming all-powerful as we speak. At midnight we will dissemble here, and relocate to the hallowed place.'

Again there came that powerful gaze around the huge chamber, as though he knew everything that went on in the world – and elsewhere.

'Friends, my master's history goes back a long time.

'It began in 1209 when an army of thirty thousand knights and soldiers from northern Europe attacked the Languedoc, a mountainous area in the north-eastern foothills of the Pyrenees in what is now known as southern France. Crops were totally ruined, towns and cities were destroyed, and the entire population were put to the sword. This was done on so vast a scale that it may have been the first case of genocide in modern history.

'The papal delegate at the time, for make no mistake this wholesale slaughter was condoned and instigated by the Church of Rome, wrote to his superior, Innocent III and stated contentedly that "neither age nor sex nor status was spared". In the town of Beziers alone at least fifteen thousand men, women, and children were slaughtered. After Beziers they swept through the Languedoc, and then Perpignan went, Narbonne, Carcassonne and Toulouse. The army of the Pope left a trail of death, blood and absolute carnage. Not too different to the exploits of the Templars in fact.

'This "war" lasted for forty years and was known as the Albigensian Crusade and it was a crusade in reality for it had been called by the Pope himself. His army wore a cross on their tunics, like the crusaders in Palestine, and the rewards were the same for those who had chosen to fight in the Holy Land. They were given remission of all their sins, complete expiation of penances and an assured place in Heaven. And of course, all the plunder they could take.

'In this crusade one did not even have to cross the sea. But why had this even taken place? At the beginning of the thirteenth century the Languedoc was not recognized as part of France. It was an independent principality with a language, culture and political institutions that had little in common with the north. It was ruled by noble families; the counts of Toulouse and Trencavel. There flourished a culture that was the most advanced and sophisticated, and could even be compared with Byzantium. Learning was highly esteemed, with philosophy, poetry, the teaching of Arabic, Greek and Hebrew, and esoteric subjects were studied avidly.

'They had an easy view of religion, and the Church of Rome held no high esteem in this place, for they had a history of corruption. There were churches where no Mass had been said for thirty years. Priests ran businesses or large estates, and one archbishop of Narbonne had never visited his diocese. Despite the church and its corruption, the Languedoc reached an apex of culture not to be seen again in Europe until the Renaissance.

'It was said that the Languedoc was infected by the Albigensian heresy, and although they were non-violent, they constituted a threat to the authority of the Church of Rome. The northern nobility had always coveted the wealth of the Languedoc and it was not hard for the Church to recruit the vast army that destroyed a peaceful and harmonious culture.

'In prehistoric times the area around Rennes-le-Chateau was considered a sacred site by the Celtic tribes who dwelt there. The village itself was once called Rhedae, taking its name from one of the local tribes. The Romans developed a large community there, with mines and therapeutic hot springs. They too considered the site as sacred and several pagan temples have been unearthed there.

'My master was a man of some consequence in Rennes-le-Chateau at that time, and although he had no title, he was the leader of the whole region, a man whose proud ancestors had fought off many would be aggressors through the ages, for legend had it that the Languedoc possessed treasures beyond compare. He owned property in the town and had many productive fields outside. He was fifty years old, as he still is, with a wife twenty years his junior who was regarded the beauty of the Languedoc. His three children, two boys and a girl, had been born with their mother's looks and their father's astonishing intellect.

'When the hordes from the north swept down he girded on his armor and marched out to meet them at the head of a small determined army from the town. It was no contest, and after a heroic stand all were slaughtered on the spot, except for my master. They dragged his bleeding body back into the town and forced him to watch while the noble knights from the north raped the women, his beloved wife among them, then handed them over to their foot soldiers. They slew the children in front of their mothers then burnt the women alive in the town square.

'As a final act of merciless revenge against the leader of the heretics, they left my master alive. One of the greatest mistakes the Church of Rome has ever committed; perhaps the greatest. The gallant troops of the Pope stripped the town bare, taking all the loot they could carry; but none of it was treasure in the sense of the word. Not the stuff of legend, not the vast mountain of gold and silver and precious jewels. Yet, who to ask about this treasure? For they had slaughtered the whole town: but wait, there was one man left alive, and who better to torture and question than the leader. Alas for the plunderers, he was nowhere to be found. He had vanished into the fields then into the mountains to the east.'

He paused. His bulky figure took on a glow, but it was not the glow of goodness and piety, it was the reflection of the pits of hell.

'It was there, hidden deep in the mountains where he could gaze down on his former home and remember that he made his pact with the real Father, Lucifer. And the Father heard, for is the master not alive today? 800 years after the time that will go down in infamy against the Church of Rome and the "Holy War" that was begun for plunder, for more wealth to be added to the coffers of the Papal fortune; and all in the name of the Catholic religion, and its war on heresy.'

I was remarkably still for an ex-altar boy. I found myself actually agreeing with some of the stuff the prick was saying, for I remembered other times, like the Inquisition of Torquemada, and the invasion and decimation of the ancient civilizations of Mexico by the Conquistadores, egged on by their priests and monks.

But the feeling did not last for long, and I was never that gullible to believe that the forthcoming ceremony was for the good of mankind.

Au contraire, Mon Amis as the Frogs would say.

Oblivious of my tight little feelings, Zoltan Milos pushed the gas pedal a bit heavier and he was quite aggressive in his attack.

'Roman Catholicism is the biggest cult in the world:

There is nothing in the Bible about purgatory

There is nothing in the Bible about praying to dead saints

There is nothing in the Bible about praying to statues

There is nothing in the Bible about not eating meat on Fridays

There is nothing in the Bible about worshipping the dead

There is nothing in the Bible about digesting Jesus' flesh and blood.

'From whence then, down through the ages, do the Popes get their authority to deign to put themselves above God and the Bible with their sanctimonious preaching's and idolatrous instructions? I will tell you – from man alone. Their God, the supposed supreme being of the Christians, has no say in these manifestations of their religion on Earth.'

He paused after this tirade. He even looked down, as though with humility, though I knew this was the last thing this man might suffer from. Man? Perhaps not that even. Maybe he'd become the same as his master, though for different reasons. God knows the Compte had reasons enough to hate Catholicism.

I had a feeling that the party might be drawing to a conclusion, and bent my own cowled head in a copy of Milos's, though not in mock humility. I checked my watch, a little after ten.

The tall priest's next words confirmed it, and I slowly began to withdraw to the doorway, and I could detect the suppressed excitement in his voice as he spoke his message of encouragement for the disciples of the reclusive Compte. Disciples who had supposedly been waiting their whole lives, and possibly the lives of their entire lineage going way back. Milos's next words confirmed this.

'Tonight will see the fulfilment of two millennia of hopes, dreams and unquestionable service to the master and the Great One himself. Our families and allies above will be waiting for us now, although unaware of why you have all withdrawn momentarily from the party. We do not want to warn anyone who might attempt to disturb us this night, so at precisely eleven o'clock we will proceed in convoy to our holy place. Tomorrow will see a new dawn – OUR dawn.'

He turned and raised his arms out from his sides in a gesture to the wall behind him, and only as the lights above brightened on dimmer switches from some unseen source, did I see the signs and symbols painted in large colorful letters above. The last time I'd seen them, in the Chateau Revanche, they had meant nothing to me, but now, thanks to Antonio, they did.

As they obviously did to the people around me, for they all raised their arms above their heads and intoned something in an unfamiliar language. So absorbed were they in their own little ritual that I managed to get back to the curtain unobserved. It was a good job that I did, because the last thing I saw before letting the curtain fall was the assembled multitude throwing back their cowls and greeting each other warmly. I could only stare for a moment as I found I recognized so many of them; well-known and high-ranking personages from all walks of life; politicians, policemen, celebs, people in the news and people who were not.

I engaged in a bit of scurrying up the passageway myself and made it just before the great doors were opened behind me and they came bustling through. I got back to the upper regions of Houghton Hall without event and wondered absently what had happened to my erstwhile back-up boys.

I could hear the music from the ballroom at the front of the great house and it sounded like the party was in full swing. As I turned to the rear of the house, and my means of exit, a dark shape appeared before me. A tenth of a second before my right fist found his face the grave voice of Antonio spoke quietly.

'Scusi Signore, we had a spot of bother as you went down below.'

The spot of bother turned out to be a couple of the household security guards who happened along soon after I'd gone "down below". They were about to follow after me, although unaware of my presence, when the boys in black decided to take no chances and so took them out. They were now lying trussed up behind a long settee in one of the drawing rooms at the front of the house.

'That makes three who could be discovered at any moment,' I whispered brusquely. 'So let's get the hell out of here.'

I saw another figure appear at Antonio's shoulder as I went back along the passage to the scullery window where we'd gained entry. I stood on the draining board and put my head to the window. To my dismay the place was lit up like the main strip of Vegas on a Saturday night.

I jumped down and explained the situation. 'Someone may have found the guy I left in the cleaning cupboard at the bottom level.'

The two never said a word, but Alain jumped nimbly onto the drainer and peered out from the side for a minute. He crouched down and spoke softly.

'They have a row of lights shining inwards on the house. I think if the right hand two are gone we could negotiate the lawn.'

'What do you mean, "If the right hand two are gone?" How do you expect to find the main light panel before they find us? Anyway, I expect they've got a guard on it by now...'

'I will take the right one,' Antonio said, also giving that nimble leap onto the draining board.

As though on cue both drew out pistols from the backs of their belts, and I could see that the barrels were long, with silencers attached to the ends. Wordlessly they extracted metal frames from their jacket pockets. These pulled out into hollow stocks that they attached to the pistols. They each now had an improvised type of machine pistol, but as they now added a small scope to indents in the frame stock, I saw they had in fact a pair of sniper weapons.

'Be ready, Signore Harry,' Alain said and they both moved up into positions at the window. Two faint plops, almost instantaneous, and the lights went out. As both priests disappeared through the scullery window I was right behind them. We spread out as we raced across the lawn but no shots were fired, no voices were raised, and we were over the wall and driving away in the Merc without further incident.

I'd already phoned Heather on her unique little cell and told her it looked like it was all on. It would happen at midnight, and she said that was what she'd expected. Puzzled as I was I left it at that and said I'd get in touch later.

We picked up Patrick at the rendezvous point on the A345 turnoff for Amesbury. As we drew near to the main A303 crossroads a police roadblock stopped us. Two police cars, lights flashing, were pulled across the road to the left, preventing any traffic from going down to the henge. The first thing that struck me was that someone had turned off all the lights. Usually, as you approached Stonehenge from any direction you were struck by the remarkable sight of the massive stones brightly displayed by a shining circle of light.

Now, just a faint glow came from what looked like the centre of the circle.

'Problem there, is it officer?' Patrick leaned across the driver, Alain, from the passengers' seat.

'Sorry, father,' the young constable leaned in the driver's window. 'Our orders are to stop all traffic going past Stonehenge. There's another roadblock at the A360 crossroads and another on the join of the A360 and A344 on the back road past the henge, so no one can get through to Stonehenge tonight.'

'Ah, now, and why would they want to stop a few priests from visiting the old henge on All Hallows Eve, for goodness sake?'

The constable laughed self-consciously. "Oh, it's not aimed at you, father. Every year at this time we get an influx of people from all over the country wanting to get into Stonehenge to celebrate the old pagan rituals on All Hallows. They break through the wire, dance around all night with drink and drugs, and leave a right mess behind them in the morning.'

'How does that explain the long line of cars that will be making their way through your cordon soon?' I asked from the back seat.

'I don't know what you mean, sir,' the young cop straightened up. 'I know nothing about that happening tonight. Now, you can go straight across, or turn right, or go back down this road.'

'Right yis are then, officer,' Patrick gave his touch of the blarney. 'You're only doing your job now, after all. Goodnight to yis.'

'Sniveller,' I muttered and told Alain to drive straight across the A303 keeping on the A345. We passed Woodhenge on our left, lying about two miles northeast of Stonehenge. I've seen it in the daytime and it consists of a large circular bank with a ditch inside, and inside of this are six concentric rings for holes, which apparently led to the theory that it was once a roofed building supported on wooden posts, but little remains today. We then turned left at the next crossroads and went through the little hamlet of Larkhill, and we stopped at a lay-by as we left the houses behind.

We began to discuss our plan of action.

I went first. 'I think they'll be coming up the A360, over the A303 then down the A344 where they'll all park. We need to get in there just before they do, and I suggest we go

314

from here across the fields. But it's going to take more than the four of us to get in among that lot, nick the two pieces of prized objects and scarper. That's if Patrick feels up to moving rapidly across the countryside in a clandestine fashion for a couple of miles.'

'As though I haven't done it all before, me boy, in a past life,' the little priest grinned at me, but I sensed some bitterness there. Someday he and I must have a long chat about Northern Ireland I decided, but now was not the time. 'You're right, of course, Harry. Which is why we have arranged back up. There'll be some more of Alain and Antonio's mates dropping in on us soon.'

'Dropping in? As in parachutes, roping from helicopters, or what?' I said, a touch of acerbity in my voice.

'You'll see,' he smiled. 'I understand you've also contacted your friend in the Met.'

'How the hell would you know that?' I was totally gob smacked by that one.

'She told me,' he said smugly, and then changed his tone when he felt my glare. 'Heather was brought into all this some time ago, Harry. The story goes back a long time and we are talking about good and evil. The one is obviously in competition with the other. We're not talking about Catholicism or Jesus Christ or Popes, whatever. Yes, I'm a priest, but not because I believe in the preaching of a prophet named Jesus, but because I believe in God, the one and only. My people, for want of a better word, you can call Gnostics if you like, but that doesn't even begin to explain it. The Pope himself is one of us, and for you, and I mean no disrespect, the simple tale is God and the Devil. It's really that simple. Tonight we have to stop something occurring that could finish the world, as we know it. Close it down if you like, from a world of God's choosing, to that of Lucifer. Let's leave it at that and go and see what we can accomplish in the name of the one true God.'

I was baffled, confused, and in a way disappointed. So much bullshit: all about God and the Devil. Well, hadn't I had that planted in me most of my life, and still with no conclusions on my part?

'So what's Heather's thing in all this?' I asked.

'She was investigating the strange disappearance of the owner of Houghton Hall a while ago, and got too close to the answers. Her boss, as a supposed reward for her efforts, put her in charge of the investigation into the Society. She found that it all tied up with Houghton Hall, and was shot for the knowledge she'd gained, but the way the shooting took place pointed to only one man; her chief in the Met. He'd given her the job so he could keep tabs on her, and when she got too close...bang. We were looking into all enquiries made about the Hall and interviewed Heather Frankton in secret. Since then she's been our contact, though only now has she gone back on duty.'

'And she's bringing in more troops, eh?' I thought for a moment. 'That still leaves us as the main retrieval group, yes? So what are we waiting for?'

'Me to change my boots, laddie,' Patrick growled from the front seat and we climbed out of the car and opened the boot. Patrick took out a stout pair of boots and bent down for a while. Both Alain and Antonio took out long cases and I knew exactly what they contained.

'Okay, we're as ready as we'll ever be.'

We left the Merc and proceeded across the fields. A faint glow gave us direction and we made our way cautiously, Alain and Antonio leading the way with their machine pistols at the ready. I had my Steyr and God alone knew what the little priest was carrying.

The fields had just been ploughed and it wasn't an easy task walking over them but we were soon above the road that looked down on Stonehenge. The scene was set. Cars were drawn up along both sides of the road and down to the tip of the long triangle formed where the A344 met the A303.

Beacons were burning inside the henge itself, embedded in the ground in the inner circle of the giant stones and giving a soft light that rose to cover the massive uprights in a bas relief of reflected light. As though part of the henge itself cloaked and cowled figures formed a huge circle around the outside of the uprights, standing completely still. The same inside the henge itself, these though were wearing white and were obviously the chosen few from the multitude. Whatever!

I could see the lights of the police roadblocks on the main road but they had obviously made no attempt to prevent the large convoy of cars entering into the area. High-ranking police officers had to be involved, indeed.

There came a not particularly loud sound from some long drawn-out woodwind instrument. A procession began moving into the light from the eastern end of Stonehenge. All wore white robes and had cowls over their features. A tall imposing figure walked in front, holding a long staff with what looked like a gold serpent on the top. Behind him came a smaller, yet equally imposing figure, dressed the same but wearing a thick chain around his neck with a heavy circle dangling below his sternum. His hands were clasped in front of him but not in the standard way of praying that the churchgoer would aspire to. His hands were one over the other as in the way of an Aikido master, such as Stephen Segal is wont to do on the movies.

Behind came about fifty people, in pairs walking side by side, but it was the first two that I paid attention to. They walked about twenty paces behind the second figure, which I took to be the mysterious Compte de Revanche, and one carried the skull I'd purloined from the Chateau. The other, smaller, figure carried a black violin. Both carried their prizes with reverence.

I frowned as I stared at the one holding the Strad, for the cowled figure looked familiar in some way. I shook my head and touched Patrick. He turned his head to me without really looking and shook his head.

'Not yet.'

The procession arrived in the middle of the great circle of stones and fanned out around the altar. I never remembered any kind of altar in the henge before, and then I remembered about the Slaughter Stone. The ancient doorway to the site was formed by the so-called Slaughter Stone, which had fallen long ago at the entrance to the earthwork surrounding the henge. This huge sarsen stone had now been moved and lay in pride of place in the centre of the circle of stones.

Very apt, I thought, for what they had in mind.

The tall figure of Zoltan Milos, one-time Signore to the Vatican, stepped to the rear of the altar, and off to one side. The person of significance, whom I assumed was the Compte, took up his place in the middle and in front of the altar. The two people bearing the violin and skull went behind the altar and positioned themselves in the middle.

The man in the front of the altar stepped forward and threw back his cowl. Suddenly I believed his publicity; that he was hundreds of years old, for he looked every year of it, every month, every week in fact. His voice was also that of an old man, but as he began to speak it gained in vibrancy, and his appearance also changed. Suddenly he looked much younger and the years diminished as he began to speak.

'A long time ago I was greatly wronged, and for restitution and vindication I turned to God. The God of the Christians, perhaps? I think not, my friends, for that God is a recent thing, as are most of the Gods of the present creeds on this Earth. No, I'm talking of the one, supposedly "true" God, and it was to him whom I prayed.'

His voice had taken on a timbre all of its own and I had to admit, from our position on the bank above the henge, it was definitely awesome.

'HE REJECTED ME,' he screamed, and I was sure the whole of Salisbury must have heard it. His voice softened. 'So I went to the other omnipotent deity, he who was cast out by the one who rejected my plea for help. And HE accepted me, and told me I would live for a very long time but would build such an order that no one could tear it down. AND at the end of it all, we would bring HIM back on Earth and we, who assemble here tonight, will be accepted unto his right hand, and WE will take our rightful place in the Heaven on Earth that will be ours. THIS VERY NIGHT, my people!'

His voice had risen to gigantic proportions, and I was becoming very apprehensive on what we had taken on.

It got worse.

The Compte stepped to one side and the smaller figure with the violin began to play.

I believe I admitted before, to Andi actually, that I liked classical music though only the more popular stuff, as I didn't really understand, or have the appreciation for the heavy stuff. This was heavy stuff, but how could you not be drawn to it, get lost in it even.

I received a blow on the side of my head, a definite shock to the system, and angrily I turned with an upraised fist.

'Pay attention, man,' there came the intense voice of Patrick Sullivan. 'That stuff is bewitching; surely you know that?'

I grunted something but couldn't get the sound out of my head.

The violin had taken on a personality of its own, the person holding the bow (I learned later that it was a Corelli, made in 1700 a year after the violin itself was made) had an amazing consanguinity with the instrument. Watching the playing was almost like being a voyeur at an intimate climax between two people, and it made me feel self-conscious for a moment.

But only for a moment, for in that time I suddenly recognized familiar traits about the maestro before us.

'My God, Patrick, the person playing the Diabolus, it's...'

'Andrea, I know, Harry. I'm sorry, lad. She never mentioned that she was a gifted virtuoso of the violin, I suppose? That she is also probably one of the few people in the world who can get a certain pitch from a Stradivarius, and only a Stradivarius? No, I didn't think so.'

Stunned as I was I remembered why we were there, and I tried to put thoughts of little Andi behind me. But they kept intruding, and I found myself thinking back to the many anomalies along the way; all those little things that I hadn't really put together properly but which now came back in full focus. I also thought of other things between us, the touch of her taut little body, the way she...

A new sight on our horizon stopped my defeatist train of thought. Two cowled figures came forth into the circle of diminished light. Between them they half-carried a young girl of about 17 or 18 years. She was blonde and would have been beautiful if in control of her own destiny, but the way she stumbled along bearing a salacious half-smile told of her drugged state.

'The virgin sacrifice,' Patrick said tonelessly, and I suddenly realized he was serious.

'You're going to stop this, surely,' I said in an outraged voice, sounding almost indignant even to myself.

'Of course we bloody well are,' he hissed at me. 'We're going to shoot the bastards, and then all hell will break loose, so get ready. As soon as the Compte goes down they'll be all over the place: the knights shooting at anyone and the rest trying to get away. Zoltan Milos and Andrea

Scolari are the ones we want. They are the targets after the Compte.'

'I'll do better than get ready,' I muttered. 'I'll be back so don't start without me.'

Holding my small pack tightly on my back I crawled back from our position and touched Alain on the shoulder. 'I need you,' was all I had to say and he followed me without a word. I was definitely beginning to like these two able young men of the cloth.

We moved around out of the filtered light from the giant circle of stones and dropped down onto the bypass road of the A344. Before us was a mass of cars stretching back on both sides of the road to the crossroads where the A 360 met the A344. That was it, there was no other way out.

My phone went off, but I didn't have a phone, then I remembered Heather's. 'Where the hell are you, Brogan?' She hissed down the line.

'And good evening to you too, darling,' I managed to get out. 'Not even a "hello", and what about radio silence concerning names and all that?'

'Can it, Brogan,' came the terse reply. 'I have a lot of people standing by for your word that something big is going to happen. We have the Armed Enforcement Squads from three counties on immediate standby in the area. What can you tell me, and for God's sake have something we can act on?'

I glanced at Alain who gave a tight smile and a Gallic shrug, neither doing much to reassure me about my, suddenly, pivotal role in all this.

'I take it the powers that be who are involved in all this have sealed off the area and used their authority to keep it tight. Okay, tell your bosses that it's all going down as we speak.' I gave her a quick rundown on the situation, from the ceremony to the number of cars ready to disappear

321

into the night from both directions along the A344. 'It's going to happen soon, Heather. They've got a young girl as sacrifice and if you know even a quarter of what I do about all this then you know they'll do anything to finish out tonight. When you come in watch out for young men wearing priests' outfits. They're the real thing and on our side; they're Patrick's boys. I'm just above the henge, on the A344 and we're going to stop anyone leaving the scene, as you fuzz love to say.'

'You know too much about what we love to say, Brogan,' and I could sense the amusement in her voice, despite the tense situation. Talk about fickle; I was in love again only minutes after finding out that the love of my life was at the top of the whole diabolical heap. Christ, am I shallow or what? 'For your information, we also have the Army on standby at Bulford Camp along the main road towards Andover.'

'I know Bulford; went there as a guest instructor in another life.'

'Of course you did; take care, Harry,' and she rang off.

Harry, now, things were looking up on the home front. The dream of every lad in Liverpool used to be to get in with the landlord's daughter; free ale and anything that came along – or not. As long as there was free ale in it, though I had to admit that we'd never planned on her being a copper, and a D/I at that.

'Harry,' I came out of my meandering bag of thoughts and realized Alain was talking to me.

'Sorry, mate, what was that?'

'We have not much time left. What is your plan?'

'Ah, plan,' I was suddenly back in the frame. I whipped my pack off my shoulders and handed him a pile of spiky objects. 'Careful, these are called "caltrops" my friend. Hastily knocked up my gifted self when I went back home,

322

out of four inch nails welded together. Originally called "caltrops", another name for a snare, a gin or a trap for the feet, but used by the military around 1519 in the form of an iron ball armed with four sharp prongs, placed so that when thrown on the ground it has one always sticking up, and was excellent to fuck-up the enemy cavalry. Works just as well today with the modern cavalry of the motor car.'

Alain held one of my improvised caltrops up and whistled softly. 'We live and we learn, Signore. What do you want me to do with these ingenious gifts?'

'Go to the other end of this road and place one tight against the front of the front tire on the inside wheel. When they take off, in a hurry I should imagine, the tire will blow and cause the car to pile into someone else. You have enough to do the first four or five cars on either side, and I will do the same here. That should be ample, my friend.'

Alain inclined his head and disappeared along the road on his mission.

I began my own sequence of accident control, or mis-control, by moving quickly on the insides of both lines of cars, pushing the caltrops close in to the front tires. I had just enough to manage four on either side, and then took off back to where Patrick and Antonio were waiting, the little priest seething with impatience. 'Where the hell have you been to, Brogan? Things are getting to their peak now, man.'

At that moment, Alain appeared behind him and I grinned. 'Tell him where we've been, Alain, see if he cares.'

I pulled out the Steyr and checked it.

The Italian priest spoke quietly to the Irish priest in Italian; following which Patrick looked at me and gave a grudging smile and a nod.

'Clever bastard, are you not?'

I gave him a wry smile back then things became serious as we all gazed down on what was taking place on the Slaughterer Stone. The effects of the drugs were still on the young lass and she was still out of it. She was humming softly to herself and totally unaware that the white-cloaked figure of the Compte behind her was holding aloft a dark dagger of antiquity.

'Antonio,' the little priest said quietly, and it was both an acknowledgement and a command at the same time.

The taciturn priest lifted the cover from the case he was carrying and withdrew another nylon-clad case. Unzipping it he withdrew a square aluminium box, its hasps locked with a combination padlock. He rotated the tumblers, opened the lid and exposed a scoped Thompson Centre Contender pistol where it lay in a cut-out in the foam. The end of the barrel had been threaded for the fourteen-inch beer-can diameter suppressor that lay in its recess. The top of the ammunition box, labelled "300 Whisper" could be seen where it nestled in the foam. Silent as a whisper, no supersonic crack...and deadly accurate out to 200 yards. Unless you're within ten feet, and paying attention, you have no idea that anyone shot anything.

Within moments the big Contender pistol rested on its butt, the barrel supported by a Harris bipod. The long black steel cylinder of the suppressor threaded onto the barrel ruined the single-shot pistol's clean lines and made it look front-heavy.

But I wasn't fooled for a minute – I knew the gun was the business and knew that it would do that business. I remembered that Antonio was the biathlon champion so I also knew that he would be the one to do that business.

Alain had also been working on the far side of Antonio. He took off his case and withdrew what I recognized as a Heckler & Koch MSG90, with a 5 round magazine and a Hensoldt telescopic sight. A variant of the MSG90 with several custom features, which included a threaded muzzle that wore a screw-on silencer and a low-signature flash hider; and the sound suppressor worked well.

I was just thinking what a formidable pair of priests they were, when Antonio loosed the first shot without any prior warning. Then I saw why he had no time for any such warning before he'd committed that small piece of lethal metal to the scene below.

It struck the Compte in the forehead as he was in the act of bringing the knife down in a vicious arc and into the poor girl's chest. What happened next stopped Alain taking his shot at Milos, and left the rest of us gaping like village idiots.

For the Compte transformed before our eyes; he'd thrown back the cowl of his hood at the beginning of his rant, and had appeared as a rather sophisticated man in his fifties; greying hair, aristocratic face, and hawk-like nose curved defiantly down on all who would dare gaze on his countenance. Now he looked his age – his REAL age. What had Zoltan said, somewhere around the year 1209? And how old had he been then? My God, the man must be around 830 years.

Now he began to break up, to crumble, disintegrate; literally decompose before our sight. His form rapidly decreased and diminished in volume and height and substance – as he returned to the dust from whence he came, and from which he had evaded all these centuries. It was from whence we ALL came, and would all return to eventually when our allotted span and reasons for being here were gone. Within a few seconds it seemed he became just...mere grey dirt and white dust.

The horror for me was gazing down into his eyes.

For as his body fragmented and virtually ceased to exist, the eyes retained their spark, their glitter and intensity until the end; until they were only expunged in the seconds that his body disappeared into the earth itself.

I think that was the moment when I began to believe. Really believe; not just the sights that were before me, but everything that had happened since that day in Bermuda, when I'd first met Zoltan Milos.

The night turned into a riot, worse than the most terrible soccer matches ever, and not unlike the First day of the January sales at Harrods. The single shot from the MSG90 was the catalyst to what followed, for the sight of their evil Messiah, suddenly disappearing before their eyes into a heap of dirt and dust had done more than horrify his most ardent followers. There had been no sound, and of course no blood for whatever else the Compte might have been, human he wasn't and yet he had disappeared before their eyes at the moment he was about to plunge the ancient dagger into the breast of the innocent young girl.

Surely at that moment they began to question their faith in the Master of Darkness that they had spent their lives working for. The robed rabble, for such they'd turned into, took off in different directions.

Figures began to move into the circle wearing quasi-military garb and all heavily armed. They began to argue with the crowd, trying to persuade them to remain where they were. Other figures were moving in now, and I saw hard-faced men with dog collars emerge from the low mist that had sprung up around the massive stones of the henge. The first group turned and began to lay down fire and I saw one or two of the priests go down before they too opened up. Lights suddenly beamed down from above, causing even more consternation among the crowd.

I caught a glimpse of the markings and they were police helicopters. At the same time I saw the lights of vehicles coming in from either end of the A303 and more arriving on the back road. The cars there were trying to take off but not succeeding too well; thanks to my little devices. Tires were giving off popping noises as the 3 or 4 inches of heavy gauge nail penetrated heavy rubber; as some who had put their foot down as they roared off skidded sideways into their neighbours, others screamed forward a few feet then moved sideways, again either blocking the road or running into someone.

Struck by a sudden epiphany I began to look around frantically, for I suddenly noticed that Milos and the smaller figure of the violin player, if it WAS Andrea, had disappeared. So why was I not surprised? We had all been distracted by the horror of seeing the Compte die in such a horrendous fashion, despite having been almost primed for it by the preceding tales of his longevity; though of course nothing could have quite prepared us for the actual shock of his demise as it played out. I blamed myself for losing focus on the main chance of getting them both, for they would have been the most desperate to escape capture, especially if they still had the Diabolus in their possession. For it could still be used once more to carry out the ungodly plans that Milos had always intended.

A familiar voice broke through my crowded thoughts.

'Attention, all Police Officers. This is D/I Frankton, heading this operation. Watch out for the men in dog collars; they are priests and on our side. I say again…'

Some people, the hardier ones, got away across the fields, some, the cannier ones, moved straight across the main road and headed towards Salisbury.

'Shall we join them?' the little priest was already on his feet and moving down the small incline to the circle of stones.

The two priests and I followed on. Two men stepped from behind one of the giant pillars, machine pistols raised but they were too late. Alain and Antonio shot both without breaking stride. Another came in from the left side and I back-fisted him as his weapon was being raised. We reached the altar where two more of Milo's' little army appeared to be on guard but I could see no reason for this. The blonde girl was still strapped down and I could see several of Patrick's newly arrived theological hit men fighting their way in.

'Go now or die,' I hissed at the two men and they hesitated. 'Too late,' I muttered and shot the nearest one with the Steyr. I turned to the other but Alain had beaten me to it and the man went down.

I pulled out my knife from the leg sheath and cut her free. God knows but the poor creature was still smiling and cooing softly to herself. I lifted her up and turned; to look straight into the hazel eyes of Heather Frankton.

'Brogan, am I just in time to prevent you running off with your latest acquisition?' she asked quietly.

'All yours, Inspector,' I handed over my burden and Heather gently set the girl on her feet, but her limbs were beyond control. The detective-inspector called out sharply and two policewomen arrived to take over the intended victim.

I walked with Heather over to where Patrick was issuing orders to some of his team.

'Inspector Frankton,' he beamed. 'How nice to finally see you.'

'Signore,' she said formally. 'We've been working on this for a long time.'

'We have,' he nodded gravely.

'Whatever you've been working on for so long,' I butted in. 'It still isn't over. I'm going back to Houghton Hall. This thing can't be over until we get them.'

'Who...?' Heather began to ask.

'Milos and Andrea,' Patrick supplied.

'IF its Andrea,' I protested weakly, and even I knew how weak it was.

'You know it is, lad,' he said softly. 'Anyway, go on along with you and take the two lads for company. Are you interested in joining them, Inspector?'

Heather Frankton looked around at the scenes of mayhem taking place and nodded her head. 'I'll get one of my sergeants to finish up here first, Signore. I'll send someone with you, Harry, so you can get past the police officers on the gate at the Hall and I'll catch up with you there.'

I admitted to being somewhat disappointed at Heather; after all, this was something she'd apparently been working on for quite a while, and now we were coming to the dénouement of the whole thing and she wasn't exactly in a rush to get things finished. I called to Alain and Antonio and we headed back across the open fields. When we arrived at the Mercedes Alain got behind the wheel and I got in beside him in the front passenger seat. Antonio took the back. As we were about to take off a car came up behind us and flashed its lights.

'Bloody hell,' I growled. 'I bet I know who this is.'

A fist banged on my window and I wound it down. 'Hey, Brogan, I'm supposed to be coming with you. You'll never get in the house without me, you know. We've got officers on the gates.'

'I know that Millerchip, but we've been in and out of there already tonight. Still, climb in and we'll enter through the front gates this time; be a nice change.'

He got in the back and we drove rapidly back to the A303, crossed it, and back down to Salisbury. We went through the city quietly as there were few cars around at that time of night. When we arrived at the hall we found the gates closed and two uniformed policemen standing watch outside.

'Right, detective inspector,' I told him over the front seat, 'do your thing and get us in fast.'

He left the car full of importance and flashed his warrant card to the two police officers. The gates were quickly opened and we swept through; then at my word we kept on going. I heard a cry from outside the vehicle, which of course we ignored and we carried on up the drive to Houghton Hall itself.

'I'll go in the back with Alain,' I said. 'Antonio, see if you can get in through the front and join us below,'

We disappeared around the back. I had the Steyr and Alain had left his rifle in the Merc, favouring an automatic which he drew now and checked. We found the back door closed but unlocked and proceeded with caution. Without discussion Alain and I moved through the house using the basic covering procedures, one moving forward at a time and covering the other as he moved.

Arriving at the cellar doors I proceeded down first, with the priest keeping close behind and watching the rear.

We dropped down to the lowest level and along the corridor without incident or even seeing any other human being. Coming to the massive doors I slowly opened the right hand one and pulled it back on its well-oiled hinges. As before it made no noise and Alain followed close behind as I went up to the curtain.

I drew them open just enough to peer through.

Milos was standing on the dais in front of a number of people as before. This time, however, the numbers were greatly reduced, and I doubted if any more than fifty were present. Alain crouched below me and also watched through the curtain. Some still wore their robes and some did not. No attempt was made to hide their identity any further.

The chant began on the dais, Milos initiating the sound and his audience following suit. Then the strident chords of the violin cut through the human chant, effectively stifling it with its increased power, pushing the chant into the background, driving it behind a wall of superior noise. The people present continued but the sound of the violin rose above it all.

To say that the violinist was an expert would have been to oversimplify the performance of a lifetime that was taking place before us. The notes rose and fell, from sublime depth rising to exquisite heights. I had no knowledge of the notes or their execution, nor how it was all put together, but I had enough musical appreciation in my bones to recognize the good stuff when I heard it. Gradually the chanting fell away and the vast chamber became the ideal acoustical venue for such incredible musical sounds coming from just one violin.

But of course, it was hardly JUST a violin. For it was not even JUST a Stradivari – it was THE Stradivari Diabolus itself, the black instrument of legend and the stuff bad dreams are made from.

I walked forward with the priest Alain by my side, and the crowd stood back silently to let us through. As the path ahead cleared we threaded our way to the dais and there was the small figure in the brown robe, hood cowled up over its head and face, playing the Diabolus as though it was part of her – as though each had been made for the other. As I said, I admit to a cursory interest in classical music, but only in its most commercial forms. This was way beyond my meagre comprehension of what the instrument might be halfway capable of.

It was dominant and subdominant; supertonic and subtonic; it was mediant one minute, that is between the tonic and the dominant, then the spread chord of the arpeggio, the notes herd one after the other from the bottom upwards as well as from the top downwards. The straight into the appoggiatura, or the "leaning note"; for having a harmonious status it is not an ornament in the same sense as the timeless acciaccatura. The music changed into mordant and my blood ran cold with its effect. All of this musical gob speak was told to me afterwards, of course.

I knew Bochelli and Pavarotti, and that Welsh bloke, Bryn something or other; and that was it.

The figure with the violin tossed its head back and with a feeling of revulsion in my stomach I saw that it was indeed Andrea, who had already seen me and stared right at me now as she attacked the Diabolus with a fierceness and wild bestiality that she had never brought to our lovemaking. In truth I did not believe it was the same Andrea, the little Andi that I thought I had loved.

I stood before her and mouthed just the one word, "why?"

I thought I saw tears appear in her eyes for just a moment, but it was for just a moment and then it was replaced with a look of pure malevolence. Her playing never faltered and she kept on producing the most incredible music. It was then that Zoltan Milos spotted me. His speed was phenomenal as he came over the front of the dais and backhanded me with one of those shovels he kept on the ends of his arms.

I rolled over and made to get up but a dozen figures hurled themselves on top of me. I just had time to see Alain go down with a similar number clinging to him. Only their numbers kept them from tearing us apart for each got in the way of another. I straightened out and began to roll violently from side to side, and then when I'd made a reasonable space I continued the roll rapidly to the right. Knocking people down left and right I managed to get clear of my main attackers and was halfway to my feet when a size twelve from Milos hit me with solid force on the left temple.

Before the lights went out I saw an unsettling look come on the Signore's face, and realized it was the semblance of a smile. I supposed it was the best he could do.

I awoke to the sound of someone playing a bass drum somewhere nearby. Very nearby; then as my faculties slowly returned the drumming came even closer, then it was in my head and I realized it wasn't a drum but one bugger of a headache.

Next I discovered that I was paralysed as well; until I worked on my arms and realized that they were only tied. What a relief, I was only tied and not paralysed – what a choice. I was seated in a darkened room and as my head cleared somewhat, I felt there was someone else in the room with me.

'Who's there?' I called into the darkness.

'Alain, Signore Harry,' the voice croaked from behind me.

'How are you, Alain? And cut the Signore bit, hey?' I groaned back through the reverberations in my head.

'I...am well, Harry, but I think my arm is broken.'

'What's your status, my friend?' I asked.

After a few minutes he replied. 'I am in a wooden chair, with my arms and legs tied to it. I think I have the left arm broken, the lower part.'

'Okay,' I said slowly. 'We have to get together, you and me.'

I tried to sound positive, as though I had a plan, but the insufferable pain in my head was very distracting from establishing pure thought.

'I'm going to try moving the chair backwards, try and keep making some kind of noise so I know where you are, *capacitarsi di*?'

'*Capacitarsi di*,' came the weak voice of Alain. My Italian was coming on, I thought proudly, and then remembered where it had come from and frowned.

It wasn't easy. We were on some kind of stone floor, which helped as I began to wriggle backwards but I soon realized that they were stone flags, or large tiles, and it was hard negotiating the joins, where the mortar had disappeared many years before. I had to wiggle the chair one way then the other to negotiate the join.

I eventually reached Alain and moved behind around his back. My searching fingers found the ropes, and then the knots, but that did not make it any easier. The knots were tight and presumably done by experts in the art of bondage.

'Not easy,' I muttered as my fingers failed to loosen even one knot. The clever bastards had poured water over the rope, a vegetable fibre one at that, which meant that the rope would tighten, knots and all as the fibres dried out.

'Why are you not able to untie us, Harry?' the priest said after a while and I felt embarrassed to reply. But I did, as he deserved that at least.

'*Non problema*, I already have a broken arm,' Alain said and I heard his chair turn and as he threw himself backwards.

There was a crash and an ominous silence.

'You f...' I began angrily, then felt fingers untying my bonds, albeit awkwardly. '...lovely fellow.'

I was untied in seconds and we checked each other out, and what we were carrying. Absolutely nothing. Our weapons were gone, including my knife from its ankle sheath.

We found the door after groping our way around the room. Prizing it open gently we emerged into a corridor smaller than the one leading into the main chamber or vault.

'I think we are behind the dais, Harry,' Alain whispered in my ear and I found myself nodding in agreement.

We moved to the end of the corridor and again found a set of doors that divided off a curtain. The noise from the other side was familiar; as it should have been, for it was the Diabolus still being played, though now at a diabolical rate, and that is not intended as a pun.

Andrea was performing as though her life depended on it; and maybe it did. Milos was now in the middle of the pentagram, or was it a pentacle; I never know the difference.

The ex-Vatican Signore held his arms out and upwards and was mumbling to himself, while the music of the violin became more and more bizarre even to my non-appreciative ears. The remaining sycophantic acolytes had fallen back against the walls and the main space of the vast amphitheatre had become a mass of smoke or mist.

I moved into the arena once more, Alain close to my side. No one saw us, and no one gave a damn about us. We were invisible to the crowd for much bigger things had their attention now. And I do mean much bigger things.

It came from nothing, or below the ground itself, for who could tell?

It rose slowly, as though on an open elevator, though it was nothing man-made that brought it up. It was hard to describe, although it was a monster with all the traditional appearance and accoutrements, such as wings, horns, tail and scaly skin, there was a depth of intelligence in its eyes that made you want to tear your eyes away. But you could not.

I admit now, as I did then, that I had no clue about what to do next.

But Alain, the warrior priest, did. He shot the man standing next to the fiddle player, the tall figure of Zoltan Milos. Just like that. I didn't even see him aim his pistol, but the shot took the man through the left side below chest height, and he faltered and dropped in the crowd. Maybe the shot was meant for Andrea and missed, so I went after the slight figure with the violin swinging in the left hand and the bow in the right, each hand keeping a tight hold.

Before I reached it Milos appeared again, towering above everyone as he snatched both violin and bow.

In that moment, when the playing stopped, the monstrous creature began to change. It was no longer fifteen feet tall, with wings, scales, tail, and horns – the whole damn thing, as I'd seen it; or as I THOUGHT I'd seen it. Now it was nine feet tall and had the appearance of an angel from the world of fictionalised art, with wings, beautified features and all. Then the music began again, although Zoltan Milos himself wielded the bow this time. He must have been in pain but held the violin back into his shoulder and began sawing away with the bow. As the music continued, and changed, so did the creature; and although it kept the overall appearance of an angel, its seraphic and cherubic features transformed, or transmutated – whatever, and the aquiline nose became bulbous, the eyebrows thickened and merged, the ears tapered back and the body took on an overall obscene and obese appearance.

As the violin reached crescendo the horrible creature appeared to grow in stature again. The next metamorphosis was that of the Christ himself; half-naked, arms akimbo, crown of thorns, and of course, eyes brimming with tears.

'How do we stop this...thing?' I muttered to no one in particular, but Alain heard me.

He was firing as we moved forward and Milos took another bullet in the back and the violin fell to the ground as he went down with it.

I then saw the slight figure of Andrea who was also moving away when a bullet struck her in the back of the head, piercing the cowl and throwing her forward as though slapped by a giant hand. She took two stumbling paces forward then appeared to simply crumble, and when she reached the ground there was no movement, no final twitches or jerks, just a pathetically small figure in a brown robe, taking up no more space than a child would.

Then I saw the tall figure of Zoltan Milos going berserk.

His head whipped around and he saw us immediately. The ferocity on his face was incredible and his movement was even more so. With a speed that belied his huge, awkward frame, he was on us, tossing Alain aside as though he was a window dummy.

I moved in with rights and lefts to the body, all of which he ignored, and a big fist the size of a ham sent me sprawling and I knew that headache was going to make a quick return.

Expecting to be engaged in fight for my life I was surprised to see Milos turn to the still figure on the floor and put his arms around it.

'Where is my music?' a mighty voice boomed around the high vaulted place. The great beast had diminished in stature yet again and was now only the size of a man. It had taken on an anthromorphic shadowy form; and I realized with some otherworldly wisdom that I suddenly became aware the voice had not come from this thing in front of me.

The big priest ignored the demon he had used up so much of his life trying to summon, yet his next words made a lot of sense of so many puzzles and anomalies over the past weeks.

'My daughter,' he cried. 'Why have you killed my daughter?'

So many things were apparent to me when I heard those words, and they reminded me incongruously of the final words that Jesus allegedly spoke from the cross, 'Father, why have though forsaken me?'

Heart rendering words, and no less than the ones spoken now from the lips of the one time Signore.

Milos gently laid the lifeless body onto the cold stone flag of the underground vault, reached out and slowly took up the Diabolus. He plucked the bow from the floor; the same one that later turned out to be the Corelli, again one of the best. But wasn't everything around here?

The de-frocked priest began to play the Diabolus. Like his daughter, if such she was or had been, Milos was a gifted violinist, for that he could play the instrument well was beyond dispute, and the strident notes of discord cried out in that cavernous place.

There were no niceties now in the playing, any subtle beginnings and eloquent themes to show off the impresario's acquaintance with the instrument, but he banged straight into the discordant sounds that soon became the notorious tritones Andrea had told me about. Again, this knowledge came to me later, relayed from the attentive ears of the priest, Alain.

A cowled figure came from the side of the dais, holding aloft an object that I recognized as the skull I'd taken from that other crypt in the mountains of France.

I looked from the violin to the skull, and to the summoned figure on the far side of the pentacle, and it was now flickering incandescently before us. I saw the assembled followers, the descendants of families who had followed faithfully down through the centuries. Following…what? The rival of God himself? Lucifer, the Devil, Beelzebub…? How could they latch on to a being that did not even know its own name that it had to have so many? At least the Christian God had only one, and that consisted of only three letters to make it easy.

At that moment I also noticed that Milos had left the protection of the pentacle.

The so-called followers were looking decidedly apprehensive now; not at all the ecstatic worshippers who were so steadfast at the site of Stonehenge, and who were now about to realize their lives desire; for they were in the final stages of something that was begun so many years before at the behest of their ancestors.

Some were now edging towards the massive doors at the exit; which were now flung open as a horde of police personnel piled in. They were lead by a glaring Millerchip, now wearing a yellow safety vest with the single word Police stitched on the front and back.

'Everyone keep still,' he was yelling. True to form everyone was ignoring him. The sheep were running in all directions, but suddenly several robes were tossed aside and submachine guns were in evidence. They were firing at the new arrivals; who were mistakenly trying to protect the innocent by not returning fire.

'Millerchip,' I yelled through the confusion. 'There are no innocents here – open fire, man.'

His head turned in my direction but I could see he was out of it, being momentarily as confused as the robed figures running hither and thither. I lurched to my feet and checked on Alain, who was wounded but still capable. I hauled him to his feet.

'Millerchip,' I yelled again. 'Tell your men to return fire, for God's sake.'

He turned in my direction and a bullet took him in the body. He went down like a sack of the old proverbial; and I saw reinforcements coming in through the big doors. Lead by Heather who apparently had heard my instruction and had no problem in dealing with it. I heard her screaming at the cops who were already inside and they responded instantly, cutting down on all the armed men in robes.

I turned towards where I'd last seen Milos, Steyr in hand but saw it was not needed.

The creature had sprung up to full size again, but there was a shadowy alter-image superimposing itself over its shape; and becoming stronger by the second. I can swear now, years later, that it was the shape of the Devil himself. The creature had been only what it was meant to be, a decoy sent to fool whoever had summoned it into false belief in case their intentions were also false, and the aim was to destroy Lucifer.

Milos was still playing, oblivious to what was going on around him. The Diabolus was suddenly plucked from his grasp and thrown away to skid across the dais where it slid over the far edge and fell with a shrieking sound as though it was still being played. The man who had been behind all of this, the man who had used his own daughter in his terrible ambition, training her from birth to be a major player in the acquiring of the Devil's approbation, gave a terrible cry as he watched the fabled violin disappear.

It was all falling apart and he had lost his daughter for nothing. Zoltan Milos was beginning to realize it now and he stared at his monstrous creation and held his arms out in supplication.

'Why, Lord?' he called out, and although his voice maintained much of its timbre yet it was broken from its former strength. 'Why do you not appear before us in your glory and receive our glorification of your being, and your return to earth as our God.'

'Fool,' the voice boomed out, and it was inside our ears as well as outside in the great hall. 'You have angered me with your incompetence, for you have failed to get things as they should be. There are rules in the universe but I do not expect something like you to understand them. Your playing was inept, you do not have the skill to give me the notes I require, and which only your offspring is capable of producing.'

IS producing? In the present tense? The words gave me pause but they did not sink in properly as I had managed to reach the still form of Millerchip and hefted him under the arms, then managed to get him upright and slung him over my shoulder in the traditional fireman's carry. I turned to make for the main doors and found two bastards standing in front of me with Uzi's pointed at my chest.

'Would you accept that I'm a para-med type person who just happened to recognize someone who's been shot and am taking him to a hospital near-by? No, I thought not.'

I saw Heather Frankton before I heard the noise of her small ladies-type gun going off. I think it was an old-fashioned S&W .32 stubby, but I really wasn't too concerned other than whether it could do the business in the present circumstances. Heather proved that it could.

She appeared before us as an avenging angel, (hey, there's a form of romanticism in me, you know), gun in hand and voice very authorative. I just loved that last bit. Both arseholes chose to ignore her of course; gorgeous looking bird with a small piece of weaponry didn't come close as far as they were concerned.

Their mistake.

The first spun towards her and his knuckle was going white on the trigger as she shot him in the head. No hesitation, no fucking about – she just shot him in the head, the weapon turning in the same instant to point at the face of the second man...who obviously had a death wish as he spent no time debating the point but brought the Uzi around in a small curve to aim at the detective inspector, but of course she was already there.

'Don't,' she said, and I would repeat this in court later, of course, as the major witness against police brutality. Then she shot him as the Uzi came up, and why not?

'Let me help you, Brogan,' she said, moving in on the other side of Millerchip, well out of it now as he suffered with his pain.

'I think I should be helping you,' I said quietly and she glanced across at me.

'Maybe later,' was all she said and I was actually nonplussed for a moment. I hadn't been nonplussed for a long time, I can tell you.

It wasn't actually a noise that took us out of our mutual bonding thing. It was a scream of the utmost terror and despair, as Zoltan Milos realized he was being taken to the opposite of where he really expected it all to happen for him.

The Devil, Lucifer, or just his representative; whatever, appeared to get a shitty on and Milos suddenly went upwards into the air, though not quite reaching the high barrel vaulting.

'You thought to cheat me, human dregs,' he did not appear to speak but I think we all got the message, for it was in our ears, our heads, all over. The big guy really DID have a shitty on, and I just hoped at that moment that it wasn't with me. Milos hit the hard stone paving slabs from a height of about fifty feet and lay there. Ironically he was only an arm's length from his daughter's body; a body I had once taken pleasure in, and with. Anyway, she was now dead, not that the fact made me feel any better, but any waste of a life depresses me. I held that thought very briefly as I turned to check out Milos and to make sure he was dead. By the shape of his head I concluded that he was.

After all, they say the Devil takes care of his own, don't they?

I then turned Andrea over onto her back and to my ultimate shock I saw it wasn't Andrea but some slightly built man with a narrow face and a large third eye in the centre of his forehead where Alain's bullet had emerged. The thing had been planned long ago for just such an eventuality and she'd managed to get away in the commotion.

With mixed feelings I returned to Heather, still holding onto the detective inspector from Special Branch, and grabbing his other side although for some very nasty reason I couldn't quite understand why I was bothering, and made for the door. The commotion behind me was just that, a commotion. She was terrific, fighting them off left and right; shooting where necessary, and kicking people in the nuts if the shots weren't going right.

I think I fell in love about then; oh, I know I'd thought I felt the same way about little Andi a short time before, but I don't think I would have been quite the same if I had known about her earlier, or maybe I'm just fickle – whatever.

We gained the comparative safety of the door and as I reached it I almost collided with two policemen.

'Ah, who says there's never a copper around when you need one?' I beamed. 'Lads, this is Detective Inspector Millerchip of Special Branch and he needs looking after. He's wounded, took a body shot in there. Get him out of here fast and take care of him; he's one of yours.'

The oldest of the pair looked as though he was going to make the huge mistake of arguing the toss but Heather shoved her warrant card under his nose and snapped something at him. 'Yes ma'm,' he coughed out in one word and he and his mate carried the unconscious man out between them.

'What fine men you have under your command, Inspector,' I said by way of a snappy retort to ease whatever tension might have built up between us. Apparently none had because she bestowed upon me that beatific smile and shook her head.

At the head of the stairs were lines of policemen and women on either side, quickly segregating the escapees into two groups; the good guys and those who weren't.

'I'm telling you I'm Superintendent Shaw and I'm wearing this garment because I have been engaged in undercover work on these people for a great length of time. I demand you release me at once so I can begin identifying them.'

'I suppose you've noticed that their voices get posher and posher as they climb the giddy heights of promotion, haven't you?' I whispered to Heather in as loud a voice as I could muster.

'Of course, I have,' she came straight back at me. 'Very few pull it off, though. Take this gentleman for example, Harry...' She was walking up to the distinguished looking man in the brown robe.

'...He says he's a police superintendent, and he undoubtedly is; but he also says he's been carrying out undercover work with these people and I know for certain that he's not, but he thinks that his rank will make everyone believe what he says. As they say on the tele; you're nicked, mate.'

As I walked past behind Heather the superintendent spat at me, 'You damn fool; I'll have your badge for this.'

I stopped and looked into his eyes, giving him the "killer squeeze" as I call it. 'What badge, arsehole?' I winked at the cop putting the handcuffs on him as I walked off, and he grinned back, no doubt thinking I was just being abusive to a senior officer. I was, but he didn't know to what extent the abusive bit went.

'How did you know that Super wasn't really in there undercover?' I asked Heather.

She looked at me steadily; then said sarcastically. 'Perhaps because I've been in charge of this investigation for two years and we've never been able to get anyone in there. As I said before, we've never been able to get anyone into their hallowed circle, for like the Hell's Angels founder members only, or in this case families that go back a long, long time, and whose loyalty has always been devoted to their organization and their long-time obsession to put the Devil on the throne that rightfully belongs to He who created it all.'

'My God,' I stared at her. 'You really DO believe in it all.'

'MY God, Brogan,' she snapped. 'You don't have one, remember?'

'I'll ignore that but I'm deeply hurt,' I sniffed. 'So, now you've got all those behind it all?'

'No,' to my surprise she shook her head and shrugged. 'The Compte was always the figurehead of the organization, and Zoltan Milos was always the administrator, the "gofer" if you like, for them, but I always felt there was someone else, a main man or woman.'

We thought about that for a moment or two, but no suggestions were put forward by either of us. 'No offence, Heather,' I said finally, and in as straight a voice as I could, 'but why would they appoint a relatively young, and newly promoted inspector in charge of what is a world-wide organization, or conspiracy.'

'Good point, Brogan, you're not just a cute, ageing Lothario after all,' she gave a grim smile. 'The superintendent back there is only part of the plot. There are far more high-ranking people back in the Yard, and they were the ones who gave poor little me the "wonderful opportunity", and I quote, to go places. I'd been an inspector for a year when this "wonderful opportunity" came up, and I was a female. How could they go wrong; inexperienced female officer, of quite a junior rank as far as investigations like this are supposed to work. But they made a mistake.'

There was a long silence while Heather looked around and checked that the large amount of manpower at her disposal wasn't being wasted. Satisfied, she turned back to me.

'I have to ask,' I said. 'Why did they make a mistake?'

'They never checked me out properly,' she shrugged, an eloquent gesture. 'Oh, they did their homework as far as the job was concerned but not my private life. You see, Brogan, I've always been a devout Catholic. This came from my mother, as you wouldn't find Dad walking past a church on the same side. I also have a confessor that I've know since a child; a friend of the family you might say. Patrick Sullivan.'

'Ah,' I said wisely. 'That does explain a lot.'

'We both believe there is someone else behind all this, someone who has been in power at least as long as the Compte, someone who was always there, and saw it all through the ages.'

'You are talking someone who has lived a long time,' I frowned. 'I heard the spiel from Milos about the Compte's hereditary history, but found it hard to get to grips with the 800 year old bit.'

It was the very attractive looking detective inspector's turn to frown back at me. 'Excuse me, but weren't you in there just now? Didn't you see what I did? You couldn't have missed the big ugly bugger that killed Milos, and who did you think that was, or where it had come from?'

'Er, maybe it was a hologram, or we were all hallucinating when we saw what you think we might have seen,' I said feebly. Very feebly.

She stood and looked at me. Women are bad enough but women police...people, well, they're something else.

'You saw what you saw, Brogan, so don't try and play me.' She said finally. 'We both saw it and so did Father Alain, who is also a witness, to what happened in there.'

'Things happened,' I acknowledged. 'I'm not sure what but surely it could have been some kind of mass hypnosis, couldn't it?' I realized that my last words were slightly pleading.

'You really believe that, Brogan?' It was the way she was looking at me as she asked the question that made me nod.

'Can I take a rain check on that one?' I said hopefully. Again that steady look, but to my surprise she actually smiled.

'Why not? You've been very helpful to us, Brogan, so how about we give you a meal on the house?'

'On the house?' I asked. 'You're going to buy me a meal? Oh, goody. Can I bring a friend?'

'I'M your friend, Brogan,' she said demurely. 'Just remember that and don't push it.'

I didn't.

CHAPTER FIFTEEN

Why should the Devil have all the good tunes?

Rowland Hill
1744 – 1833

"Confounded be all they that serve graven images that boast themselves of idols."

Psalm 97

Which is how we wound up in this lovely little Italian place in Salisbury the following evening about eight pip emma, after having spent a very long day answering questions, identifying people and signing statements.

I should not have chosen the restaurant really, although of course you must realize by now that I love Iti food. No, it was just the thought of Italian without little Andi around. But of course, when the taste buds start salivating, what can you do? I know, not a lot.

'I hate to spoil your appetite, Brogan,' Heather said as we started into a couple of martinis. 'But Signore Sullivan will be joining us for dessert.'

'A bit late for saying Grace, won't it be?' I suggested cleverly.

'Not at all, Brogan, he's coming because he likes dessert – not saying Grace.' As she spoke I got the feeling that I'd just been reprimanded.

The entrée arrived and we tucked in. I had ordered the platter of antipasta and Heather was being boring with a prawn cocktail. The antipasta was okay, but the prawn cocktail looked delicious. Why is it that we always fancy whatever anyone else orders in a restaurant? It always happens to me, and I get quite irate about it.

'Prawn, Brogan?' Heather asked nicely and to my everlasting shame and weakness I actually snatched it from her proffered fork. 'Nice,' I murmured.

The main course came and being a smartarse having already been to Italy, I'd ordered the Carbonara, with the pancetta, cream, paprika and Parmesan, and of course with the tagliatelle noodles. It was nothing like the stuff I'd had in Italy that night with Andrea, and just thinking of her, and that night, gave me a fit of the glooms. Naturally Detective Inspector Heather picked up on it right away.

'It REALLY tastes that bad, eh?' she attempted to inject some humour into the situation.

I looked up from my plate and gave a weak grin. Weak grins seemed to be all I could manage these days.

'No,' I said. 'It's not the food, which is a poor imitation for Italy, but the last time I had this, and the first I must say, I was with Andrea, and all things were different.'

'I imagine so,' she said without sarcasm, and sipped her Frascati. I almost gave a shudder at her choice of wine and had imbibed a long draught of my Chianti. At least that was real Italian. 'Why did you pick this place, Brogan, some kind of self-flagellation?'

I smiled, actually at a bit of a loss to explain. 'Not really, I think it's more a moment of *finito* more than anything profound.'

'I can understand that,' she said in a tone that convinced me she really could, but also realized that was not the time to push the point. I left it at that. Things were getting too personal anyway.

We'd both finished as much as we were going to eat of the Carbonara, and as though he'd been lurking around the corner just waiting, Patrick Sullivan appeared.

'Not too hungry then, folks?' he commented, plonking himself down without asking and looking at our unfinished plates.

'Always looks better on the movies, doesn't it?' I murmured.

'Isn't that the truth of it,' he said without conviction. Rubbing his hands together he said, 'Now what's on the menu for dessert?'

'Whatever your little heart desires, Padraig.' I said warmly, but he wasn't convinced by my little burst of sincere camaraderie. Shame really, as I always though I did sincere very well.

'Humm,' he murmured as he grabbed the menu from the waiter's hand, albeit with a gracious smile. 'Oh, my goodness, you have Crème Brule. Yes please, two.'

'Greedy bugger,' I muttered and ordered exactly the same for myself. Heather declined with a condescending smile. Well, she would, wouldn't she?'

We ordered black coffee too and they arrived promptly with the Crème Brule. Glancing around I saw that the place was already emptying, proving the general belief that the British are a nation of gobble-and-goers.

'So, where do we go from here, Patrick?' I interrupted the little priest in his most intimate face-filling moment.

'Ah,' he said with some relief in his voice and I realized I'd just dropped myself in it again. 'We need to go back to Rome, the Vatican to be exact, and trace her from there.'

'What's this "we", white man?' I asked in my best Tonto voice.

'Oh, come on man, for God's sake, now,' he growled, although it did not come off too well as he was licking the spoon before delving into his second dish of Brule. 'You've been chosen by the divine one himself. How can you refuse?' He put on an indignant look, spoiled by his pulling the Brule in front of him and beginning the delving.

'Difficult, I know, but I can probably manage it,' I glared at him and fervently hoped he'd get a large lump of caramelised sugar stuck in his little Irish throat.

No such luck; the little bugger probably WAS on the side of the angels.

'Why the vestal virgin, then?' I mumbled, for want of anything more profound to mumble.

'Vestal virgin?' he looked up from his Crème Brule briefly.

'The young lady they were about to use in the ceremony,' Heather reminded him, he had the decency to actually put his spoon down for a few moments.

'Simply a courtesy approbation to the Gods of the henge, aimed at the ancient druids, those who came before and ruled Stonehenge and its mysteries,' Patrick said grimly. 'Therefore not needed when you got back to the house and its blood-soaked cellar. Just the violin and the skull of Judas for their little ceremony to unit them with their lord and master.'

'The skull of Judas,' I repeated dully.

'You brought it back from the Chateau,' he pointed his spoon at me.

'Allegedly,' Heather put in. 'The skull of Judas.'

Oh, goody, it might not be then.

Then I dropped the bombshell of the evening.

'So, which one of you good people has the Diabolus?' I asked.

The D/I and the Signore looked at each other.

'I thought...' Patrick began, and Heather shook her head.

'No, I thought you had it,' she said quietly. I could sense shock in her voice.

'My God,' I stated the obvious. 'The little bitch must have somehow got her claws on it again and disappeared. And how about the skull of Judas?'

'Ah, now,' the little priest smiled, but I saw the narrowing of his eyes. 'There are many theories of the death of Jesus Christ; so numerous that we don't have time to even begin to go through any of them right now. Harry, you were trained in Catholicism, were you not? As an altar boy you must have had many questions, none of them properly answered at the time. Am I correct? Now tell me what you think you know about the death of Christ.'

I didn't like the way he posed the question, but gave a polite answer anyway.

'I personally believe that he was a good man, but only a man, and thought himself a messenger from God, a Messiah, possibly even thought of himself as THE Messiah, and wandered the countryside with a bunch of his mates preaching nice things and doing nice things, when he could. The bad guys got hold of him and tortured and executed him in an unpleasant manner. End of story.'

'Hmm, oversimplified, as is no doubt your way, Harry,' Patrick allowed the little smile to remain around his mouth but I noticed it did not extend to his eyes. 'Heather, you also had a Catholic upbringing. What are your thoughts?'

'I...I'm somewhat confused these days, Signore,' she said, and I could see the confusion in her eyes. She was no longer the confident hard-nosed female cop. Religion will do that to you. 'I believe Christ lived, of course, for there is too much evidence for him merely to have been a legend. Like Harry I believe he was a man, but not JUST a man. For his teachings to have existed for thousands of years he must have been QUITE a man. I...get confused over the Resurrection and the Ascension, but not over what followed. His mission, his teachings, his existence on this Earth lived on after him, but in such a way that he had to have been filled with goodness, and that had to come from only one source.'

Patrick dipped his head. 'Very good, Heather, very good. However, there has been a lot of religious thought, and speculation, given to the theory that Christ did not die on the cross, but that a substitute volunteered to take his place. That he in fact married and began a bloodline that has been secretly procreating down through the centuries – even to the present day.'

'Yes,' Heather agreed, to my surprise. 'As popularly brought out in the *Da Vinci Code* and in *Holy Blood, Holy Grail*; and not to mention a couple of hundred other books before and since.'

'But I don't understand why a man like Christ, a prophet, would either allow himself to endure all that torture stuff, or allow it to happen to some other poor sod,' I sipped cold coffee and held my hand up for more around the table.

'A little brandy would be nice,' said the shy little priest. 'A large one would be even nicer. Keeps the cold out, you know?'

354

'It's not cold, it's bloody summer, but yes the brandy seems like a good idea,' I agreed and Heather's hand went up and received prompt attention unlike my own.

'An Egyptian peasant in 1945 was digging near the village of Nag Hammadi in Upper Egypt and came across an earthenware jar. It contained what we call codices, papyrus books or scrolls, and there were thirteen of them bound in leather. They actually used some of them to stoke their little peasant fire, but fortunately some were smuggled out of Egypt, and eventually wound up in the right hands. To cut a long story short, it wasn't until 1977 that the scrolls were printed in an English translation. They contained the famous, and perhaps notorious, Gospel of Thomas. You may be aware that the four standard Gospels of Mathew, Mark, Luke and John are contradictory to say the least, but the Gospel of Thomas, the Gospel of Truth, and the Gospel of the Egyptians, are mentioned by the very earliest Church Fathers. Most of the texts in the Nag Hammadi scrolls are no later than AD 150.'

'Interesting,' I said without sarcasm. 'No, fascinating in fact, but all this has to do with...what, exactly?'

'Forgive me, ah,' the little priest's face lit up as the fresh coffee and brandy appeared. 'I was merely supplying the smallest bit of background about Christ, which will come full circle to the question you asked, Harry. In one codex, the Second Treaty of the Great Seth, Jesus is depicted as he was in the heresy of Basilides – basically that he escaped death on the cross by a clever substitution. It is now popularly believed that the person who gallantly volunteered was one Simon of Cyrene. Early Muslim chroniclers' write of Jesus hiding in a niche of a wall and watching the crucifixion of a surrogate for himself, and this agrees with the fragment from the Nag Hammadi scrolls.'

'Very controversial stuff coming from a man of the cloth, a Signore of Rome no less,' I observed in a neutral tone.

He shrugged. 'Other religions are more forthcoming with their research findings. For example, in the Koran Jesus is mentioned thirty-five times, and is called among other titles, "Messenger of God" and "Messiah". They acknowledged him, and still do, as a mortal prophet, one who came before Muhammad, and as such was indeed a spokesman for a single supreme God. Like Basilides and Mani, the Koran 4:157, also maintains that Jesus did not die on the cross; "they did not kill him, nor did they crucify him, but they thought they did."

'As I said, Patrick, all very interesting, but you're telling us all this now...why?'

'You asked a question about the skull of Judas, which is still in their possession by the way, and why do you think they want it?'

'Because of its inherent evil,' I replied. 'If it is indeed the skull of Judas Iscariot then it must be one of the most evil relics on Earth, for he was the man who betrayed Christ.'

'Ah,' the little priest drained his brandy glass. 'But was he, and did he?'

'You're doing it again, Padraig,' I pointed my own half-full glass at him, more to see the greed in his eyes than to intimidate him. 'Talking in riddles.'

'We need to ask ourselves "why",' he said, steepling his fingers in a pedantic manner.

'Which I've been doing since you came in,' I muttered but he ignored me and carried on regardless.

'Why the elaborate ruse to show that Jesus was more than mortal man, the Son of God, in fact? The Crucifixion, the Resurrection and the rest; to make him appear to be more than he was, certainly, but also to initiate and perpetuate the myth of the Messiah. During the first century Palestine was a hotbed of squabbles over dynasties, internecine strife and always wars, either between small family tribes or the full-scale kind. The second century saw a unified Judaic kingdom but by 63 BC it was all messed up again and ready for conquest. Enter Pompey, and the Romans took over. There then came revolts against the Roman rule and it was all on again. Jesus lived around 35 years, which coincided with the beginning of a turmoil that went on for another 140 years. D'you think perhaps I could have another little…?'

I raised my hand and the waiter appeared like good little Italian waiters do. Their pasta sucked but you couldn't beat the service. Patrick and I had brandy and coffee and Heather stayed with the coffee.

'Now then, where was I, oh yes. As I said, it continued for another hundred years after Jesus' death, and it was his own desire that a Messiah would come to deliver his people from the oppressive Roman rule. Only history and the accident of misplaced semantics applied this term exclusively to Jesus. The Greek word for Messiah is Christ or *Christos*, and in either Hebrew or Greek simply meant "the anointed one". David, in the Old Testament, when he was anointed king he became a Messiah or Christ…'

'Is this going…?' I began, glancing around the now empty restaurant, except for us.

'Somewhere? Of course it is lad, and stop interrupting. It was actually the mundane political meaning that was meant when they began calling him "Jesus the Messiah". This of course pissed off the Zealots and the rest of the Jewish factions, proclaiming him a false Messiah. It was not the Romans who were behind the "death", if such took place, of Jesus. For many reasons that I'll enlighten you with sometime, the Romans actually saw no harm in Jesus, and in fact it's down on record that his shenanigans in the temple with the money-lenders made them chuckle more than a bit.'

'And the skull of Judas Iscariot?' Heather said with infinite patience, obviously also getting bored with the profound revelations of the man from the Vat.

'The reason we allowed the skull to be taken is for the same reason that we didn't worry too much about the somewhat battered violin. It must surely have been damaged when it hit the dais and bounced off it. You saw the Dark One tonight, people, and you saw his wrath when thing's did not go exactly right. The Diabolus, in the hands of a less than perfect violinist, even of Milos's standard, did not produce the notes in their correct form, so the ceremony was useless. If we are also right about the skull, then that too would upset the big lad.'

He drained his brandy, which he had been sipping slowly along with the coffee.

'If the crucifixion and resurrection of Jesus, whether the supposed substitution took place or not is irrelevant, then from beginning to end it was all a contrivance, and Judas Iscariot by informing the officials where he would be that night played a major role. Not against Jesus, but as one of his most intimate confidants. The rest of his disciples were left in the dark, don't you see? Even Peter played along unwittingly, by denouncing him three times. Therefore, Judas was a good man, and has spent over two thousand years being unfairly judged and condemned as the great betrayer. Who calls their sons Judas any more? No one. And isn't the very name a description of one who betrays another? No, if what we believe is true, then presenting the skull of Judas Iscariot to the Dark Angel will unleash his rage and ire more than anything else. For, if anyone, Lucifer knows his own. Now, when are you leaving for Rome, Harry, lad?'

I shrugged, well used to the little priest's sudden change of tack by now. 'What good would that do; she wouldn't go back there surely? Everyone and his dog will be looking for her.'

'She's a remarkable lady, that Andrea,' Patrick shook his head. 'Bounced through several degrees and a doctorate, speaks about four languages, plays the violin as well as any virtuoso in the world, and also took acting classes while in college.'

'You mean...' Heather began.

'Yes, my dear, she spent more time doing makeup than performing on stage, so I am well informed. Getting in and out of Rome will be no trouble for her, especially with the contacts she has. Most likely got a couple of extra passports by now. She will be making contact with Cardinal Warkowsky I imagine.'

'He's her boss?'

'No, Harry. She is HIS boss. Andrea Scolari, or Andrea Milos as she should be called, was brought into this world for one thing only. A union was made between Zoltan Milos and a leading female member of one of the oldest and illustrious royal families of Europe. The lady died some years ago, but she had little or nothing to do with the upbringing of her daughter, so I think we'll let her rest in peace. But do not have too much sympathy for her as she knew exactly what she was doing from the beginning, and WHO she was doing it for.'

We talked about my return to Rome for a few more minutes, then Patrick and I returned to the hotel and Heather went to wherever good little lady detective inspectors go for the night. I suspected she still had a lot of reports to finish off.

'You knew she still had the violin, didn't you, oh crafty one,' I said to the little priest before we went to our separate rooms.

He nodded quite open and blatantly. 'In order to use it for its purpose what do you think she'll have to do with it?'

'Why, get it repaired I would think.'

'Exactly, me boyo, exactly. So now you know where to start when you get back to Roma,' and he went in his room leaving me gazing at his door rather stupidly.

The next morning I rang my son early, expected to listen to a confused piece of invective but instead a bright and cheery voice greeted me as though he'd been up for hours. I didn't go into details but told him I was off to Roma again and would he be able to get down and keep an eye on the house, and the fox? Fortunately he could and would. I thought about it for a moment then told him about Andi, and to keep a lookout for her. Not that I thought she'd be coming back to Merrie Olde England for a while, but you never knew. Next I rang Fabio in Rome and he promised he would drop everything and be standing by.

Patrick drove me personally to Stanstead airport in my car, with Antonio and Alain coming behind us in the Mercedes. Ostensibly it was to pick up Patrick as we were leaving my Rangerover at the airport, but I suspected it was to keep a watch on my person, just in case anyone with revenge in his or her hearts were still lurking around. Patrick said he'd put my car in the long stay car park and would pay for two weeks in advance.

With the Papal Seal being flashed around in front of me, my little carry-on and I were through the security gates and settled on the plane in no time at all. By the time the pilot was yanking back on the stick and we were in a steep climb over London, my little eyes were closing and my last waking thought was how I could get my hands on one of those handy little Papal Seals.

Just before I fell asleep I remembered I already had one, of sorts.

We landed with hardly a bump and twenty-five minutes later I was in Fabio's new Mercedes and heading into Rome. I enquired about his family and we exchanged inconsequential chitchat. His English had certainly improved even since last time and he modestly admitted that he was taking lessons from a venerable old retired English teacher.

'It is good to see you again, Sen... Harry,' he grinned with a typical burst of Fabio enthusiasm. 'And so soon after the last visit, yes?'

'Yes,' I said. 'As happy as I am to see you again, my friend, it is a bit too soon.'

'Ah,' he said knowingly. 'The lovely Signorina Andrea, yes?'

'Yes, but not for the reasons you might think, Fabio. That little...tell me, have you seen anything of her since my last time here?'

Fabio shook his head and glanced across at me. 'I have not seen her since the last time you and she were together. Surely such a good couple have not split up, Harry? Is there a problem between you and the Signorina Andrea?'

'Signorina Andrea IS the problem, my friend,' I said softly. In a précised version, suited to his English and religious sensitivities I gave him a general outline of the story so far. I think he got most of it, for what Fabio lacked in formal education he made up for with his street-wise education in the gutters of Rome. He was shocked, he said sadly, to know that the beautiful Signorina was in league with Il Di'avolo himself, but as I was a friend of Il Papa I must surely win the battle for my soul.

He had it a bit mixed up but had the essence of it all so I didn't disillusion him. We drove to the little hotel I'd stayed in before near the Vatican. It was gone eleven and Fabio invited me to lunch with his family but I declined, saying I had things to do and he didn't push it.

'But I insist that you dine with us tonight, and I will pick you up here at 7 of the clock, yes? You have my number Harry, and I am at your disposal for as long as you need me. Comprendere?'

'Comprendere,' I agreed. 'But whatever happened to Capice?'

'Hah, that's only something the Italians in American movies made up, no such word in Italian, Ciao, Harry.'

I was chuckling as I watched him drive away for his family lunch. I had at least one friend in Italy anyway.

But how many enemies, I wondered.

I was welcomed back warmly by the proprietor and his wife, booked in and took my hand grip to my room, the same one as last time overlooking the narrow street outside; just enough room for a medium sized truck. I didn't know whether that was a good thing or a bad thing. I spent a few minutes with the local Rome telephone book, yellow pages edition. Like England it was a separate volume, unlike France that has a separate book for each Department with yellow pages at one end and white residences at the other. I thought I'd just throw that bit in to show what a well-travelled man of the world you're dealing with here.

Hoping to get some business done before the whole of Italy stopped for lunch, again like France and Spain, I splashed some water on my face, brushed my unruly mop of hair back. I say that to annoy my eldest brother, Tom, who is beginning to just show signs of being hirsutely challenged, and who used to tease me as a child about being a little sissy as my mother liked me with long hair. She apparently wanted a girl-child on the third throw, and if she had her way I'd probably have been wearing dresses too. At the end of the street I grabbed a cab, as the Yanks say in movies.

We drove to one of the main shopping districts and I paid off the taxi. I found the street I wanted just off the Via Veneto, where I had no trouble finding *Musica del Mondo* – Music for the World. According to the phone book, and the blurb on the window, it was a legend in its own diary, being the largest purveyor of musical instruments, both ancient and modern, in the known world. Whatever they didn't have, they would get. Quite an ambitious statement, but when I entered the shop it was hardly an overstatement. It was another Tardis, medium-size outside and humungous inside. Not that I'd know but I'm sure there was at least one of every known instrument from every known country.

I asked to see the manager and handed over a card. Not just any old card, but a heavily embossed black card containing a miniature of the Papal Seal over the Vatican colors. The one I'd remembered on the plane and which had been presented to me before I left the presence of the Pope himself, and he told me that its presentation to anyone was an immediate direction to the recipient for full co-operation to the holder of the card; in other words a miniature Papal Seal. Patrick had told me that they were not given lightly.

Signor Bersgoni was short, fat and sweaty, and very reminiscent of Carlo Ponti in his heyday or a taller version of Danny de Vito in the present day. He was immaculately dressed in a pin-striped suit, white shirt and silver tie, black Gucci's with tassels, and the lot set off by an enormous deep red rose in his lapel. His English was very good and his opening words positively fawning.

'Signore Broogan,' he came forward and bowed deeply as he returned the card, handling it with the same reverence he might have shown to a relic like the tibia of St Francis, for example. 'It is an honour, Signore. Only twice before in my life have I seen such a card. Many years ago, in the days of my father, a great Cardinal in the service of Il Papa came to inspect our humble premises for the quality of the instruments and he was not disappointed. We are now the foremost suppliers to the Vatican Orchestra, and I have my people searching all over the world for the right instruments.'

Bersgoni had the proud look of a father whose first-born had just learned to shit accurately in its potty for the first time. It was his next words that brought on the palpitations in my chest.

'The next time was just a few days ago, when a beautiful lady came in. She examined my violins and played on a few to test their resonance, but on every one she shook her head sadly. She trifled with only a few notes but it was enough to impress upon me that she was a very fine exponent of the instrument, a virtuoso no less.'

'Let me hazard a guess,' I said carefully. 'She asked if you knew an expert violin artisan, a modern day luthier no less, who could carry out very fine repair work on an old and priceless violin and she would be prepared to pay whatever it took. You then sent her to Cremona, to one of the fine artisan houses dealing in such things. Yes?'

'No, Signore,' he said in surprise. 'That is, yes, Signore. Actually, yes and no. You are right that she did indeed request the name of such a person, but I did not send her to Cremona.'

'And why was that, Signore Bersgoni? I thought that Cremona still had the best of such experts,' I enquired softly. I still held the Pope's card and as I spoke I blatantly manipulated it between both hands, though perhaps I needn't have bothered. Signore Bersgoni was eager to please, not I of course, but Il Papa.

'Because, Signore Broogan, there lives here in Roma an old artisan who is superior at his craft than any of the esteemed luthiers of the great Cremona. Many have come here to seek his advice and knowledge.'

'And you can give me the name and address of this man?' I asked carefully.

'But of course, Signore Broogan,' he beamed. We were obviously good mates now because he loved saying my name, even if he did keep getting it wrong.

Armed with the name and address of the great artisan I thanked Bersgoni and took my leave, promising to pass on a word of his invaluable assistance to the great man himself.

He ushered me personally to the door, effusive in his thanks for my doing him the honour of gracing his humble threshold with my presence, etc, etc. I was glad to get away.

I sat at one of the many sidewalk cafes on the Veneto and drank cappuccino while I collected my thoughts on what my next plan of action would be. So far I'd struck it lucky. I knew that Andrea would have to get the Diabolus repaired, and not just any old repair, but one that had to be perfect, for the horned one would not be too pleased if they mucked it up again. Apparently they needed Andrea, who had been brought up to play the Devil's sequence like no one else on earth, for even her father, Milos, had failed to enact the right interpretation of the notes.

The Diabolus was also required of course, and in pristine condition. Perhaps after, and I referred to the slip of paper Bersgoni had given me, Signore Maggini had repaired the violin it would be even better than before. Andrea must be stopped, although if the little priest was right about the skull, perhaps she would stop herself.

But I knew I could not take that chance with what was at stake.

That night I was rudely made aware that Andrea Scolari was cognisant of my presence in Rome.

I had conversed briefly with the Pope's assistant, Cardinal Lumbrozzi, and he said Monsignor Sullivan had already brought the Holy Father up to date and he, Lumbrozzi, was of course privy to it all. He told me that Warkowsky was under close observation but as far as they were aware Andrea Scolari had not made contact with him. Which proved nothing, as perhaps our conversation had been bugged; who knew what went on in the Vatican with its mysteries and intrigues, or maybe she just had spies watching all incoming flights at the Rome airport.

The premises of Signore Giovanni Maggini lay a short trip outside of the city of Rome so I decided to make it the next morning. I phoned Fabio and arranged for him to pick me up at 9 am.

That night, for some perverse reason that I couldn't exactly fathom out, I decided to eat in the little Italian place where Andi and I had eaten together the first time, and what seemed so long ago now. *Ristorante* Fratello was the same, the two brothers who could have been identical twins and the two sisters who could not have been more different, one short and round, the other tall and thin. I wondered unkindly which cuckoo had flown into that little nest.

They were very busy and did not appear to remember me, for which I was grateful, and I enjoyed a solitary meal at a small corner table and watched as the Roman night went on around me. Couples not even trying to be discreet as they held hands and exchanged a kiss now and then, and the occasional couple trying to be the opposite as they also showed affection and gave the game away by glancing around surreptitiously before indulging. Family groups abounded in the place, all were laughing and chatting and eating and drinking; apparently all at the same time. It was a delightful place to be, though not if you were alone.

I ate a small bowl of minestrone, followed by a lovely dish of moulded Parmesan risotto with chicken-liver sauce, washed down with an excellent Lacrima Christi from the Campania and nurtured from the volcanic soil around the Bay of Naples. I read that on the bottle and thought it rather apt, as the literal translation is Tears of Christ. I finished with coffee and Strega, paid the bill and wandered off into the night.

I was somewhere off the Via di Pia Angelica when the Blues Brothers decided to strike. I call them that because both were wearing dark blue suits with light blue shirts and matching blue ties. Their shoes were black, just for contrast, and they both wore hats. One had a fedora, which looked as though it had seen service as an extra in *Angels with Dirty Faces*, and the other wore a cloth cap like my old man used to wear in the dockyard. I suppose the wine and the Strega had something to do with it but I couldn't control the titter that came forth from my lips. What were they like, for God's sake?

'You're amused, eh, buddy?' Fedora snarled. Actually he tried to snarl but his lisp, though only slight, made it more of a purr than a snarl. This made me titter some more, and the thought that I wasn't laughing but tittering, made me even worse. Their overall shape and size and fitness level, not to mention potential for violence, had not escaped me, despite the tittering. Both were on the big side, Cloth Cap was the larger though he also had the largest gut, and both looked mean, if such a word could be applied to a couple of ridiculous take-offs for the Blues Brothers. Only Fedora had spoken so far and I placed his accent as Bostonian, quite similar to the Bronx if you weren't too into American accents, but quite discernable if you were. I was. So little Andi had been recruiting at home.

I made an admirable job of controlling my titter for the moment, though it wasn't easy.

'What do you two chumps want, exactly?' I enquired, moving forward in a nonchalant fashion.

'Chumps?' Fedora hissed. His hiss was a lot better than his snarl, given the lisp, but I couldn't be bothered complimenting him on it at that time.

'Yes, you know, like clowns, arseholes, dickheads – all the above and more,' I smiled now as I'd gained the distance I wanted.

Fedora reached for the absurdly obvious bulge alongside his left armpit and I stepped in and hit him with a right forearm to the side of the jaw. I spun to my right and kicked Cloth Cap between the legs and he developed a commendable high octave note that Ivan Rebroff would have been proud of. As he doubled over I recovered the foot and lifted it in his face in a drop kick that my rugby-playing brother Dick would have been proud of.

As I turned it was only instinct that made me duck at the same time, and Fedora's fist whistled over my head. I straightened and my head took him under the chin at a speed that snapped his head back. Unfortunately, for Fedora, his tongue had protruded a bit between his teeth, and he spat out teeth and half an inch of tongue as he smashed backwards into the pavement. Maybe I'd done him a favour and it would get rid of the lisp, though I doubted it. That's part of my trouble; my big heart is always looking for a good outcome in every situation.

I'd been so engrossed in sorting out the Blues Brothers that I'd failed to hear the close proximity of the siren and it was only as the blue light began to interfere with my night vision that I responded. I held my hands well away from my sides and tried to look like the frightened victim of a mugging. I don't think I did it very well for both cops levelled their *pistolas* at me at once. Without being told I went down on my knees and raised my arms above my head.

One of the cops went over and examined the unconscious men. He straightened and spoke rapidly to his colleague, and to my surprise they both laughed.

'Please, Signore, stand and put down your arms,' the one with the pistol trained on me said, though I noticed it remained in position. I did as I was told. 'Please tell us what took place here.'

I shrugged. 'I was going back to my accommodation and these two suddenly attacked me. I think you will find they are both armed.'

The second cop nodded and held up a couple of automatics. 'You must have been very quick, Signore, to have put them both down before they could draw their weapons. Are you armed, perhaps?'

I told them I wasn't and allowed myself to be patted down. I'd purposely left my few bits of armoury in my room, a fact for which I was now grateful.

'As you say, officer, I'm just very quick, as my ex-wife used to observe.' I gave my winsome smile but I don't think they were too appreciative. And then I had one of my epiphanies.

'I'm going to reach inside my pocket, gentlemen, and as you already know I'm clean of weaponry, you'll appreciate that I'm not a threat.'

The one with the gun still pointing at me nodded and I withdrew the black embossed card of the Vatican. I had been wondering if it had any significance to the local fuzz outside of the Vatican City, and within seconds had the answer. They asked my name and when I told them both cops replaced their guns immediately and almost stood to attention.

'We apologise, Signore Brogan,' the one who appeared to be the senior said, with an elaborate bow. It was only then that I realised my name was on the card but in some kind of coded wording. Probably Latin.

'Please,' I said with largesse. 'You were only doing your job. Now, you appeared to know these two men, is that so?'

'Si, they are Americans and we have been watching them since they arrived in Roma. Up until the present they have done nothing against the law, but now...thanks to you, Signore Brogan, we have them on criminal charges and can send them back to America. *Il deportare.*'

'Good, gentlemen,' I said somewhat condescendingly, 'I'm pleased to have been of service, and perhaps they'll pick on someone their own size next time.'

I felt it was wasted on them but what the hell, as long as the Blues Brothers were out of the frame I could care less. I refused the offer of a ride to my hotel and risked the rest of the walk back.

Am I brave or what?

The next morning by 9:30am we were driving out of Rome to the southeast and heading for the countryside around Frascati. Just before lunch we arrived in the small village of Moderno, although it was about as modern as the catacombs or my eldest brother Tom's left testicle. We located the workshop of Signore Maggini without too much trouble. It was a surprisingly spacious building, attached to a surprisingly spacious house.

The master himself appeared as ancient as his house. He was tall but not stooped, which was surprising considering his occupation, and he too spoke good English.

After we had been introduced he gave me an unabashed appraisal, no shyness on his part at all.

'In 1942 I was a prisoner of war in England,' he said without preamble. 'I liked it there and found the people very kind. They did not treat us like prisoners but felt sorry for us because we were in a war that was not of our choosing, that is, the ordinary soldiers. We just wanted to get back to our families and our lives. Somehow the English people knew that, and they took pity on us. How can I help you, Signore Englishman?'

'Your name,' I said with a smile. 'It is familiar to me because I have been studying the history of the violin, and the great Stradivari.' As I said the last word the old man seemed to freeze and his eyes glazed over. He waited.

'Sir, your name is Giovanni Maggini, and if I remember correctly there was a Giovanni Paolo Maggini who was once a pupil of Gasparo Bertolotti, who was always called da Salo after his birthplace.'

'You are right, young man,' the old luthier nodded. 'Bertolotti, or da Salo, built violins with a powerful tone but his style was so primitive that he was once thought to be the instrument's inventor. However, as he was born in 1540 he would have been far too young. The violins made by his pupil, Giovanni Paolo Maggini, retained his overall shape but flattened the archings. Many people say that the violas made by these two have never been bettered.'

He was sitting in a battered old chair in his workshop, and took time out now to fill his pipe, yet another old relic in the scheme of things.

'I am a descendant of that Giovanni Paolo Maggini, young man, and I am regarded now as the foremost artisan of my kind who is left in the world of violin making.'

He spoke without false modesty, nor was his tone boasting, obviously a man who knew his worth and was saddened that on his demise much of it would disappear forever.

'Now, what can I do for you?'

I produced the black card once again. He took it hesitantly and held it in his hand, somewhat awkwardly I thought.

'You have met Il Papa?' he asked quietly, and I nodded. 'I too met him, once, a long time ago. Not the one now but one before. He told me that I was indeed the finest luthier in the world and I believed him.'

'And now you have the opportunity to prove it,' I said. 'By repairing the Diabolus.'

He looked up at me, his eyes opaque. 'How do you know?'

'I work for Il Papa, remember?'

'You plan to destroy it,' he said as a statement, not a question.

'Yes,' I told him. 'For the good of mankind, and at the direction of the Holy Father.'

371

'It seems a monstrous thing to do,' he said resignedly. 'You know it is a Stradivarius, made by the hands of the great one himself.'

'But commanded so by the false one himself,' I reminded him. 'Who do you pledge your allegiance to, Maggini; the one true God or the impostor who wishes to usurp the place of the true God? Where do you think it leaves mankind, the puppets in this monumental game of organised chance? Please, you must recognise the truth when you see it.'

'Truth?' his voice changed, became younger and defiant now. Before my eyes he too changed, became visibly younger and more confidant, until I was looking into the eyes of a man whom the centuries had not neglected, only made old to establish his purpose in the scheme of things. 'You would not know truth should it appear before you in the trappings of eternity. You dare to bring me this, a symbol of the bond between man and the usurper? You were close to the truth before, Brogan, but like all small creatures you refused the evidence of your own eyes. I AM Giovanni Paolo Maggini, the original. I served under da Salo for many years and was present when the mediator of the great one came calling. I listened and heard the offer of life eternal in exchange for the production of a violin that would be without comparison in the world of man. But it was too soon, and da Salo did not have the skill. For my sins, neither did I at that time. Later would come a man who possessed all of those skills in abundance. Stradivari. It was to be almost a century and a half later that a stranger would come calling on the great luthier on a dark and dreadful night, and would cajole the master into using all of his skill and all of his adroitness to produce the Diabolus.'

By his wild eyes and overly effusive manner I could see that the man had lost it, and if he hadn't then he soon would. I needed to know where the damn violin was now.

'And over the years, Signore, these skills you had back then, primitive as they may have been at the time, have been honed so that you now believe yourself the equal of the master himself; Antonio Stradivari, no less.'

'Fool,' his voice had become stronger now, and it reverberated around the high-ceilinged workshop. 'Because I tried my best but was without the knowledge that came later, the Devil's mediary gave me the gift and said that one day they would call on me, and the skill I would have acquired over the centuries. It was I who approached Stradivari on that dark night, and it was I who inveigled him into abandoning his purity to make the Diabolus and in so doing gave him the gift of those skills to manufacture the world's best instruments for over thirty years. But the fool had misgivings, and he renounced the Di'avolo and his future coming. His reward was to have his gift of longevity withdrawn, and he died old but unprepared. Fool.'

'You've already said that,' I reminded him. 'Now, I need to have that fiddle, my friend, with or without your bloody permission. Have you finished its repair, Maggini?'

His eyes took on the glow of a piece of well-burnt charcoal and his gaze was over my shoulder. The incredible sound of a violin suddenly being taken to its top level of achievement by an expert came pulsing through the vaulted acoustics of the huge workshop. I whipped around and there was Andrea cuddling the Diabolus to her shoulder, neatly tucked under her chin, and playing like the prodigy she was.

'If music be the food of love, you little bitch,' I muttered.

'Harry,' her voice seemed to span out over the sound of the violin. 'How wonderful to see you, and what a survivor you are. They were some of my best people, you know?'

'They were incompetent arseholes,' I muttered. 'Surely with your contacts you could have got some of the real hard blokes. You know, the ones with the forked tails and little knobbly bits on their heads.'

'Not allowed,' she said nonchantly, still working the bow like she was in the Albert Hall. 'Shame, but there you have it. Incompetents only this week, I'm afraid. But this time you won't get away with anything so easily. I did love you, Harry, in my own way, and I hope that makes you feel a little easier when you go.'

'Go?' I gave a false frown. 'I haven't planned to go anywhere, darling.'

As though on cue, which it largely was, a heavy plant pot with the most gorgeous geraniums came through the big window at the front of the building. I went for the now quite youthful Maggini. Youthful he was at that moment, and with the vigour of that youth and the accumulated strength of some five centuries he merely swatted me like a fly. I took umbrage at being dismissed so contemptuously and went charging back in again. A series of left hooks to the ribs followed by a right hook and he smiled and hit me with a clenched fist this time. Now that hurt, so I knew it was time for different tactics. I think I mentioned Modern Pentathlon once? Well, there were no horses around, and no pistols, but I had noticed the crossed swords above the huge fireplace at one end of the workshop. I turned and ran, using a wicker chair as a trampette and snatched one of the swords as I elevated up against the fireplace.

To my delight it was in the form of an epee, the duellist's weapon of choice. I had no compunction about using it on an unarmed man; after all he'd had five hundred years to prepare for me, hadn't he? The blow behind the head was unexpected to say the least, and although I felt the movement behind me and rolled forward, it still took the wind out of my sails. In fact it left me becalmed in still waters, you might say.

It was all that Maggini needed to get to the other epee. Unlike me he did not need the boost of the wicker chair and must have broken a dozen high jump records when he went for it. As he landed he drove it into the small of my back; or tried to. I rolled and clambered to my feet. I swished the blade and pointed it in his direction.

'Signore, you have been watching too many of those Hollywood movies, have you not?' the one-time violinmaker now turned killer laughed. One thing I take a fervent dislike to is being laughed at.

Especially by five hundred year old men.

He also swished his blade and went down into the ritual position, right foot extended and left leg pointed to the left in a very uncomfortable stance, both legs bent for balance. His right arm was extended and his left was raised behind him in a really puffta position, but I knew there was a reason for that.

'We have had a tradition of duelling for a long time, Brogan,' he said with a disarming smile. 'Like the French we are very good at it, though I think that we Italians are superior. These are epees, the classic duelling weapon, you know.'

To his surprise I also moved into the classic fencing stance. 'Yes, as a matter of fact I DO know. The French call it the *epée*; in old French it was known as the *epée*, in Latin the *spatha* and in Greek the *spathe*. The exponent of the *epee* is called an *epeeist* and in Modern Pentathlon it takes only one hit to win. I think in the duel it is the same rule, Signore, just the one hit, and of course a hit with the point is valid on any part of the opponent. I used to compete in Modern Pentathlon some years ago.'

'Really?' he smiled and moved into the attack at the same time. Very sneaky, no salute with the sword, no touching of blades, just a fully fledged bounce off his rear foot and extension of the arm, body and legs thrown forward in a lunge, or what is called a *fleche* in fencing circles. I countered with a *redoublement* and counter parry, changing quickly to a circular parry and launched into *trompement*, a series of offensive blade movements to deceive the opponent's parries.

He returned to the on guard position after the lunge but then went straight into a riposte and almost had me, but I countered with a reprise and returned to the guard forward position. I stepped back and watched Maggini carefully. He appeared to know his stuff while I was rusty as hell; God knows how many years it had been since I'd held a sword of any kind. Still, I had the advantage.

You see, in pentathlon it was never like traditional contests with foil, epee or sabre, where you have the luxury of the best of nine hits. In pentathlon *epee* it is the first, and only, hit to count, as it would be in a real duel such as we were engaged in now. Because of this we were taught some pretty unorthodox techniques – dirty tactics in other words.

I waited in preparation for *a prise de fer*, and which he obliged by beginning an attack and I took his blade with envelopment followed by a *croise*, then to his surprise I stepped back.

He could not believe his luck and came right back in with arm extended in a *fleche* or a spring off his rear foot. I went down on my back leg and took my sword hand into supination, which is with the fingernails upward, but more than that. I held the end of the handle in a tight grip that gave me a four-inch advantage and angled it upwards. It entered his lower abdomen but was not a fatal wound. That came when I moved forward and drove the rigid triangular blade through his body until the *coquille*, or guard, stopped it going any further.

I put my left foot against Maggini's upright body and pulled my blade out. As it came free I sensed rather than heard a person behind me. In one movement I reversed the blade and thrust it behind me to the right, placing the heel of my left hand on the end of the handle and helping the force of the movement. I heard the shocked gasp and as I turned I found Andrea holding her left side where my blade had entered.

It was not a fatal wound, but the thin dagger she flung nearly was, as it took me high on the left side of my chest only inches above the heart. I passed out from the pain for a minute or so, and came to slowly with the plaintive high notes of the Diabolus ringing in my ears.

I didn't know how long I'd been unconscious but Andrea had made the most of the time, but again, I suppose she'd assumed me dead. On a makeshift altar of a workbench with a large book on it, the skull resting on the book, and several black candles threw an eerie light on the skull itself. Andrea stood before it with a look of joy on her face and the light of adoration in her gleaming eyes.

I tried to move but had no strength as I felt the blood oozing out of me. The notes rose to the crescendo they had on that night in Houghton Hall, and only then did I notice where the violinist's gaze was fixed. In the darkest corner of the workshop I could see smoke curling up to the high ceiling. It gathered together, became a congealed mass; and then began to take on corporeal form. Within seconds it had become the shape and appearance that I'd seen the previous time. The winged form, the triangle-shaped tail, the demonic face and red eyes; and then it simply vanished and a gentle looking man in a white robe, with long white hair and beard took its place.

Andrea stopped playing and her face took on a look of puzzlement.

'You think I really look like the popular image you just saw before you, child? No, how could it be, remember I once took my place along He who calls himself the One God, so it is only natural that I look like him, is it not?' His voice was kindness itself, a gentle voice that conveyed great warmth and harmony. 'Over the eons it amuses me to appear from time to time to men in the guise they have always imagined me in.'

He, it, the figure, moved forward to stand in front of the makeshift altar. 'You think to bring me back to my rightful place on earth, child? Is it not so? But despite the hundreds of years your society has had to prepare you have made a mockery of that which is written down in the Great Book.' The voice was still gentle, still warm, and when the change came it was a great shock, even to me who was almost out of it.

'YOU HAVE BROUGHT ME INTO THE PRESENCE OF ONE WHO WAS BELOVED OF THE CHRIST,' he screamed. 'JUDAS WAS THE ONE WHO ORGANISED THE WHOLE SCHEME THAT MADE JESUS IMMORTAL TO HIS FOLLOWERS AND THOSE FOLLOWERS HAVE BEEN MY CURSE FOR ALL TIME.'

I didn't quite understand it then, but got the message that Patrick had been right, and the plot to reinstate the Devil on Earth had just taken a dive. Andrea got it also, a bit ahead of me and made a bolt for the door with the Diabolus in tow.

'CHILD,' the voice stopped her by the door and despite herself she stopped and turned around, gazing defiantly at the one she had worked so long and so hard for. She knew it was over, and also knew there was nowhere she could hide on this Earth.

The skull rose in the air then smashed down on the workshop's hard wooden floor. At the same time a large jagged piece rose and hovered in front of Andrea, before flying forward and cutting deeply across her throat. Blood spurted and she tried to scream but could not get sound past her torn vocal cords. Both major arteries were slashed on either side of her throat and her lifeblood divested itself from her body in a very short time.

Before I went into unconsciousness again I thought I heard words in my head, 'you are not dead, mortal, so be thankful it is not yet your time. Neither was this your victory, but was caused by the vanity of those who would harness me for their own needs...' But I could never be sure.

I woke in a hospital, white sheets and white-coated professional looking people scurrying around me and I knew immediately I could not possible be in the Britain of today.

Fabio was sitting by the bedside and was on his feet as soon as he saw me.

He had gotten me out of there, into his taxi and driven me straight to the Vatican where he showed my black card and asked for Cardinal Lumbrozzi. I was now a patient in the Vatican infirmary and on the mend.

I spent three weeks in the hospital bed. I made two phone calls and told people that I'd had a slight accident but would be well soon and not to worry about me.

During those quiet days I had many conversations with myself about what had taken place in the last few months, and always asked myself the same question.

'Why?'

'Why?' little Andi would answer me in my delirium. 'Because it was the reason I was born, Harry. I was to be the one who brought Him back. I spent my whole life training for...it. My father taught me...'

I would stay there, holding her hand and gazing down at her olive beauty. At first I blamed her father for his Trilby-like control over her, but realised that all along she had been her own master and the things she had done had been in the full knowledge of what she was about.

She would always die then, just before I would wake up.

I then pleaded to be sent home. No chance. The best I got was to be taken by ambulance to the home of my good friend Fabio, where his wife made the most of having a pliant and weak person to take care of. Finally the doctor examined me for the final time and pronounced me fit for air travel.

One last chore awaited me before I would board the 747 for home.

A call to Lumbrozzi that night and I was received into the Vatican through the back door with my parcel; the parcel that Fabio had the presence of mind to pick up off the workshop floor, where it lay close to the body of Andrea Scolari. When I left it was with the promise that everything had been taken care of and I had *Il Papa*'s thanks and his blessings.

By 10 o'clock the next morning I was saying goodbye to Fabio at the Da Vinci Airport and once more was dozing as the plane exaggerated its climb for altitude over the great city of Roma. I promised myself that I would be back soon, only the next time as a *touristi*.

The hostess brought me a double whisky and soda and I saw her smile wryly as she saw the few tears spilling down my cheeks. She obviously though I was filled with regret at leaving the beautiful city, or perhaps at leaving a lover. Perhaps both of these reasons would have been enough to cry over, but of course neither would have caused such emotion in my own cold heart.

It was more likely the regret I'd felt ever since I'd watched Cardinal Lumbrozzi set fire to the Diabolus, mumbling the right prayers or incantations over the ashes, and then covering the lot in holy water. What was probably the greatest creation of Stradivari the luthier, and worth at least £20 million, now gone up in smoke.

That was why the tears were in my eyes, but I couldn't tell her that, could I?

CHAPTER SIXTEEN

"I am the LORD: that is my name: and my glory will I not give to another, neither my praise to graven images."

Isaiah 42:8

"The lofty looks of man shall be humbled, and the haughtiness of men shall be bowed down, and the LORD alone shall be exalted in that day."

Isaiah 2:11

'Hey, Dad,' a voice came from the parlour.

Having recognized the voice I wandered through and met an extraordinary sight. My son was sprawled out on the couch, feet up on my coffee table, working on a huge pizza and drinking one of my cans of Guinness. Granted he was sharing the pizza with the fox, which was also up on the couch, also sprawling, and both looked at me as though I was the intruder.

'You're giving Lupus pizza?' I protested mildly. 'He's a hunting animal.'

'Aren't we all?' my son said facetiously. 'But at heart we all love pizza, don't we? Have a slice, we'd hate to waste it, wouldn't we, mate?'

'And can I have a beer too?' Now it was my turn to be facetious, but it was returned with a nonchalant wave of the hand.

I went to the kitchen, grabbed two cans and returned to the living room, where my son and my best pal were watching some mindless cop drama. I put one down on the coffee table, just out of range of a lunging hand, and opened the other one. I took a deep quaff and placed it down as I reached for a large slice of the succulent looked pizza. I then slumped back in my favourite easy chair.

'I don't suppose you've corrupted him to booze as well, have you, sunshine?' I grunted.

'Nah, he doesn't like spirits or wine,' Phillip grinned at me. 'But he's very partial to Guinness, aren't you, fella?'

The reply was an enthusiastic tongue slurp on the side of Phillip's face, and only then did I notice the bowl in front of the fox. The tongue returned to the bowl and that answered my question about corruption. I decided to give up and spent a few minutes chewing on the pizza, which was surprisingly good, and guzzling Guinness from the can.

'So, how did you get on this time, Dad?' Phillip asked with an air of nonchalance that didn't quite come off. 'I understand you did okay.'

'And you've been listening to who?'

'To whom,' he corrected me. 'Your friend Heather rang a few times, and last night she rang to say you were all right and coming home. She also told me to get the place ready.'

'Ready for what?' I asked. 'It's never unready, as far as I'm concerned. Anyway, what have you been doing to "get it ready" for someone of my impeccable taste?'

'Haven't actually started yet,' he admitted. 'Since I got here we've been going on walks that seem to take ages, and then we get back late. And today again we've been rambling and didn't get back until late, so feeling a bit peckish I drove into the village for pizza...'

'Since when did a bloody fox need taking for a walk, anyway?' I bit down on a piece of pizza and had to admit it was very good.

'Actually it was me who needed the walk and Lupus showed me some interesting stuff around the countryside. It's amazing this place where you live, you know?'

'I do know,' I smirked at him. 'It's why I live here, remember?'

'Of course it is,' he grinned.

'Condescending little prick,' I reached for the last piece of pizza and heard a light growl from the couch.

'He likes the hard crusty bits on the outside,' Phillip said apologetically.

'So do I,' I mock grumbled, but broke them off and threw them across the coffee table. None of them touched the material of the couch for they were neatly plucked from the air by a pair of huge slavering jaws. Ye Gods.

'Heard a good one last night,' Phillip suddenly got excited. 'I know how you're a fan of Tony Blair and that nice Mr. Prescott.'

He grinned as I prepared to throw a cushion at him.

'Tony Blair called John Prescott into his office one day and said, "John, I have a great idea! We are going to go all out to win back Middle England."

"Good idea PM, how will we go about it?" said Prescott.

"Well," said Blair, "we'll get ourselves two of those long Barbour coats, some proper wellies', a stick and a flat cap, oh and a Labrador. Then we'll really look the part. We'll go to a nice old country pub, in Much Something or other or one of those villages and we'll show we really enjoy the Countryside."

"Right PM," said Prescott.

'So a few days later, all kitted out and with the requisite Labrador at heel, they set off from London in a westerly direction. Eventually they arrived at just the place they were looking for and found a lovely country pub and, with the dog, went in and up to the bar.

"Good evening Landlord, may we have two pints of your best ale, from the wood," said Blair.

"Good evening Prime Minister," said the landlord, "two pints of best it is, coming up."

'Blair and Prescott stood leaning on the bar drinking their beer and chatting, nodding now and again to those who came into the bar for a drink. The dog lay quietly at their feet.

'All of a sudden the door from the adjacent bar opened and in came a grizzled old shepherd, complete with crook. He walked up to the Labrador, lifted its tail and looked underneath, shrugged his shoulders and walked back to the other bar.

'A few moments later, in came another old shepherd with his crook. He walked up to the dog, lifted its tail, looked underneath, scratched his head and went back to the other bar. Over the course of the next hour or so another four or five shepherds came in, lifted the dog's tail and went away looking puzzled.

'Eventually Blair and Prescott could stand it no longer and called the barman over.

"Tell me," said Blair. "Why did all those old shepherds come in and look under the dog's tail like that? Is it an old custom?"

"Good Lord, no," said the barman. "It's just that someone has told them that there was a Labrador in this bar with two arseholes!"

I had to laugh, and then of course it was too late to reprimand him for his language.

'Very good,' I grinned. 'Just don't tell that one in front of Heather.'

'Why not?' he asked innocently. 'She was the one who told me it in the pub last night.'

What could I say to that?

'Oh, by the way, Dad, you have a dinner invitation tonight. At the Dartmoor Pony, Heather said she's got a couple more weeks off, thanks to tying up all the loose ends on the violin thing. She wants to show her appreciation for the help you gave.'

'The help I gave...? Of all the bloody cheek...'

'She said you'd react like that,' Phillip laughed. 'She said she'd thank you properly tonight.'

'Aren't you going?' I did my Roger Moore thing with my right eyebrow in mock surprise. 'Forgive me for asking; only you seem to have caught up to everything that goes on around here.'

'I do, don't I?' he grinned again. 'But in answer to your question, no, I don't want to be a party-pooper, as they say in our late colony in the Americas. I think the lady Heather would like you all to herself.'

'And what do you think, Phillip.'

'Gee, I'm flattered, pops. No, seriously, I am.' He frowned. 'I don't remember anyone asking me what I thought for a long time – if ever. What do I think? I never took to your other lady friend, Andi, and I'm sure you noticed but neither did Lupus, did you feller?'

He fondled the fox's ears and the big guy seemed to nod, but it was probably just in appreciation of having his ears fondled.

My son gave me a very grown up look. Not surprising, given that he was now actually grown up, but you know what I mean.

'If you let this one get away you really ARE an arsewipe. Dad. She's amazing. For a cop, and of the female type as well.'

'Copess, even,' I glared, but couldn't keep it up for long. 'You like her then?'

'Not 'alf,' he said in an exaggerated Cockney accent. 'If she was only ten years younger.'

'She'd still be too old for you,' I pointed out.

'Hang on, what about all those Hollywood actresses, then? Demi Moore, Renee Zellwiggler, or whatever. They've all got toy boys.'

'Hate to burst your bubble, pal, but look at the toy boys. I could fancy some of them myself.'

I received a double Roger for that but he added that cheeky grin that I'd been unable to resist when he was a kid, and I gave in.

'So, how's your mother and what's his face?' I asked to change the subject.

He shrugged, and became all adult. 'She's my mother and I love her, in a filial kind of way, but I don't like her, Dad. Albie got more than he bargained for, you know? He probably deserves it, cuckolding you and all, but I'll give him this; he's never raised a hand to me, or her, though God knows the poor bloke must have been tempted a few times in her case. I'm sorry for all those years you missed me growing up, but we're together now and I think we can make the most of it, and lay time past to rest.'

'Christ, how did you get so wise, so young?' I asked softly.

'Having no father and a mother who was never there,' he said softly, though not in a self-deprecating way. He told it as it was and I respected him for it. 'Tell you something though; you've been the only one that didn't climb on my back about switching varsity courses, and wanting to become an actor. Albie said I was a suppressed fairy and mum said I was throwing my life away. I should have done it long ago. I could have been Harry Potter in the movies.'

I didn't know what to say so I helped myself to another piece of pizza; dutifully tore off the crusts and walked across and fed them to Lupus – God forbid that he should have to get off the couch – and sat back down again.

'So, how was it really, Dad?' Phillip asked seriously. I told him the story, just as seriously.

'God, Dad, you've been in hospital all this time and you never told us? We would have been worried sick.'

'Exactly why I never told you,' I shrugged. 'Now, how about a walk after I've had this?' My son nodded. 'That's if the fox can manage to waddle along after all those pizza crusts.'

'Ah, that was the famous Brogan sarcasm, wasn't it?' he said sagely. 'You must teach it to me sometime, pops.'

'It comes naturally,' I said with a mouth full of pepperoni and anchovies, a helluva combination. 'A gift like mine can't be taught.'

We sat there while I finished the pizza, Phillip drank his beer and the fox climbed off the couch and licked himself like a dog, balls and all.

'Why do they do that?' I asked my son.

'Because they can,' he replied, and I was proud of his quick repost and sarcasm.

A chip off the old block.

It was only when I arrived at the pub that I realized it was Saturday night. I'd phoned Heather to confirm our dinner and she told me she was continuing her recuperation now that it was all over. She never mentioned it was Saturday night. All over Britain it was the same scene in the local pubs and The Dartmoor Pony was no exception. There was a folk group locked into a corner in siege formation and the place was heaving.

I stood in the door for a moment to get my bearings and Heather's father waved from the bar. The folk group consisted of four men and two women and they had just concluded their last number. The hair on the men were as long as the hair on the women and the only distinguishing difference was the beards; on the men that is.

'Now for a blast from the past for all you oldies out there,' a big man with a beer belly that must have cost a fortune announced in a surprisingly high-pitched voice. 'The Land of Sandra Dee, people, and hardly a folk song but we like it so shut your gobs.'

This was acknowledged by a lot of blown raspberries and good-natured remarks, some quite amusing.

They were good instrumentalists and played anything from fiddles, accordions and those little Irish drums played with a small stick. Seven Bellies, the leader, had an excellent voice as he began the song.

Long ago and far away,
In a land that time forgot,
Before the days of Dylan
Or the dawn of Camelot.

There lived a race of innocents,
And they were you and me
Long ago and far away
In the Land of Sandra Dee.

390

Oh, there was truth and goodness
In that land where we were born,
Where navels were for oranges,
And Peyton Place was porn.

For Ike was in the White House,
And Hoss was on TV,
And God was in his heaven
In the Land of Sandra Dee.

We learned to gut a muffler,
We washed our hair at dawn,
We spread our cloths on lines to dry
In circles on the lawn.

They all could hear us coming
All the way to Tennessee,
All starched and sprayed and rustling
in the Land of Sandra Dee.

We longed for love and romance,
And waited for the prince,
Then Eddie Fisher married Liz,
And no one's seen him since.
We danced to "Little Darlin",
And Sang to "Stagger Lee"
We cried for Buddy Holly
In the Land of Sandra Dee.

Only girls wore earrings then,
And three was one too many,
When only guys wore flattop cuts,
Except for Jean McKinney.

And only in our wildest dreams
Did we expect to see
A boy named George with Lipstick
In the Land of Sandra Dee.

We fell for Frankie Avalon,
Annette was oh, so nice,
And when they made a movie,
They never made it twice.

We didn't have a Star Trek Five,
Or Psycho Two and Three,
Or Rocky-Rambo Twenty
In the Land of Sandra Dee.

Miss Kitty had a heart of gold,
And Chester had a limp,
And Reagan was a Democrat
Whose co-star was a chimp.

We had a Mr. Wizard,
But not a Mr. T;
And Oprah couldn't talk yet
In the Land of Sandra Dee.

We had our share of heroes;
We never thought they'd go,
At least not Bobby Darin,
Or Marilyn Monroe.

For youth was still eternal,
Our life was yet to be,
And Elvis was forever,
In the Land of Sandra Dee.

We'd never seen the rock band
That was Grateful to be Dead,
And Airplanes weren't named Jefferson,
And Zeppelins weren't Led.

Beatles lived in gardens then,
And Monkees in a tree,
And Madonna was a virgin
In the Land of Sandra Dee.

We'd never heard of Microwaves,
Or telephones in cars,
And babies might be bottle-fed,
But they sure weren't "grown" in jars.
Pumping iron got wrinkles out,
And "gay" meant fancy-free,
But dorms were never coed
In the Land of Sandra Dee.

We hadn't seen enough of jets
To talk about the lag,
And microchips were what was left
At the bottom of the bag.

Hardware was a box of nails,
And bytes came from a flea,
And our rocket ships were fiction
In the Land of Sandra Dee.

Buicks' came with portholes,
And sideshows came with freaks,
And bathing suits came big enough
To cover both your cheeks.

Coke came just in bottles,
And skirts came to the knee,
As Castro came to power
In the Land of Sandra Dee.

We had no Crest with Fluoride,
We had no Hill Street Blues,
Girls all wore superstructure bras
Designed by Howard Hughes.

We had no patterned pantyhose
Or Lipton herbal tea
Or prime time ads for condoms
In the Land of Sandra Dee.

There were no golden arches,
No Perrier to chill,
Our fish were not called Wanda,
And cats were not called Bill.

Middle age was thirty-five
And old was forty-three,
And ancient were our parents
In the Land of Sandra Dee.

But all things have a season,
Or so we've heard them say,
And now instead of Maybelline
We swear by Retin-A.
And they send us invitations
To join AARP,
We've come a long way, baby,
From the Land of Sandra Dee.

So now we face a brave new world
In "slightly" larger jeans,
And we wonder why they're using
Smaller print in magazines.

We tell our children's children
of the way it used to be,
Long ago and far away
In the Land of Sandra Dee

A voice said softly in my ear, 'Movies are better than real life. If you go to enough movies then movies become real life, and real life becomes a movie. Jules Feiffer said that in 1969.'

'I know, and I'll have you know I grew up in the movies, lil lady,' I said in my John Wayne voice.

Heather looked gorgeous; for once wearing a non-masculine outfit, light fawn trousers, not too tight in the fashion of a hussy but not too loose either. She wore a wool knit beige top and brown shoes with straps around the ankles. She bestowed a kiss on my right cheek.

'You look...'

'Gorgeous, you were going to say,' she finished for me, tilting her head to a coquettish angle.

'No,' I sniffed disdainfully. 'Actually I was going to say "autumnal", but you've spoiled it now.'

She laughed and put her arm through mine. 'Why don't we eat dinner in the back, this place is too crowded.' And she turned and led the way around to the private entrance to the pub.

Mindless wimp that I am I merely followed on behind.

ends.....

Made in the USA